The Siren of Paris

David LeRoy

To all of those who rest as 'Known Unto God,'
may the Lord be with you.

ACKNOWLEDGEMENTS

The Siren of Paris is due in large part to the work of several editors, and I am very thankful to the talents of Thom, Jennifer, and Chris. Yves provided insight regarding my questions about Saint-Nazaire. Vickie, Mark, Charlie, Theresa, and many other friends have listened to me go about the story with encouragement and patient endurance. Tupelo coffee house's friendly staff provided a place away from home distractions to write. Valerie's group critiques helped improve the text. My writing coach Sarah has always been there for me and I am very grateful for her encouragement
.

FORWARD

It is somewhat fitting that *The Siren of Paris* begins with a funeral. In the same way that a funeral acts as the end of one life and the beginning of another, or the closure of one chapter before the page is turned to the next, so the characters of David LeRoy's novel live their lives at the very watershed of two distinct epochs of history.

The book's central character, Marc, is already a man out of place when he arrives in the Paris of the late 1930's. It is a city caught between the old world and the new, on the cusp of a conflict that will begin with cavalry charges, only to come to be defined by the airplane, and then ended with the atomic bomb. Marc's Paris retains the grandeur of its pre-First World War heyday and the *fin de siecle* - the time that the French would recall as *le belle epoque,* or "the beautiful era"- this was the Paris of the Moulin Rouge and the can-can, and artists like Proust and Gauguin, but by the time of the novel its sheen has been dulled.

The World of the Siren of Paris: France in the 1930's

The indescribable losses of the 1914-1918 conflict and the Great Depression have left it injured when Marc arrives, and there is a pervasive feeling in the book that the coming storm from the east will be worse still. Nevertheless, Marc encounters a hardy stoicism and fatal optimism, what the French themselves would term *elan*- the flair, panache, and bravery to face whatever storms may come and then rise again to fight another day.

This was nothing new to the Parisians of the time. The conflict with Nazi Germany was seen as almost inevitable, but it was merely the latest act of a long rivalry which dated back long before the First World War, to the Franco Prussian War of 1870-71 and the Napoleonic Wars before that, even, in many educated French and German minds, all the way to the ancient days of the Roman Empire.

Then, when the Roman world had looked like it would last forever, invaders from the east, the Huns, had stormed across the Rhine frontier and laid waste to all around them. The citizens of Republican France could identify with the plight of their ancestors as they themselves faced Imperial Germany, whose Kaiser openly called on his soldiers to fight in the same spirit as the ancient Hunnic horde. Perhaps this shared cultural nightmare explains in some small way why the French were later so reluctant to confront the German crossing of the same river in 1936, when elsewhere, alarm bells sounded that the latest round of hostilities was about to commence. To them, Nazi Germany seemed little different, its anti-Semitism worthy of little comment and even matched at times in a France where many had bitterly opposed the election of the Jewish Leon Blum as Prime Minister a short time before.

In a strange regard, the French were resigned and acquiescent to the international developments of the 1930's, and people were weary of reading everyday about the latest crisis. France had, after all, been defeated by Germany in 1871, and Paris itself bombarded and occupied in that war. The people had starved during the siege, and cats, dogs and even the animals of the zoo were slaughtered to feed them. When it was finished, the Germans had gone home, and in the decades following the French capital had risen again as the most glamorous and cultural city in Europe, with the evocative nickname-"the City of Lights". Defeat was something to be endured and then overcome unendingly, a sentiment that France's future allies in Britain and the United States found hard to comprehend.

In the same way, it had been Germany's turn to feel defeat in 1918, and once that war had been settled with the infamous Treaty of Versailles the year after, Berlin had recovered and even overtaken Paris as the most exciting city on the continent. Its cabarets and artists, its architecture and science were reborn after the defeat of what people in 1939 still called the Great War.

For its part, Paris had also made an attempt to return to the good times and forget the annihilation in the trenches. Its reputation for the good life and art remained intact through the 1920's and even into the 1930's, but there is something poignant in the fact that many of the great names from this period were, like Marc, exiles from their own countries. Hemingway and Fitzgerald traveled from the United States; Joyce and Beckett came from Ireland. Even the dancer and singer Josephine Baker was an American by birth.

This influx of talent was demonstrative of the hole left in French society by the First World War. Though Russia had suffered by far the most casualties, with Germany a distant second, France had lost proportionally more of its men than either. From a population in 1914 of roughly forty million, over four million (that is one out of every five men in the country) had been wounded, with nearly a million and a half killed.

These statistics are almost unimaginable in a modern Western country today. To put it in perspective, in the four years from 1914-1918, one hundred thousand more Frenchmen were killed than the United States has lost in *all* of its wars since 1775. After such a sacrifice, many simply felt that they had nothing left to give. Added to this, the domestic political turmoil and depression of the 1930's caused such disillusionment that many of the same people wondered whether they should have bothered in the first place.

There was a feeling, moreover, that the battles and casualties of the next war would be something different, perhaps even worse again. In the First World War, ordinary people in cities far from the frontlines had been killed by enemy attack, as newly invented airplanes demonstrated their potential for causing death as well as wonder. The Germans had even used airships, or

Zeppelins as they called them, to attack London, which was not only far from the battles then raging in France, but safely, it was thought, across the sea on a different island.

The widespread use of poison gas in that war, as well as the potential for the newer, modern airplanes of 1940 to reach almost any city in great numbers, put a fear in the minds of ordinary citizens that was quite unprecedented. Marc and the people around him found themselves in a war older than the very countries they were born in, but a conflict which was now going to be fought in a wholly new and terrifying manner.

That is exactly how the battle plays out in the novel, but LeRoy places the focus of the book away from the war itself, in the cities behind the front lines. The first half *of The Siren of Paris* describes an often forgotten episode of the Second World War, the plight of the refugees in the war's opening days. Millions of people were dispersed and evacuated before and during the German attacks in 1940, with children at the forefront of the desperate flight. In Britain, millions of them had already been separated from their families and moved to safer locations in the countryside in anticipation of the air raids and bombing that was expected to start as soon as war was declared.

In the cities and towns of France, Belgium and the Netherlands, however, there was nowhere to go. Many who could afford it moved to the ports where they could board ships to get them to safer locales, while foreign embassies worked frantically to get their citizens and their families out of harm's way. The work of the real-life American Ambassador William Christian Bullitt Jr. is dramatized to startling effect in the chapters of The Siren of Paris dealing with the German invasion and the evacuation of Paris, and they give a revelatory insight into the confusion and hysteria, which blanketed the city at the time.

The already vast and complicated process was made worse by the fact that the German onslaught, which would come to be called *blitzkreig* or "lightning war", had sidestepped and confounded the armies of France and Britain, which were hopelessly wrong-footed in May and June 1940. Their generals and governments had gone into battle in 1939 and 1940 thinking that it was to be a replay of the First World War. In such a conflict, fought over years rather than weeks and months, it was assumed that the resources of the French and British Empires would eventually overwhelm and starve their almost landlocked German opponents. Unfortunately for them, the generals of the German Army had other ideas, and after a feint against the Low Countries (Luxemburg, Belgium, the Netherlands) to draw in the best of the combined British and French forces, they moved their tanks through what had hitherto been thought of as the impassable terrain of the Ardennes forest.

It is hard to imagine the shock that must have been felt when the German *panzer* formations came rolling out of the woods and straight into the fields of France that day. Many books and novels have tried, but few have managed to convey the visceral trauma and fear that must have gone through the Allied countries like a collective shudder. Winston Churchill later recalled the horror he felt upon learning there was no reserve force to protect Paris as the greatest upset of his life. The tanks streamed on through the flat, open terrain of the countryside, with the armies sent to fight them racing to catch up behind.

Marc

This is the world that *The Siren of Paris's* protagonist Marc arrives in at the outset of the story. Though French born and half French himself, he has a curious relationship with the country where he would like to settle. His fluency in French and English helps him to move in wide social circles, both Anglo and Francophone, but it also means that he never feels truly at home with any group, even his closest friends. He forms a close relationship with the Parisian model, Marie, but even with her, there is a divide both of his and her making.

This feeling of separation is reflective of his rejection of the social stability that life with his family entailed. They had a lucrative, yet dull life pre-ordained for him, but his determination to escape leads him to literally cross an ocean and throw himself into the bohemian existence of an artist.

Though he does his best to escape it, the world of his birth and his status continually intrude into his new existence, and once war is declared, he gravitates, almost against his better judgment, into the American diplomatic corps. This revolt against his instincts, albeit back to a natural habit, is to cost him dearly as he and those around him dither in the face of the coming German occupation.

Marc's internal conflict over the correct path to take in extraordinary circumstances gives rise to the book's central themes: guilt and its ability to haunt those who suffer from it. Throughout *The Siren of Paris*, we are faced with guilt in all of its facets. Marc's conscience is troubled initially by his perception that he has let his family down by leaving and pursuing the artistic life. This weighs on him and contributes to his inability to truly enjoy what should be an envious existence. Later, he is plagued with an existential self-loathing brought about by his ability to survive where others close to him and many thousands around him did not.

Guilt is also ever present in the book's sections, which deal with the battle for France and its subsequent occupation. The frenzied retreat that Marc and his friends embark on brings myriad instances of death, often in the most random and horrific of circumstances, and they are helpless to stop it. This death comes from the skies haphazardly and cares nothing for whether its victims are young or old, civilian or military. Even the religious orders are subject to its whims, as is shown in the tragic character of Sister Clayton.

Through these experiences, the reader sees that the guilt of the survivor can be even more damaging to the survivor than it is even to the perpetrator. LeRoy does not only examine the formation and irrationality of guilt, however, but in the characters of those who turn on the people they once in different times professed to love, so the absence of guilt is also examined. The cognitive dissonance and the methods that a person uses to justify their actions to themselves and others are explored in all their duplicitous callousness.

Betrayal and Collaboration

This is the second of the lesser-known areas of the Second World War that *The Siren of Paris* explores. An unspoken topic in France for decades and largely forgotten in the Allied countries, which were not occupied, the collaboration of citizens with German occupation forces in France was alarmingly widespread. It took official form in the French government formed under Marshal Petain and which operated from Vichy, but thousands (6,000 in 1944 Paris alone) of Frenchmen and women actively aided the Germans either in uniform or undercover as spies and informers. In the book, characters who had earlier met and talked easily at cafes and restaurants are now suspicious and careful of what they say to one another.

This new world of occupation is deftly handled by LeRoy also, its claustrophobia and deprivation painted in immaculate detail right down to wooden soled shoes that Marc, the former artist and diplomat, is now reduced to wearing. Occupied Paris is a shell of itself, where the old markets sell old food and the black market has now become king. Operas and plays are still staged, but the spirit of the city has now been truly diminished. Those who oppose the authorities do what they can to save downed British and America airmen from arrest and Jewish families from deportation, but they live in fear of the slipped word or the tip off from someone who they may once have called a friend.

For the collaborators, the choice is simple, France was made weak by republicanism, Jewry, and degenerate behavior, and so it must be made be made strong again. To do this, the elements, which caused its downfall, have to be eradicated. The insight into the thought processes of the characters who carry out this betrayal are some of the most fascinating and chilling of *The Siren of Paris* and are a lesson in how those whom history regards as monsters live with themselves and their decisions.

Redemption and the Hereafter

The endurance of Le-Roy's cast of characters transcends both life and death into the world of paranormal, which is highly fitting, because war is a paranormal storm of chaos and death that always leaves a scar upon the soul. *The Siren of Paris* is a book littered with the ghosts of the past, most strongly at the book's opening and close. For its characters, these ghosts exist in the truest sense of the word, but as all in great books, it is left to the reader to decide what is real and what is not.

In times of immense stress, such as war, there are many accounts of the appearance of friends and loved ones, in places far from where they could possibly have been at the time. Eastern cultures take this spiritual presence for granted; Cambodia's capital city, Phnom Penh, for example, is known by locals as the "City of Ghosts", but it is less discussed in the more superficial and scientifically minded West. In *The Siren of Paris* Marc has similar experiences, such as Allen's appearance at his bedside and again later on with John. Much like real life anecdotal accounts of similar spiritual occurrences, his friends appear happy and at peace, comforting him and helping him come to terms with the very real fate that could await him at a moment's notice. Eventually, after many trials, Marc will allow himself the same comfort and finally be at peace with the past and the choices he has made.

The Siren of Paris avoids battlefield cliché and the lives of the political leaders to focus instead upon the suffering and choices that every ordinary person who lived through that awful conflict had to make in order to survive. It is a book for readers who want to be treated to a view of an oft-told story in a completely new and original light. LeRoy avoids tanks, guns, and generals, to focus upon passenger ships, refugees, nuns, animals, and orphans. The triumphant victory of the classical hero over the great enemy is absent, and is replaced instead with the haunted guilt of the survivor, suffered in silence. The Paris, which had promised love, becomes the Paris of betrayal. LeRoy creates for us the world of the vast majority, the everyman, at the crucial point of history when the boredom and restlessness of the "phoney war" gave way to hopelessness and regret for millions. In this way, it is essential reading not just for anyone with even a passing interest in the events of the largest war in human history, but also for the endurance that people, even the people that pass by on the street every day, are capable of. In the great tradition of the historical novel, *The Siren of Paris* opens a door for us into the past and allows us to glimpse the soul of humanity put to its greatest test.

Damien Peters
University College Dublin
BA (Hons) English Literature, Drama and History,
MA, History
(damien.peters9091@live.com)

CHAPTER 1

Saint-Nazaire, France

"May the Lord be with you," the priest's voice rang out to all gathered at Marc's graveside in September 1967.

The cloaked man stood taller than all others gathered, with the hood of his smock pulled over his head. He held in his right hand a staff with a round clock mounted on top.

Marc stood beyond the gathering, gazing back upon his grave. He saw his only sister, Elda, surrounded by all his other friends from France. The body of his soul beamed a reddish-golden light, as he anticipated the final moment he would leave in peace. He strained to see the face of the priest obscured from view under the hood.

"And also with you," Marc whispered, looking toward the release from his life.

"Let us pray," the priest asked softly. With a rush, the first eleven souls then appeared around him. They had come from the graveyards of Angoulins-sur-Mer, Les Fortes, Saint-Charles-de-Percy, Saint-Clément-des-Baleines, Saint-Palais-sur-Mer, Chatelaillon- Plage, Saint-Sever, Traize, Brest, Saint-Hilaire-de-Talmont and Saint Pancras. They wore drab olive-green uniforms, with kit bags ready for war, but they were soaked to the bone and only a few had boots. The dial on the clock stopped as a moment of Marc's life flashed before him.

"I no longer want to see you, Marc. It is finished and over," Veronica said to him outside his dorm room in the winter of '39. Marc recognized this is why he dropped out of medical school. Once she cut her bond with him, he decided to run. Marc's soul turned a dark red over the pain of her words.

"O God, we pray you lead us to truth, deliver us all from violence, battle, and murder, and from dying suddenly and unprepared," the priest said as he glanced up from his hood and then down again before Marc could catch his face.

A second group of twenty-two souls gathered by the grave. They came from the graveyards of Bretignolles-sur-Mer, L'Aiguillon-sur-Mer, Port-Joinville, Les Sables-d'Olonne, Nantes Pont du Cens, Sainte Marie, Yves, Piriac-sur-Mer, Olonne-sur-Mer, Coulac and Charroux. Among the soldiers stood one woman dressed as a nurse, a Belgian boy and little girl, all with no names.

The clock came to a second stop. Marc glanced back upon the moment of his life.

"I can watch out for myself, you know. I am not small anymore. You should go," flashed with lightning speed in front of Marc. She was only eight years old at the time, yet Marc could see she held herself silently to blame. His soul constricted as the time on the clock once again started. His light turned to blue.

"O God, we pray for those who suffer in silence with guilt, and for those who suffer with shame, regret, and remorse."

"I have seen enough," Marc called out to the priest. Another thirty-three souls arrived from the graveyards of La Couarde-sur-Mer, La Turballe, Saint-Denis-D'oléron, Sainte-Marie-de-Ré, Olonnes, Bouin, Saint-Gilles-Croix-de-Vie, Aytré and Barbatre. The clock slammed to a stop.

"One-way ticket for first class, June 14, crossing on the *Normandie*, please," Marc asked the ticket agent, smiling satisfactorily over his decision. Marc's soul stepped back from this moment of his life. The self-knowledge of his motives as a younger man churned inside of him. The time upon the clock rolled on again. The light of his soul turned a dark purple.

"Please, let this go, it is just the past," Marc called out to the priest. The priest held the staff steady.

"O God, our time is in your hands, and we pray that you look upon us with favor as we, your servants, begin another year of life."

Sixty-five more souls appeared in a flash from the graveyards of Le Bois-Plage-en-Ré, Château-d'Olonne, Saint-Hilaire-de-Riez, Ile d'Yeu, Beauvoir-sur-Mer, Saint-Georges-D'oléron, Ars-en-Ré, La-Barre-de-Mont, Dolus, Saint-Trojan, L'Épine, La Plaine-sur-Mer, Noirmoutier-en-l'Ile, L'Herbaudiere, and Le Clion-sur-Mer. Marc felt the pull of time upon him as it stopped again upon his life.

"Happy birthday, young man. Better get a move on it. You have a ship to catch today," his mother Lynette said to him the morning he left for France. The words pierced him as he perceived the truth that she drank herself to death from worry in the spring of '42.

"Why must you show me this? Is this my judgment?" he yelled back at the priest. The light of his soul turned a dark green. The priest looked up only slightly through his hood at Marc. The clock began to move.

"O God, whose glory fills the whole of creation: Preserve and protect those who travel from every danger and bring them in safety to their journeys' end," the priest called out.

An additional 233 souls of men, women, children and soldiers from the graveyards of Saint-Nazaire-sur-Charentes, Les Moutiers-en-Retz, Prefailles and La Baule-Escoublac flashed around Marc. He felt the compression of the approaching time as the clock slowed to a stop. A sense of dread now replaced his fears.

"When you get to Paris, let Ambassador Bullitt know you are in town. He would be glad to see you. We were classmates back in college before the war," his father said to him as the car pulled up to the French Line Pier. Marc smelled the sea air as the image flickered before him. He understood that his father never believed art school to be serious. The pain of his father's last words to him before he passed of a heart attack in '44 brought Marc to his knees. The priest's eyes peered back through the hood upon Marc's uplifted face of anguish. The clock dial started to spin.

"O God, we pray for those who have died. May your love and light keep them eternally yours in peace and life without end," the priest said softly without breaking his gaze, as everyone who had gathered whispered their own names. Marc then swallowed hard as another 370 more gathered from the graveyards of La Bernerie-en-Retz and Pornic to join the other souls. The clock stopped.

"You should have left Paris, Marc, and never returned," she said before the charges were read to him by the Gestapo officer. Marc groaned under the weight of this most painful moment, feeling a mixture of regret and shame. The light of his soul turned dark as obsidian and the clock began to run.

"Make this stop. I have forgiven her," he pleaded. The priest then removed his hood to bear his face.

"O God, the Father of all, who commanded us to love our enemies: Lead us both from hatred and revenge and, in your good time, enable us all, who are known unto you, to stand before you in eternal peace," the priest said, looking directly at Marc. The words ripped through him in shock waves, fracturing him on his side three times, and once down the middle. The time upon the clock came to a dead stop, but Marc noticed that the second hand now ticked forward with temporal time.

A number unknown rose up from the sea, the beaches, and ditches to join the 859 gathered from their rest on the land. Marc stared in disbelief at the priest's face before him. With all of his strength, he strained to whisper, "Why?"

"May the Lord be with you," the priest said, his tone gentle as the clock reached June 18, 1939, eight thirty at night. A fear greater than the judgment of hell filled Marc, as he realized he would now watch his life during the war all over again.

The S.S. *Normandie*'s bow parted the sea as she carried her passengers toward France that Sunday. Marc dressed for dinner in his finest tuxedo. Before taking the last dinner at sea, he entered the chapel of the ship for his evening prayers.

"And may you, my Father in heaven, keep my family in your protection. I pray for my mother, Lynette, my father, Eldon, and my little sister, Elda. Amen," Marc kneeled alone in the chapel. He made the sign of the cross as he rose to leave for dinner.

CHAPTER 2

Marc crossed the foyer to the large double doors entering the main dining room. The maître d' escorted him through the large three-deck-high room, lined on each side by massive crystal light sculptures. Frosted crystal columns flanked the towering walls. Gilded golden crossbeams covered the room's ceiling. Bas-relief carvings of peasants, farmers, kings, and soldiers decorated the sides of the entrance.

La Paix, a tall bronze statue of a woman extending an olive leaf, towered over his table. Marc frowned as he searched the room for his traveling companions. None could be found within the nearly empty cavernous room. A silly thought crossed his mind that he somehow had the wrong time for dinner.

Marc's black hair, parted to the right side of his head, flawlessly hugged his scalp, a stark contrast to his body as he slumped into the chair at the empty table. His eyes scanned the tables between the light sculptures, squinting with disappointment.

Dora descended the staircase, walked over to his table, and said, "I forgot to tell you that on the last night, we like to dine at the grill. We can speak English there without any fear."

Marc left the lonely waiters and sprinkling of passengers in the golden room to follow Dora up the staircase. Fifty years old, Dora appeared far younger with her hair pulled back into a small, tight bun. She glided through the dining room in a long, slender cream-colored evening dress. Marc walked with a spring to his step and smiled as he loathed the idea of eating alone on the last night. Dora met Marc on the first day out and immediately adopted him into her circle, but he did feel a tint of self-consciousness for he stood out among them, at nearly half their ages.

"Race you," Dora said at the base of the stairs to the aft foyer.

"You will not," Marc said.

Marc climbed the stairs and lost her as they both ran across the foyer to the doors of the grillroom perched upon the aft deck of the ship.

"It feels damn good to have a man chase me again," Dora smirked at Marc as she swished side to side.

"Marc, were you the rabbit or the fox?" David said with a smile as he looked up from his menu.

"You know the answer to that question," Nigel said. He put down the wine list.

Once they'd dined, Dora tapped her wine glass with her fork. "It is time for a small celebration." The Café Grill did not have one single empty seat. Some passengers sat at tables with extra chairs. The room was loud, as if they were inside an Irish pub. David's long, thin face looked up with a curious smile in his bright gray eyes. Nigel rested his head of thin gray hair upon his hand as his round face studied Dora's intentions.

"Crossings for the gods," Dora said, raising her glass to her friends.

After each one stood and proclaimed mockingly the number of times they had safely crossed the sea with the help of the gods, David stood. "I, David, have crossed the sea with the help of the gods thirty-two times."

Nigel teased David. "Tell us your secret to such luck on the waves, old friend?" Dora sat back in her chair and cocked her head to the side. Marc noticed that David's hand had a slight twitch to it, even as he strained to smile.

He looked out over his friends after a pause and said, "It is simple. I never sail British!"

"Here, here, my friends! A toast—never sail British!" Dora said, raising her glass to meet the other three. The gaze between David and Dora told Marc there was more to the toast than he could grasp.

"Now, let us dance." Dora rose from the table as they left the Café Grill for the lounge. Marc followed Dora, her arms locked with David and Nigel, down the long staircase into the smoking room. Passing into the lounge, the air sparkled with the tune of *Now It Can Be Told*. Four fluted light pillars surrounded the dance floor, but only a few were dancing. In the four corners of the lounge, glass murals stretched the entire length of the walls.

While dancing, Dora asked Marc, "So, does she have a name?"

"Does who have a name?"

"The woman, silly."

"There is no woman. Remember, I am single."

"Marc," her eyes narrowed and she tilted her head back to look up at him, "a young attractive man like you does not just run off to Paris for nothing. Either you are running away from a woman, or running toward one," she smiled. "Maybe both! Am I right?"

"Her name is Veronica and we broke up this winter," Marc said, his eyes glancing up and away toward the band.

"I see. And the other one?" she pushed.

"There is no other one. Besides, the breakup is really a blessing."

"How so?"

Marc then looked back at Dora's face as he warmed up to her charm. He reflected upon her charisma, which made her beauty all the more enchanting, even if she was in her fifties.

"I was a premed student and hated it, because, to be honest, I was only doing it to make Veronica happy. I think this change will be good for me. I have always loved art and this will be my choice. I let her make all my major decisions. It felt good, but it was not actually good for me."

"Oh God, Marc, please be careful."

"Don't worry. I don't think much will happen with Germany," Marc said. He believed she had switched to the war talk he had read in the papers.

"I am talking about the women of Paris."

Marc glanced at each corner of the room as he danced, quickly studying the massive panels of glass painted in gold, silver, and platinum leaf, with designs of ships, gods, and goddesses.

"A game?" Dora said, poking him.

"With you?"

"We will guess which one the other likes best," she said, glancing at the murals.

"You go first."

Dora pointed to the one called the *Birth of Aphrodite*, a collection of massive, tall ships, with a woman rising from the foam of the sea.

"You're good," Marc nodded, smiling.

Marc then pointed toward the one called *The Rape of Europa*. Dora shook her head side to side and then pointed behind Marc to a set of large pocket doors separating the lounge from the smoking room, decorated with a golden lacquer mural spanning the opening. Horses, women, and angels flew through the sky to catch stars and blow wind, a radiant golden sun at the noonday position in the sky.

"It is incredible. I have not noticed it before. Why this one?"

"The sun reminds me of hope," she said. The band played a new number. "I think you really believe your story about art school," she said, turning back to him.

"Oh, you think I am a shipboard spy?" Marc joked, matching her dry wit.

"That would be grand. Then you would know who you are and what you are doing. You are sexy enough to get secrets out of anyone." Marc averted his eyes from her stare and glanced at the murals. Her tone turned serious. "Paris is not the place it might seem to be."

"I know what you mean. I can speak fluently, and, besides, I belong there."

"How so, handsome?"

"I was born there," he said, with a nod.

Dora laughed out loud. "That explains this thick, dark hair." She ran her hand over his head. "Marc, I was born in Baltimore, but I do not belong there. Paris is my home, but I am still an outsider, even after living there twenty years. You may be Parisian-born, Marc, but belonging there is another story."

"What called you to Paris?" Marc stared into her right eye.

"A relationship. I thought it would solve everything."

"Must have been some love?"

"I would like to think so."

"Well, I think you are being a bit rough with me," Marc said.

"What a nice idea, but that will have to be another time." They continued to dance in the center of the floor between the frosted light columns. "Why did you want to leave Veronica?" Dora pressed Marc.

"Actually, she left me," Marc said.

"You must have given her everything she wanted. Don't answer that. I am sorry. I can be insensitive when I drink too much," she looked down and then up, a blushing smile warming her face.

Dora held Marc's hand as they walked over to David and Nigel talking with some passengers. "Ready to have a nightcap in the smoking room?"

"Brilliant idea," David said.

They sat in the thick, brown leather chairs in a semicircle, Dora in the middle. Her back faced a giant golden lacquer wall mural. Their raucous laughter echoed through the empty room as they drank, smoked, and joked.

"Please, please, can we have a bedtime story?" Nigel begged Dora.

"Ah, how can I say no to my lovelies? I will tell you a bedtime story," she said in her dry, nasally voice.

"Goldilocks and the Three Bears were in Paris."

"Oh shit, they are so screwed," David said.

"Hush, hush now."

"Dora, is this going to be another Jewish tale?" Nigel said.

"And they needed to get a room, so Papa Bear, in German, asked someone on the street for a room. But the man said, '*Parler seulement francais*.'"

David's and Nigel's laughter filled the large room as passengers continued to dance in the lounge beyond the pocket doors. Marc could see his friends were drunk, but was amused all the same. The cocktail helped him to drop his guard for a bit.

"Mama Bear went to another and asked in Italian for a room, but got the same response. Then Baby Bear went to another and asked in English, but again, the answer was no," Dora continued, never once breaking character.

Nigel continued to laugh. "Maybe they should have gone to Spain. I hear the war is now over."

"Hush now, children. Please. This is a serious story," Dora said with a small smile.

"So, Goldilocks finally says, 'Fine, I will take care of this myself,' and she goes over to another Parisian and comes back straight away and says, 'Good news. We are staying at the Palace Hotel.' The bears were amazed. 'Goldilocks, what did you say?' I just said in Yiddish, 'Get me a room or I will close your bank.'"

David and Nigel broke into laughter. Marc found it amusing but was perplexed by the joke's meaning. Nigel turned to Marc. "Never do this. It will not work for you unless you are in a little red dress with three bears. The French will blow you off."

David could barely speak as tears streamed down his face. "Dora, I had no idea Goldilocks was Jewish. Who would'a known?"

Marc gave each of them a warm good night after Dora finished her story. The others headed back to their rooms, but Marc decided to take a walk. Before he left the smoking room, Dora caught him and said, "I am sorry if my story seemed a bit rowdy. I have had a bit to drink. I want you to keep in touch when you get to Paris," and then pushed into his hand a small piece of paper. "I know you speak French very well, but it is important to have friends. Here is my number and address. It is not what you think, although I could use a young man. In all seriousness, I want you to know that you can contact me if you need a friend."

"No problem, I understand, and I would like that," Marc said, holding her hand.

"I never asked you where you will be studying," Dora said, looking embarrassed.

"Oh, I am at Fontainebleau from the first of July to the first of September, and then I am not sure. I could be at the École Nationale Supérieure, or I might be starting at the Ateliers Académie Julian. I have not decided," Marc said, his eyes lighting up.

"Those are wonderful schools, Marc. I can introduce you to my friend Sylvia Beach. She owns a bookshop called Shakespeare and Company," she said. She smiled and held his hands.

"We can meet after the first of September, when you return to Paris. I can't wait to introduce you to all the other lost Americans. Oh Marc, what do you need?" she asked.

"Dora, I have everything taken care of. I don't need any kind of help, but thank you."

"No, that came out wrong. I meant to say, what do you need to be happy?"

"I don't know. Friends. Finding love would be nice."

"You don't know, do you? I know."

"Oh, you need to get some rest," Marc said.

"You need freedom. That is why you are coming to Paris. Freedom. I lied about the relationship. Oh, there was a lover, but my other lover, freedom, is what kept me in Paris."

Marc began to chuckle and then kissed her on both cheeks. "Sleep well, my new friend," he said. Dora turned and left for her cabin.

Marc walked out on the promenade, around the nighttime decks. The impact of his decision to leave for France rested uneasy in his mind as he leaned over the rail, looking out at the black sea. The smile he wore for the others had waned while he considered his choices. He continued his walk to shake off his doubts.

Entering through the doors to the upper aft foyer, he stopped in front of the bronze statue in the center of the staircase. He noticed that it was different from the one in the dining room. The bronze woman gazed forward in a proud and defiant pose, holding a wreath to one side.

Marc asked a passing steward the name, and he said, "*La Normandie. She is France.*"

"And the wreath?"

"For the fallen of war," the steward replied as he continued toward the grillroom. Marc studied the statue, taking in its full presence.

Descending down the stairs, he walked slowly around the edge of the smoking room, studying each of the massive murals. One had peasants taking in the harvest; another depicted Egyptians on boats sailing the Nile. Marc took a chair facing the large mural of horses where Dora had entertained them with her story. Two men on horseback chased five other horses and had caught one with an outstretched rope. It rose from the floor to ceiling of the room, about three decks high. Though Marc's eyes were heavy, he was not yet ready to retire, instead studying the mural, holding onto the sweetness of the evening, thankful he was not left to dine alone.

The lights of the *Normandie* blazed alone through the waves. Wind whistled through windows of the promenade. A couple left the main lounge to their cabin for a drink. The mighty *La Paix* stood faithful in the dining room as the lights extinguished one by one. Marc awoke to a steward in French, "*Il est tard, monsieur.* It is late sir, one thirty. You fell asleep."

"Wait, my watch says twelve thirty," Marc said.

"Eastbound, we lose an hour each night, remember?" the steward said.

"Oh yes, I forgot. Thank you for waking me." Marc then made his way through the halls to his cabin and left the golden horses alone for the night.

In the morning, Marc could not help but notice just how few passengers were departing the ship at Cherbourg. He purchased his rail ticket to Paris and turned toward a long line of passengers waiting to board the ship heading westbound. The line of travelers wrapped out of the dock and down the street. Marc glanced at all the anxious faces as he made his way to the train station.

CHAPTER 3

"Marc, Marc," a voice called out from the bustling Metro crowd. Marc turned, but could not see who had called his name, and doubted if it was even for him. As he turned back, he heard his name again. David emerged from behind a crowd of young school children.

"Shouldn't you be out at Fontainebleau?"

"Hey, yes, I am heading back now. I came into Paris to line up my next flat," Marc said, shaking David's hand.

"Dora said the same, plus that she had been showing you off around town," David said as the crowd of young school children moved around them.

"Ah, yes, the gang. How is Nigel?"

"Good. He is out of town right now on some banking business. I have been busy as well. I have a new supplier and have been lining up the contracts back in the States."

"David, I need to catch this train."

"No problem. When you are in Paris, we can meet up at Dora's for a Sunday brunch."

"You bet."

Marc patted David's shoulder and left to board the train that would take him to the southeast side of Paris.

On board, a woman moved through the cabin toward the rear, passing row after row of school children. "Are all you little ones going on a holiday?" she said as she passed.

"We are going south in case the Germans bomb the city," a boy said, looking up at her.

"That is absurd. Nothing will happen, but you have a good trip all the same."

After making a connection back to Fontainebleau, Marc spent the evening drawing.

"How was Paris?" his roommate asked.

"A bit tense. It appears they are sending the little ones out of the city."

"The drama of it all. I bet that was the government's idea. Always trying to convince us of the impending doom."

"You think it is all a hoax?"

"Don't you?"

A light breeze entered through the open windows of the third-floor life-drawing classroom the following afternoon of September 1, 1939. Marc could not quite figure out if the room at one time had been a drawing room, dressing room, or parlor. The gold leafing of the plaster molds was barely visible. The mirrors held cracks in the gilding. He knew it was not a valuable room; otherwise, it would never have become home to an art class. The entire school might be held within the servants' quarters, but Marc preferred not to ask and instead allowed his imagination to run wild.

"They say in the papers nearly 16,000 children have now left the city," Marc overheard from a discussion next to him.

"I believe they are now passing out the gas masks," another student said in a hushed tone.

"Take out a pencil and a sheet of paper. Place it to one side of your desk where you cannot see it," the older instructor told the students. "Now, please, eyes forward. Marie, can you please remove your robe and give the class a comfortable pose? I want you to draw the contour of Marie's body, without looking at the paper. This exercise will be seven minutes." Marie gazed confidently in the nude, auburn hair with brown eyes, her figure full and hourglass.

"Why can't I look at the paper?" a student complained from the rear of the room.

"How will I know if I am drawing her right?" one of the female students echoed.

"You won't know," the instructor retorted.

"This makes no sense to me," another complained.

"This is the final? You have led us to a point of drawing without looking?" another complained bitterly.

"Do as I ask. And now, silence. My God, all of this worry and fuss over a certificate of attendance. You will get your paper but, right now, focus on Marie. Draw her slowly. Do everything you can to overcome the desire to check your work. Do not look at your hand, paper, or the pencil. Just look at the model."

When the instructor turned his back, nearly everyone in the class looked, including Marc. The temptation inside him became overwhelming but the glance at his page did nothing to relieve his frustrations, fears, or doubts.

"Who just looked?" There was silence. "Liars," he chuckled with a smirk. The time was finally over. "Now, let's take a look."

Sighs and murmurs filled the room. Students glanced away from their drawings. The man in front of Marc turned his paper over.

"What do you see?" the instructor demanded.

"I see a really shitty drawing," a woman in the middle of the class said, her tone sharp.

"Excellent. Who else?"

"Mine looks good, not perfect, but good," another student replied.

"Were you looking?" he asked.

"No, I did just as you asked," the student answered.

"Amazing. Maybe later you can demonstrate for us this miracle gift you have," the instructor said. A few laughs floated amongst the students. "The purpose of this exercise is not to draw what you think you see, but what you actually see. Most of the time when we draw, we are focused upon the paper instead of the model. You look up with a glance, and then look down at your paper and continue to work. But you are not drawing the model. You are drawing what you think you see as the model. This exercise is not about training your hand, but your eyes. Unless you really see your model with all your sight, you are just drawing from your imagination."

Marc studied his own poor example. The shape he had drawn was nearly unrecognizable as a human form. He felt irate with himself as he stared at the distorted proportions and contorted lines.

A sound could be heard outside in the hallway, muffled by the door.

"This is the foundation of my class if you continue with me at École Nationale Supérieure des Beaux-Arts. You know how to draw, but you lack the ability to see," he continued.

The noise became far greater outside the class. People in the hall spoke loudly; the stomping feet of someone running down the corridor grew closer.

"Marie, please replace your robe," the instructor said, and then walked toward the noise.

As the door opened, Marc heard, "Guerre! La guerre!"

"Stop! Silence, please. I have a class in session. Have you gone mad?" Students from other classes poured into the hallway.

"No, sir. I was told to tell everyone of the war."

"What war?" he asked.

"France. France is at war with Germany. If you have a radio, turn it on. They are calling up the troops." The students gasped, and their teacher stood in the doorway, stunned.

That night, Marc's roommate packed for the front. "It is all a farce. I am going to be bored to death," he complained bitterly. "France is not Czechoslovakia, or Austria."

"The war is not official yet. France and Britain made demands, but nothing is official until the third," Marc said to him.

"Perhaps I am packing for nothing?" he snorted.

Marc left in the morning for the city to take up his next flat. People bustled about, making preparations for the war. Sandbags lined the fronts of prominent buildings; posters announced air raid stations. Marc stopped and joined a crowd gathered in front of one of the posters. As he read, it occurred to him that it said nothing different from what he'd heard on the radio or read in the papers, yet, somehow, none of it seemed real to him.

Nigel complained to Marc in the café that night while having a smoke. "This is absurd. Suddenly now, everyone is bustling about as if the loudmouth himself is at the border, but the entire German army is in Poland. This is just another short crisis. I am sure there will be a new agreement in a few weeks."

"I hope you are right," Marc said. "If all the students are at the front, how many classes will there be?"

"Oh Marc, if you get bored of drawing lovely naked women, you can join the troops at the front and earn your glory and honor. It is the hero's calling, you know, and you are a citizen of France, so you can be drafted in case the calling does not come through," Nigel teased. Marc suddenly remembered he was born in France. The thought struck him as odd that he could be called up for the draft.

"Oh, I have the dogs of war in me, but I prefer not to feed them and, besides that, the French don't know what to do with a man born in France, yet a citizen of the United States. I don't even have a French passport," Marc crushed out his cigarette.

"Smart. No worry Marc, you will find your glory another way I am sure, but, as for me, I have no dogs left in me at all," Nigel said, a look of bemusement on his face.

"Are you leaving soon?"

"Of course I am, even though I'm sure everything will work out. But if this doesn't calm down, I want to be on the other side of the pond." Nigel looked out to the street.

"Well, I have class in the morning all the same," Marc said. "If I do not see you before you leave, I hope you have a safe trip."

"You will see me. I am not leaving that fast. David will be back and I will be at Dora's for lunch. Don't stay up too late dreaming of all your drawings," Nigel said, and left the café.

On September 2, Marc saw a line out the door of the travel offices of the Cunard Line agency. He found this odd for a Sunday. Then, as he turned the corner, he saw the same with the French and Italian Line offices on Rue Auber. As he passed en route to the opera house, he heard excited conversations with the ticket agents. Marc caught the back of Nigel's head among the would-be passengers.

"You must have something?" Nigel said.

"I do, just not in cabin class. I can get you on the *Champlain,* in tourist, in two weeks' time," the agent said, looking over Nigel toward the door.

"Any larger ship? What about the *Ile de France*?"

"No, all booked. If you want bigger, then maybe check with Cunard next door," the agent said. Nigel looked down at his shoes, searching for a decision to come. He had just left the Cunard office and already knew they had no solution. The conversation was exactly the same, just in a different language.

The morning of Tuesday, September 4, all the papers were filled with the fantastic headlines. Marc could not avoid them if he tried.

"*Athenia* Hit!"

"EMPIRE AT WAR!"

"*Athenia*, Terrible Loss of Life!"

"10-year-old Girl from Canada a Victim of German Wolf Pack."

"28 Americans Among the Dead."

"What does it say, Marc?" Dora asked him from across the table.

"More of the same. It was dark, and that perhaps it was a mistake. It seems more people died trying to get over by boats to the rescue ship than from the blast of the torpedo. One flipped, and another was sucked into the propeller of the ship," Marc said, scanning the article.

"Right up the rear staircase," David said, staring at his tea.

"They think because the ship was zigzagging with lights out, the U-boat believed it was a cruiser instead of a passenger vessel," Nigel said. He looked up at Dora.

"Right, and passenger ships do look so much like naval cruisers. It could have been the British, to bring America into the war." David looked at Nigel.

"Well, what a world this has become." Nigel's face twitched.

"I think staying is better than trying to go," David said, his face stark and serious.

"I am not so sure, David. I think we should at least consider making some other plans to leave," Nigel responded, worry thick in his brow.

"Well, if you need a place to stay, you are welcome to stay with me," Dora said. Marc sat quietly listening to his friends. He pondered his own plans at the same time. There was no pressing need for him to return to America, and Paris was safer than a lifeboat at sea. Marc looked up from the paper at David and Nigel, more worried for them than for himself.

"Let's wait and see what happens. Everyone is upset right now about this *Athenia* thing and in a few weeks, the whole storm could blow over. We might be worrying for no reason," David said, looking over at Dora.

After dinner, Marc decided to join David to make a call back to the States. Brought to a small oak desk at the Paris international telephone exchange, Marc read the instructions of how to make a call. The entire room appeared to be nothing but Americans the evening of September 4. David had just made his own call home to his wife. Marc explained to his family his reasons for staying and they agreed it would be safer than risking a trip. Marc passed a long line a few hundred souls long as he left the exchange that night.

"Did you get inside?" David asked Nigel.

"Yes, of course, but it took a bit," he answered in an irate voice.

"And, what did you find out?" he pressed further.

"Everything is canceled. They are giving refunds, but I did not take mine. I think it is better to let the money sit with them so when things open up, we are on the list of paid passengers." Nigel waved his hand.

"That is wise. But, I'm worried. I would not underwrite these ships and I am sure that is what is going on," David commented.

"What do you mean?" Nigel looked perplexed.

"All these ships are underwritten with insurance in the event of a disaster. I would not take the risk, and who do you think ultimately is behind all that money with the insurance underwriters?" David explained as he pointed to Nigel's chest.

"There are thousands, you know, all searching for a way home," Nigel said, waving his hands up in the air.

"It does not matter, Nigel, if it is thousands or millions. If no one is willing to risk the money for those ships, they are not going to take us home." David looked directly at Nigel's face, trying to catch the attention of his eyes.

"You're right. I never thought of it that way," Nigel said, defeated. "I felt sorry for the agent. He just looked at me and said 'I cannot help you.'"

CHAPTER 4

Marc looked to the front of the classroom. The semicircular, wheeled stage held no model. The instructor had just finished passing out bottles of ink and long wooden dowels.

"Attention, please, attention. Listen to me," the instructor rapped a stick on the desktop. "I am not unaware of what is taking place outside these walls of École Nationale Supérieure; however, the standards of instruction will remain the same. If you listen to every radio report, read every newspaper, and run to the underground every time you hear a siren, you will have no focus in this class and you might as well leave."

The students stared without any emotion at the instructor. Marc looked out the windows, crisscrossed with tape. As he turned back to the front, Marie, again in her robe, came through a door with her back to the class.

"Today, you will stand as you draw. Break the dowels I have given you. I want you to draw on the full sheet of paper on your desk. You must focus and draw with your entire body, not just your little hands. Any questions?"

The students stood and uncapped their bottles of ink. Some removed their gas mask canisters from the top of their desks. Marc spread out a large sheet of paper upon his table.

"Excellent. Marie, if you please," the instructor pointed to the cushions on the stage. She removed her robe and turned to face the class, as she lay nude across the cushions.

First, a student gasped. Another let out a laugh. A murmur rippled through the room. Marc's face grinned like a fox. The instructor turned toward her and cupped his hand to his mouth. Marie looked up at him, wearing nothing but a gas mask as she tilted her head to one side.

"Always up on the latest fashions," he said with a smirk.

"But, of course," she said, and pulled off the mask.

Marc took the dowel and dunked into the bottle of ink, looked up at Marie and then began to mark the page, all the while grinning with admiration.

Later that evening, Marc met Dora for dinner.

"Do you think this war is serious?" Marc asked her.

"What war? There is a war? I had no idea!"

"Dora, stop teasing." Marc scrunched his brow.

"Marc, for the past hour, all you have talked about is your art class and Marie. Do you realize that? I have not even met this woman, but I feel like I could draw her myself," Dora said.

"It is nothing. I think it is just due to the fact that I have to look at her so much."

"You mean look at her while she is nude, right?" Dora smiled as she stared at him.

"Yes, yes, nude. I understand what you mean, but it is not going to go any place. She is the model and I am the student." He averted Dora's stare.

"You really do like to tell yourself stories, and I think you believe them," she said as the food came to the table. Marc nodded thanks to the waiter.

"Have you seen Nigel or David recently?" he asked with a genuine sense of concern in his voice. Dora paused for a moment to consider her words.

"Not with Marie, but yes, and they are staying put. Neither of them are happy about it, but Nigel's own bank has recommended it. David, well, he is not eager for it," she said, looking to the side.

"Why does David not want to get home?" Marc asked quietly.

"He wants to get home. I think he wants to get home desperately, but David is cautious about travel. He has been burned, so that is always in the background," she answered. "They were talking about South America the other day. There is a possibility of getting out through Lisbon. But, you know, I have to agree with David."

"Germany said they did not sink that ship. Do you think the British did it to bring America into the war?" Marc studied her reaction.

"Marc, it does not matter who or why the ship was hit if you are a passenger, and that is where David is coming from."

"I took the job."

"With the embassy? How did you land that?"

"My father knows Ambassador Bullitt, and he suggested it before I left New York."

"Can't you just relax and enjoy Paris? I did not know you needed the work."

"I don't need the money, but I do need the work."

"You're lying, you know. I am not a fool," Dora said.

"What?"

"You are doing it to impress someone, and I think we both know whom." Dora raised her eyes while she stared at Marc.

"Dora, are you a professional psychic, or just a part-timer?"

"Eat, and have some wine."

"There is a package that needs to go to the British Embassy and, when you get back, I think there is some translation work," the secretary said to Marc. It was his first week at the American Embassy in Paris.

"I know you," a tall, young man said as he received Marc's package. "You live in my building, right?"

Marc thought for a minute. "Yes, I think I do. Are you a student?"

"I was before all this mess. My name is Allen. And you are?"

"Marc ... Marc Tolbert."

"Where are you from originally?" Allen said with a Manchester accent.

"New York. I am here for a year to study art."

"Well, let's get together, chap, for drinks sometime. I have never been to New York, but would love to hear about it. Plus, it is always nice to find someone whom I can speak English with."

"Marc, you are a savior," Sylvia said to him as he entered the door to Shakespeare and Company.

"Oh, have I done something?"

"Yes, you have come too soon, and now you are going to help me set up for the reading," she said, smiling as she rushed about the cluttered bookstore. She stood shorter than Marc, even with her square heels. Her hair parted down the middle, curls puffing out on the sides.

"Well, everything has worked out for the best, then. I came early because Marie cannot make it, but will meet me afterwards. So, these are the chairs?" Marc asked.

"Yes, those are the ones. Have you read Andre Gide before?" she asked with excitement.

"No, but I have heard of him. He is an interesting character. What will he be reading tonight?" Marc set up another chair.

"*L'école des femmes*, published in 1929," she said, just as Nigel walked through the door.

"Will Dora be able to make it?" Marc asked him.

"No, she would not tell me why, but I believe she's on a date. She's always so tight-lipped when she has found a hot one."

Just before everyone had arrived, Allen walked through the shop door.

"Well, twice in one day, imagine that," Marc said, smiling.

"It is a small city if you speak English," Allen said, looking at Sylvia.

After the reading, Marc asked Allen if he would like to join the group for drinks. Sylvia, Nigel, Allen, and Marc walked to the café where Marie had agreed to meet Marc after the reading.

"So, you see, Eveline has fallen in love with the worst sort of fellow one could imagine," Sylvia said as they walked.

"It is a very odd work, but brilliantly insightful. Andre certainly has captured how blind love can be," Allen added.

"I thought the reading was going to be an English book by Joyce, and I am shocked, Allen, that you understood," Marc said.

"I am not in Paris by mistake, Marc. French is a wonderful escape from English, and I take it at every chance I get," Allen bumped against Marc.

"So, how does it all end?" Marc asked Sylvia.

"Oh, that is in book two. Eveline makes a series of choices to escape from her love, which leads her to an early death," Sylvia said jovially.

"Oh, that never happens," Allen said.

"Of course not, Allen, never at all," Sylvia smiled warmly and poked Marc in the ribs.

"How does he know these things? After all, he does not chase after women himself," Marc complained, just before they reached the café. Allen opened the door for Marc and Sylvia to pass through, and, as Marc looked through the restaurant, Marie caught his eye and waved.

"She is lovely. Do you know her?" Sylvia asked.

"Yes, she is a model, uh, I mean, student at the university."

"Well, it appears she wants you to join her. Mind if we tag along?" Allen said, his tone snide.

"We'll all join them. They are all students from my class."

After a round of drinks, the conversation turned again to the war.

"The problem is not with Germany but with France. We have seen this coming for a long time and refused to do anything about it. Now it is here at our doorstep, and we still act as if we have no idea what to do," Marie said.

"It is absurd. They have called up all these troops to do what? There is no fighting at the front. There is no invasion of France. What can we do now that Poland has fallen? Are we expecting to conquer Germany and then liberate Poland?" another student chimed in.

"Well, you know, Britain will save us!" a younger woman said, stirring the pot, aware of Allen's nationality.

"Oh, is that so?" Marie retorted. "England is just taking advantage of the opportunity and that should not surprise anyone here," she said, looking directly at Allen. Marc frowned at Marie, but she only smiled back.

"I agree, it is a farce, as politics and wars always are," Allen said in perfect French to the surprise of the other students. "I am just surprised we are still even talking about this war. It should have been over the day after it began, and certainly by the weekend. Don't they know we have a life to live here in Paris?" Allen finished, not breaking eye contact with Marie.

"Marc, I have a question for you," Marie said.

"Yes," he said nervously, wondering if the argument would escalate.

"I model for another class, and the male model has been called up. There is a session tomorrow night and I need a model for some classic poses. There will be a few seven-minute poses and likely one longer pose of thirty or forty minutes. I think you would be perfect."

"I have never modeled before," he stammered.

"Oh, it is cake. Don't worry. Besides, it will give you a new appreciation when you are drawing your subject. It is important to know what life is like on the other side. Your work is very good and this will make it even better. What do you say? Class is at six in the evening. "

"Uh … what kind of poses?" he asked, relaxing a little.

"Classical," Marie said.

Marc arrived before Marie. The instructor showed him the dressing room. Marie entered a few minutes later.

"Are you nervous?" she asked.

"A little," he said, shaking out his hands. "I'm not sure how I will do."

"I am always nervous just before, but it goes away." Marie removed her blouse and dropped her dress.

"Do I strip here?" Marc looked left and right nervously.

"Of course. I know. It is odd, but it makes sense since we are going to model together." Her slip dropped to the ground.

Marc removed his pants and shirt, neatly folding them before putting on the robe. He found himself getting slightly aroused, but quickly focused on an art object in the window, willing his arousal to pass. The full impact of the stupidity of agreeing to her request hit him as his heartbeat quickened.

"If you get hard, don't worry. It is not like the first time," she joked.

"Thanks, you're really helping here," he grimaced, realizing she saw through his act.

"I am just trying to help you relax, Marc. You have to see the humor in all this at times." She laughed a bit more as she put on a dressing robe.

"We are ready," the instructor called. Marc and Marie walked into the center of the room to the circular stage, around which sat twenty students behind easels.

Marc stood over Marie like a soldier in the first pose. Then Marc posed, looking back at Marie as she was turned away. Marc sank to a point where he became relaxed posing nude with her. It seemed as if the students' eyes disappeared, as if no one else was in the room and he was safe with her.

"Marc, I need you to put this around your neck. Don't worry, we will not pull it." The instructor gave him a rope. "Marie, you are going to be standing above him, with this staff extended over him. Make sure it is comfortable for you."

The instructor turned to his students. "Now, class, when you combine two classic poses such as this, it adds a new element to the composition. There is a relationship to ponder."

Marc posed, lying horizontal on the stage with his right arm bent at the elbow, torso straight, his legs crossed and extended, and his head bent downward with the rope around his neck. Marie stood over him with a vertical staff and her head slightly downturned, yet looking directly forward.

"Marc's pose clearly is the classical death of Gaul," the instructor explained, "but Marie's posture is intentionally uncertain. Is she his rescuer, or betrayer? Is she the one who pardons Gaul, or condemns him?"

The long scream of the air raid sirens rose throughout the city just then, and the lights started to go out through the districts of Paris.

"And the reason the pose is neutral is that the composition is stronger if you leave the question of the relationship to the viewer," the instructor said. The whining howl grew louder as sirens closer to the building joined in the chorus. Shouts and hollers filled the streets outside the windows.

The instructor took a deep breath of frustration and ran his hands over his face and hair. He said, "Can one of you get the lights? It appears we have another blackout."

CHAPTER 5

"Congratulations to everyone for passing the class. Your grades have been posted and I am very pleased," the professor said. "In spite of all the distractions and events over these months, you have kept your focus, and it shows in your work."

That struck Marc as a serious understatement. Paris seemed like the same city, but the small details told a different story. Masking tape crisscrossed the windows of all the classrooms. Marc, like everyone else, carried a long cylinder that contained a gas mask. Sandbags surrounded various buildings and hugged the sides of the Arc de Triomphe and the Obelisk in the Place de la Concorde.

Russia's attack of Finland surprised the Allies, and the response of the Parisians was to raise funds to support the Finns and, strangely, wear Finnish fashion to show their solidarity. Marc found it unsettling that the public of Paris seemed to believe fashion would overcome in the end.

"There is one final exercise to complete this class, and, although it is ungraded, it will be the final test of your skills." The students looked back and forth to each other, perplexed by this last announcement. Marie, smiling, came out from behind the screen and took a seat on the stage. "Please take out a large sheet of paper and be sure to use your best stick for this drawing."

"What is he up to now?" whispered a student behind Marc.

"You are going to draw Marie as she changes positions. She will hold a position for a few moments and then move into a new position," the instructor said. A few laughs came from the students. "There is no way you can draw her entirely at any one time. Instead, I want you to stack each sketch you make on top of the other." The idea of this struck Marc as even more absurd than the first request.

"So, I want you to use one sheet of paper, and your very best stick with ink, and as quickly as you can, draw Marie while she dances. This will be our final exercise together." The instructor then looked toward Marie with an approving nod. "This is called a motion study and I do not give this to every class upon completion, but only to students whose talents impress me." He held out his hand to Marie. "Enjoy."

Standing on the platform, totally nude, she began to rotate slowly, taking a posture and then changing it, making sure to give everyone in the room a chance of seeing her front, side and back.

Marc started to draw, sketching out a hand, a foot, but then never having enough time to sketch out the full body. His frustration grew over not drawing fast enough. How in the world was he going to do this? What was he learning? He studied Marie, and noticed her smile as her gaze passed him. He wondered if anyone knew in the room. Then he let go of his thoughts, and dunked the pen into the bottle of ink. He decided to focus on the hands.

Marie changed her hands each time she broke her pose and moved to another position. It was the most expressive thing of the entire dance. Each pose seemed to end with her fingers in a certain position. Marc would then sketch out some trunk movements and legs, but most of his drawing focused on positions of her arms and hands. He released his thoughts, stopped thinking of how he was going to draw her hands, and allowed the pen and his hand to draw what was before him.

Marie's legs danced over the platform and her hands undulated in the air like a bird. She seemed like liquefied crystal, brought to life. None of the poses were static. She never stopped moving the entire time as each position of her hands only lasted for a few seconds.

"Stop. Thank you, Marie. Now, let's take a look," the professor called out after five minutes had passed, the students' faces trancelike after trying to follow Marie.

"Yes, this is good," he said as he passed one table. "Very nice. You're learning to let go and not to worry about details," as he passed another student's sheet of paper. "You are just getting down the basis of the core shape," he said to another.

"Oh, this is incredible," he said as he came to Marc's table. "Everyone come over to Marc's table. I want to talk about this." As the students gathered, Marie pulled on her robe. "See. This is what I am talking about. See how he has captured the core movements in these expressive lines? And, look, the only details are these small little movements for her hands. His entire focus has been on what was truly moving, which were her hands, and the core is sketched, but does not change much. The only way Marc could have done this was by letting go of the need to be perfect, letting go of the need to draw everything." The professor continued, excited, "And once he let that happen, the separation between what the eye sees and what the hand draws falls away."

"Marc, you need to keep this drawing. It is fantastic," the professor said. "This is the reason you came to Paris."

Marc returned with a glass of wine for Marie as she stood near the entrance of the embassy's grand ballroom. Garland hung over the windows; partygoers commented about the large, decorated tree.

"Are you all right?" Marc asked.

"Yes, of course, just a bit nervous. I had no idea you were so well connected."

"Underneath all the masks, they are just like you."

"Is that so?"

"If you don't want to talk with someone, just say you only speak French," Marc said, turning to look at her smile.

"And if they speak French better than I can?" she volleyed.

"That is an unlikely problem with this crowd." Marc rolled his eyes.

Ambassador Bullitt came over to him. "Marc, there is someone I would like to introduce you to. Marie, you look beautiful, by the way. Can you come over here for a minute?" he asked before walking toward the center of the room. "Dr. Jackson, I would like you to meet Marc Tolbert. You may recall his father, Eldon, during the war. Marc, Dr. Jackson works at the American Hospital in Paris. I believe you were born there."

The man towered above the other party guests. His stoic face searched the past for this name Eldon, until he said, "Oh yes, your father went to Yale with Mr. Bullitt. This is my wife, Torquette, and my son, Philip." He introduced a far shorter woman and a young boy of about fifteen.

"Yes, that is correct. He met my mother here in Paris in '17," Marc said. "And, this is my girlfriend Marie. We are both students at the university."

"Well, you are taking after your father now, and myself. What are you studying?" Dr. Jackson asked.

"Art. It is a break for me. To be honest, I was enrolled as a premed student back home, but I needed a break," Marc said.

"Is that so? And there are no art schools in America? You had to come to Paris, now of all times?" Dr. Jackson countered.

"I had no idea all of this would happen. Seemed like a great idea at the time, and I have no regrets. After all, I would not have met Marie." She smiled at him.

Torquette took Marie's hand. Marc overheard her whisper in Marie's ear in French, "You need to kidnap him. Hold him ransom until the Americans join the war. I know just the place to hide him." Marie laughed out loud.

"You may think you are now an art student, but I have news for you, young man. You will be back in med school before you know it," Dr. Jackson said, after glancing at his wife.

"I am not so sure. Maybe you are right. Are you staying in Paris or going back to the States?" Marc said. Talk of returning to medical school made him uncomfortable.

"We cannot go back. It is not even a question. I know they are telling Americans to leave, but how? Even if we could get a ship, I am afraid that will not work out for us." He looked at his wife.

"I know what you mean. Do you think we will join the war soon?"

"I sure hope so. I don't know what the holdup is now," he responded. "But that is not going to save you, Marc," he said, smiling. Marc looked perplexed. "You are heading to med school regardless. I took a break, too, you know," Dr. Jackson continued, charming Marc with his humble attitude, more in keeping with a farmer from Maine than a doctor in Paris. Marie and Torquette continued to speak in French, gesturing at the large Christmas tree and the various guests in the embassy ballroom.

Marc felt a tug on his jacket. He turned expecting to see Marie, but he met Dora's smile. "Excuse me, sir, but do you know where I can get a room?" Dora asked, in a dry, nasally tone.

"Dora, Merry Christmas. Yes, of course, and you will not even have to close my bank," Marc said with a smile, not missing a beat in the conversation.

"You know this woman? Marc, she is notorious. Your father would be so proud," Dr. Jackson, grinning.

"Yes, I know Dora. We met coming over last summer," Marc said.

"Marc, Nigel and David are going to be here for New Year's and we have a tradition, well, sort of. Actually, we have never done it before. But, would you like to join us for Mass at Notre Dame on New Year's Day?" she asked, stealing a look at Marie.

"Dora, I had no idea you were Catholic," Marc said.

"Of course, if you already have plans with someone," she said, nodding.

"Oh, excuse me. How rude. Marie, this is my friend Dora whom I told you about. Dora, this is Marie," he said.

"Marie, you are even more beautiful than Marc described," Dora said with a refined French accent. Marie blushed.

"Well, I hope to see you on New Year's," Marie, said, while leaning into Marc.

"Surrender, she has you cornered and there is no way out," Dora whispered and left with a warm look in her eyes.

CHAPTER 6

"Marc, do you have that announcement translated yet?" the staffer asked him, leaning over his desk.

"Yes, the rush job this morning? I am just finishing it now."

"Great. The ambassador has requested to speak with you once you have it ready. You may go in now."

Marc thought this was odd and wondered why the ambassador wanted to see him about a simple translation job.

"Marc, please take a seat," Ambassador Bullitt asked him. He then took the sheet of paper with the translation in his hand and studied it. "Very good. This reads well, and I think it does the job. I need to speak with you about something else," he said, removing his glasses. "I am asking each staff member if they would like to go or stay. I will not make the decision for you, but I think it is important to consider and I want every staff member to know that I do not expect you to stay on here, given these circumstances."

He had never considered the fact that the minute the sheet of paper he had just translated reached the papers in France, there would be a rush of Americans making arrangements.

"I have decided to stay. I understand you do not expect it, but I want to. I would rather work here than go back home and just read about it in the papers." Marc's face was set, eyes meeting the ambassador's.

"Have you spoken with your family?" the ambassador said.

"Yes, and they know," he lied outright, nearly resenting the question since it implied he could not make his own decisions.

"Very well. I am glad to have you and I absolutely will need the help. Not all the staff will be staying. I will be rearranging the workload shortly," he finished.

That morning, Marc delivered sealed envelopes to the papers containing carbon copies of the announcement to be printed in the following day's edition.

"Americans seeking to evacuate the war region are to proceed to Genova, Italy, to embark upon the *George Washington* or *Manhattan* commencing in January. Valid passport required or 1040 United States tax form. The State Department encourages all Americans without urgent business to leave immediately."

"Marc, it is great to see you. Happy New Year, friend," Allen said to him as he entered the crammed nightclub. "Where is Marie?"

"She had something going on with her family and is exhausted. It has been nonstop parties. She gives her regards," Marc said with some embarrassment.

"Ah, it is because I am British!"

"You know how the French are."

"Of course I do. Well, I am glad you are here, my friend. That is a smart ad you placed in the papers," he said, raising his eyebrows.

"Oh, yes. Once that hit, things went through the roof. The ambassador put me in charge of it all. If someone calls with questions, I am the one on the spot. Frankly, I had no idea how many people are trying to get home."

"Ahh … it is foolish. This is not going to last much longer," Allen said, his tone dismissive.

"What do you mean?" Marc asked, trying to listen to him over the loud partygoers.

"The war is over, friend. It is at a standstill now. Look, Germany only wants sure fights. Just the quick wins, but with the British and French up along Belgium to the north and the Maginot Line to the south, where are they going to go?" he said, Marc listening intently. "And another thing—did you see those photographs of what the Finns did to the Russians? They are amazing." Allen looked excited and confident.

"No, I have not had a chance. In today's papers?" Marc asked.

"Not sure, but, Marc, they stopped the army dead. Soldiers were frozen dead throwing grenades and firing shots. The Finns slaughtered them. The entire army, frozen in place."

"Well, the Americans who want to go are mostly the ones who had their plans canceled in the first place, and I suppose that is a good thing. All my other friends here in Paris have no intention of going anywhere."

"Are you going?" Allen asked.

"No. I am staying. I agree with you that the war is over and it is just a matter of time before some agreement is reached. By the time I get home, I will be turning back," Marc said.

"How many Americans are over here?"

"In Paris, thirty thousand, and I suspect at least that number spread throughout the rest of the country. They are just sending two ships, so even though they tell people to leave, well, it's not practical," Marc said, looking over the crowd toward the front of the room.

"Thirty thousand. Who would have known? Could you imagine if they all wanted to leave at once?" Allen said. A voice rang through the crowded nightclub full of British soldiers.

"One minute till midnight!" the speakers boomed. Men and women cheered and started raising their glasses.

"Here, get a glass," Allen gestured to Marc.

"Ten, nine, eight, seven," the partiers counted. "Six...five...four... three... two... one! Happy New Year!" The crowd went wild.

"Victory in '40!" a bellowing voice called out, and nearly everyone around said in response, "Victory in '40!"

On New Year's Day, Marc and Marie met Dora, Nigel, and David outside the Notre Dame Cathedral. David smiled and nudged Nigel when he saw Marie. They sat in the pews facing the South Rose Window. Marc reflected upon everything in '39, upon how much had changed. Only a year ago, he was with Veronica at just such a New Year's service back home in the States. Now, he was in Paris, his whole life changed. Marie wore a decidedly fashionable dress suit with matching jacket. Marc beamed with pride over her sense of style as he watched her next to him.

The usher reached his row and he stood to join the line for the sacrament. Dora did not stand. A wind chilled Marc as it passed through the empty windows. Nearly all the stained glass windows in the cathedral had been removed just after the start of the war. As he reached the altar, the howl of the air raid sirens filled the morning air outside the walls of the cathedral. He left his gas mask canister back at the pew. David and Nigel stood in front of them. All the other people seemed unfazed by the sirens. Marc took Marie's hand at the altar, before the priest came with the sacrament.

"The body of Christ, the bread of Heaven." One priest passed, giving the host to the kneeling believers, their palms raised.

"The blood of Christ, the cup of salvation." The second priest followed with the wine. Marc relished the intimacy of sharing the morning service with Marie and his friends. He looked up and noticed the last of the Rose Window still had not been removed.

He rose to return to his pew. Some of the people in the line wore their gas masks. Dora had donned her own mask while Marc took communion. The minute he saw her, the seriousness of the air raid disappeared.

"You look very stylish," Marie said to Dora in French as she removed her mask from the canister and put it on.

Marc watched the scene play out before him as people negotiated between the demands of their faith and the demands of the alarms. When it was time for the final collect, Marc surrendered to the unusual service and put on his mask. Above and beyond the joke of it, and the sirens, the entire time Marc stared at the single window remaining on the south façade, wondering why it was so remarkable that it should be left in place.

"Sir, that window, does it have a name?" he asked the usher as they left the cathedral.

"Yes. It is called the *Descent into Hell*," the usher said.

"Good God, why is it still in the church when they have removed all the other windows?"

"They tried, but the workers want nothing to do with it. People, you know, can be superstitious."

CHAPTER 7

Dora looked up from her plate and directly at David. "You should be thankful, and I think you are being a bit dramatic," she said, rolling her eyes.

"I am thankful. July is just six months away," he answered back, looking surprised by her tone.

"I wish I could do better, but you must understand, David, there are a lot of people trying to get home," Marc said and sipped his wine.

"I understand and this is not about you, Marc. I am just weary and anxious," David said quietly.

"Maybe Lord Haw Haw can advise you on a ship?" Dora smirked.

"Germany calling, Germany calling," Nigel said in a thick, mocking tone. Dora laughed out loud and then placed her finger in front of her mouth, feigning embarrassment.

"Who is Lord Haw Haw?" Marc asked.

"You don't know? How can you not know?" Dora blurted out. "He is better informed on the British than the BBC."

"Dora, Marc has Marie. Only we single fuddy-duddies need Lord Haw Haw to warm us up at night," Nigel said next. "Lord Haw Haw is broadcasted from Bremen, Marc, and just over 25 percent of the British public tune into him nightly."

"Yes, and just fewer than 75 percent of the British public lie about it each night," Dora said next.

David picked at his food. "I wish I could be so light about it. The waiting is a burden."

"Stay busy, David. I have all kinds of work now with the bank. Just look at this as an opportunity. Besides, by the time your date comes up, this could be over, and we will be back on a ship together returning to America," Nigel continued. "They're going to sue for peace. They have to. They stumbled into this war and I am sure they are looking for a way out of it." He cut into the plate of duck. "In spite of the high-pitched rhetoric for the newspapers and the speeches on the wireless."

"Marc, they don't want to have France," Dora said.

"Germany calling, Germany calling," Nigel said with a low voice.

"Stop it, stop it. Some more, please," Dora begged, laughing.

By January, the Sunday evening dinners had become routine. Marc's job as travel liaison to Americans in France eclipsed any casual study of art he continued during the evenings. There were only two ships per month, and a horrible backlog of passengers from September waiting to leave back for the States.

Marc walked into Ambassador Bullitt's office the morning of Tuesday, February 6, 1940, and sat down in the chair opposite him. The ambassador appeared to be deep in thought as he read a memo.

"Sir, you asked to speak with me?" Marc finally said, wondering if Bullitt had noticed him enter.

"Yes, sorry." He looked up at Marc and took a deep breath. "How are you doing? I know you are very busy with the ship list."

"I am well. It is coming together now and overall. There are those who believe they should be an exception to everyone, and be placed first, of course. Everyone has a special story as to why they need to ..."

"There is something I need to ask you," Bullitt interrupted, "and before I say anything else, please understand that this is not my idea." Marc fell silent. "I understand you know Arnold Wells from Harvard who is Sumner Wells, son—I believe you roomed together and are friends."

"Yes. How did you know that? Is there something wrong?"

"No, nothing at all. Mr. Wells has asked if you would assist him on some business he has here in Europe. He needs a personal secretary to accompany him to Italy and Germany, and he has requested that I approach you regarding this work."

Marc sat silently for a few seconds, searching for the words to respond. "I am not in the State Department. Why would he ask me? Shouldn't he have someone more experienced?" Bullitt stared back at him. Marc's stomach began to churn as he realized the manipulative nature of the interview.

"I have only met Mr. Wells twice. I saw him once at a Harvard function, and then at his house for a Christmas party," Marc said. "Why would he request me on this and whom is he meeting again?" Bullitt held Marc's gaze. "This makes no sense. Did my father get involved with this in some way?"

"Your father had no part, and I resisted the idea of even asking you, but all the same," Bullitt paused, searching for words, "Marc, Mr. Wells requested you not because of what you can do, but because of who you are and represent." Marc looked even more perplexed.

"We have no horse in this race or bets at this table. The people who should be talking, the ones with the most to lose, cannot speak to one another." Marc grew slightly more anxious as Bullitt continued. "In times like these," he waxed in a theatrical tone, "people such as Mr. Wells are able to visit with all of the players in the casino, because we are perceived as neutral, with no bets to win or lose." He started to smile at Marc. "He is hoping to stir these leaders toward seeking a peace agreement."

"What is so special about me that Mr. Wells would want me to be his personal secretary?" Marc asked, deciding to go straight to the core of the matter. "Mr. Bullitt, please explain to me how a dropout premedical student, now art student, would be so important to Mr. Wells."

The room fell silent for a moment, except for the bustle of the city traffic outside the window, below on the streets. The rain pattered against the window as the wind picked up.

"For one, you were born in Paris," Bullitt said with a smile. Marc's face turned blank. "You come from a well-connected and important family in America." His grin widened. "And in the highly delusional world of diplomacy, he believes your presence along his side will create a perception in the strangely deluded minds of those whom he is meeting, that the government here is interested in talks." Bullitt's smile spanned the entire room.

"That is absurd," Marc said curtly. He rolled his eyes in astonishment at the harebrained plot.

"Absolutely absurd, Marc, and I could not agree with you more." Bullitt tapped his leg with a nervous twitch and took a deep breath.

"I am more shocked that he even knows who I am in the first place."

"Why do you say that?" Bullitt tilted his head to one side.

"Speaking with Mr. Wells is like talking to a wall. He can look straight through you."

"I know what you mean. I would not blame you if you decide to pass on this adventure."

"Whom is he meeting? Will this trip be long?" Marc asked, resignation heavy in his voice. Bullitt paused, his eyes shifting from one wall to the other.

"The trip will not be long. He is leaving in a week on the SS *Rex*. Friday they make the announcements of this trip," he said, next picking up his pace of speech like a salesman closing a contract.

"I am not sure whom he is meeting, but I am sure they are officials of his own level. The papers will make the trip into more, of course, which you know is what the public wants, but Mr. Wells is an undersecretary, so," he paused briefly, "I imagine you will be meeting equally boorish bureaucrats. Italy and Germany are being gracious about his adventure, but they did not ask for his visit, so I would not get your hopes up for anything exciting to happen." Then Bullitt's face turned stoic again.

"Do I need to keep this to myself?" Marc asked.

"No, not at all. Well, that is not exactly true," Bullitt paused. "Tell anyone you care to. In fact, I would encourage you to do so, because there is nothing secret of Mr. Wells' trip but, please, do me a favor—when you tell your friends," he grinned like a fox, "explain to them you are not supposed to."

Marc smirked. He had never seen the ambassador act so silly before and began to second-guess this entire adventure.

"It is about perception, Marc. Perception is reality in our business." Then he asked with disinterest, "Do you know any German?"

"Some. I can follow a conversation, but I cannot speak it very well."

"Excellent. You are just his secretary, nothing more, so, you are making notes, and don't worry if they are wrong. It does not matter, and the less you speak, the better. Besides, no one will ask you any questions. The questions are Mr. Wells' problem."

"Is there anything else, other than travel plans?" Marc asked. He could clearly see by Bullitt's unusual expression that he believed the trip to be a hopeless adventure and resented that Mr. Wells had used his influence to obtain Marc's company. At the same time, Marc rationalized that it would be easier to just cooperate than answer questions later back home.

"Uh, no," Bullitt smiled and finished with a strong tone of voice. "No. I am sure you will be bored, but do try to enjoy the trip all the same."

CHAPTER 8

Marc could not pull off the same stupid game that Bullitt wanted him to with Marie. "It will not be long, and it is just office support," he told her, leaving out the part of it being a secret.

"He will fail. Nothing will come of this trip. I hope they are paying you well," Marie said curtly.

That Sunday, Marc casually let out the news of his trip over dinner with Nigel, David and Dora.

"You are going where with …" Dora stopped dead in mid-sentence. She clasped her mouth, which had fallen open.

"I told you they needed a peace," Nigel added self-righteously.

"Do you think they will be able to get the parties to talk?" David asked.

"I have no idea. I am just going to take notes for him and look mouse like," Marc said. "Oh, and I am not supposed to tell you, so be sure to let everyone know, please."

"You are French. They will see you as a symbol." Dora then stopped again. Her eyes widened and her face paled. "I thought you were being a smartass when you said shipboard spy."

"Dora, you are blowing this completely out of the water. I know what you are thinking and it is not true," Marc said, exasperated. "I am an American citizen, and Mr. Wells knows my family. He requested me because I went to Harvard with his son. It is nothing but an old boys' game, and no one is going to see me as anything but an idiot with a notepad."

"Does the premier know about you going?" Dora whispered.

"Why should he?"

Later that same evening at the pub where the Anglos gathered, Marc shared the news with Allen, expecting a sensible reaction.

"You know what this means?" Allen said over his pint.

"Allen, it means nothing at all." Marc now regretted agreeing to the trip, because everyone had read something more into it.

"You are going to get a promotion. This is a test. They are grooming you for another position, Marc," Allen said, smiling. He beamed with pride. "Someday, I will be able to say, 'I knew him when.'"

"You're drunk," Marc said.

"Actually, I was just thinking of ordering another to celebrate."

Marc stood at the end of the gangway of the SS *Rex*. One by one, men and even one woman came off the ship, but time dragged. There was no solid stream of disembarking passengers. Instead, people left the ship as if they had somehow just stumbled upon the gangway as a way to escape. Down along the dock, a line of passengers with baggage waited to board.

Mr. Wells came down the gangway, cane in hand. A few photographers moved in to take his photograph. The scene felt surreal to Marc due to the contrast of how few passengers left the ship compared to the thousands of passengers waiting to board.

"Do you have the banking records?" Mr. Wells asked Marc.

"Yes, you just saw them. You want to see them again?" Marc asked.

"Yes, and there should be a report in that briefcase about copper production and smelting," Wells said with a dry tone.

"Have you spoken with Arnold lately?" Marc asked after a few hours more of watching Sumner's obsessive record review.

"I am not sure who he is going to support. He has been talking a bit with James Farley and, of course, with Garner and myself, but I am sure they are in the race," Sumner said, never looking up from his documents.

"I was not aware that Arnold would play a role in the election. Is he running for office?" Marc asked.

"Arnold, right. No, of course not. He is well and he gives his best," Sumner said, finally looking up. Marc wondered if his decision to surrender to the request had been a serious mistake.

"Whom are you meeting again?"

"I am not sure. They haven't told me." Sumner shrugged his shoulders as he pored over his reports.

"You have no idea? You came all the way to Rome without any plans?" Marc pressed again.

"These meetings are often very loose and dependent upon the needs of the moment. I am sure everything will go to some plan," Sumner said, without cracking any character or smile. Marc now knew, without any doubt, he had made a serious mistake agreeing to this trip. He knew some Italian, yet Sumner had never once asked him regarding his language skills.

Monday morning, February 26, he accompanied Mr. Wells to his first meeting. Down a long, enormous hallway, a horribly obese, gray-haired man struggled to walk down and greet them. Mr. Wells shook his hand, and then they followed him back to an equally cavernous office. Marc found the contrast between Mr. Wells—tall, slim, well-dressed, with a cane—to the overweight man who should have a cane, remarkably strange. After sitting down and taking out his notepad, Marc realized this man whom he failed to recognize, actually was, in fact, Mussolini in the flesh.

Mussolini insisted upon speaking English, while Mr. Wells responded in Italian. Sumner's voice, void of all emotion, gave Marc a headache. He prayed they would reverse their choice of languages so that Italian could remain a romantic language to Marc. Mussolini spoke English at a relaxed pace, appearing as if it were his native language.

"Again, who are you meeting in Germany?" Marc repeated to Sumner on the train as they left Rome en route to Germany.

"Oh, I am not sure. They did not give me a solid agenda," Sumner said as he studied his notes. Marc heard the same avoidance in his voice he'd heard on the train to Rome.

"Whom would you hope to meet with?"

"What do you mean? I am just the undersecretary, Marc, but sometimes people read more into it than that. The Germans are different. These meetings will be lower level," he said, looking up and then out the window.

"I would like to prepare myself, Mr. Wells. I agreed to accompany you, however, not to be just led around in the dark."

Just then, as the train pulled into the Munich station, Sumner's attention never left the windows. He grew even quieter, withdrawn, corpselike, as he studied the flags and people.

"Is there something you see?" Marc finally asked.

"Yes, just not sure what to call it," Sumner answered back. The tone caught Marc off guard because it hit him as sincere, unlike the typical avoidance he'd heard before.

Marc was shocked by Ribbentrop's behavior during their meeting. Mussolini acted thoughtful, and spoke softly at times. Marc poured himself into taking notes for Sumner Wells, as the German official ranted and raved. Mr. Wells continued in the same lifeless, monotone voice, except this time in German.

After a two-hour-long diatribe, Marc's ear was tuned to the German language, spurred on by a hint of fear. Afterwards in the hotel, over dinner, Sumner explained to Marc that Ribbentrop had lived in America, worked in the United States for a while, and spent a lot of time around Montréal before the First World War. Marc's nerves were still wrecked from what seemed like an endless machine gun barrage of German words.

"He can speak English as well as you or I, but he spoke only German to make a point," Wells explained, "and he is the one who refused to let anyone have a copy of the notes from Munich. That is why I requested that I bring a secretary. I told Ribbentrop that I could not take notes and carry on a conversation in German at the same time," he said. Marc pondered if Ribbentrop's rant was an attempt to draw out some emotion from Sumner. He then realized that Sumner knew all along he'd be meeting Ribbentrop.

"I see. Whom are you meeting tomorrow?" Marc asked coolly.

"I have no idea. This may be it. We might be back on a train to Belgium. But if there are more meetings, he will inform me in the morning," Sumner said as he took a glass of wine.

"This diplomacy business is a lot like prostitution. You just show up and turn on the light," Marc said, looking directly at Sumner as he drank his wine.

"Marc, you might have a future," Sumner said. He smiled and raised his glass for a toast.

Marc and Sumner found the powdered wigs odd at the Reich chancellery. Marc swallowed hard and fidgeted in his chair, waiting with Sumner Wells in the hallway. "Whom are we meeting again?" he pressed.

"Someone. I have not been told. They just gave me this appointment and nothing else was said," Sumner said, a slight quiver in his voice. Marc continued to ponder his remark about prostitution the night before and what an unusually successful career Mr. Wells has had, given his dry personality.

The door opened to the office and a medium-height man with slick, dark hair walked out and shook both Sumner's and Marc's hands. He then eagerly invited them in to take a seat in his massive office. Marc at first believed he would wait in the hall, but the man insisted that he join the meeting and take notes. He was warm and friendly, which was a complete turn from Ribbentrop. He spoke evenly and without any dramatic ranting and raving of the previous meeting a few days prior with Ribbentrop. His voice had a rhythmic cadence at times, and Marc felt uncomfortable that he found himself attracted to this voice when compared to Sumner's monotonous German shuffle.

Hitler then turned directly to Marc and asked in German, "Do you believe the people of France and Germany can know peace?"

Marc glanced at Sumner Wells, confused by the question.

"Marc is my secretary. He has no diplomatic post with France," Mr. Wells answered.

"I know that, but he was born in France, and is French, and I am asking him as a Frenchman: does he believe France and Germany can know peace?" Marc's stomach fell and he suddenly realized Dora was right.

"Marc, I believe he wants to know how you feel personally," Sumner said.

"Yes, exactly correct." Hitler then turned to a tablet of paper. "It says here you were born at the American Hospital in Paris, on June 14, 1919. I know you are an American, but you are also French." Marc's mind turned blank. "Do you believe the French and German people can know peace?"

Dora came to his mind, when he danced with her back on the *Normandie*, and then he said, "I believe it is always a hope, like the sun rising."

His answer pleased Hitler. "When you return to Paris, I hope you share that hope with whomever you meet in the government," and then he continued on for another forty-five minutes, confessing that he never wanted this war that had been thrust upon him. He never again asked Marc a direct question, and Marc resumed his note-taking duties.

Once outside the Reich chancellery, Mr. Wells spoke. "You did very well in there. I am sorry that you may have felt you were put on the spot." However, the complete lack of any emotion gave Marc serious doubts about Mr. Well's sincerity. Marc resolved in himself to not share this meeting with anyone when he returned to Paris. The meeting with Rudolf Hess seemed anticlimactic after Hitler. However, the meeting with Goering, Marc found disconcerting.

Goering's entire appearance countered everything in Marc's mind of the stereotypical Nazi. His hands looked like the claws of a swollen badger that had raided a pirate's treasure trove of elaborate jewelry. On one hand he wore an emerald that was at least an inch wide. His uniform was white, unlike any other official uniform Marc had seen while in Berlin. Marc took notice of the artwork that he had placed on the walls of his badger den. Goering stopped mid-sentence with Mr. Wells and walked towards Marc.

"Marc, it is amazing, but I must confess to you that I don't believe it is an original," Goering said to him in the hallway.

"How can you tell?"

"It is too clean and neat. Over in America you may not know this but, in Europe, art students would study by copying originals. Often, their work exceeded that of the artist."

"I had no idea."

"Do you think there is anything you can do about the situation?" Mr. Wells said, attempting to recapture Goering's attention.

"There is nothing that can be done. Our air power is superior to all of Europe combined. They are lunatics you know."

"They are just attempting to defend themselves from what they perceive as an aggressor."

"I was not referring to the French or British. Marc, there are several artists living in Paris you should take note of and, if you can, try to collect. Have you met Picasso yet? I know his work is degenerate, but it is superbly degenerate and that must be admired. I would smuggle some, but you must understand my circumstances."

CHAPTER 9

The train approached the border of Belgium and, after customs, it continued on toward France. Marc felt a wave of relaxation come over him as the train left Germany. Sumner Wells barely spoke on the train to Paris. He did not pore over notes or obsess over details. Marc's mind gradually reflected upon the trip.

"It is strange," Marc said, staring out the window.

"What?"

"In Italy, we only had to meet one person, and that person was the head of state."

"Yes."

"But in Germany, we met four, including Hitler."

"You are very observant, Marc."

"And, I am still uncertain of who exactly is in charge of Germany."

"You have read my thoughts," Sumner Wells said as he turned back to Marc from the window. "You should return with me to America. When we get back into Paris, call the Italian Line and let them know," Sumner Wells said casually.

"I see, just like that? Who will run the travel desk at the embassy?"

Sumner Wells did not respond. He continued to look out the window as the landscape passed by. The train steward came by and offered drinks.

"Yes, please," Wells grunted. "Make it two," as he looked at Marc. "I just believe it is a good idea to leave. Have you thought about working in diplomacy? You did very well," he said, his voice even, without ever looking at Marc.

"Has this been helpful to you?" He turned to Sumner as he stared out the window, lost in his Scotch. "Mr. Wells, was it helpful to have me along, as a citizen of both France and the United States, in these meetings?"

"Yes, of course, but Marc," and after a long pause Sumner said, "they are beyond all help."

An hour later, Sumner had several drinks down. "Is there anything else that I should know about before we get back to Paris?" Marc asked.

"Only that you had met several assembly members and the premier before the trip, and will meet them privately after this trip," he said, his words somewhat slurred, "but don't worry. It does not matter. It is just the story we floated. But ..." He paused and then never finished his sentence.

"What about others? Do you think I could call the Italian Line and get passage for others?" Marc asked.

"You can try, but I doubt it. I think I have played my cards and lost. Actually, they are the ones who have lost," he said.

Marc had to help him walk when they arrived in Paris.

"There he is," Marc heard as he reached the platform with Sumner.

"Grandpa, Grandpa! You are so ill," the man said dramatically, and Marc recognized him as Bullitt—in disguise.

"So good to see you, my son." The nun kissed Marc on his head and drew in close to him, taking the cane away to hide in her smock. "His fever is very high, so very sick." She spoke loudly for others to hear. Mr. Wells looked on the surface just like any other middle-aged man; however, his cane set him apart and had become his calling card to the press. Without the cane, he could pass unnoticed through the curtain of doubt.

"Make clear, my father is very ill, please," Bullitt said, as the four of them walked past the reporters looking for Sumner Wells' arrival from Germany.

"We will take him directly to the hospital, do not worry, my son," the nun said.

No one spoke of the smell of hard alcohol that wafted through the car. Marc held his mind in check as the silence in the car built into an uncomfortable roar.

"I should have told you he drinks," Bullitt said as the car drove through the darkened Paris streets. "I thought you would know, but, well, I am sorry."

"How did you know?" Marc asked, still shocked by the ruse at the station.

"He told a porter on the train in Belgium, who called ahead," Bullitt said. "When did he start?"

"Before the train left Berlin," Marc said coldly, understanding just how much a failure Sumner Wells felt the trip had been.

The trip accomplished nothing and Marc realized there would be no peace. He did not follow Sumner Wells to Britain, but instead stayed behind in Paris. He focused upon the travel logs. Sunday came, and Marc joined his friends for dinner.

"When are you leaving?" he asked Dora.

"I am not. I don't need to get back to America, that is David and Nigel's problem," she waved her hand dismissively and snorted.

"It is your problem, Dora. This is not going to end with any peace agreement," he said. She looked out the window at the street. Marc became frustrated at her denial over the danger of the war.

"Marc, they have to have peace. They have no choice," Nigel said in a strong direct voice. "The first meeting is always a failure. This is just the start of the process," he continued to preach. "Mr. Wells always gets drunk on trains and you are reading too much into it."

"What is he like?" David asked meekly.

"Dry as dust, and just about as much life," Marc said, believing he was asking about Mr. Wells.

"Odd, he speaks well enough on the wireless," David said next, obviously referring to Hitler. Marc froze for a second inside. He weighed the consequences of his friend's reaction if they knew he had met Hitler.

"I never met him. I just waited outside," Marc lied. "At the hotel, in fact." Marc regretted that, wondering if they believed his lie. "I have a problem," he said, trying to get Dora's attention.

"What is it?"

"Mr. Wells met with Leon Blum, and I have now close to three thousand of the most vile and nasty letters I have ever read in my life," Marc said, hoping that she would see that the same anti-Semitic attitudes in Germany were now in France.

"Are they addressed to him?"

"Yes, of course," Marc said, wondering where this would end up next.

"Then he should read them. He should read every single one of them. Your job is not to hide his eyes," she said with near disgust in her voice.

"Dora, are you the least bit worried about these kinds of attitudes?"

"Marc, if I was to move every time someone said or wrote something anti-Semitic, I would be living at the bottom of the sea."

Monday morning, Marc approached the ambassador regarding the letters.

"This is not South America, and he wanted to come over here. Therefore, they are his to read. He needs to understand the significance of meeting with certain individuals," Bullitt said. "He would not listen to me, so let him live and learn."

Sumner surprised Marc as he started to read the letters. Marc did not think he would pay much attention to them and would just brush them aside. He read for nearly two hours straight without saying a word. Marc noticed that he had stopped and closed his eyes. Marc recognized the same emotional storm of frustration and despair in himself. Sumner then said out loud to no one, except to himself and maybe Marc, "I am amazed that this poison of the mind knows no border."

Roosevelt spoke in glowing terms of the diplomatic trip. Marc's routine returned, but every time someone would stall or delay booking on the American ships, Ribbentrop's raging fit, that Germany would never accept anything but a full surrender, haunted him. Finland settled with Russia.

Marie found the meeting with Leon Blum more troubling than with Adolf Hitler, which hurt Marc's feelings. Sumner was back in America by March 30, and Marie could not meet Marc that night for dinner. He spent Wednesday evening with Allen and his British friends from the British Expeditionary Force at an English pub in Paris.

The warm tone of the tube radio filled the room. The men echoed back to the radio like a church choir, "Germany calling, Germany calling," laughing out loud, with shouts and hollers. The voice told of the important papers found in Poland that proved that America was anything but a neutral power. Lord Haw Haw's thick British accent sickened Marc, as it scolded America for attempting to drive a wedge between Germany and Italy.

But it was the next bomb blast of words that hit Marc the hardest.

"Ambassador Bullitt in these papers is quoted that he considers the French the first line of defense of the United States."

Marc walked to the bar and said, "Double Scotch, straight up."

Then, not long after that, Marc ordered another round. Allen stopped joking with Marc, and then he had to walk him home that night to his flat.

CHAPTER 10

David did not hear Lord Haw Haw that night on the radio, but he did read the papers. "America No Longer Welcomed at the Peace Table," flashed across papers in both French and English.

"Do you think this means they might target our ships?" David asked Marc over Sunday dinner.

"No, absolutely not. It just means they are rubbing our noses in it to make themselves look big."

"But, Marc, if they say we are not neutral, then those flags on the ship mean nothing."

"David, Germany has enough war already, it will be safe," Nigel said, trying to calm him. Dora sat silently and just observed.

Before Marc left that night, he cornered Dora. "Why is he so preoccupied by these absurd fears?" Dora looked down first and then back up at Marc.

"Some things never leave people," she paused. "They are like eternal moments." Marc stared at her. "David has a moment like that, and all we can do is just listen to him," she said. Marc pondered her words. He knew she was holding something back about David out of a sense of protection.

The Italian Line advertised a sailing, but then canceled it. Eventually, they did both at the same time; they made an announcement that all voyages were canceled, and then released a poster that stated "Full Steam Ahead." The confusion and frustration did not matter for most, because the price exceeded their means. David, however, rushed upon the opportunity.

David stood in the line that wrapped out of the Italian Line ticket office and down the street.

"Two thousand dollars?" David gasped.

"Yes, sir, that is correct," the agent responded quickly.

"American dollars? I just want a standard cabin, not a suite," David continued, his face blank.

"Sir, it is American dollars, and that is for a standard cabin," the agent explained. David's face then contorted in shock.

"That is insane. Why are these fares so outrageous?"

"Sir, there are no passengers going east, and the insurance is very high. We have to cover the expenses for the ship round-trip. So, I understand, I could never afford these rates myself, but there is nothing I can do about it."

"How much is third?" David asked.

"Berths are seven hundred dollars," the agent said quickly, while looking at the others in line.

"I will take it," David paused and realized he did not even have this much money now left in his bank account. He would need to get a loan.

"Do you want a ticket, sir?" the agent asked. David just walked away without answering. He walked back to the Opera Metro station, and stood on the platform in disgust. The train came, the passengers boarded, and the train left with David standing on the platform. He climbed the stairs back to the street and made his way toward the Place de la Concorde and the American Embassy.

"They would never fire on the Italians," David said over and over again to Marc. His eyes appeared to be looking past Marc, to someone behind him. He spoke quickly, with a tremble in his voice. "Is there any way that I could get a travel loan through—" He paused. "I know they would never fire on the Italians," he repeated softer, and he appeared like a child.

"I tried to get a ticket, but the rates are too high," David added.

"What was the date of their ship?" Marc asked.

"May 28. Not sure which ship. I think the *Rex*," David said. Marc could tell by David's behavior that he would starve himself and likely sleep on the streets to take this ship.

Marc took out his wallet and looked, then told the secretary he needed to run an errand. He walked to the bank and took out the money for David to get a ticket on the *Rex*. "You owe me nothing. Just try and slam some sense into the other two." Outside the bank, David broke down in tears and then ran back to the Italian Line offices on Rue Auber.

Sunday came again, and Marc welcomed the break for dinner with the gang, but missed the jovial conversations of the past.

"Marc, those ships are floating targets. They have huge American flags on them, and they are stopping them at Gibraltar for hours. Sometimes even a few days," Nigel said, dismissing him outright about taking David's slot in July. "Don't you think the British would like it if America would join the war? It does not have to be a German torpedo. Any torpedo could do it under the right circumstances."

"I think you are ..." Then Marc stopped. He had tried to keep this thought from his mind over the months as he directed Americans to Genoa or Lisbon. He knew there were risks, but did not take seriously that a ship would be fired upon.

"When are you leaving?" Dora asked David.

"Well, the ship leaves on the twenty-eighth, but I want to get down there sooner than that, so I am thinking of leaving May 15." Marc did not know why, but the simple fact of having a ticket gave David a complete new sense of peace.

"And what about you?" Dora looked toward Nigel.

"I still have business with the bank. If things turn, they have assured me they will make the arrangements," Nigel responded, shrugging his shoulders.

"I see. I heard you had a nice time with the LeRoy family," Dora pressed.

"I did not realize you knew them. Are they ..."

"Yes."

"You mean the family involved with bauxite and aluminum production? Are you sure?"

"You have been a very busy boy running all about France for your bank," Dora said, toasting her wine glass.

"Dora, I think you know why, and I am impressed. Next time I will clear my appointments with you." Nigel smiled.

"They are very nice. I hope she is not wearing that silly perfume, Chypre, anymore. I got her some Shalimar last time I visited."

"I believe that was her scent at dinner," Nigel stared back into Dora's eyes.

Marc began to feel a greater sense of disconnection with everyone around him. "This is not going to last forever, you know," Marc said.

"Dinner?" Dora asked.

"No, this false peace. Soon, there will be no need to argue," Marc said, and no one replied.

Marc took Marie's hand from across the table during dinner that same week.

"But I do love you," Marc pleaded with Marie.

"I know, but Marc, it is not right. We cannot do this just so I can leave with you. What about my family? What about my life?"

"Marie, they could come as well."

"Marc, you are overreacting. France is in no danger. I will marry you when there is no threat of running away. Not just to run away."

"Then, you accept. We are engaged." Marc looked at her.

"Yes, of course I do. I love you, but I do not want to do this just to run away. After the war, like your parents," she smiled at him. Marc cherished the promise. It pleased him to think that he had found her at last and now he knew eventually they would marry. He also took a certain pleasure that his life would follow, in a sense, his parents' lives. "But, for now, we must tell no one. It is a promise, for later, Marc. For later, after this war."

CHAPTER 11

"It is a classic overreach," Nigel said when Germany invaded Norway.

"I suspect they must have overlooked the country," Dora said when Germany invaded Denmark.

"Thank you, Marc. You have no idea what this means for me," David said as he left for Italy with the ticket Marc had bought for him.

"They have now taken on a fight they cannot win," Allen said to Marc when Germany invaded Belgium on May 10, 1940.

"No, no, nothing serious. I want to see the Walt Disney parade. It seems like everyone has seen it now in Paris. Please, we can see something more serious next time," Marie said, using just the right tone of voice that would win her case that Wednesday afternoon of May 15.

"If there is a bunch of kids cutting up in the theater, remember, I told you so. What about *Goodbye, Mr. Chips*? I hear it is very interesting, but it might be in English."

"I can understand English. I have not heard of it before. You are just so stubborn about French." She poked him and he leaned in to kiss her. "No, I want to see a cartoon."

"Then let's. It will be good for me, too," he decided. They bought the tickets at the box office and walked inside for the show.

The theater had an art deco interior. People of various dress packed the rear part of the theater to take in the daily newsreels, which were free so long as the viewers did not sit down. One newsreel had just finished as Marc and Marie seated themselves in a pair of seats in the middle.

"I am looking forward to this weekend." Marc took her hand and squeezed it.

"I have created a monster in you," she whispered into his ear and nudged her nose against his earlobe.

"You have indeed," he turned and gave her a long kiss, then said in a childish voice, "I love you."

The screen of the theater came to life with the black-and-white headlines of the newsreel. People in the back of the theater jostled to see if the headlines were new or old.

"Militiamen follow in fathers footsteps" flashed over the screen as two lines of soldiers marched in the snow. "The twenty-ones have reached France. And on the snow-clad surfaces where their fathers once tread, they stride out with weary step."

"My God, this is so old. I can't believe they are still showing this one," Marc complained to Marie. She had never seen this newsreel, because it was produced for the British. Her eyes took in the sight of the young, cocky British striding across snow-covered fields, rifles in hand.

"Roll out the barrel, we'll have a barrel of fun! Roll out the barrel, we've got the blues on the run," the men sang with hearty voices. Some in the audience joined in the chorus. "Zing, boom, tararrel, ring out a song of good cheer. Now's the time to roll the barrel, for the gang's all here."

"The British sure love their songs," Marie leaned over into Marc. He leaned into her closer, a smile on his face.

"That's the song of this war, the song that these militiamen will be remembered by when they are veterans. They are a splendid type of fellow and it is funny to think that twenty-one years ago, they were called war babies." Marc could not wait for this tired newsreel from February to be over. He never liked it and each time it played, he liked it even less. "People wondered if being born at the end of a long war, if their nerves would be affected." Men crawled on the ground and made their way over the field with rifles at the ready.

Marc used the time to look at Marie. She stared religiously as the images flashed on the screen. Her face bore a serious frown. "Not much sign of that today as they bear arms in the defense of freedom against the Nazi war machine."

"Even their news is kind of cocky," she said to Marc.

"I like Allen, but when he gets with the rest of them, they can be a bit much," he said as he looked back at the screen. It went black and then the lead started for another newsreel. Even more people now stood in the rear of the theater. "The British and French move into Belgium" flashed across the screen.

"I have seen this one," Marie said, continuing to hold Marc's hand.

"And now the advance of the British Expeditionary Force. These are the pictures that have a supreme sentimental interest for British audiences as the custom's barriers rise on Franco-Belgian boundaries and the mechanized troops move forward." Horizontal poles across the border road rose to allow trucks, tanks, and artillery through the town as people lined the streets. Silence fell in the theater as people studied the images. Marc held Marie's hand in his lap.

"For long, the British solider had religiously avoided this dividing line, since to trespass on neutral soil meant internment. Now that the die is cast and the balloon has gone up, he is welcomed across the boundary like a savior, and this, of course, is the character in which the Belgian people know the British Army all along, remembering 1914 and 1918. It is no wonder that anxious folk of the invaded Low Countries give the British Tommy a heartfelt cheer as he passes."

Old and young, men, women, and children lined the streets of villages, waving as the transports passed by. Marc stared longer at the screen and noticed details he had missed when he had caught this newsreel two days earlier. People shifted in their seats in the theater and the light from the doors at the rear became obscured by the people who poured in from the street to watch the news.

"It is the same gallant army with a difference. This time it flashes by in vehicles, tanks, armored carriers, lorries spaced out in regular intervals so as not to present a bomber target. There is evidence indeed that Nazi bombers have been feeling for the path by which the BEF will advance. Bomb craters in the road and demolished houses, these tell the story."

The camera spanned a street where some of the houses had sustained heavy damage and where debris littered the street. "Of course, there is a different story sometimes in the relics of Nazi bombers brought down by the RAF." Soldiers carried proudly the rear tail fin of an airplane emblazoned with the swastika.

"So, history repeats itself and the British Army for the third, fourth, and fifth time goes to fight in the Low Countries." The last line irritated Marc, and he was sure Marie as well, because he recognized the over-the-top bragging in the statement.

"And history repeats the pitiable scenes of refugees streaming westward from the war area." People streamed down a road in wagons, on foot, or with horses, a city in the background. Just then, the screen went bright white and the sound cut off. "Film, film," called out several voices in the crowded theater as the lights flashed on.

"The film must have broken," Marc said, as he looked back at the projector room. He could hear the film reel slapping against the projector. The lamp then went dark as an usher came to the front of the theater.

"It will be just a minute," he said in both English and French.

The crowd stopped their chorus of complaints and the usher walked to the back of the theater. The screen came alive again. A cannon fired. "S." A second fired, "C." Then a third fired, "A." "Service Cinémathèque Agencier" flashed over the screen. The newsreel was French.

"Eleventh of May, morning in France: Our civilian population count is already 150 deaths and almost 400 wounded from that dumping of bombs from planes as systematic as blind in its rage on a number of our cities and villages having no military value," the voice spoke with a frantic speed.

A car rushed down a street. Men held a hose of water on the rubble of a burning building. A baby carriage rested on the edge of a second-floor flat where the wall had fallen away. A total silence fell over the theater. The film had sound but there was no narration. The sound of distant rifle shots rang out through the speakers.

A single woman with a cart walked past a burned-out storefront. An old man stared aimlessly at an overturned truck crashed into a building. A cabinet full of dishes was open to the street and the wallpaper blew in the wind where the edge gave way. The film spanned house after house where walls had been blown apart, revealing the personal items of the people who once called them homes. People shifted from side to side as they studied the screen in a trance. The wind was the only sound on the film, then the noise of a plane passing overhead. Marie let go of Marc's hand and put it in her lap. Marc looked straight ahead and did not turn to her. A young child began to cry a few rows in front of them, complaining that she wanted to see the cartoon.

On the screen, young school boys in uniform searched through the broken walls of their school. A man grabbed bicycles out of the wreckage of his business. An old woman and her daughter loaded a cart outside of a two-story building with pock holes all across the front. The screen flashed scenes of young and old men, women, and children picking through their houses, loading what they could carry.

Two minutes passed before there was a single voice on the film. The room felt like it was holding its breath. Marie's hand covered her mouth. Marc grew uncomfortable with the silence. A mother got up with her son and made for the rear of the theater. By now, a few of the children in the theater had become upset.

A man sat outside his house with a bandaged foot. Another man pulled on the jacket of someone dead in the street. A woman with a head bandage wandered through the wreckage. Policemen pulled at bricks, trying to free a trapped person. Others carried a man down the street on a stretcher. It was too much for another woman and her two children sitting near the front. They got up and walked down the aisle. A second person followed her as she cried, pulling the children who complained bitterly of not staying to see the film.

Marc studied the screen as a church appeared with part of the roof gone. In the pews was a briefcase and purse left in a haste. The wall collapsed into the pews until it reached the lectern, like an ocean wave rising upon a beach. Marie could not look away from the screen. Another man near them got up and left the theater, pushing through the crowed back rows of standing people. The newsreel continued without a single voice. Marc wondered if the projectionist would check the film to make sure it had fed correctly. He was puzzled by the lack of voiceover. Rapid gunfire barked out in the distance. The wind whispered through the speakers.

A sign outside a building said "no school today." People swept the floor of a building clearing debris. "May 10, eating too much will make you ill," flashed as it was left scrolled in French on a school chalkboard, followed by "5689 divided by 23…" A woman got up from the center aisle with a crying young girl. Marie whispered, "My God," under her hand as the shock of the scene overtook her. A child's bag hung on a peg. Another student's bag rested on the top of a desk dusted with shattered glass.

A child with an eye bandage cried on a hospital bed. A young boy with a head and nose bandage smiled to the camera. Nurses cared for another bandaged woman covered in a bed. She was wearing smart clothes, as if she had been at the bombed-out church.

Five eternal minutes passed before a single voice was heard over the speakers. The march of raw footage across the screen had become too much for many of the parents and children in the theater. A few tried to calm down their children, but even some of the adults struggled to hold back their emotions. Marie got up and started for the aisle. Marc followed her out through the people standing three deep at the rear doors.

"They lied to us," Marie said to Marc in the lobby. "They lied in the papers. They tell us what we want to hear." She started to cry.

"I am sure the truth is someplace between the two. They don't tell us everything, because they don't want people to panic, but it looks like they hold back too much," Marc said, as he realized he could not sugarcoat what he had just experienced. He wanted to comfort Marie, but was not even sure if it was wise.

"We are going to lose. We are going to become those people on the screen," Marie continued to cry.

Marc tried to calm her down as they left behind a mother with two young children.

"That will not happen, Marie, please."

"Marc, how can you promise that?"

CHAPTER 12

On the morning of May 20, the ambassador called the staff together. "This is not a solution to our problem and it is not meant to cause a panic." The staff stared at him stoically.

"We need to do something to give people confidence, and I know you may believe this absurd, but," he went on as the morning light filled the room, "if they are insistent they must stay, then this will give at least some identification to them."

The staff stood silently looking at the table in front of them. Stacked were bundles of red tickets.

"Take their names, businesses, locations, everything you can get about them on these forms," the ambassador said. "Then copy the key information onto one of the red certificates and give this to them, and they are to put it on their door fronts." The ambassador scanned the faces of the staff to discern their morale.

He watched them as they looked at the forms with total silence. He closed his eyes for a moment.

"Does anyone have any questions?" he asked the staff.

"Do we have any assurance from them?" Marc's voice cracked with emotion.

"What do you mean?" the ambassador responded.

"Is there any diplomatic assurance that these certificates will be respected?" he asked in a quiet and low tone.

"I am not going to lie. We have nothing, but this. We are remaining open. If it comes to the point that they arrive here in Paris, I will be in a position to directly communicate the meaning of the certificates," the ambassador's voice stammered. "I cannot force Americans to leave, but I cannot abandon this post, either, so this is a solution that helps me to know who is left in Paris, and gives me some ability to identify and represent them to the occupying forces."

"When does this start?" Marc choked out another question.

"This morning. I put the notice out to the papers last night. I expect they will find their way here over the next few days, but we should be ready this morning," the ambassador finished.

Marc went with the secretary to unlock the doors. To his surprise, there were already forty to fifty people outside waiting to come in.

"Take this and then place it on your door," Marc said to Nigel after filling out the form. Nigel took the certificate in his hand and looked it over with an odd expression. He then took something from his pocket and pressed it into Marc's hand.

"What is this?"

"It is yours if you need a place to go. The rent is paid up for the year," Nigel said to Marc without any smile. "Do you have the latest on travel?"

"Wait here." Marc went back to his desk and looked through the notices. "Genoa, June 2, but that is far away. If you miss that one, they are sending the *George Washington* to Lisbon and Bordeaux." He then looked at the other dates on the paper. "Well, you can afford it, I am sure, so May 28 out of Genoa, the *Rex* is leaving, along with the Conte." He then looked up. "Bet you wish you'd gone with David now."

"Yes, I feel like an idiot for not going with him." Nigel's face squinted as if he had swallowed a lemon.

"Look, that is not going to help you now. Do you think you could get to Genoa in eight days?" Marc asked him next.

"It is tricky, Marc. I'm not sure. The train station is a mob right now, and there is no petrol, but I might be able to make it," Nigel said.

"Well, I just think Genoa is a good bet, because there is the Italian Line and the United States Line running, so, if you are going to get stuck someplace—" Marc stopped and looked further.

"Look. Bordeaux is just for Americans. At least that is what we believe right now. But that is not until June 10. What about the *Clipper*?" Marc asked him next.

"Well, I don't know. Lisbon is damn far away and through Spain. I guess I am just going to start out and see how bad it is out there and wherever I am closest, I will choose at that time." Nigel then left the embassy, but before leaving Paris, he stopped off at his flat to nail the red certificate to his door.

That night, Marc put the keys in a bowl of colored glass from Biot he bought in the summer of '39.

"Which side of the doorway?" Dora asked Marc the morning of June 1.

"Whichever. It doesn't matter."

"Well, I want to make sure I do this right. I have not ever had to do this before in all my years here, so I figure I have only one chance to get this right."

"Dora, I wish this was a time for jokes, but, you know."

"Oh, I know. I know all too well." She then took out an envelope and gave it to Marc.

"What is this?" He opened it and looked at the bundle of francs. "Oh God, what is this for?"

"In case you need it for anything, because these are yours." She then passed him the keys to her apartment in one of the exceedingly nice districts of town off of Foch Street.

"So all that talk of staying to the end and fighting off the Germans was just talk?" Marc balked.

"Oh, damn right, it was. This is no place for me. I am smart enough to know better, and I sure wish some other stubborn Jews would see the same now." She then looked up. "This Goldilocks is ditching the Three Bears and heading south."

"Do you have a plan?" Marc asked next.

"Lisbon. It is too late for Genoa," she said. "I think I would miss it, but Lisbon, at least, has options. Yes. So, I would leave you the car but I need it, even though I am not sure where I am going to get petrol yet. There is more than enough money for anything the apartment might need, and you, my friend." She kissed him goodbye and she left the morning of June 1.

That night, Marc locked up the francs in his dresser drawer and put the keys with Nigel's in the glass bowl.

"Stay here, and try to act American," Marc said to Marie as she reached the line for the red certificates. He returned then from his desk with a completed form. "Here, sign this," Marc pushed the form across to her.

"But my name is not Elda?" Marie asked, perplexed.

"Miss, these certificates are for Americans only, so please do not share them with your French neighbors," Marc said with an official tone.

"Absolutely not. I would never do that," Marie said, trying to sound convincing.

Later that afternoon, the ambassador said to Marc, "I do hope Elda will be safe here in Paris." Marc froze, searching for words to explain.

"How many have taken up the certificates?"

"Just over five thousand Americans, sir."

"That we know of, and if a few French have need, well, who is to judge? It is war, after all."

"Yes, I think I understand."

"Marc, don't forget."

"Forget what, sir? I am not sure I understand."

"Don't forget to fill one out for yourself. Unless, of course, you have made other plans."

"Oh, yes, thank you. I am rather tired and would have forgotten."

CHAPTER 13

June 2, 1940

Genoa, Italy

David walked down the narrow streets of the old port of Genoa, past several of the small vendors, reaching the steps of a large Moorish-styled church. Upon entering, he sat quietly in the back as he watched what appeared to be some kind of small, private ceremony. Time stood still as he stared at the front of the church but never gazed up at the cross. After about an hour, he got up and walked back again to the train station to look at the board and consider his options.

"David, David! Is that you?" called out a voice behind him. He turned and it was another American friend of his from Paris.

"Larry? What are you doing here?" David said as Larry moved through the crowd with his wife, his young son, and even younger daughter.

"What do you think? I'm here for the same reason you are. Trying to get home," Larry answered back. "It's good to see someone we know. It has been a mess getting here and I didn't think we'd make the ship." David looked down at Larry's two children and then caught the eye of his worried wife.

"Are you on the Italian Line? We can walk down together."

"It's canceled. They are all canceled," David said, trying not to look panicked, but his face turned white with fear.

"What? Are you sure?" Larry asked in disbelief.

"Look, go, go right now down to the US Line's desk and get on the list for the SS *Manhattan.*" Larry's face was serious as he heard David's emphatic tone. "Do you have your passports? They will even take just tax papers." David waved his hand toward the docks. "Go, now. I will meet you down at the dock in an hour or so," and, as he said these words, Larry and his family quickly disappeared from him in the crowds of refugees coming from the latest train into the station.

David walked back toward the church again. He meandered slowly down the narrow streets and passed underneath the medieval gate towers until he came to a small courtyard. He climbed the steps of an unusually small chapel, its interior made of rose-colored marble. It had five rows of chairs inside and, as the door shut and the sound of children playing outside subsided, he saw that he was entirely alone.

He sat down again in the back row, looking forward, slowing raising his eyes until he saw the cross. After twenty minutes, he kneeled. His stomach rumbled, as if he were going to vomit up all of his fears. Then he whispered the words to a god he had not spoken to for twenty-two years. "Oh God, please, help me get home."

June 2, 1940

Vichy, France

"Dora, the *Post* wrote that the State Department says, if you missed the *Manhattan* on June 2 from Genoa, to go to Bordeaux for the *George Washington,*" her sister said from the other side of the Atlantic. Dora cupped her ear to drown out the noise of the callers in the busy international phone exchange. The room was packed and crowded with all manner of travelers speaking different languages.

"That is too long. I am going to go south to Lisbon."

"But Bordeaux is closer. Please don't," her sister pleaded.

"I will call you again when I reach Spain, but my plan is to get out on the Pan Am *Clipper*. Look, I need to go. I love you and will be home soon. Don't worry," she said as she hung up the phone. She then looked at all the people, each one trying to reach a loved one or make their own arrangements. It reminded her of a busy Christmas Eve on the East Coast of America, yet without the joy.

June 2, 1940

Tours Train Station, France

Nigel woke as the train came to a stop. All of the passengers stood and waited to leave the car. He was still half asleep but stood and left the car all the same. The connecting train waited on a separate platform. After sitting down, he realized that he had left his bags in the previous train car.

He ran quickly back to the car. His bag was nowhere to be seen. He heard the whistle of the departing train. He looked frantically through the car. Perhaps it had moved? He searched the front of the car. The whistle blew a second time and much longer. Then three short snorts and he heard the conductors make a last call. He ran back to the rear of the car, thinking it was on the rack. He returned to his chair and looked underneath for the third time. He could hear the train leaving the station.

He sat down and started to punch the seat in front of him. He pulled back his hand after his knuckles caught the edge and cut him. Nigel looked up to see if anyone else was coming to the empty train car. He then remembered and checked inside his jacket. He pulled out his wallet: thirty-five francs. It was not enough for another train. His mind began to race. He could feel a sweat coming over him. He hit the chair again and it snapped back at him. Then he curled up in the seat next to him and began to cry, hoping that no one would enter the car.

June 2, 1940

Genoa, Italy

On June 2, Larry, with his family, and David boarded the SS *Manhattan*. As the ship docked in the morning, he could see the giant American flags painted on both the bow and stern. Along the amidships section in bright white letters read, "UNITED STATES."

"Here is your number. Are you traveling alone?" the officer asked him. A desk had been set up just before the gangway.

"Yes. Well, no. I know this family," as he looked behind him.

"Are you a relative?" the officer pressed.

"No, no, just friends." David glanced at the ledger as the officer looked over his papers.

"I don't have any cabins, but I can put you together with them if you like. I have the smoking room and the lounge. We are trying to keep young kids inside yet close to the boats," the officer said, writing his name in the ledger.

David looked back at Larry and his wife Margarette. "It will be fun." He then looked down at Larry's young daughter. "Like a camping trip. You like camping, right?" Then he turned back to the officer and said in a soft, dignified tone, "We'll take five together for the lounge, please," while he focused his mind upon the rose-colored marble altar of the church back in the port.

"Here are your cot numbers," the officer said, and passed back their papers.

June 2, 1940

Paris

Marc left the Metro and started to walk toward the embassy. He noticed people on the street reading flyers strewn everywhere on the ground. He picked one up and started to read the warning of the approaching bombardment.

"Is this real?" he asked the secretary when he walked in.

"Yes, maybe. To them, it is real," the secretary nodded toward the lobby filled with people in all sorts of dress waiting to apply for American visas.

After dinner, Marc sat with Marie's family around the radio. No one spoke a word, each one lost in his or her own world, poring over the meaning of every French word. The tension on the dial was too much, and the station would slip. Marie's father got up and then tuned it back into the official station.

"Go to sleep, I told you two," Marie's mother told her little sister and brother.

"But we can't. It is too loud," the little girl said.

"Marie, please," her father said next.

"Come with me," Marie said, and took them back into their room. "Now, you need to sleep, and be good." She tucked them both in, and then sat for a moment on the edge of her brother's bed. Then she heard it. Then another one followed the first. She got up and went to the window and stood in front of it in silence, holding her breath so not to smother the noise of the next one.

She opened the window to the warm night. She stood listening, while her brother and sister stayed in their beds.

Marie's mother left the room next. Marc listened to the radio with Marie's father, his attention utterly absorbed by the reports.

"*Un moment, un moment,*" Marie's father said to Marc as he left the room, but Marc barely noticed as he stared into the frogeye tube of the radio panel. After a few minutes, Marc awoke from his trance of radio reports, realizing he was alone in the room.

Marc listened for their speaking. He heard nothing but the warm voice of the radio. He stood up and walked down the hallway toward the open door to the children's room. Marie stood at the window with her father. Her mother sat with her little sister on the bed. No one spoke. Marc walked into the room toward the window to try and get a glimpse of what they were looking at down on the street. Then he heard them. They were soft and distant, like the muffled backfires of a car. A louder and closer one snapped his ears to attention. The shelling just northeast of the city softly drowned out all other sounds, including the frantic radio reports.

When Marc left that night for his flat, the streets were alive with people packing cars. A couple argued about getting money before the Germans took over the banks. In the Metro, no one spoke. It seemed to Marc that the air had been removed from all of Paris. People lined the floor of Marc's station to sleep that night in fear of the approaching bombs.

CHAPTER 14

June 3, 1940

Paris, France

Bullitt was at a meeting, and Marc was at the embassy speaking with a frantic Belgian woman who claimed to have an American brother in New York. Marc doubted the story, but was sympathetic to her desperation to leave France. He noticed that the father stayed outside while she pleaded for a visa, and that her husband looked like a traditional Orthodox Jew.

The sirens then began to blare in the streets and a man came running into the embassy, yelling in French to get underground to the basement.

At first, Marc thought the man was overreacting, but when another woman came running across the street and entered the building, he could hear the drone of the planes. Before he had another moment to think, the blasting of the anti-aircraft guns began throughout the city.

The entire staff and all the people waiting rushed to the basement. Marc gave his gas mask to the daughter of the woman from Belgium, and helped the father try and put it over her face as she screamed and fought off the mask. Everyone then looked up at once as the shock wave of a bomb could be felt, even in the basement of the building.

June 3, 1940

Gibraltar, United Kingdom

David sat on his cot in the first-class lounge. The ship had been stopped in Gibraltar for hours. Larry had gone out for a smoke along the deck as the ship rocked gently back and forth in the calm seas. His son, Robert, sat with his little sister, Majdouline. Margarette asked the steward how much longer the ship would be waiting before they were allowed to pass.

Majdouline then asked, "Is it time yet?" Her voice broke just over a half whisper.

"No, it is not time yet." Then Margarette asked another question of the steward.

"Mum, is it time yet?" she demanded a little louder in French.

"Majdouline, what do you want?" And then Margarette bent down to listen to her whisper in her ear. "No, no, of course not. Robert, will you get your sister a little book to read from the library?"

Outside on the deck, leaning against the rail, Larry asked another man next to him, "When do you think they will be done with this inspection?"

"I hope soon. The British are being absurd Asses, if you ask me," the man grumbled.

Two officers walked past them and the other passengers on the deck heading aft.

"I hope they are going to start the engines," Larry said, unsure if the man had heard him.

"But Mommy, I can't read," little Majdouline complained as she sat on the cot inside the lounge.

"Robert, will you read it please?" Margarette stood. "I will be right back. I am going to find your father." She walked into the main foyer outside the lounge and spotted David coming in from the promenade deck.

"David, have you seen Larry?" she asked him, looking around.

"Yes, he is on the other side, through those doors." He pointed to the starboard side doors from the foyer.

"Can you go sit with the kids for a minute? They are getting antsy. I need to get Larry," she asked. David went back into the lounge.

As David sat on his cot, Robert said, "*The Tale of Tom Kitten*. Look, Maji, see the kitten with the blue shorts and jacket?" She looked at the front of the book and smiled.

Outside on the deck, Margarette looked up and down for any sign of her husband. She then recognized his jacket from behind as he leaned over the rail.

"Larry, can you take Majdouline for a walk?" she asked.

"Why, what is wrong?" he looked through the windows of the lounge.

"She just needs to get out a bit and I think she will calm down with you taking her," she continued.

"Is she upset?"

"Yes, she is picking up on how tense everyone is waiting here. I think if you take her, she will do better."

The afternoon sun filled the large lounge. Most of the chairs and tables had been moved to the sides of the room. Passengers sat in small groups talking or playing cards. Life jackets served as pillows on most of the cots.

"See, Tom Kitten is too fat for his suit and needs more buttons," Robert said. His little sister laughed.

"Read me more, Robert," she asked him, seeming relaxed.

"I will be right in. Let me finish my smoke," Larry said, looking down the deck where the officers had entered just a moment prior.

"Mr. Drake Puddle-duck has Tom's clothes, Maji. See?" Robert said as she giggled.

Margarette stepped back into the lounge through the doors of the foyer. David rose from the cot and walked over to meet her.

"How is she doing?" Margarette asked.

"Fine, fine. They have been reading and she is laughing. You worry too much. Did you sleep well last night?"

"No, of course not. Did you?" she asked.

"Well, not exactly, but tonight should be better," David answered, looking out through the windows.

Robert paged through the book, carefully showing each small illustration to his sister.

"See, look, Maji," Robert said. Robert then turned to the last page of the book.

"The clothes all came off directly in the pond, because there were no buttons, and Mr. Drake Puddle-duck and Jemima and Rebeccah have been looking for them ever since. See, look, Maji." He held up the book for his sister. Her smile fell away and she stared intensely at the page. She started to cry and then took the life jacket from underneath her cot and started to put it on.

"What are you doing?" Robert asked.

"What's wrong?" Margarette demanded as she rushed over from the doors. "Majdouline, what is wrong?"

"I am not stupid. I am not going to lose my clothes," she cried as she struggled with the jacket.

"What did you say to her?" Margarette turned to Robert.

"Nothing, I just read her the book. See?" He turned the pages.

"Majdouline, dear, no one is going to lose their clothes. Calm down, please, for mommy," Margarette pleaded, trying not to be overheard.

"What is wrong with that little girl over there?" a man turned to the woman sitting next to her on a cot.

"I don't know, but she is upset," the woman peered over.

"Are they putting on their life jackets?" he asked as he took his vest from the front of his cot.

"I bet they have seen a U-boat. You know, I saw one myself this morning," the woman said, pulling her jacket out from under the cot.

"Good idea," another woman said as she pulled on her vest.

"Maji, nothing is wrong. Calm down, please," Robert pleaded quietly and looked through the room. He then whispered, "You are frightening the others. Please behave."

"Daddy is going to take you for a walk," Margarette said, forcing a smile.

Larry began to pull himself away from his conversation with the other passenger and turned toward the foyer entrance.

"We got lucky, I suppose, to get to Genoa in time. Ventimiglia was a riot and, had it not been for our American passports, I don't think we would've made it," Larry said.

"I sure hope we get going soon. We're sitting ducks out here," the man said, looking out over the afternoon sea.

"Well, I need to take my daughter for a walk," Larry said. His eye caught a man leaving the foyer with a life jacket on, followed by a second person wearing a vest. He dropped his lit cigarette and made for the door.

"David, will you get Larry for me?" Margarette turned to David as she tried to stop Majdouline from crying.

"Why is your life jacket on?" Larry asked a fourth passenger he caught leaving the lounge.

"U-boats. They saw a U-boat," the older man said. Larry nearly knocked David over as he came through the lounge door.

"Larry, will you …" Margarette stopped as she saw his face.

"Get the jackets on. There is a U-boat," Larry said, with no attempt to protect Robert or Majdouline from hearing him. His words snapped through the lounge like a bullet. They each quickly donned jackets and then left the lounge, followed by many others. Passengers gathered on the boat deck, searching the afternoon sea for some hint of what was to come next.

The two officers returned to the bridge after their inspection, each wearing a life jacket.

"Take those off. You are going to frighten the passengers," the captain barked as he emerged from the navigation room.

"We thought you ordered it." The officers looked at one another and then back at the captain. "They told us we have seen a U-boat." The captain's face turned red with a grimace and expression of disgust. He took a few deep breaths and then took the microphone. "Request permission to leave now. U-boat." He then looked out over the bridge and started to walk back to the navigation room but stopped. He turned and picked up his pace toward the radio room.

"Yes, that is correct. Can you advise us how much longer?" the radio room officer said to the British officer on the other end. Just then, the captain took the transmitter from his hand and hit the button.

"Five minutes more. Starting engines in five minutes. We have a U-boat in the area," and then silence.

"Sir, there is no U-boat. I have not been advised of any U—" Then the sound stopped as the captain hit the mic again.

"You can keep the fucking mail. We don't need it if you are going to let us take a hit like some goddamn sitting duck," followed by total silence on the other end.

"Over on the port side," one passenger said to another.

"Really?" the man asked the other man passing to the starboard deck.

"I saw it myself, just missed us," the woman said with a confident snort.

"Do you think …?" Margarette looked up at David.

"Think what?"

"Well, that there really is a U-boat."

"Probably not," David said, glancing back and forth over the passengers, "but I have to believe there must have been something. Otherwise, the crew would be calming everyone down."

Robert held Maji's hand, and the Puddle-ducks of *The Tale of Tom Kitten* rested face down on the cot, alone in the lounge.

CHAPTER 15

June 3, 1940

Paris, France

Marc decided to walk home instead of taking the Metro. He approached one of the main boulevards that led from the east train station. All along the road, people carried whatever baggage they could manage. A few were injured. Marc stood on the side of the street and watched as they passed. At first he was going to cross over, but then decided to join the crowd and walk for a bit.

He knew after a few moments where they were going. He could overhear them speaking among themselves in French or Dutch. After crossing the Seine, and walking a few more blocks, Marc briefly lost track of time. It had not been long, maybe only twenty minutes or so.

The crowds grew denser. There was less room to walk on the sidewalks or even the street. In another block, he could see the façade of the station in front of him. He did not walk any further, and instead turned around.

He walked against the crowds coming down the street, turning his back to the south train station with a horde of people before it. A herd of goats being led by a peasant farmer did not faze him, because livestock had now become common in Paris.

After another thirty or so minutes, he stood in the street below his apartment. Bricks crushed a car on the other side of the street. People took what they could from the building. Marc stood in shock, as he looked directly up into the parlor room of his fourth-floor flat. He made his way in through the door and up the marble staircase as others were coming down.

Marc opened the door to his apartment, and the evening breeze gently flapped the drawing he'd done of Marie back in early December. He turned over the armoire, pulled out the clothes, and packed his bags. He found the keys that Nigel and Dora had given him. The bowl's rose-colored glass lay shattered on the floor. He stuffed the francs from Dora into his jacket.

Marc felt cold and detached as he gathered his belongings. He fully accepted the loss of the wall to the outside street below. It did not bother him at all that he was not sure where he was going to stay. He had two sets of keys, after all, for two other Parisian apartments. *They could not have got all of them,* he thought to himself.

Nothing could take his mind off the crowds at the south station. The desperate voices, the stares of the other refugees looking to flee the city, echoed in his mind. Before he left the apartment, he looked around. He saw the drawing again on the wall, and remembered with a small laugh what the instructor had said. "This is what you came to France for, Marc."

He took a deep breath and decided to leave it on the wall, turned and made his way down the stairs, thinking of sleeping that night at the YMCA. He knew it would be crowded, but it was better than sleeping alone in an apartment if another raid should come.

June 5, 1940

Bordeaux, France

Nigel walked through the masses of men, women and children moving toward the city. He could see the Bordeaux skyline in the distance. The bus he had taken ran out of petrol five miles back. On both sides of the road, refugees plodded forward toward the city. Some pulled handcarts containing what belongings they could carry; a few had horse-drawn carriages.

People talked, but in a hushed tones, as if their voices could somehow draw down the planes. As they began to approach the outer parts of

Bordeaux, the mood became somber. From time to time, a car or truck would pass, but this was rare.

Nigel crested a small hill and in front of him was a scene he was not prepared for. A truck lay on its side in a ditch. About thirty yards in front of that, two dead horses stretched across the road. Beyond the horses laid a dead farmer who appeared to be maybe fifty years old. No one spoke a word. People just kept moving toward the city. In the distance, Nigel could see a column of smoke come from south of the city and knew that meant a bombing raid.

A teenaged girl walked with her father in front of Nigel. A truck sped by in the opposite direction, just as a second truck was coming from behind Nigel and the girl. The truck swerved to miss the oncoming vehicle, and the truck's mirror struck the girl in the back of the head.

She fell to the ground, rolling into the ditch on the side of the road. The father yelled in horror and Nigel ran to see if he could help. The father took the girl into his arms and began to rock her back and forth, yelling for anyone to help. Nigel removed his wallet first and then took off his jacket to give her a pillow. He tried to see if the girl was bleeding on the back of her head and then pulled back. The rear of her skull collapsed inward, mixed with blood and hair.

More trucks and cars passed, but none stopped. Others came running forward to see if they could help, but it was pointless. There was nothing anyone could do. Nigel felt horribly sick to his stomach and helpless as he started to walk away. The girl had died in her father's arms, but the farmer refused to leave her on the side of the road.

June 7, 1940

Hendaye, France

The train came to a full stop. All the passengers rose at once. Dora clutched her bag tightly. The conductor yelled out, *"Gare des Deux-Jumeaux, la fin, la fin."*

She was exhausted from the transfers since leaving the phone exchange in Vichy. Limoges, Périgueux, Bordeaux were now behind her. This was the end of France and the beginning of Spain. The tracks were different in Spain and she now needed to change trains again and go through the border crossing.

She walked quickly to the line, which was very long. She barely remembered the questions regarding her passport and travel plans. She sat for three hours on a bench, waiting for the connecting train. Once, she considered leaving to get a drink, but another hour went by and she had not moved.

The train arrived. She boarded it with the other passengers. The cars appeared nearly identical to the French, or at least inside. She clutched the armrest, focusing on her index finger. She never looked the passenger across from her in the eyes. Her lip quivered and she gazed out the window at the passing countryside.

It had been four hours now, but she could not shake it. The woman was gone. In Bordeaux, Dora boarded a direct train for the border. It was extra money, but worth it to her in order to avoid all the stops. The woman across from her had come from Tours.

"Mum, I am hungry, please," her little ones pleaded for some food. But the woman had none left. The older sister then left the car to go buy some bread for the family while the mother waited. The boy was maybe four years old, and the little girl was five or six.

The train's whistle blew and the car began to move forward. The woman looked frantically out the window calling, "Ranette! Ranette!" and then ran to the front of the car. She pleaded in French with the conductor to stop the train, but he said he could do nothing. She screamed Ranette's name over and over again out the door, looking for her amongst the hectic hoard of people moving in every direction.

Passengers tried to calm her down. "You can turn around at the next station," one suggested.

"She is old enough and she will be fine," another man said, trying to help her see that it was not the end of the world. It was true. Her daughter was at least a teenager.

The woman sobbed relentlessly, for hours on end across from Dora. Her two children tried even to console her between their own tears. Dora held the little boy in her lap and the little girl climbed into the lap of the man sitting next to her. There would be no turning around because the train was direct to the border with no stops.

The woman would look up from time to time at the window and would murmur "Ranette," even though it was hopeless. No one knew where her husband was. Maybe he was a soldier at the front.

Dora thought to ask where her husband was, but then didn't, out of fear that he had been wounded or even worse. Instead, she thought about what she would do if it had been her who had lost her daughter at a train station in the middle of a war. Dora could see in the woman's reaction far more than just a single drama of separation, but a breakdown brought about by the cumulative loss of a long, unknown journey.

Dora gave her a handkerchief and tried to comfort her. Others in the car attempted to bring some relief to this woman. Soon, the car was silent except for the click-clack of the tracks and the sobbing of this woman.

Dora clutched the armrest, holding it firm. She sank her spine against the core of the seat, to give a posture that seemed strong for the children. Dora could not let them down or break her masked belief that everything would turn out fine.

Dora was still clutching the armrest of her chair on the train leaving France behind. She focused on her breathing and her index finger held so tight to the wood, she could have drilled through it. But the woman was now gone, and Dora was in Spain. Only the landscape outside passed by. She still felt the little boy in her lap. She still saw the woman sobbing and crumpled across from her. Dora still heard her call out her daughter's name: "Ranette!"

The train came to a stop. Passengers rose to exit the car. The conductor called out, "Madrid, Madrid."

June 9, 1940

Paris, France

"You work at the American Embassy?" the little boy asked Marc in French.

"Yes, and my friend, Allen, over there, he works as a translator at the British Embassy," Marc said as he pointed.

"He is the one who brought us here," the boy then said from his position on the floor of the Paris YMCA. "That is my papa. He has a big factory that makes planes that fly in the sky," the little boy said, pointing and then spreading his arms wide to show the size of the factory. Marc looked and noticed that the man-tall, slender, gray-haired-was speaking with Allen. Next to him was another boy of about eleven years old and another girl with long, blond curls.

"What kind of planes?" Marc asked.

"Uh, I don't know. I am from Belgium. Where are you from?" the boy asked next.

"New York. And is this your dog?" Marc petted the golden retriever sitting next to the boy.

"Yes, this is my dog, and this is my little sister and her dog," he said in a rather simplistic way, almost as if he were younger than his actual age.

"You have a very large family." Marc smiled at the young girl.

Allen then looked up, and then the father. Marc heard the air raid sirens outside of the building.

"In here, now, everyone downstairs now!" Sister Clayton yelled through the room. She looked to be about thirty-five years old, wore glasses, and held a no-nonsense attitude.

Everyone stayed that night in the basement and the air raid sirens announced the arrival of another group of bombings soon after 10 p.m. Marc woke in the morning unsure of the time and found the little boy snuggled up against him.

In the morning, Marc stood half awake, while the ambassador spoke to the staff.

"Anyone who wishes to leave should do so now. I am choosing to stay on, but I do not expect this of you. Please just let me know," he asked.

Marc wondered to himself, if I stay, I wonder if it would be safer to sleep in the basement of the embassy than at the YMCA?

"Sir, may I ask you a question?" Marc stood before the ambassador in his office. "I was wondering if you know if ..."

"Marc, I have no idea. None. I don't know at all what I am doing," he said, going through his papers. "You know, they are going to make me mayor. They are all leaving and they are giving me the honor of mayor," he mumbled to himself.

"Sir, I was going to ask you whether, if I need to, I could stay here, at the embassy."

"There is nothing at all for a situation like this. It has never happened before. And all they can say in DC is leave. No one has left this post, even during the revolution. I have no idea. I am sure this is the end of my career, but I don't care anymore. Someone has to stay and try and maintain some order."

"Can I?" Marc asked.

"Can you what?"

"Can I stay here if I need to? My apartment has been bombed and I have been staying with the YMCA, but I might need to move soon."

"Yes, of course. Absolutely, I had no idea your apartment got hit. I almost got hit last week, too. Maybe it was the same plane that got your apartment?" The ambassador looked down again at his papers. "Have you spoken to your father?" he asked as Marc was leaving.

"No."

"You should. Call him on our lines if you need to. Oh, and ask him for his prayers," Bullitt said as he ransacked his desk.

The streets that afternoon began to fill with cars and carts. People began to leave the city en masse. The shelling now could be heard during the day and night. The softest of the bombs were as loud as the loudest ones only a week ago.

Marc tried the bank, but the line wrapped around the street corner, and he gave up trying to wait, instead counting the only money he had left. The francs from Dora he almost turned away became all-important to him. The Germans had been broadcasting into France that they would confiscate savings accounts as their first action in occupation. Every bank through the city had huge lines of desperate people who now believed German radio more than their own nation's official news.

Marie surprised Marc when she came to the embassy that day.

"What are these for?" Marc asked.

"My father said you can stay there if you need to," she said, holding back tears. "I have to go with them. I have to go, I cannot stay," her eyes watered. "The government is leaving and he needs to follow them, to help set up the new assembly, but it won't be long, and then I can come back, Marc. But if you need a place."

"Marc, you need to go. Don't stay," she then pleaded.

"Marie, we are the only ones left. In about an hour, Bullitt becomes mayor of the city. I cannot ..." He paused, trying to find his emotions.

"You can. It was a promise, Marc, for after the war. Bullitt's problem is not your own. You can go, and should. I am not staying here for you, and it is unfair for you to stay here for me." She then quickly kissed him, and walked out of the embassy.

"Marc, Marc," Bullitt called from his office. Marc quickly walked in to see what he needed.

"Can you do a cable? Have you done it before?" he asked him and gathered papers from his desk.

"Yes, I have done them. What do you need sent?"

"Here, this," he handed Marc a single sheet. "Send it to Hull and Roosevelt. I have to go meet with the police and fire departments."

Marc went into the cable room and checked the line to make sure it was still live. He then sat down to the table and started to type out the message on the secure cable typewriter.

"Start: Hull; Roosevelt; This embassy is the only official organization still functioning in the city of Paris except the headquarters of the military forces, Governor and the Prefecture of Police. Phones still on. Stop."

CHAPTER 16

Morning of June 10, 1940

Paris, France

Marc drove the car as they passed street after street filled with people piling their belongings into carts and cars, preparing to leave the city.

"They said that they would wait. Did you get the cable out?" Bullitt asked Marc.

"Yes, I tested the line before sending. I got a confirmation it was received," Marc said as they pulled near Notre Dame.

"You should leave today," Bullitt said as they walked inside. Marc thought it was an odd statement because it seemed pointless to him. Marc already knew the details of travel for leaving the war zone, and the window to leave had already past.

Inside the walls of Notre Dame Cathedral, Ambassador Bullitt knelt in front of the priest as he held his hand on his head and gave prayers. It was a horrible scene for Marc to behold, filled with bitterness for all who were present. Bullitt sobbed as the responsibility now rested on his head. The French government had left during the night and the only solution that seemed reasonable was to give Bullitt the duty as honoree mayor.

Marc returned to the embassy with the ambassador after the ceremony at Notre Dame.

"Allen, I thought the British Embassy had left?" Marc stood in front of his desk, across from Allen.

"We are. This afternoon. When will you be back to the YMCA?" Allen quickly responded.

"Do you need to leave your keys?"

"No, Marc, you are coming with us."

"Allen, I can't. Bullitt is now the mayor. We are the only officials left. Look, I would help you, but I can't. It would be like abandoning a post."

"Look, Marc, I need your help. The nuns and staff are coming and so are the Belgians. We are going east to Saint-Nazaire and the government is sending an evacuation armada of ships," Allen said as Bullitt came into the room.

"You can land in Britain and then over to America through Ireland, but this is it. We have to leave today, and I need your help with the others," Allen pleaded.

"Go," Bullitt said to Marc. "I have the official French police and fire to help. As soon as I am done here, I am leaving south."

"But," Marc hesitated, thinking.

"We cannot wait another day. In a few more hours, Marc, it is going to be impossible to leave the city," Allen said.

Marc then took out of his desk drawer the wad of francs from Dora and put them in his jacket. "I should make a call," he said next. Marc took up the phone and started to dial the number, using the direct line. "This will be just a minute."

"Can you call England?" Allen asked Marc. "Is it a direct line?"

"Yes, but wait," Marc said as he rang for the operator.

"I want to let my family know if I can get out on a line. What is wrong?" Allen asked him, looking at the phone.

"I think it's dead." Marc hit the button a few times and listened, then gave it to Allen.

"They cut the lines. They are dead now," he yelled back to Bullitt.

"Goddamn them! I told them to wait. What am I supposed to do without any phone lines? I told them I would give them the go-ahead, and now this!" Bullitt's voice roared.

"Time to go," Allen said, and they left out into the morning streets. A herd of cattle crossed in front of the Place de la Concorde, taking the same route south Marc and Allen were going to take to the other side of the river.

"We are leaving with a company of the BEF. I think on trucks. By following with them, we are sure to get aboard a ship," Allen said breathlessly as they neared the YMCA building.

Inside the YMCA, the refugees put together their belongings, preparing to meet up with the soldiers.

"When will the trucks be here?" Marc asked Allen.

"There has been a change of plans, I will be right back," he said as he ran back over to speak with the commander of the unit.

"Only what you can carry," Allen said to the refugees. "This is too much."

"It is the food, we need to bring some food," Sister Clayton said to him.

"Then Sister, let's break it apart and put it in different bags. We need to make sure that everything is distributed in case we get separated," Allen said, sorting through the bags of bread, cheeses and vegetables.

"Here, this is yours. Put this in your bags," the nun said to one group.

"Be careful. Pack it so you don't lose it. We don't know when we will get more," Allen said to the president of the airplane company, as the little Belgian boy hung close with the other children.

"Here, hold my hand," Marc said to the small young Belgian boy as he held his sister's hand, with the dogs following. "Gardez, don't let go, and watch out," Marc continued in French.

"What is your name?" Marc asked the boy.

"Cricket, because I chirp," the boy said with a bright smile.

"What an odd little name, but what is your real name?" Marc pressed.

"Look, it is beautiful," the boy said, pointing in front of them as they walked down the street with the others toward the south Montparnasse train station.

As they approached the rail station, Marc looked up, and his face changed. Between trucks and simple cars, he saw terribly expensive cars with doors open, just abandoned in the streets surrounding the station.

"Someone is going to get lucky if they snatch this one," Marc said as they passed a white Silver Cloud Rolls Royce.

"No one wants it, Marc. Besides, it is probably not from Paris but out of town," Allen said.

Allen focused as he walked quickly among the people. Marc's anxiety increased as the party approached the sea of refugees. He was not sure if everyone would stay together and, even if they could, if this was exactly the best idea.

People crowded the train station to board various trains. Others camped out waiting in hopes of getting on a train. In every direction, Marc could see lost eyes. Some were looking for a train, some were looking for a relative, and some were simply set inside, looking for no place at all. Marc could feel his own eyes become just like everyone else's: helpless, lost, and scared.

"Sir, sir, can you help me? I have lost," a man said to Marc.

"Maurice, Maurice, where are you?" a woman's voice screamed above all others.

"Attention, attention, please! The train for Tours is departing in ten minutes," came across the station speakers.

"Please, please, I need to get to Lyons! Please, I will pay you," a woman begged Allen just in front of Marc.

"We are taking the 81. Stay close. Many of the staff should already be there," Allen said to Marc as they moved through the crowds of men, women, children and soldiers on the bustling platforms as they boarded the trains. Some had bags. Some looked as if they had fled with nothing. The station felt like an anthill that had been dusted up.

Just before noon, all of the people from their group made it to Train eighty-one. The third car back appeared to have some staff already on board. All of the train cars were totally overcrowded. There were maybe nine passenger cars in all, and several boxcars, and every one of them was standing room only. Cars one and two held soldiers from the BEF on top of the roofs.

Mr. Lugoux's heart nearly stopped at the sight. He had already experienced the loss of his airplane factory in Belgium, and the trauma of fleeing by road with his family to Paris. He quickly thought that he could ride on top with his older son, while his wife and daughter could ride inside the car with the other children.

Inside the car, Sister Clayton's eyes took a minute to adjust to the scene. At first, she saw no seats available for her staff of the Church Army, and the YMCA traveling with them. She pushed through the middle aisle to the front of the car, as the others followed. Some moved a bit to let the younger children sit down. Everyone else accepted they would need to stand.

Grabbing the boarding rails of car three, Marc and Allen made for the roof via the ladder. On top of the train car were already about twenty men and two women. A young man took Marc's hand and helped him up. Marc could see all through the train station and just about every train he saw had people on top of it. Marc started to reconsider his decision to leave with Allen. He was no longer sure it was safer to leave Paris than to hold his ground and stay in the city.

Engine eighty-one's whistle blew loud and long.

"Welcome aboard, young man," an older man in uniform said to Marc as he sat down and looked for something to hold onto.

"Here, hold this. Right under the inner window line, you can hold there," he said, studying Marc's features.

Allen sat down next to Marc and said hello to the man and apparently knew him, but did not introduce Marc.

Across the rail station, a train pulled out slowly. Marc stared, mesmerized, as the overcrowded train left the station with every car piled with men, women, and children on top. For most of the week, he had stayed away from the station. He had interacted with other Americans and people who were traveling, but he had no idea exactly what it felt to be as desperate now as everyone else to leave Paris.

The June 3 bombing raid had shaken him up; the one on the night of June 9 made him numb to the world. The whistle blew a second time, the train lurched forward just a bit, and then stopped.

"What is your name?" the man asked.

"Marc," he said, "and this is my friend from the British Embassy, Allen."

"Nice to meet you, Marc. Yes, I know Mr. Lee well. Are you an American?" the man asked in a thick accent.

"Yes, sir. New York. I was here as a student when the war broke out and have been working for the American Embassy."

"Good for you. What were you studying?" His conversational tone was a pleasant relief to the hectic station.

"Art, drawing, some painting. When I came to Paris, it seemed like a good idea. Now, not so sure," Marc said, looking out again and taking in the panorama of the station's bustle.

"Excellent. I wish I had studied art more," the older man said.

"What do you do?" Marc asked.

The whistle blew now three short times and the cars began to move forward ever so slowly. Train eighty-one was the next to depart. Marc grabbed the top of the windows hard, making sure to hold steady to the train's roof. After looking forward through two other car roofs full of people, he glanced around the entire train station at the surreal drama that was playing out in what was once such a stuffy environment.

"I am in between jobs now, so to speak," the man said.

"Sorry to hear that. A lot of people are in the same boat, including me. What did you do before you lost your job?" Marc asked, trying to focus upon not losing his grip.

"Oh, I did diplomatic business for the United Kingdom," the man said in a voice of defeat, just as Engine 81 cleared the roof of the Paris station.

June 10, 1940

SS Manhattan, At Sea

David awoke on the deck chair where he'd spent the night. Passengers gathered on the rail as the ship passed the Nantucket lighthouse. It would not be much longer, he thought. He gave up his cot to a woman who did not want to stay below in her cabin. Larry was still asleep next to him, and Robert as well. The girls were inside, but the woman had a daughter and an older mother. It seemed like the right thing to do. It was not that cold out.

It had been the strangest trip ever. There was no class distinction on the ship at all. People were exceptionally polite to each other, but somber. Most had not removed their life jackets since Gibraltar. No one complained about any inconvenience. There was none of the drama he had seen during all of his previous thirty-two Atlantic crossings. Everyone aboard seemed to be of one mind, and that was thankful to be heading home. David mused to himself that he was only nine months late getting home, but that was better than never.

He got up and went to the rail, wearing his life jacket. He closed his eyes and smelled the morning fog. He found the face of his parents in his mind, on the morning of May 7 so long ago. He promised them no more. This would be his very last trip over the pond, and he thanked the gods for the safety of his thirty-third voyage.

CHAPTER 17

June 11, 1940

SS George Washington, At Sea

"Ten minutes" was the signal that came as the ship came to a full stop at sea. The first officer on the bridge frantically signaled to the U-boat. "American, United States."

"Ten minutes," a terse response came back.

"Don't they see the flags?" the captain said.

"The lights are on, I checked," the first officer said.

"Keep signaling," the captain said. He then walked back to the panel with the watertight door switches that had already been activated. He then switched over the large toggle switch to the ship's alarms.

Nigel awoke to the alarm ringing throughout the ship. He quickly put on his life jacket, as did the four other men piled into a cabin meant for two. The hallways filled with passengers in pajamas and nightgowns.

"May I have your attention, please: All passengers muster to the lifeboat stations," blared over the intercom. The ship's sirens grew louder up on the boat deck in the early air of just after five in the morning.

People spoke in hushed tones, only a few words to each other. Nigel walked from his cabin into the hallway and made his way to the main staircase. He exited onto the port promenade deck. The lifeboats had been swung out and the doors had been opened already. It was almost as if he never stopped moving or even needed to wait as he stepped onto the boat on the ship's side, sliding over and making room for two women and a teenaged boy.

"Can't they tell we are American? We have flags on the side of the ship, for fucking crying out loud!" the second officer said as he came across the bridge from the port side.

"Get this out now. It is our position," the captain said to the radio officer.

"What is the time? Are they going to warn us before they fire?" the first officer called out on the bridge.

The only noise Nigel could hear was the wind, and it was gentle. The sound of the ship alarms seemed to disappear, as if his mind had shut them off. People moved around in the boat a bit. Some cried, though they tried not to be heard. There seemed to be just this sense of destiny about everything. And time seemed to fall away. People moved and sat together. He had never seen so many people do one thing so quickly without saying but a few words.

"Clear to go. Sorry," came back from the German U-boat.

"Full ahead." The captain called out. The ship's telegraph cried out with a series of bells as the officer moved the handles forward to full ahead.

"That's it? They stop us, threaten to blow us to the sky, and then clear to go?" the first officer said.

"I don't care. Maybe they thought we were a Greek or French ship and that is why they stopped us. I am just thankful now they can see those flags," the captain said.

"Are the passengers back onboard?" the captain asked twenty minutes later.

"No, sir, most are still in the boats," the first officer answered back after returning from the wing bridge.

"Well, let them stay a while, I suppose," he said, a sort of bemusement on his face.

"I think they will, sir. They seem to like it in the boats right now," the officer said, looking out toward the sea.

"No harm. If it makes them feel better, let them stay," the captain mumbled to himself.

June 12, 1940

Loire Valley, France

The train broke down about eighty miles out of Paris. At first they thought it was going to get going again but, soon, a line of German fighter planes spotted the train on the tracks. As the planes dived in, bullets pierced through the roofs of the cars as people piled out of the windows, the rear and front doors and ran in all directions to take cover in nearby fields. Marc and the others slid almost like cats off the top of the cars and onto the ground around the tracks.

"Under here! Don't run!" Allen called out. Marc threw himself under the train on the tracks.

"Is this safe?" Marc heard someone ask.

"No, but safer than out there," Allen said next.

"What if they bomb the train?" Marc asked.

In front of them, a woman yelled in pain and held her leg, which had snapped just above the ankle.

"Then we don't have to worry about the war anymore," Allen said. He scooted out from under the train, grabbed the woman under the arms and started to drag her back as she screamed in pain.

Another plane dived alongside the train and he could hear the guns shooting as they approached. Above him, he heard several yell in pain as bullets ripped through the cars. It sounded as if two men fell to the floor inside the coach. The bullets reached the engine and he could hear steam hissing from the boiler that had been hit.

The planes did not come back for another run. People slowly started to get up and walk out of the fields. Some were shouting for friends, relatives, or children. Marc and Allen, along with all the others, climbed out from under the train car. Everyone in the engineer's cabin was dead. A woman sobbed in front of a small child. Marc could barely bring himself to look but was relieved it was not the boy from Belgium.

The woman Allen had dragged no longer screamed. He did not see the wound, and was not sure if she was hit before or after she broke her leg. The front of her dress, however, was soaked in blood. Sister Clayton offered some prayers over her body before they gathered their bags and set out on foot across the field toward the road where other refugees walked and pulled carts.

"Are you scared?" the Belgian boy asked Marc as he walked behind Allen.

"Hey, there you are. Where is your family?" Marc asked, faking a smile.

"We are all safe," the boy said, his dog by his side.

June 13, 1940

Lisbon, Portugal

"Miss? Miss?" The man stood over Dora. At first he was gentle and then became firmer in his tone.

"Yes, sorry, I was asleep." She looked up at him.

"Would you be ready to go right now?" he asked her quietly.

"I thought you said there were no openings?" Dora asked, perplexed by his question.

"One of the passengers who had booked ahead has not arrived yet. No others on the waiting list are here or know yet, and you have been waiting, sleeping here, and I thought I would come to you first," the Pan Am agent said, and it was clear he was trying to be kind to her.

Dora had never flown before. She had an opportunity once to take the *Graf Zeppelin* to Europe, but decided against it and instead traveled with a group of friends back to France aboard the SS *Paris* instead. She was not sure what to expect as the large, four-engine flying boat, the Pan Am *China*

Clipper, started to move faster and faster over the choppy river, bouncing along in the water.

"Steward, question, please. We are not flying to China, right? I mean, this plane is going back to America?" Dora asked.

"Yes, of course. Oh, you saw the name on the plane," he said.

"Yes, I don't want to fly to China," Dora said.

"No worry. We have had to move some of the planes off the other routes to get everyone home, miss. You are not flying to China, but back to the States," the steward said to her in his friendly southern accent.

Even though she had not had much food during the nearly two weeks since leaving Paris, the sensation of flying did not give her any incentive to eat. Instead, she just looked out the window near her. The passengers took turns in the center lounge for breakfast and lunch.

Someplace past the Azores, over the Atlantic, another female passenger asked her, "Are you going home?"

"No, not exactly. I am going to see my sister," Dora said after a bit of a pause.

"Are you an American?" the woman asked.

"Yes, but my home is in Paris," Dora went on as she continued to stare out the window.

"Oh, I see. I am sorry," she said.

"Yes. It is a damn mess," Dora murmured over the drone of the plane's engines.

"Yes. It most certainly is." The woman's voice held a hint of sadness.

"Are you going home?" Dora asked.

"No. I am going to visit a friend."

"I see."

About an hour later, after another round of passengers took dinner in the center compartment, the woman said to Dora, "Aren't you hungry? You should eat."

"Oh, I will be fine. I am just not feeling very social or hungry," Dora lied. She had become angry stewing over the storm the woman's questions awoke inside her. Dora had been running for two weeks, never looking back at Paris, her friends, home, or the loss. Her sadness turned to anger, and the anger felt like a bowling ball in her gut.

The woman looked out the same window and then casually asked Dora, "Are you Jewish?"

The bluntness of the question shocked Dora, then she thought about it for a few minutes. "If by Jewish, you mean that I have lost everything including my home and friends then, why, yes, I am."

"Yes, so am I," the woman said, looking out the window.

Dora looked at the woman with a hesitant glance. The woman did not look back from the window.

"I have rebuilt before, and I will do it again. I am beginning to believe that those who are possessed by nothing possess everything, most of all freedom. I am sorry if I sounded curt. It's just been very hard. Up until now, I thought I was fleeing France, but actually, it feels more like I have been pushed out," Dora said.

"I know what you mean." The woman cracked a forced smile.

"Are you going to eat?" Dora asked her, for she did not go with the others for dinner when the steward came through the cabin.

The woman just shook her head ever so slightly, and she remained like a granite statue for the rest of the flight.

CHAPTER 18

June 14, 1940

Le Mans, France

"Get in, get in," the soldier said from the top of the truck.

"Where are you chaps heading?" the lost soldier asked.

"The same place you and everyone else are going. Away from France," Allen answered back.

It was early yet in the day and the soldier had just dropped off a group of men, so the truck was empty. Marc, Allen, the president and the two sisters from the YMCA, as well as the other Belgian refugees, climbed into the first truck. The rest piled into the second and third trucks. The convoy had gone out to retrieve the unit, which had gone missing after the train broke down.

The roads were clogged with all sorts of abandoned trucks and cars. As the truck turned a corner just after Fontaine-Milon, heading next to Angers, Marc never expected to see a group of elephants moving down the road. The truck slowly maneuvered around the herd as it marched along with the circus members, encircled by hundreds of refugees.

"What the bloody fuck," Allen murmured.

"I, I cannot …" Marc then stopped and looked toward the sky. Others then started to turn and look in all directions for the source of the sound.

Five bears walked in a line, each linked to the other. Behind the bears, a few families followed who did not appear to be with the circus. Back further from the bears were two horse-drawn carriages with several lions in them. And then there were the towering elephants that were mixed in between the bears, lions, and other refugees. Mahouts guided their elephants down the road. The elephants seemed to hold the space for the group with a stately consciousness.

Everyone seemed to be connected and lead by them as they walked with a certain determination and careful grace. The expressions upon their faces seemed to mirror the exact somberness of the refugees. Walkers would part for the elephants as the circus made its way down the crowded road. Then everyone began to scatter from the road in every imaginable direction, though no one seemed to know exactly from which direction the sound of the planes was coming.

"Get out! Take cover!" the driver yelled. Marc looked for Allen when he hit the ground. Then he looked at the others running to find a spot to hide. He turned, and just then, a Russian sun bear slammed Marc to the ground, pushing the air out of his lungs, as it ran over him and into the woods.

Within a few minutes, two elephants laid dead. The bears ran in every direction. One of the horse-drawn lion carriages had overturned and had crushed a boy, maybe six years old, and his father.

Marc rolled over on the ground and tried to find his breath. They must have thought those elephants were trucks, he thought to himself, because there could be no other reason to fire upon a traveling circus.

One of the truck's engine compartments hissed with the steam of the shot-up radiator. Marc huddled next to the soldier, who trembled violently. The Dutch girl sobbed and shook her mother.

"Can it be fixed?" Allen asked the officer as they opened the truck's hood.

"I think so. It's just a hose and we have some tape," he said as he pulled a kit out of the truck's cab.

Galway, Ireland

June 14, 1940

SS George Washington, At Dock.

Nigel sat at the bar of the SS *George Washington* where it was stopped in Galway, Ireland, to take on more passengers.

"Need another, friend?" the bartender asked.

"Pass. I have had enough. Do you need anything?" Nigel asked.

"On the house, friend, captain's orders."

Nigel left the bar on the aft boat deck. He walked to the rail overlooking the stern section of the ship. Sailors struggled with hoisting rafts up over the rail from the dock. On the other side, three rafts were stacked upon one another, lashed down to the deck.

As he walked forward along the deck, he passed a small group of workers with the ship's engineer. Nigel stopped on the deck and looked back to see what they were working on. The hatch to a service panel had been removed, and cables ran from the panel up over the deck to the top of the roof.

"We need an 80-amp fuse," he overheard. The engineer walked past him toward the forward decks to get the fuse.

Nigel looked up and saw the large flood lamps lashed down on the roof that pointed up toward an enormous American flag stretched between the ship's two funnels. Inside, people moved all about the cabins with luggage in tow.

"Sir, we need you to move to the lounge. Everyone in your cabin will be staying there. Here is your cot number, and if you can remove your luggage, please," the steward asked him as he reached the cabin.

"What is this about?" Nigel asked.

"We are taking on more, and many are children, so, we need the cabins. I am sorry," the steward said and then left.

On reaching the main deck foyer, Nigel saw the line of new passengers boarding the ship. On one side, life jackets were stacked clear up the wall. Nigel stared as each family member was given a life jacket, and instructed on how to put it on.

In the lounge, Nigel put his small package of emergency clothes he was able to get from the Red Cross under his cot. All of the furniture had been moved to the center of the room and stacked. He spied another pile of life jackets in one corner, along with blankets.

Nigel made his way through the crowds of new passengers in the writing room, smoking room and library. "May I have a Scotch, please?" he asked the bartender.

"Where you from?" the bartender asked.

"Paris, well, America, but have been in Paris for the past year."

"When did you leave Paris?"

"End of May, I think. Maybe it was early June? I don't really remember."

"You really should have a double."

Out of habit, Nigel reached for his wallet in his jacket. But then he realized he was not wearing a jacket, because he had given it to the girl who had been hit by the truck. The bartender waved his hand, reminding Nigel that the drinks were on the house, but his mind only focused on the girl's head.

"Scotch again?" the bartender asked. Another crewman came in with more cases of alcohol.

"More supplies, and should be enough. We have another 852 now aboard, maybe more," the crewman said to the bartender.

"Yes, please, a double," Nigel said.

June 14, 1940

Outside Nantes, France

The truck pulled into town. One of the officers got out and moved to the back of the truck. "You chaps, come with me."

Marc and Allen climbed out and said, "What are we doing?"

The town was deserted, the streets completely empty.

"This is not a good sign. Do you think the Germans might already have come through?" Allen asked the officer.

They went to a restaurant and the doors were shut, but there was someone inside. The officer pounded on the door. "Open up! BEF here." The man came to the door and opened it for him.

"We are looking for food. I have several thousand francs. I have a few children in the back who need something to eat, and several men and women," but the man then pretended not to speak English and, even as Allen spoke perfect French, he ignored them.

"Wait here, I'll be right back," Allen said and then went to the back of the truck. "Sister, I need you," he said to Sister Clayton.

"Will you talk to him, please?" Allen asked her as they walked up to the restaurateur.

"We need food, sir, not just for us but for the little ones. Don't you believe in helping others as Christ helped you?" she said in a supremely cool tone.

The man crumbled under the weight of her lecture and would not look her in the eye. He brought them back into the rear of the restaurant, and they collected some supplies.

"What's in there?" the officer pointed to the door of the large walk-in refrigerator.

"More stores if we need them. Want to see?" the owner said, smiling.

"Yes. Do you have any milk?" he asked as the man opened the door.

Marc and Allen stood in shock and the officer said, "What the bloody fuck is this?" the British Officer said to Allen. Marc's entire face dropped, and Sister Clayton grabbed the cross that lay upon her chest.

"The Germans eat off the fat of the land. When they come, they are going to take everything. We are not shooting dogs just to keep the streets clean. We are going to need something to eat as well," he said, as if the answer was obvious.

Inside the freezer, lined up on all three sides upon the shelves were the corpses of dogs of all breeds, many clearly pets.

"I have not had time to skin them yet, but if you need one," the man said.

"Let's go. We'll pass on the dogs," the officer said quickly.

The man shut the door and stood in the back room as the officer, Marc, Allen, and Sister Clayton returned to the trucks.

June 14, 1940

Paris, near midnight

The streets were totally clear. Ambassador Bullitt rehearsed in his mind his words. This was a bitter cup for him now. The trains had stopped. Had it not been for a chance call from Switzerland to the embassy, the Germans would have been shelling the city by now. Instead the night was silent, except for a few lookers.

A single car drove out to meet the Germans. "We are kind of winging this, you know. There is nothing in the diplomatic handbook for such things," Bullitt said to his driver. Bullitt shook the officer's hand and then assured him, along with the acting police chief of Paris, that the city was open, and there would be no resistance. No traffic moved in or out of Paris that night.

"Can you recommend a hotel?" the officer asked. Bullitt was not prepared for this question. The police chief wondered if it was a joke.

"There are many. You can take the best, I am sure," said the police chief, deciding that the officer was immensely serious.

"There is an excellent hotel just across from the embassy on the Place de la Concorde," Bullitt said next.

"Excellent. Please take us there," the officer said.

June 14, 1940

Between Savenay and Saint-Nazaire, France

Marc lay in the back of the truck with the others from the YMCA, along with some British soldiers and a few employees of a Belgian aircraft company. It was about 1 a.m. and though they had been traveling for hours, they were not yet ready to bed for the night. And they were not alone. All along the valley road were others still on the move. Everyone seemed to be going someplace, anyplace, wherever they could get in a hurry, with a great determination.

"I am really looking forward to getting out of France. When I get home, I am going to go straight to Elizabeth's house and spend the night. I have not been able to write her for two weeks. She probably thinks I am dead," Allen said to Marc.

Marc stirred from his self-loathing mood. He played over and over in his head the number of times he could've left France. He resented himself for staying too long, just for Marie. He even doubted the sincerity of the promise of engagement.

"How long have you been together?" Marc asked.

"Two years now," Allen said, looking up at the stars.

Marc could see his mother, father and sister in his mind's eye. Sadness washed over him as he remembered how Marie had promised to make him dinner this night.

"I am twenty-one, now," Marc said, more as an afterthought.

"Really? Well, cheers to that, my friend. Bet you will never forget this birthday, will you?" Allen said.

"No, I don't believe I will," Marc said as they drove toward Saint-Nazaire. "Marie and I are engaged," he then said.

"What? When? You never said anything," Allen said, looking directly at Marc.

"I know. It is just a promise for after the war. We were not going to tell anyone," Marc said next. "It probably means nothing."

The truck then pulled off the road and the officer driving it said, "Let's sack down for the night, but someplace off the road away from the truck just in case."

"Marc, don't say that," Allen said, surprised by his friend's attitude. "You've been in a mood for a while now. Are you stewing?"

"What do you mean?" Marc said as he climbed from the truck. He and Allen began walking away from the road with the others.

"You've been in a mood since the bear hit you," Allen said cautiously. "You think too much."

"What does that mean? The little shit knocked the wind out of me, Allen."

"That little shit rides a motorcycle, Marc." Marc turned toward Allen. "While you were analyzing the entire situation, trying to make the best decision, that bear knew it needed to run for its life."

Marc sat on the ground with the others gathering to bed down for the night. Allen looked closely at Marc. "Are you feeling okay?"

Marc looked up, tears in his eyes. He laughed to himself and said, "I can't even ride a motorcycle. You're right, Allen," he continued laughing while others looked at him as if he had lost his mind. "The bear did put me in a bad mood."

"He needs some rest," Sister Clayton said as she passed with the little Belgian boy and his sister and their two dogs. "He is going slaphappy from the strain."

CHAPTER 19

June 15, 1940

Saint-Nazaire, France

After breaking camp that morning, the group drove the last few miles into the port of Saint-Nazaire. Marc studied the soldiers marching on the road as the truck passed them.

"I thought, Allen, that most left at Dunkirk," Marc asked.

"These are the support troops, and other units not cut off at Dunkirk."

"But, over the radio, they said everyone."

"Of course they did," Allen said, and then looked over the side toward Saint Nazaire in the distance. The truck crested the hill, and Allen saw thousands of men in front of him amassing in fields around the port city.

"Where are you coming from?" the officer said as they stopped on the road just outside the city.

"Nantes," the driver replied.

"Any Germans yet?" the officer sounded more like the guard of a camp.

"None on the ground, but in the air we had quite a few close calls."

"Drive down over there and put the truck in drive, before you get out," the soldier said.

All along the road by the beach, soldiers were taking trucks and driving them into the open sea. Marc watched the odd carnival of men shouting as they drove the trucks and lorries into the surf.

"Are we siphoning the petrol?" Allen asked.

"No need. I am nearly empty, anyway," the officer said.

"All out back here," Allen called to the front.

"Oh hey, and there you go, my lady." The officer then jumped from the truck as it drove down the beach into the surf. Just fifty yards away, another truck drove toward the sea. And all along the shore in front of them were trucks and vehicles either sticking out of the ocean, or buried in the sand from the previous high tide.

Marc could not help but be captivated by the scene. As they walked toward the port, hundreds of trucks and cars laid abandoned. Many had open hoods and it was clear that they'd been sabotaged. A large bonfire soared into the sky as quartermasters burned supplies that were to be left behind. Along the town and docks, the city was overtaken with scores of fleeing soldiers and refugees.

"Sister, I think we are best heading back to stay with the other men near the airway," Allen said to Sister Clayton.

"The children cannot sleep out in the open. I'm sure the local church can put us up. Even if we have to sleep on a floor, it is better to be inside," she protested.

"Well, you could be right, but Marc and I are going to go back and hang close to the soldiers, because when word comes it is time to get on a ship, we need to be with them," Allen said.

"We are not going to be far, but stay in the town and I am sure we will find you in the morning," Sister Clayton said as they separated that day.

It was early yet, and the men pouring into the airfield looked like a ragtag of souls. Marc and Allen ended up walking back into the port and even taking in a movie to help the time pass. Air raid sirens made their calls and a plane dived in on the port, but nothing terribly serious happened that day. Throughout the night, sleeping out in the open with the other men of the BEF, Marc and Allen noticed the constant flow of new men arriving at all hours.

It was the afternoon of the following day that ships came into port. Marc and Allen rushed with the soldiers of the airfield down to the port, looking for the other members of their convoy from Paris. Long lines formed as boats took the men out to the ships. A hospital ship arrived and offered to take men aboard if they abandoned their gear, but they refused.

"Should I go look for them?" Marc asked Allen.

"It really is not that important. They are going to catch a ship by the same dock we are on. It is not as if there are fifty ways to get out of here. They might have got out to a ship even before we made our way down here," Allen said, while waiting in the line.

"You're right. I never thought about that," Marc said. He watched more men pile into the lines down at the port.

At ten that night, the port master shut down the line. "The lights will draw the planes! Shut off those lights!" he yelled as he passed the lines.

It started to rain, and Marc and Allen crowded under the eave of a building with a group of soldiers. Several men ran over to the barrels, and used a tarp to create a small refuge from the soaking.

"Wherever Sister Clayton and the others found to stay, I sure hope it's dry," Allen complained to Marc. Marc pulled at Allen's coat and pointed toward the wine barrels.

"Let's get over by the wine. At least if they're hit by a raid, we can get drunk as we die," Marc joked. They made their way over to find a dry spot to sleep for the night.

"Boys, time to muster up to the dock," the shouts came at four in the morning.

"Holy Mother of God, one bullet, Allen, and we'd be done for," Marc said, amazed at just how stupid he'd been to not pay better attention. The barrels were not wine but paraffin.

After joining a long line of soldiers, Marc and Allen finally boarded the fifth trawler to take the men out to one of the evacuation ships. Marc looked out to a single-stack liner as the small vessel took them out over the bay. It was about five decks high with a sweeping profile. The funnel was dark grayish black, the portholes blacked out with paint.

"I feel bad, Allen, that we're separated now from the others," Marc said as he looked up the side of the ship.

"Marc, there are going to be dozens of ships. Just look over there," Marc pointed to a two-stack liner about a mile away. "No one is going to be left behind, but I cannot help who, how and when everyone gets aboard a ship home."

"Rank and unit?" the officer asked as they crossed the threshold.

"I am in the diplomatic corps, and so is my friend here, from the American Embassy," Marc said. The soldier looked perplexed, as if he couldn't decide what to do next.

"Like officers, except we're civilians working for the embassy," Marc explained.

"Excellent, yes. Here are your cabin numbers and a ticket for the dining room," the officer said.

They made their way down to C Deck and to their assigned cabin. Allen opened the door and there were already two men inside. One of the men had a white Angora rabbit on his chest and the second read a book through his thick glasses.

"Welcome," said the man with the rabbit.

"The bottom bunks are yours." Soon after Marc and Allen got settled in, another group of men came to the door and had tickets with the same cabin.

"Sorry, we are all out of room," Allen said to the weary young soldier. The hallways filled fast with soldiers trying to get from deck to deck and cabin to cabin. Each of the men carried a duffle or sack of some sort with their gear. The voices of commanders pierced the thin wood walls of the staterooms.

On the docks later that morning, civilians mixed with soldiers in line for a boat out to one of the ships.

"Sister, should we wait for Marc and Allen?" Mr. Longoux asked her as they approached the trawler on the side of the dock.

"I'm sure they will get aboard a ship fine. We cannot wait," she said to him as the line drew closer. "Have you seen the two little ones?" she asked, looking out over the crowds.

"No, they walked off again. They will be back, I am sure," he said, scanning the line.

Crossing the threshold of the ship, the officer then asked, "How many and are you all together?"

"I have two families here, with women and children. There are two sisters from the YMCA, and the rest are with the Church Army."

"Right. I will give the cabins to the families. How are the rest of you with the lounge?" the officer asked.

"If the lounge is heading back to England, it will be a splendid place to stay," Sister Clayton said, smiling.

"Welcome aboard, Sister. Always good to have a woman of prayer aboard," he said.

"My honor. What is the name of this ship?" The sister asked.

"RMS *Lancastria*," he answered.

"Well, then, may the Lord watch over and keep her," Sister Clayton said as she left down the hallway.

Marc rested on his bunk in the cabin on C Deck. Outside the door he listened to the men move back and forth down the hallway.

"This way. The forward hold is through that bulkhead." "Move along, move along." "Is there any food?" Voices came through the wooden door as they passed.

"Are they serving food?" Allen asked.

"Yes, I got our names on the list," Marc left, followed by John, the young, bespectacled Scotsman. Marc felt a restless need to leave the cabin.

"What are you reading?" he asked John, trying to make some small talk as they moved down the hall.

"*Ulysees*. It is a strange book, by James Joyce," he answered back. He was shorter than most Scots Marc had met. Marc wasn't sure if John was younger than he was, but he couldn't have been much older.

"I know the author and the publisher back in Paris. Do you know the other fellow well?" Marc asked him, fighting through the passageway as men heavy with gear looked for various cabins.

"Horus? Yes, we trained together. So you say you know the author?" John said to him.

"I have never heard anyone called Horus from Scotland before." Marc looked perplexed.

"Oh, that is not his name. Just my nickname for him," John responded.

"Why does he have a rabbit?" Marc pressed.

"For his daughter. He wanted to bring her something back, so he picked up the rabbit along the way," John said.

"Did you have trouble getting out of Paris?" Marc asked, wondering how one had time for souvenir hunting while in retreat.

"Never got there. We have been out here nearly the whole time. In charge of supplies," John said as he gave their names for the dining room. "That is why I call him Horus. He bragged he would watch everything like a hawk. So, what better name for a hawk man?" John smiled through his wire glasses.

A gangway extended from the trawler to the single-funnel liner. Soldiers and various civilians crossed over to the open passageway.

"Hold it there, kiddies. I can't let you bring the dogs aboard. Against the rules," the officer said at the threshold of the ship. The Belgian boy and his sister looked confused and then he started to hug the golden retriever. A gray-haired woman stepped forward and, in French, began to explain what the officer said to them.

"But, he must. I cannot leave them. It is not right that I should be allowed to save my life yet let my best friend go," the boy said in extremely fast French, crying and using the back of his hand to wipe away tears. His sister clung to the mane of her own dog.

The officer could not bear to take in the gray eyes of the boy. "I suppose regulations are meant to be broken. You can come aboard," he finally relented.

"Can you take on more? There are two thousand still waiting back at the dock," barreled across the sea from the captain of another trawler full of refugees.

"We are all full now, overcrowded. Go to one of the other ships," the officer yelled back from the gangway threshold.

"That's it! Shut up the hatch," he said to the crewmen.

"What is the count?" the first officer asked.

"Count? I reckon I don't know, sir. I stopped counting at seven thousand," the steward responded.

"Bloody hell, we really are overloaded," the first officer said as he walked down the hallway toward the front of the ship.

Sister Clayton walked out onto the promenade deck, past the place where the men had stacked their rifles. Over the bay, another large two-stack liner stood anchored in the sea. Just about this time, a single German plane entered the sky around the ship and dropped a bomb. On the decks of the *Lancastria*, soldiers stared as the bomb took away the bridge of the ship just a few miles away.

Return gunfire could be heard coming from the liner. Another plane came near the *Lancastria* and dropped a series of bombs, but they missed the ship and splashed into the sea just to the port side of the ship.

"Oh dear God, help us all," Sister Clayton whispered as the soldiers cheered that the bombs had missed the ship.

From the inside cabin on C Deck, Marc heard a thundering cheer coming from the upper decks. He did not know it was for the bombs that had missed their target. The planes then left as quickly as they'd arrived, leaving just the liner several miles away with a smoldering, smashed bridge deck.

About three-thirty in the afternoon, Allen, Marc and his two cabin mates got the call for the dining room. Marc had been petting the rabbit and gave it to Horus, who then put it on the bunk and told it to stay, promising to bring back some food.

"Be good now and stay put," Marc said, as he left the cabin to join the group walking toward the dining room. He passed both young and older men and, most of all, the tired. Reaching the main dining room, Marc was shocked at just how crowded the entire ship felt to him. In every direction, through passageways, stairways and rooms, soldiers stood talking or just waiting.

Marc looked at the menu card. He couldn't explain it, but all the way down into the dining room, he kept thinking of the previous year with Dora, David, and Nigel. He started to wonder if they were able to get out and then stopped worrying as he realized they had left weeks before him. But it seemed odd that he couldn't shake it. David would come to his mind and he could see him just as he was before he left for Genoa. *He was smart for getting that ticket*, Marc thought. Marc then looked down at the menu card and read the name *Lancastria*.

"I've never heard of this ship before," Marc said to John.

"She is a Cunarder, British," John answered back, looking out over the crowded dining room. David's words flashed in Marc's mind from that night the year prior on the *Normandie*.

"Never sail British," Marc could see in his mind's eye. He shook the chill off his back and pushed the memory aside.

"They changed the name sometime ago. I can't remember the first name, but *Lancastria* is the second name," Horus said.

"Allen, the others made it aboard. I saw Mr. Lougoux's youngest children with the dogs earlier. I cannot say I really like him that much," Marc said, looking at the card.

"What do you mean? He is a fine fellow," Allen asked.

"It is just that he dotes over his oldest son, but pays no attention whatsoever to his other boy and little girl," Marc said, irate at Allen for not seeing the neglect.

"Marc, those are not his children," Allen said, looking directly at him.

"What do you mean? The little boy told me that was his father," Marc said, surprised by the statement.

"He knows, he knows. They followed them from Belgium. He thinks their parents might have been killed on the road fleeing, because they nearly were killed themselves. He's not sure, and felt sorry for the two, but all the same, they are not his children," Allen finished.

"I had no idea. I just assumed that …" Marc said.

"Look, friend, it has been a long trip. What do you want from the bar?" Allen asked. After getting the order, Allen left and joined a long line of men who were waiting at the bar for drinks.

"Nothing to worry about. They missed us," the steward said to another group of men near Marc's table. It caught Marc's ear and he wondered what ship the steward was talking about.

"We are a lucky ship. We just got back from Norway and not a scratch on us." Marc looked over at the steward.

"You're safe on this old gal!" he then walked away to the galley.

CHAPTER 20

"Don't sell my seat. I'm going to the head," Horus said as he left the table.

Marc's senses seemed to intensify as he became ultra-aware of his surroundings. A deep sense of anticipation filled his chest but he could not pinpoint what it was that he was expecting. The memory of David on the *Normandie* the previous year spooked him. But his eyes were now open in a way they had not been when he boarded the ship.

"This ship is overcrowded," he said to John sitting across from him.

"Damn right, it is. A lot of men sure are in a hurry to get home, and damn glad to be heading home." John then turned to talk to someone passing.

"Do you think it is—" Marc stopped mid-sentence because it was pointless. John's back was turned and the room was so loud, he could hardly hear his own words.

Mr. Lougoux and his son walked out from the lounge out onto the promenade deck. The Belgian boy and little girl walked past them with their dogs, as he pointed his sister toward a beautiful chrome bicycle. It sparkled in the sun while strapped to the side of the railing.

"Papa, it appears everyone from Paris made it aboard," his son said to him.

"Yes, it does. See, everything works out for the best if you don't worry about it," Mr. Lougoux said with a smile, as he looked at the bike and patted his son on his shoulder.

"Do you hear that?" his son asked him.

"Uh, yes, where is it?" he said as he looked toward the sky.

"George, George, over here!" John got up from the table to walk across to a soldier. Marc felt a slight nausea in his gut. He wondered if it was due to hunger or if he was starting to get the flu.

On the stern of the ship, men started to get up from lying down on the deck. "Someone get the guns!"

"Where is it? I can't see it for the sun!" another man hollered. Then a sharp whining noise filled the air.

The first bomb hit just aft of the funnel. Sister Clayton was thrown to the deck. The second bomb hit directly into the second cargo hold. The little Belgian boy and girl fell against the bulkhead to hide.

The ship rocked heavily and, even down in the dining room, it was clear that something was wrong. Marc held the sides of the table. A few of the men slipped on the floor as the ship rocked.

The third bomb ripped through several of the decks and penetrated the dining room. After a horrific flash, the pungent smell of coralyte filled the air. Marc had been blown several feet away from the table. Screaming filled the room as china flew and crashed to the deck. A sugar bowl whacked Marc on his back after flying through the room from the blast. He yelled out in pain as it thudded against his body.

After regaining his balance, Marc looked for John, but he was gone. Only perhaps ten seconds had passed and everyone scrambled to make for the dining room doors and out to the main stairwell. The ship rocked back and forth heavily. Marc's vision became myopic as he focused through the smoke to follow the soldiers.

"Hurry, hurry! Make way, make way!" Mr. Lougoux said to his wife and the others in the lounge. Another family had a small child already in a life vest. The men parted so to allow them through the lounge out to the stairway and up the boat deck.

"Will it hold us?" his wife asked as they climbed. The timbers cracked under the weight of all the soldiers. Out on the deck, they climbed into a boat that had been swung out from the ship. Another group of soldiers came and started to fill the boat. But then the boat flipped over, and Mr. Lougoux fell toward the sea in midair as his son held his hand.

Sister Clayton clung to the side of the rail, looking down into the water. Men climbed up on top of the rail and jumped with full gear and life vests on. She looked down and saw each of the men snap their necks as the vest would fly up and catch their helmets.

"No, no, look!" She held a young soldier back from jumping into the sea. "Take it off, or you will snap your neck," she said to him.

A large group of women with children then came out on the deck as she turned. "Oh dear God," she said as the frantic passengers started to fly over the railing. From the deck above, a lifeboat fell halfway from the davits, pointing straight down to the sea.

"Come along," the Belgian boy said, holding his dog. He could see the water pouring over the bow of the ship from near the bridge. "They say the stern always goes down last," he said to his sister as they walked aft past the chrome bicycle.

Allen stumbled to his feet. He looked around, trying to gain his focus in the dark. His head felt empty and his ears rang so loud, he could barely hear anything outside. He started to stumble down past bodies laid out dead in every direction. He caught a light down the hallway as it started to fill with water.

Marc, making his way to the stairwell, was caught up in a huge crowed of men pouring out from passageways and cabins. The gear they carried with them added to the confusion and congestion.

Marc reached the staircase and heard a cracking sound from above.

Snap ... snap, snap ... crack ...snap. He looked up and saw that a part of the staircase was separating from the upper landing. Another part of the staircase had already snapped, causing the stairs to sag. The sheer number of soldiers and their gear was causing the stairs to fail.

Marc became sick with panic on how he could climb the stairs before they fully disconnected. A long, loud grinding sound could be heard from above, within the next round of stairs, and was followed by a very loud snap muffled by the sound of falling men and duty bags, shouts and hollers, as the stairs began to collapse.

Another soldier, as Marc hesitated to climb the stairs, pulled him back to cut in front of him. Just as the separation from the upper landing became complete, the stairs crashed down on the man in front of Marc. Marc fell backwards into the soldiers behind him in the foyer as men and gear poured down from above.

Marc pulled himself up off the deck and scooted away from the stairs.

"Is there another staircase?" one soldier said, frantic.

"Rope! Anyone have a rope up there?" another called above the yelling.

Out of the corner of his eye, Marc caught a glimpse of a man followed by another crewmember as they passed through a small hatchway. Marc went for the hatch, and was followed by another man. He entered a remarkably small crew stairway leading up from the engine room.

Marc turned on the stairway about four times until he came to an open hatch door that landed on the promenade deck on the starboard side of the ship. A group of guns stood in a stack on the deck right outside the main foyer landing. Just as another group of soldiers came out of the main foyer doors to the deck, the guns came entirely loose and started sliding across the deck while discharging, hitting one unlucky fellow square in the head as he fell back dead into the crowd trying to escape the ship.

Marc stumbled against the bulkhead and looked down the deck as a lifeboat slid down the side of the ship.

"Everyone to the port side," came over the ship's intercom. The ship started to lurch heavy to port, and Marc's eyes widened with fear as the view of the sky now became a view of the sea. Men, women, and children who had gathered around the boats lost their footing and fell into the sea in front of him.

Marc fought his way back through the ship's rooms to the other side, along with men desperately looking for a way to get out.

Marc came out on the other side of the promenade deck, acutely aware of the growing tilt of the ship as his weight pressed against the bulkhead.

"She is going over! She is going over!" a young soldier yelled in terror. Marc knew he needed to act quickly and so, before the deck became so slanted he couldn't climb it, he made it to the railing just next to the chrome bicycle.

As he reached the railing, he pulled himself over and turned back and saw several soldiers trying to reach the side. He held out his hand to help pull them up and over the railing. About five or six made it up and over this way.

Each one grabbed the bike handles to pull themselves over, and as they did, they'd accidently pull the bike's bell. *"Bling-ging, bling-ging, bling-ging,"* went the bell each time a soldier climbed over the rail onto the side of the ship's plates. The sound of its cheerful, childlike tone made Marc think of what a delightful afternoon it would be for a bike ride on the side of a ship.

CHAPTER 21

Allen struggled to keep his balance inside the dark room as he waited to get through the porthole.

"Get back!" the man yelled.

Just then, the light went out through the porthole and water began to rush inside.

Sister Clayton made her way aft, coming upon a man stripping out of his trousers and shirt, dropping his drawers as he prepared to jump over the side of the ship. He turned and looked at her with embarrassment.

"This is no time for modesty," she said as she started to pull off her hat. The ship then lurched, throwing both of them against the rail. They floated away from the rail as the ocean came up and over it.

On the side of the ship, Marc could see a group of lifeboats that had made it free. Around the ship, he saw bobbing heads of men, and sometimes women, in the sea. "Who would lash a life vest on a dead man?" Marc pondered.

In the distance, Marc saw the cruiser that earlier had been ferrying troops as it approached the now-overturned *Lancastria*. But, just then, another plane dived down upon the swimmers and fired into the sea. The plane dropped some kind of bomb on the struggling soldiers.

Marc looked down the plates of the hull, toward a large crack. Through the gaping hole, oil spilled from the ship. He scanned how far the oil slick extended over the sea, and then saw that some of this oil had caught on fire. Marc watched as one man swam through the oil, trying to get out of it, as his hair caught fire. He screamed before disappearing into the black sea.

"Hand … hand…" he heard to his right. Marc looked and no one was there.

"Down here," he heard. He looked and there was a man in porthole calling for his hand. He helped him up and out. Another man was behind the first.

"Hurry!" he said. "Hurry!" The man he'd just helped from the porthole yelled down inside the ship, as he tried to help his buddy escape. Marc saw the water now rising up from the ship's submerged bow. He started to walk backwards along the side of the plates and then turned toward the aft. The propellers jetted out of the sea. Marc could see men climbing over the railings near the aft section, and up on the now-jutting propeller shaft.

"Do you want to live?" a British officer asked Marc. He snapped out of what felt like a heavy state of sleep.

"Yes," Marc pulled the words out of himself.

"Then strip out of those clothes. They are just going to pull you down," the officer barked to him, and pointed to others just behind Marc. Marc felt like the words had passed through him, as he struggled to focus amidst the panic.

All along the side of the ship, men busted through portholes and called for help to climb out. When the water reached the open portholes, Marc heard the shouts and screams of men inside the ship.

Marc took off his boots, shirt and trousers. The officer in front of him now stood fully naked. Others were stripping down, some naked, and some just no trousers on. Other men appeared like they expected to walk off the ship and across the ocean on some magical bridge. They were in full dress, and with heavy kitbags on their backs. Somehow they seemed unable to save their own lives; the idea of letting go of equipment was grounds for court martial.

The ocean continued to climb the side of the ship. The cruiser had moved away a bit from the scene to avoid the planes diving from above.

Marc slipped out of his underwear and got done folding his clothing. He stacked it neatly on the side of the ship, as if he were just going for a swim and was going to come back later to dress for dinner.

"Are you ready?" the officer called over the yelling to Marc.

"For what?" Marc thought the words first and then had to force himself to say them.

"To jump into the sea. We need to get away from the ship so it does not pull us down," the officer yelled.

Just then, across the sea of broken bodies, lifeboats, and shouting men, coming from within busted-out portholes came a chorus of rowdy British men singing out "Roll out the Barrel." They perched themselves along the protruding starboard side propeller shaft. The voices seemed to be disconnected from the scene. Marc looked out upon a dark sea of oil mixed with swimmers, bodies, smoke, and broken lifeboats.

"There will always be an England," came ringing out from a single voice of a steward. He sat along the outside part of the railing near the aft of the ship.

The water surged along the ship's side. Marc saw men climbing out from various portholes. Just ten feet from him, the glass snapped as another person deep inside the ship attempted to break free. There was a man, not thirty feet away, who could not get out of the porthole. He was stuck. Another soldier hit him on the head to knock him out so he would not suffer as he drowned.

"Do you want to live, son?" the officer asked again in a sharp tone.

Shots rang out behind them to the aft. Two officers had taken out their revolvers and then shot each other. Both Marc and the officer looked in the direction of the gunfire. Marc's eye caught another soldier who appeared to be a high-ranking officer. He perched himself near the propeller and stood as calm as could be, smoking a cigarette and looking out over the ocean as if he were at the beach for the day.

Marc looked back at the naked man in front of him and away from the scene all around him. He took a deep breath and focused his mind, trying to block it all out.

"Yes, ready," he said, as if he were speaking through a wall of glass.

"Let's go, then," the officer said as he dived into the sea.

Marc walked to the side, just on the edge of the keel, and decided to jump instead of dive. As he leaped from the ship, Marc plunged into the cold, oily water and, as it caved over his head, an odd thought occurred to him. *That rabbit doesn't stand a chance.*

CHAPTER 22

Spring, 1942

Paris, France

Torquette arranged the drapes in just the right way. She had done this so often, it was natural. Her faced wore heavy the signs of age for being relatively young. The teakettle screamed in the kitchen. She removed the kettle from the stove and there came a knock at the door.

"Bonjour, R," she said with a welcome smile in her voice. R removed his coat and hung it near the door.

"Bonjour. You look well today," he responded. "Do you need any help?" He towered over her, but was not quite as tall as her husband. His face was unreadable and his head was full of thick, black hair.

"Can you set up the table?" she asked, and returned to the kitchen.

"But, of course." He got out the chairs and the deck of cards. Beside each of the four chairs, he placed a small pad and pencil.

Dr. Jackson came through the door in silence. He put his jacket up straight away and retreated to a back bedroom.

"Where is Philip?" he asked.

"He is out with his friends."

"Later I need to speak with him." The clock chimed four, and a few minutes later came another knock on the door.

"Bonjour, Marc," Torquette answered the door in a very warm, inviting voice.

"Bonjour, my sweet. How are you today?" Marc said. He hung his jacket and put down his bag. She brought out the cups and poured into each of them some tea, and then placed in the center of the table a modest bowl of blueberries. The men then sat and Marc passed out the cards to each of them as they waited for the tea to cool.

R spoke next. "Someday I will learn this game," he smirked.

"Don't you think you're being a little optimistic there?" Torquette glanced toward Dr. Jackson.

"I hope never to learn this game. It reminds me how little I can remember," Dr. Jackson said with a grumpy tone.

"I have made this game as simple as I can for you. You don't have to play. You just keep score and I tell you the numbers and place the pegs in the holes," Marc proclaimed as he passed out the cards. "What more can I do?"

"We appreciate you, Marc, for all you do. Without you, we would have no mystery in our lives, such as watching a game of cribbage, where supposedly we are winning but have no idea how or why," Torquette responded with a smile.

"It would be rather funny if we should ever need this game," R said, laughing quietly.

"How is that?" Dr. Jackson asked.

"They will spend six months trying to figure out our code. They will pore over this board and convince themselves that each peg and every hole are a part of a greater sum," R elaborated as he popped two blueberries into his mouth.

"You're right, R. Marc, where is the railing from the ship?" Dr. Jackson asked.

"I nearly forgot the board," Marc then reached into his bag and pulled out the hand-carved wooden cribbage board and placed it on the table.

June 17, 1940

Saint-Nazaire, France

After a few seconds, Marc made his way to the surface and, due to the oil, was careful about opening his eyes. His body cringed in the cold water. All around him, men swam in every direction, but he lost sight of the officer.

"Over here!" Marc heard, turned and saw the officer swimming toward him. "We need to move out of here! We are too close."

Behind them, Marc could still hear the chorus of voices near the aft starboard propeller shaft. "Roll out the barrel and we'll have a barrel of fun! Roll out the barrel, the barrel ... and we will ..."

"Lifebelt! I need a lifebelt!" called another soldier.

"The planes are coming back!" another voice called out in pain.

"I will call soon, soon, don't worry," a man mumbled to himself as Marc swam by.

"Can you swim?" he heard a panicked voice behind him.

"Ah! Ouch! These damn plates are hot," said another as he ran down the side of the ship.

"Baby, baby, I have your baby, mother. He is safe and out of the water," Marc heard about twenty yards away.

The Pekingese dog that was tied up at the hatch door when Marc came aboard swam in front of him, holding its head out of the water.

The officer and Marc got to an oar of a lifeboat and held on. Just then, the roar of a plane could be heard as it came in on the crowd of swimmers. Marc looked back at the ship and saw the water rising along the side and spray coming from the open, smashed portholes. The dressed officer at the back stood smoking his cigarette, as if nothing were wrong.

Stu, stu, stu, Marc heard the approaching plane's guns. A string of spurts came up out of the water, through the crowd of swimmers over a lifeboat.

Marc saw two slump over, followed by another slipping into the water, and then a stream of spray came straight toward the officer and him.

Marc dived down just before the spurts arrived and then came back up to the oar. He cleared his eyes of the oil.

"Are you all right?" Marc asked. "Are you all right, sir?" Marc saw a perfect hole in the officer's forehead as he fell backwards from the oar into the sea. He took the oar and started to swim away.

Spring 1942

Paris, France

"You're right, it is brilliant. It is not just a game, but a secret and a little mystery," Torquette chimed in with a small chuckle.

Marc froze inside. He didn't like the little chat about the board, but knew he needed to let them have their fun. His stomach churned with anxiety to get them off the topic of the railing.

"I am telling you. They would send the board to Hitler himself and proclaim they have cracked the resistance in Paris," R said boldly, in a bragging tone.

"Let's hope it never gets to that," Marc said in a measured voice. R looked at Marc and then his eyes glanced down at his cards.

"So, there is someone I know who has been asking questions. The time has come to bring this up. His name is Georges. He is young, well, in fact, very young," R paused, with an odd look on his face, then said, "I think he is seventeen years old. I have known him for a while, several years, in fact, and he works with the group called the Sons of Liberty." Dr. Jackson looked into Marc's eyes with doubt about the direction of the conversation. "They produce papers for information's sake and distribute them. *Defense de la France* is the name of their track," R finished.

"Papers are not something we can do, R. You know that by now," Dr. Jackson said dismissively.

"Yes, I know, of course. I think it is reckless work as well, and if they should ever get caught, I am sure it would not be a happy ending." Torquette looked pensively at the drapes. "But here is why I am bringing him up. They want to help with downed birdies," R's voice focused.

"Birdies?" Torquette snapped back, bewildered.

"I've never told him about what I am doing, but I think he knows by intuition that I am not giving tours of Paris. He asked me if I knew anyone with contacts in Paris with the 'birdies.'"

"Do you trust him?" Marc asked R. It was odd but he had relaxed some after talking about real risks rather than imaginary heroism.

"Yes, I trust him and I know several of their group. They are cautious and careful. I don't think we are dealing with another Vidal situation." Marc had not heard about this now for over a year and cringed at the name. He'd pushed that memory to the back of his mind. Torquette looked again toward the window, and Dr. Jackson looked down at the board, taking in everything R told them.

"We need to take it slow, and careful. What has this Georges proposed?" Dr. Jackson then asked.

"Nothing yet. I told him that I have no idea how to help him. You know that I am completely dumb to such matters." R shrugged his shoulders and smirked as he glanced at Marc.

"And what do you think? Do you think they can take them?" Marc asked next.

"Birdies and birdhouses are no easy thing, but we need the help. Think on it and let me know. And don't worry, I am far more out on a limb than you, my friends," R said to them.

"That's it?" Torquette pushed him for more.

"Yes. They want to help. And frankly, I need the help and so will we all in time. It is not as if there are fewer air raids. If we are going to keep helping, we are going to need to secure some more resources," R said.

"How many are in their group?" Marc asked.

"Quite a few. I'm not sure. They are careful, very careful. The Sons of Liberty are not a fly-by-night group of kids marking up the Metro after dark."

Dr. Jackson then lowered his eyes toward the table as R continued. "They have multiple operations and cells and, from what I understand, much of it is compartmentalized so if one part is compromised, it does not compromise the whole." He sipped his tea.

"Well, what is the next step?" Dr. Jackson asked as he took out a peg on the board and moved it forward toward Marc. "Is that okay, Marc?"

"Yes, of course. You may move a peg," he said, smiling. "But I'm not sure about handoffs to ambitious kids just yet," Marc said next.

"I think the next step is to meet with him. We can do it here or elsewhere. I think they are very trustworthy and can follow instructions." R continued to sell the plan while he focused on Marc.

"Just one!" Torquette said. "We cannot have a bunch of new cribbage players all at once. It will draw attention. We don't want to attract the wrong type of players," she said, and then took a sip of her tea and nibbled a few blueberries.

"You said he is young," Dr. Jackson asked.

"Yes, seventeen, but looks even younger," R confirmed.

"Philip can bring him then," Dr. Jackson said. Torquette glanced at him, surprised. "It is perfect. They'll just think they're boys," Dr. Jackson finished. Torquette frowned but didn't protest further.

"All right, I will make the arrangements. By the way, is that one ready yet?" R asked Dr. Jackson.

"Not quite yet, but soon. I'll need a nest for this birdie, but he is still recovering right now," Dr. Jackson said.

"I'll see about gathering some twigs and string then," R said with a joking smile.

"Don't forget your scores," Marc told them as he finished his tea.

"Oh yes, let's not forget. Everyone put down some meaningless numbers," Torquette said after carefully taking away the bowl of precious berries.

Marc took the board from the center of the table and placed it back into his bag.

June 17, 1940

Saint Nazaire, France

"May I?" a swimmer asked politely as he came over.

"Yes, but just the end," Marc said with a nod. The older man took hold of the other end of the trunk.

"They should be coming back in soon," the man said in an upper-class British accent.

"The Germans?" Marc asked.

"No, the cruisers. They were coming over but then turned around. It will not be long now until they come back in to pick us up," the man said with a voice of entitlement.

Marc looked again out over the sea but lost track of time. Sure enough, a cruiser came back in to pick up some of the swimmers, but it was too far away and on the other side of the large, burning oil slick. There was no way he could swim through it and live. When he looked back, the man was gone. Did he drown or did he swim away, Marc wondered, but then took an interest in another man.

A dead soldier wearing a lifebelt floated past Marc. Marc left the trunk and swam toward the man who appeared to be fully dressed in his battle gear, a full kitbag still with him. The helmet chinstrap had cut a deep gash into his chin.

Marc struggled to get the cork lifebelt from the dead soldier. He pulled him down a bit and held him close, and was finally able to untie the belt. The man's face, nothing but a blank stare, then fell back from Marc and into the sea. The soldier sank quickly into the water with all the weight of his clothes and gear pulling him down.

Ships came in and out, picking up swimmers. A dog yelped atop of an overturned lifeboat. It seemed like only a few minutes had passed and Marc waved his hand toward a boat in the dark. He woke up on the deck, crawling up from a pile of life jackets. Marc's eyes focused upon the oil-stained faces of half-clothed men sitting around the deck, wrapped in blankets. He stumbled toward the galley. The light inside the cabin blinded him for a few moments.

"Oh, you're not dead after all," a young pregnant woman said to him.

Marc curled up in a ball in one corner of the cabin on a bench. The woman draped a blanket around his nude, oil-covered body.

"My name is Joan, and you are on the *Saint Michelle*. Do you think you can drink some warm tea? I am a nurse, and it would do you some good to warm up."

Marc nodded, and took the cup in his hands. The warmth radiated through his arms. After a gulp, he started to gag and cough.

"Careful now. You have taken in quite a bit of the sea, and a fair amount of oil," she said. Marc doubled over and began to heave up his stomach.

CHAPTER 23

Spring, 1942

Paris, France

"Robert tells me you are looking for some birds for your birdhouse," Marc said to Georges.

"It is true, I am," Georges said. R was right. The boy looked as if he could be fourteen years old. He was small and thin, built like a horse jockey.

"Bird care is not easy. Lots of feeding and caring for them, and escorting them so they can fly again," Marc said coolly. "Have you cared for birds before?" Marc studied Georges' facial features and his responses, trying to judge if he was a kid, or a man.

"Some, but we can take more now. Besides, more birds are falling from the sky. They will need nests, you know," Georges said. He looked like a young schoolboy, but it did not match the way he spoke or held himself.

"True, very true. Can you come for a game of cribbage?" Marc asked next, checking his expressions.

"Cribbage? You mean that game of cards with the funny board?" George asked, perplexed.

"Yes, that is the game."

"I don't know how to play," Georges responded, shrugging his shoulders.

"Oh, don't worry about that. I am the only one who does and, besides, it is never about the game but the company and tea," Marc relaxed a bit and gazed past Georges toward the park. The serious tone of his voice put Marc at ease.

"Yes, then, of course," Georges responded.

"Great, then. See that fellow over there?" Marc pointed to Philip, Dr. Jackson's son.

"Yes."

"I want you to meet him for a game of boules tomorrow afternoon about a quarter past three at the park. He is very nice. Play a bit and then he will bring you for a game of cribbage." Philip made eye contact with Georges and smiled.

"Philip, Philip," Marc called to him. Philip then walked over. "I want you to meet Georges. He likes to play boule. You are going to meet him tomorrow for a game in the park and then bring him back for some cribbage," Marc said. Philip nodded.

"He needs to make some friends, Philip. Be nice to him."

The following day, Georges met at the Jacksons. The conversation started to wind down over to the details of their next move.

"His name is Jean," Georges said to Marc. "He is very important to the group and he should meet you."

"Dr. Jackson has agreed. Can he come over tomorrow afternoon?" Marc asked Georges.

"Yes, but no boule and park business. Jean is very direct and busy," Georges continued.

"Fair enough. Four then," Torquette said to Georges and looked at R. R nodded with a smile of approval. Marc looked at Dr. Jackson who had just put down his phony score.

"Let's not forget the numbers," Dr. Jackson said.

"Oh, right," R said.

Marc took the board and placed it back into his bag for the bike ride home. So far, everything felt right to him.

June 20, 1940

Saint-Nazaire, France

Marc awoke in what looked like the foyer of a hotel, though he was not sure. He was groggy and sick to his stomach. His joints ached and his hands were swollen. He looked to his right and left and could see other beds with other men in them. Across from him was another line of beds holding even more men. The sheets were stained with oil. He looked into his memory as to how he got here.

I was swimming. The life jacket, it was dark, the woman, the pregnant woman, he thought to himself.

I must be dead, I feel dead, Marc continued in a quasi-dream state. He was there, but not there. He was alive but not alive. There was pain, but at the same time the pain was in the background of his consciousness. Marc moved his arm, but it felt as if his body were not his own.

He could remember the nude dive into the sea to fetch the struggling swimmer. *Was I the swimmer*? The ship pulled to the side of an overturned lifeboat. The Pekingese dog was plucked from the small, overturned boat. Then all was still.

They are dead, too, Marc looked around the room. He was sure of it. I wonder when they are going to tell me, he thought about the nurses. He was sure that he must be dead. This must be the waiting room. They are letting us get better first before they tell us, he thought to himself.

A German officer came to the front desk and talked with a nurse. She told him something and they talked for a few minutes. He was asking about some woman who was in charge.

He then walked down the row of beds and looked at each of the men. The German officer called over the nurse and asked about an empty bed. She cupped her hand and spoke into his ear. He nodded and looked up and around.

He pointed to Marc and asked the nurse about him. She nodded and walked away. The German officer took a chair and then sat next to Marc's bed.

Marc thought, *Here it comes. The one who tells you are dead must be the one who killed you.* He felt an overwhelming sense of dread come over him. He scanned his memory and thought he must have been shot alongside the officer but did not know it yet. *Maybe it was not the officer who was killed but me, and I was looking at myself instead of the officer.* Marc's mind raced as he tried to solve the mystery of when and how he must have died.

"What is your name?" the officer asked in perfect English.

"Marc, Marc Tolbert," he said, surprised that he could even speak.

"What unit are you with?" he asked next.

"I am not in the army. I was just a passenger," Marc responded, looking around. He felt an overbearing sense of dread and churning in his body. He began to shake.

"Passenger? What do you mean?" the officer pressed next.

"I am not British. I am American. I was trying to get home via Ireland," Marc said directly to the officer. The officer got up from the chair and went back to the nurse and started to talk with her.

Marc looked at them and wondered what they were planning on doing with him. A wave of nausea washed over him. He looked at his hands and arms and could see deep, dark oil stains in his skin. The officer then returned.

"Can you tell me where in America you are from?" he asked next.

"New York. Just north of New York City."

"Do you know how you got here?"

"I was on the ship that was bombed."

"Yes, yes, I know, but do you remember getting here?" he pressed.

Marc looked at him with fear. *He is going to tell me how I got here and what will happen to me next.* His stomach burned with nausea, mixed with fear and anger.

"No. I was in the sea and now I am here," he said back, hearing his voice as if he was speaking into a bucket.

The officer just looked at him and then nodded. "In a few days, I will be back. We will talk more then." He got up and started to walk away.

He turned back and asked Marc, "Who is the chancellor of Germany?"

Marc thought and then said, "Eleanor Roosevelt."

Then he asked, "Who is the prime minister of England?" and Marc knew it was Mick. Mickey? Is it Mickey?

"Mickey ... uhh ... Mickey. I think Mouse."

Then he asked Marc, "Do you remember the woman?" he asked him next.

"The mother? The pregnant one?" Marc answered.

"Yes, her," the officer responded.

"I saw her, yes," Marc said, feeling relieved and connected in a way to the officer.

"Good, don't forget her. I will be back in a few days." He then walked out of the makeshift hospital.

Marc felt ill. His body shook and he leaned over the bed, shoving his face into the bucket. He heaved, but nothing came up. His body trembled and shook until he could not heave anymore.

Allen then walked up to his bed. "Marc, you are going to be fine, but you need to rest."

Marc looked up into his friend's face and could not believe his eyes. *Allen survived!* He looked as though he'd just come back from the bar, without a scratch on him.

"I need to go, Marc, but before I leave, I want to encourage you to hang in there." Then he walked right through the nurse and out the door. Marc felt another wave coming down upon him, but at least he knew Allen had survived. *How did he do that? Walk through the nurse?* he thought.

Then it came to Marc. He understood what the German wanted. He said to the nurse who was walking past his bed.

"I am not the father. You understand me? I am not the father."

She looked at him, perplexed. "Father of whom?" she asked.

"That German is going to take me away in a few days to see the chancellor of Germany. Eleanor ... Eleanor Roosevelt. And she is pregnant, and they think I am the father."

She looked at him, stunned, and could not come up with a response.

"I am not the father, I'm telling you. It is not my baby," Marc pleaded with the woman.

Finally, it came to her and it was simple, "I believe you."

CHAPTER 24

Spring, 1942

Lyons, France

"Here, you take these over to François," he said to Marie as she picked up the plates and carried them to the press.

"Now, these copper plates bend and go over the drum," he said, installing the plates.

"Can you get me some of that paper over there to load?" Marie retrieved some of the paper from a corner.

"Now, the paper loads here, but you need to watch and make sure it loads correctly. Stack it this way and place it in the tray, and always run a test print to see if everything lines up before you hit the power and start making a run."

"See, just like that!" He pulled a sheet out from the other side of the press. "It is still wet, so be careful, but the alignment is correct."

"Now, see how much ink is on this sheet? It is not dry yet," he went on in his training.

"Yes," Marie answered back with an intense look. She smiled at him, glowing.

"The control for the ink flow is here. That is another reason for a test run for the first couple of sheets. You need to adjust the amount of ink for each page. It is touch and go, and might take a few turns before you get it right." The man giving instruction was not much older than Marie, and shorter. He was short compared to many other men.

"Have you been doing this long?" Marie asked him.

"Printing? All of my life. Before the war I used to work in my parents' shop."

"Is that where you got the equipment?" Marie asked in what she hoped sounded like an offhand tone.

"No. That shop is gone. This press came from the university," he said as he turned away to organize the supplies.

"What happened to your parents' shop?"

"They are gone now. Deported."

"Are you Jewish?" she asked, with a whispering confessional tone.

He looked at her, but his eyes seemed to turn inward, searching for the beginning and end of some story.

"No, not at all. I am French," he said looking directly at her. "I am not sure really what happened to them. One day they were here, and the next they were gone. Get used to it, Marie. It happens, you know, more than you might realize." He then brushed her cheek with endearment.

"We are ready. Now, when you are ready to make a run and have tested everything, you hit this button and watch. Watch the paper carefully as it comes out. Don't walk away and do anything else. You are watching to make sure the alignment stays correct. If it starts to get off track, stop. Sometimes after a few hundred sheets, these settings start to slip up."

Spring, 1942

Paris, France

Marc, Dr. Jackson and Torquette were seated at the table at four in the afternoon, wondering if Jean had gotten lost or if he would show. Perhaps even wondering if they were wrong and had been set up.

Then a knock sounded at the door. Torquette got up and looked out the window to see a young man, slightly heavier set than Georges. She opened the door and said, "Bonjour."

"I am Jean, I have come to play some cribbage with your club," the young man said, as he believed he was going to play cards.

"Excellent. Please come in and sit down. I will take your coat," Torquette said.

"Jean, have you played this game before?" Dr. Jackson asked him, grinning.

"Birdies, or cribbage?" Jean responded in a serious, straightforward manner.

"Well, both?" Marc said.

Jean then laughed. "No, I have never played cribbage before. It is an odd game. I am not good with cards."

"Well, you can certainly be a part of this club. Only Marc seems to understand the stupid game," Torquette said dismissively.

"Jean, how soon do you think you can have a nest ready?" Marc asked him.

"Soon, very soon. We have many men in the group. It is just a matter of working out the logistics, honestly," Jean answered.

"Logistics?" Torquette said.

"Yes. We need to know where and how to take handoffs. We are going to need to come to an agreed-upon method of communication. And, we need a single point of contact. A go-to for your group, and a point of contact for our group," Jean explained matter-of-factly. His tone seemed completely out of place for a schoolboy.

Dr. Jackson nodded and pulled a peg, then put it down into another hole on the board, smiling at Marc. "Jean, we are not really a group, but just people trying to help others in need. I hope you understand that."

"Agreed," Marc said. "I will be the single point of contact. Everything will go through me." Marc nodded as he glanced at both Dr. Jackson and Torquette, confirming what they had spoken about before Jean's arrival.

"Then it is settled. You will meet our head and he will interview you. He is the one who knows all the others and acts as our single point of contact. Georges and I are not in charge. He is."

"When?" Marc asked and took a deep breath.

"Wednesday. I will give you instructions through Georges. We need to keep things appearing normal with him, so, you will be asked to bring a package, just some books," Jean said.

"Excellent. We need a nest soon. We have too many birds right now and some need to get flying home. So, we need to get started sooner than we expected," Marc said. He was frustrated that this process was taking so long.

They finished their tea and Marc told them their scores for the game that day. He then took the board and placed it back into his bag.

July, 1940

Saint-Nazaire

"Maybe you should go south?" the German officer suggested to him.

"To Spain?" Marc asked.

"Yes, Spain?" the officer pressed again.

"Are you going to drive me there?"

"Well, no, but it is an idea," the officer said with a curious look.

"I don't know anyone in Spain. I mean, it sounds like a good idea, but how I am going to get over the border? I do not have a passport. I have no papers. I don't have any money." He turned to the window and with a voice of desperation said, "It is all out there. I am not just going to stroll down to Spain and show up at the border and say, 'Let me through, American here.'" The officer sat back in his chair, bemused by Marc's rant.

"I know someone north," Marc said.

"Oh, England?" the officer responded with interest.

"Yes. Do you think I could go north?"

"Oh, no problem. I will put you on a U-boat and they will just drop you off in Southampton. Do you want Churchill ... oh, excuse me, Mickey, to meet you at the dock?"

"So, going north is not an option," Marc said quietly.

"No," the officer said looking up with a smile, "look, I believe you are an American. If you were British, we would not be having this talk. But the fact is you were born in France. So, that makes you a French citizen as well. And, if I wanted to, I could have you arrested and put into a POW camp, or even worse."

"But I am not a soldier," Marc complained.

"Yes, yes, I know, but still, the point is, you have no passport, no proof, and even though I can radio back and check in on this or that about your story, you don't want that."

"What do you mean?"

"I mean that you do not want me to verify your citizenship, because then you are on record. Then, something must be done," the officer raised his eyes. "I don't like paperwork."

Marc shifted to one side of his chair as he looked down at the desk. He then shifted back, looked at the portrait of the French head of Parliament and back at the officer.

"We have not got around to changing them out yet. Other duties, you know. What about instead of a POW camp, you stay here a bit? I need some help with a problem," the officer said.

"Problem?"

"Yes, a problem. Your savior friend, Joan, is bugging me about the bodies washing ashore, and she will not let up. If there is one Brit I would like to send back over the Channel, it is that one."

Marc sat and listened, taking in what the officer told him, realizing just how stuck he was. He had no way of traveling south and he knew it was dangerous. Even if he could get to the border, he had no idea with whom or where he would stay in Spain. If at any point he should be stopped in France, he would be arrested without his papers. At least with the hospital, he knew people.

"I need help with the port to go between you and the hospital and morgue. I am good with French, but very good speaking English. You know French very well, and English, of course. The body issue is becoming a problem and, as much as I would not like to be the one who takes charge and comes up with a solution, that is not the case," his voice droned on. "I need to get some order of the problem so that every time a body comes ashore, I am not dealing with some hysterical French grandmother telling me that it is my job to do something."

"And you are not going anywhere soon, Marc," he said, without any hint of joking in his voice.

"Understood. What do you need done first?"

"I need some land. I need to get a place to bury them quickly. No more of this hold-and-wait business. So, I want you to talk to the church here and get me some land. I could send a German who knows better French than I do, but I would rather send you, because," he paused and took a deep breath, "this requires trust. They simply do not trust us. You are, however, an American, so my bet is that they will trust you."

"This is going to be tough," Marc said softly.

"She saved your life, Marc," the officer said in a firm tone. "She saved you and all the others from the sea that day, and she lost her baby." His tone grew intense. "But that did not stop her from keeping that hospital running, and has not stopped her from cursing me out every time I come over to speak to one of those sick Brits." He paused and looked out the window toward the bay. "She is not going to let me just sit on my ass while bodies wash up on the shore. I may not like her but I do respect her, and I also have something of a fear of her. I want to keep things here going well. If I can solve the problem at the docks, then I have a few points with her and then maybe I can come up with a solution for you."

"Where did you learn to speak English so well?"

"University of Chicago. Class of '37."

"You are an American?"

"No. I am a German. After university, I returned home for a visit and, due to the graces of the new order, I was conscripted to stay longer than I'd planned."

Marc thought for a second and realized he was right. If it had not been for her, his body would be washing up on the shore alongside the others.

"In many ways, Marc, I am a lot like yourself, except I have papers," the officer said.

"I understand. I'm sorry but I'm still a little loose in the head. What is your name again?"

"Sean."

"Is Sean German?"

"No, that is my American name. I would prefer you call me Officer Sean."

"I will speak to the church."

CHAPTER 25

April, 1942

Lyons, France

"We have a very large circulation," Marie said to the man sitting across from her.

"I am surprised, honestly."

"About what?" she asked him in a low tone.

"Well, about you, a woman so beautiful, doing such risky things as an underground newspaper."

"Yes, it is risky, but I am not alone. Barbie is a very pretty name. I like it," She looked up and studied his face. "You already know my skills."

"Do you want to go now?"

"Let's finish the coffee first. Are you married?" she said.

"Agreed. But not too much longer." He pondered her as he drank up. "Where is your family now?"

"Klaus, May I call you that? They live in Bordeaux. Once they left Paris, they took up an apartment down there. I see them. They are very loyal to Marshal Pétain, and they are devout Royalists."

May, 1942

Paris, France

Georges met Marc downstairs at his apartment. "You are going to go over to the Old Shakespeare and Company Bookstore. It is closed, of course. Go upstairs and knock. Sylvia will answer the door. She is going to give you some books of Braille."

"I know her! What a surprise. Braille?"

"Yes, just a few. Not a lot, and she will give you instructions on how to get to his house."

"What is his name?" Marc asked.

"Jacques. His name is Jacques," Georges said, patting Marc on the back.

"And then what?" Marc asked.

"You will go straight to his house, which is not far, and arrive at his door on the fourth floor at exactly a quarter after seven."

"How long will this take?" Marc studied Georges' expressions for some hint. "I would like to know everything that I am in for, Georges. I get a little nervous when I am walking into something open-ended."

"Marc, I understand but, please, when you get there, you will understand. It will take as along as Jacques needs it to take. Relax and enjoy the visit," Georges finished.

June, 1942

Lyons, France

The printing room door busted open as a squad of SS troopers bolted in. Marie threw up her hands, followed by others in the room. The printing press continued to roll out the papers.

"Schnell, schnell!" the soldiers shouted at everyone in the room. They carried them away in three separate cars, with the men separated from Marie.

They were taken into small, dark, six-by-nine cells. Marie screamed as the guards roughed her up and tossed her inside.

A few minutes later, she heard the door to the first cell slam open. A man shouted as he was dragged into a questioning room. Then a second man was dragged into the questioning room. After a few hours, they finally came to Marie's cell, and flung the door open. The guard screamed at her and pushed her down the corridor. They were the roughest with her.

She arrived in the questioning room and the door slammed behind her. Across from her sat her coffee date, Klaus, dressed very neatly.

"You have done good this time," he said to her quietly. "I am impressed. Now, if we can just figure out how to use this opportunity to get some more information out of them, even better."

Marie smiled at him. "I have some ideas. I have been thinking back in the cell."

"Good. Let's hear them," he asked her, smiling.

Marie screamed as if she were being hit, and then muffled her voice with her own hand. Then she looked composed at him and said, "Let's work toward this one—Reni—he likes me. I have slept with him now a few times. He will be the easiest to get to," she said, and then she nodded to the guard who slapped her hard on the face.

Marie yelled, and then recomposed herself. "Trust me on this. He will have to rescue me because he believes I am doing this just for him."

June, 1942

Paris, France

"Here are the books." Sylvia said as she winked at Marc. "When you meet him, don't forget that I need some back. Otherwise, I will run out." She was direct and to the point.

"You are very brave. Do I bring them back?"

"No. You go from here to his place, and then away, such as a café, or a walk," she looked up directly into his eyes. "Don't go directly home yet, and do not come back here, whatever you do." Sylvia looked tired. "Just remind him that I need some more books."

"Understood. And you look good," Marc said to Sylvia with a smile.

"Get going and don't lose my books, you foxy fool." She slapped him on the butt as he left the old Shakespeare and Company Bookstore.

He walked down several blocks and then crossed the Seine River onto the Isle de France, finally making his way to the four-story apartment complex. It was ten after seven. He entered the doorway to the main foyer, and then took the stairs slowly up to the fourth floor. The lights were off in the stairway and he was not sure of the switch location. But there was just enough light leaking through the window at the front door, and light peering down from the skylight to illuminate the handrails of the tightly twisting marble staircase.

Marc knocked on the door three times and then rang the bell. It was just at a quarter after seven.

The door opened and he could see a young man in front of him, but could not make out his features. "I am Marc, are you ...?"

"Yes, I am Jacques. Come inside."

The front hallway was dark. There was a light in the bathroom, but all the other lights were off. He followed Jacques down the hallway and then up a small staircase. Jacques was thin and of medium height.

"I have the books from Sylvia," Marc said, breaking the silence.

"Oh, yes, in here." He pointed to a small room to the right at the top of the staircase. It was packed to the ceiling with thick Braille books and papers of all kinds.

"Wait, let me check," Jacques said to Marc as he took the books from his hands.

"Oh, yes, I know these," he said, passing his fingertips across the first pages. "Put them in the stack," he said and gave them back to Marc. Marc then turned and put them down where he believed they were safe from falling down.

"She said she will need some more," Marc continued, studying Jacques' reaction.

"I bet she will," Jacques said, raising his voice slightly.

"In here," he said. Marc followed him into a small room at the end of the upstairs hallway. "Sit here, please," Jacques invited. Marc felt the top of a chair to get his bearings.

"Are we going to sit in the dark?" Marc asked, perplexed more than concerned.

"Oh shit, no. Sorry, I forget. The light button is there on the wall, by the door," Marc got up and reached over to hit the button. A lamp then came on.

One of his eyes appeared to be missing and the other looked at Marc directly, but with no sense of sight. "So, you are blind," Marc asked.

"Yes. I guess they didn't tell you," Jacques said.

"No. I mean, I should've guessed by the books, but I thought they were just a game," Marc said, looking side to side in the room and then back up at Jacques.

"They are a game. I don't need those books, but I do need some reason to meet you. It is better for the both of us that, if it comes to that, we at least can say you were here to bring me some books."

"Understand," Marc said back quickly, as if answering a general.

"Jean and Georges have spoken to me about you, but I needed to meet you in person. We need to talk and get to know each other. Where are you from?" Jacques asked.

"New York."

"Is that where you were born?"

"No, I was born here in Paris."

"So, you are French?"

"Well, sort of. Yes, I am French, but my father is American and my mother barely speaks French any longer, and I grew up in New York."

"So, you are a Teddy Boy?"

"Yes, you know that term?"

The conversation continued on for ninety minutes and covered all sorts of topics but never once did they talk about birdies, or the Resistance.

"What was the name again?" Jacques pressed him to repeat the answer Marc just had given him.

"*Lancastria*," Marc responded, focusing all his energy toward controlling his voice from cracking.

"I have never heard of this ship."

"It was not my choice. You know the *Normandie*, right?"

"Oh, yes, of course. You must be of some means traveling over on her."

"She was very nice but a bit lonely. I did meet some very nice people," Marc said, and then his voice became a soft mumble. "They've all left now, of course."

"What is the other ship?"

"*Lancastria*," Marc coughed, and then started to choke up just a bit.

Jacques paused for a moment. "What happened?" he asked next.

"Well, it sank, Jacques, and I did not get home and now I am here," Marc said, his voice as tense as a piano wire.

Jacques paused and seemed as if he had another question, but then stopped.

"You pass. We can help," he said next.

"What do you mean? Don't you have any other questions?"

"I am the gatekeeper, Marc. All of the members of the Sons of Liberty must meet me and be interviewed by me. Anyone we work with comes through me," Jacques said in a relaxed manner.

"But you are blind."

"Exactly. See, they insisted I be the leader. I see by the voice. I listen to your voice and can tell, if you are truthful or if you hiding something? I have this knack of sizing up character by just listening, not to the words, but to the sound of the words. A lot of boys who want in are just frivolous thrill seekers. They are silly kids who do not understand the risk, the danger and the price," Jacques finished and listened to Marc's breath echo against the apartment walls.

"You do know the price," Jacques said to Marc.

"How do you know?"

"The way you talk. How your voice changes. Everything changes. I see something else in my mind, something dark, and oily."

"That is amazing." Marc shivered, as he felt suddenly naked in front of Jacques.

"What?"

"I never said anything about the oil."

"Yes, see, that is why I am the leader. It is not the words, but how they are said. It is not what you say, but how your voice sounds to me. You are not some kid, and you know death. So, you pass," Jacques said. He tilted his head back and up toward the right corner of the room.

"Good, because we need help. We have some birds that need a nest, and soon," Marc said.

"I will set it up. We have a lot of contacts. There are over six hundred of us now and we are working with another group. Most of what we do is the newspaper, but we can do much more. The rules, though, are the same: Never more than two at the same time together. We never meet in large groups, or have any kind of centralized meetings. It is too dangerous. It brings attention where we do not need any attention," Jacques spoke quickly now.

"Do you have contacts south?"

"Yes, we are working out the way to get the birds home. We can set up the nest and then set up the flyaway south."

"Good, because they keep coming to the hospital. We can only do so much now. We cannot keep them long. In fact, we need to stop keeping them there, period."

"I understand, Marc," and then he paused and searched for his next words. "I am glad to have met you. You could have gone home, you know. You did not need to be here."

"No, I did need to be here. I couldn't have gone home, Jacques," Marc said firmly.

"Um," Jacques said, and then took a long pause with his head cocked to the side. "I understand. You may go now. Georges and Jean will set up the details for handoffs."

"I read your paper."

"*Defense de la France*? And how did you like it?"

"I enjoyed it. Someone threw it under the door of my flat."

"Yes. That is our way of passing on the news."

Marc left and descended the stairs slowly in the dark. Upon reaching the street, he looked both ways for any sign of someone waiting to follow him.

Jacques sat in his chair, alone, with the light still turned on. He rocked back and forth for a moment.

"*Lancastria*. There is a story in his voice," he said as he rose to leave the room.

August, 1940

Saint-Nazaire, France

Marc was back at the hospital after a long day of running errands to and from the hospital. Most of the other patients had now gone. Two British slipped out one night and the German officers gave Joan hell about it and threatened to shut everything down.

Marc cooled them off by telling them that no one knew when or how they left. The others had already died.

A man in one of the beds who had been burned in the oil slicks was still there and shaking. He had been well, and then sick. He would rally and then crash. This had gone on for weeks now.

The nurse was exhausted and Marc said he would watch that night. The man's breathing started to slow around 10 p.m. About 10:15, he stopped shaking and shivering. He had not spoken to anyone for nearly a week. By 10:20, his breathing was extremely shallow. At 10:30 p.m., he stopped breathing altogether. Marc sat by his bed and read until about 11 p.m. He then carefully checked the man's wrist for a pulse. He put the back of his hand over his face. He then pulled the sheet over the man's head and in a soft whisper, wished him a good night.

The next morning came as a surprise to Marc. "We leave at 6 a.m. Be here early," the fisherman said to Marc.

"What do you mean?" Marc said.

"I mean if you want to get across the Channel, then we are leaving at six."

"How did you know I was thinking about this?" Marc asked him in French.

"A friend."

"Who?"

"Look, why does it matter? You do need to get across, right?"

"Yes, but," Marc said as he stepped back from the man.

"But what?"

"I am not ready yet. Is there another time?"

"Look, I cannot promise another time. Don't be a fool. If you want to go, then be at the dock at 6 a.m."

Officer Sean could not keep himself from glancing at Marc during the funeral the following day. He studied him closely as the prayers were given for the coffins in the church.

"Your American pet is still tied to his chain," a German joked with Officer Sean at the pub in town that evening. "How long are you going to keep your pet?" they poked and prodded him.

"I already have tried once to let him go. I sent one of the fishermen to set up a ride for him north," the officer said after sipping his beer.

"What a fool. He just keeps digging those graves," they joked and laughed. Officer Sean glanced down at his mug, and then up at his friends.

"I don't think it is that at all." He paused. "I think he can't go," he finished, raising his eyebrows.

"Why?" another asked.

"Fear."

"I bet you rounds for a week you are wrong," someone else said to the officer.

"Oh, what do you propose?"

"I will set up another boat for him, a sure thing, and if he takes it, and what fool would not, you are buying the rounds for a whole week."

"And if he stays?"

"Then, your round is on us for the week."

Officer Sean thought to himself and considered carefully what he had seen, and then said, "Make it a month. If he goes, I buy for a month, and if he stays, you buy me for a month." The officer then pointed his finger at them and said, "And no scaring him off or any funny business. Leave him alone and let him decide."

"You're a fool. Your American pet has just cost you rounds for a month."

"I hope you are right. He needs to go, but don't count on those rounds just yet."

CHAPTER 26

March, 1943

Lyons, France

"I need you to wrap this up," officer Barbie said to Marie.

"I am trying. I think if we give it a little more time, we can get other names," she said.

"I am sure we can as well, but that is not the problem. I need you for another assignment."

"Where?" she asked.

"I need you in Paris. The problem is growing there, even more than it is here in Lyons, and they can use your skills. Plus, you know Paris."

"And some in Paris know me, as well. It will be a little more dangerous."

"Francs are not a problem. You will be taken care of," he said with some irritation in his voice.

"That is not the problem. The problem is that I did live there, and people do know me, but maybe things have changed a bit," Marie answered back. There was a tension around the entire idea but she shrugged it off.

"Oh, they have. There are very few people right now living there compared to before we liberated it from the previous filth," Marie listened to him, trying to imagine Paris now compared to when she lived there in 1940. "I would be shocked if you just happen across someone. Besides, if you do, that might be a benefit to your work."

"Yes, it could be. You're right." *But it also could be a problem,* she thought silently to herself.

"We need to get on top of it better. The usual methods are not working so well. We need someone on the inside to help, and you are ideal. You know Paris, but you have not been living there for a few years now. The old becomes new again. So, we need to wrap this up," officer Barbie finished and looked down at some papers on his desk.

"I suppose my chances are now over with you. I would have treated you well. When am I leaving?" she asked.

"Soon, very soon. I will let you know as soon as we have it worked out." He then noticed something else on his desk. "Oh, and one more thing. Don't take this the wrong way. There is no doubt as to your loyalties. But, you said your family is now living in Bordeaux." Everything froze inside her as he went on. "But we have not been able to locate them. Do you know more specifics?" he looked up and studied her face.

"Well, yes, I did say they live in Bordeaux, but they have moved since. I did not realize you would need to contact them," Marie said while observing her own voice for nervousness that would hint at betrayal.

"Well, we do not need to contact them, but I do need to confirm relatives of our operatives. Is there something wrong?" he pressed.

"They have moved since. They are now in Tours," Marie said, taking a seat across from officer Barbie.

"Do you have their address?" then he leaned in toward him.

"Maybe you can help me? I have been trying to reach them myself and when they moved to Tours, they have not sent their address yet. Do you have some contacts that might be able to search for them? I do want to get them some money. If not, I understand. I think I know possibly where to look," Marie looked at the officer with a slightly pathetic look of dignified desperation.

"I will see what I can do. It is not my job to track down the lost, but at the same time, I value your work," he said. He inhaled deeply and looked back at the forms.

Marie reached over and touched the top of his hand. "I would be very grateful to you," and smiled as she searched his face to connect with his eyes.

"Here are your papers," Klaus said, quick to pull his hand away from under hers.

March, 1943

Paris, France

Marc walked up and down the aisle of empty market tables looking for anything he could buy for supplies but, as usual, everything was gone. People were selling "vegetables," but they were crude-looking oddities for tea or soups. A sign posted warned people of the dangers of eating cats.

Leaving the market, he rode his bicycle down the streets heading back to his apartment, but decided to take a detour instead and headed over to the Metro where, from time to time, people sold goods at the station. He found a vendor who actually had some crude cheese to sell. Marc paid the francs quickly and then stuffed the cheese into his bag.

Out of the corner of his eye, he saw in the distance a woman he knew but could not place exactly. He looked for a few more minutes and thought, *Is that Marie?* He took his bike and started to move toward where she was standing but she turned and started to walk away with a man. The man was tall and French. Marc had never seen him before.

He decided to hold back and watch. It looked like her but he could not be certain. Her hair was a different style, as was her clothing. But the curves of her body appeared the same to him. He decided to move in closer.

Just then the woman and man stopped talking and started walking toward the front of the station. Marc decided to take a risk.

"Marie, Marie!" he called, but the woman did not turn and look back. Maybe he was too far away or his voice did not carry? He was still uncertain and felt like it was her, but she did not turn and look at him. Perhaps it was just wishful thinking. He watched them walk away toward the Metro and decided not to call out again.

Marc scrubbed the skins of the potatoes. They were small, and more than a few were shriveled. Dr. Jackson entered the kitchen and picked up one of the larger potatoes, turning it carefully.

"This is a nice one. Downstairs there is some dirty laundry that needs to go out. When you get a chance, take a run." Marc then waited until Dr. Jackson left the room and after a few more minutes, he removed his apron and went to the basement.

He took a large basket in the corner that was filled with linens and rolled it through the basement toward the large doors and then out to a German truck that was waiting. The driver helped him lift the basket into the back. They put in a second basket of linens behind the first, and then closed the doors.

Marc got into the truck and then the driver took off. The trip was not long, just a few streets, until they came to the back of a store. They backed up the van and then unloaded the two carts of laundry. After the truck took off, Marc waited a few minutes with the baskets.

Soon Georges and Jean came through the rear door, both carrying satchels. Marc moved the baskets over to the large washers and had started to unload the sheets until the top of the heads of two men could be seen underneath.

"It's time," Marc said.

Both men rose from the front basket and climbed out. From the second basket, a single man got out.

"Can you take another?" Marc asked.

"We only have clothes for two," Georges said to Marc.

"Well, we thought it would be a chance. If not, he can come home with me tonight, or maybe over to Sylvia's place. But, he cannot go back to the hospital."

"We can take him, just not wearing what he has on," Jean said, shrugging his shoulders. Marc looked at the man, an American. They were about the same size.

"What about this?" Marc said, pointing to what he was wearing.

Georges and Jean looked at each other and nodded.

"Fine, we will swap clothes. But I need you to send Dr. Jackson, or maybe Philip, to my apartment and get a change. I cannot go out looking like that, either. They will not care where I work or anything. They'll just see the clothes and arrest me."

Marc quickly stripped and passed his pants and shirt to the man. The man peeled off his flight suit and took off his boots. He was putting on his boots after stepping into Marc's trousers when Marc said, "No. No boots. If you are stopped, they will see that."

Marc took off his shoes. They were a bit big for the flyer, but he stuffed his socks into the front and then they fit fine.

"Don't forget I am here," Marc told Jean.

"Don't worry. I will go right after we drop them off," Jean said.

"Good luck to you guys. Nice of you to visit Paris and, next time, we will give you a better tour," Marc said with a little chuckle.

"No problem, friend, and thanks for the lift," one of the airmen said sheepishly.

"Do as they tell you. And do not talk much. Remember the French I taught you. Speak low and mumble, and only a few words at a time. Nothing more." Marc's tone became so serious; it sounded like he was scolding him. "Mumble when you talk, and low. Do not pronounce your words like you are in high school. If you are stopped and questioned in French, pretend not to understand and just keep asking for a cigarette."

"Cigarette? I don't think I want a smoke from some German if I am stopped," one of the airmen said in a cocky tone.

Marc glared at him. "Only a Frenchman would ask a German with a gun for a cigarette. It is not a joke. You need to act French if you want to get home." The flyer looked slightly embarrassed, realizing the real danger.

Eventually, Jean returned with a change of clothes for Marc and, after returning to the hospital, he rode his bicycle home. It was close to dark, and a new curfew had been implemented. The apartment stood cold when he arrived. He turned on the lights and did double-check through the flat to make sure everything was secure. He then glanced at the board on the mantel.

August, 1940

Saint-Nazaire, France

"We need to leave soon! Are you coming aboard?" the fisherman asked Marc. "What is the problem? Is there a girl you want to bring?" he then said mockingly.

Marc stood frozen on the dock, his chest tense and throbbing, his breathing shallow and fast. His skin itched as if it had caught fire. His stomach churned and threatened to spill out into the sea, just like the oil had done.

"Come along now, come along, it will be fine. No one will give any attention to such a small fishing boat," the fisherman said next, trying to coax Marc onto the boat. "In just a bit, you'll be over in England, so don't worry."

The fisherman's words struck a cord of fear so strongly in Marc's body that he could not find anything inside of him to override the overpowering need he had to leave the dock.

"Look at him. He is afraid of it," one shipmate said to another.

"He will get over it. He just needs to get into the boat first," the German agent spy said to the other shipmate. "My bud needs those rounds," he whispered to himself.

The German spy, dressed as a fisherman, left the boat and walked up to Marc on the dock. "It will be fine. I know it is hard, but you just need to take one step at a time and then you are on the boat," he said, trying to move Marc forward. "Once you are in the boat, you will see there is nothing to fear."

Marc took a step forward into what felt like a wall of mud. He then took a second step forward. The tension grew inside him and the fear churned. Then he took a few more steps until he was within just a few feet of the boat's ramp. A shock wave of mortal fear rose up from the sea and swept over him. Marc dropped to the dock, violently heaving the food he'd eaten that morning, and then the air inside of his stomach. His body trembled as if all his bones had shattered.

The German spy had never seen anything like it before and stopped trying to coax him aboard. When Marc was not looking, he shook his head from side to side for the German officer, watching from a distance, to see.

Marc crawled backward on all fours, away from the gangplank and made his way slowly off the dock like a crab that had escaped a basket. His entire body took over his mind and forced him to move away from the invisible wall that he had hit on the dock.

A few days later, Officer Sean saw Marc on the street walking. He crossed over to catch up with him.

"Have you thought of a plan yet for getting back home?" Officer Sean asked him casually.

"No. I'm not sure right now. Any ideas?" Marc asked, not glancing at the officer's eyes.

"France is a very nice country, and can be hard to let go of," the officer said. He was pleased he upped the bet to a month, but felt a bit of guilt inside about it each day.

"I believe I have secured enough land for the problem," Marc said.

"Excellent. I am impressed. It is always a good thing to be a solution to a problem, rather than be the cause."

"I will make sure, as they come in, that they are put to rest quickly."

"Well, Marc, I am glad to hear that. So, you plan to be staying for a while, it appears. Since you will be around, maybe you can join me for cribbage games? The practice with my English will be good."

"I don't know how to play cribbage."

"Not a problem. I will teach you."

CHAPTER 27

April, 1943

Paris, France

"Marc, should we be arrested, you think they would question us about the game?" Jacques asked calmly. Jean and Georges sat around the table, each holding a hand of cards.

"Perhaps, but likely not," Marc said, his tone cold.

"Let's get on with this. We have work to do," Georges complained.

"I have made contact with another house just south of the city. She can take up to two birdies at once," Jean said.

"We have lost another house, but he could only take one, so we are at least ahead," Georges continued.

"What happened? Do you know?" Marc asked with concern.

"He was not arrested but deported for the force labor call-up. He was twenty-three years old," Jean said.

"But Marc, about arrest—how did you deal with this before?" Jacques asked.

"Safe houses? We were it, and still are. Sometimes they stay with the doctor, and sometimes I have one in my home," he paused. "R has always set up the arrangements south, so I do not know them, but we have never had this many at one time."

"Tomorrow morning, then, we will be by," Georges said to Marc.

"The mornings are working out well. Everyone else is up and going about, so they blend in perfectly." Marc paused and said, "We must avoid evenings because the assumption is to stop you. I was stopped just the other night and it was not even dark."

"But what about arrests? How have you dealt with the problem of when you lose someone to arrest, is my question," Jacques asked for a second time.

Marc grew somber. "It has only happened once, back in '41. I will just say it was a real lesson."

"And?" Jacques continued to press.

"I was lucky. I was meeting with Boris Vidal and Angus from the university, and then they were gone. I did not know all the details, but I do now. It was an early paper, *Resistance*, and stupid. Some of us were just lucky, but too much risk and arrogance over courage."

"Did you have to run?" Jean asked next.

"No. I changed nothing. I went to work and kept to my routine. I have been told if they are watching, they want to see if you react, because that means you must know."

"That could be a problem because we are each other's routine," Georges said.

"We may need our own safe houses?" Jean asked.

"Perhaps, but fear will only stop us," Jacques said. "The reason I asked is because something is coming up soon. Marc, would you be able to help on the morning of Bastille Day?" Jacques asked.

"What is the game plan?" Marc asked cautiously.

"It will be our largest circulation to date. We are printing up 250,000 copies of the *Defense de la France* and will be distributing them in broad daylight on corners of the city. It is our two-year anniversary," Jacques said.

"What if you are arrested?" Marc asked in disbelief.

"That is what I am asking about. We are going to be distributing under armed guards, but we also need watchmen. We need eyes set apart and away that can give us time if they should come," Jacques said.

Marc thought carefully about the request and it made sense to him. His personal risk was low, and he aided others taking a greater risk for all. The idea of 250,000 papers in broad daylight, he found inspiring.

"Yes, I can do that," he said, "but you realize this is going to cost you. They will see and they will search after that," he said.

"Yes, we know, but we promised ourselves this goal," Georges said.

"We will have plans, of course, Marc," Jean said.

"Put me down for watchman and safe house if it comes to that. What is the date?"

"July 14," Jacques said.

"Bastille Day," Marc said.

"The date our paper began," Jean said.

"Gentlemen, this has been an outstanding game of cribbage. You are incredibly gifted players of the game." Each laughed out loud. Marc then took up his tea and made a toast, "To Boris and Angus, watch over us fools." He then took the board from the table and replaced it in his satchel.

September, 1940

Saint-Nazaire, France

"I am not ready to go yet and, besides, not sure where," Marc said to Joan.

"Well, at some point you need to come up with a plan. I can't pay you to work at the hospital," she said. "I barely have enough for supplies."

"That is not it. Besides, I have a few francs now from digging," Marc said.

"Why are you helping him?" she asked.

"The officer? What choice do I have? Either I help him or I am going to be sent off to some camp, or sent south. What am I supposed to do?" Marc answered back, his voice tense with surprise.

"I hate him. I think …" But she did not get far.

"You asked him for graves, and he got the graves. You asked him for a funeral service, and there was a service. You have been sick every day now and barely up and around. A German, not a British, and not a Frenchman, but a German organized and set up the service for nameless bodies that floated up on the shores here. What more do you want? He is no more a demon than the men who decided to overload that ship," Marc said indignantly.

"He did that? I thought you did that?" Joan turned to Marc, her face perplexed.

"I cannot do that alone. He sends me because they will listen to me. I am an American. You know the French. It does not matter how well you can speak, but where you are from. The only reason they listen to me now is because I am not British, and I am not German and I am not French." Marc smiled and said, "At least not French enough for them to distrust."

"I know some people in England," she said as she tried to sit up in the bed.

"So do I, and I think if I can get a fisherman to take me, then maybe I can stay with him. I probably would've made it over there with him if I had not been so sick, but that is the past now. And after a bit, I can get up to Glasgow and get home," Marc's voice cracked.

"Why, Lazarus, you could just walk upon the waves?" she said.

"What do you mean?" Marc asked, perplexed.

"Lazarus sur Mer, that is the name the nurses gave you. You were dead, but then rose again from the sea. They believe you are blessed."

"Blessed by an angel."

"Oh, and what angel would that be?"

"You, the Angel of Saint-Nazaire."

"Who calls me that?

"I do, because, had it not been for you, I would've still been in the sea floating dead. Officer Sean never fails to remind me how you saved me."

"Do they know yet?" she asked, sitting up in the bed.

"Yes. I got word back," Marc said.

"How?"

"Officer Sean had a friend call for me down at Vichy. So, at least they know I am well, and not dead someplace."

"Maybe you are right about him?" she said, and then a new wave of cramps overcame her.

April 1943

Paris, France

Marc stood looking at the board of messages in the market, walking past the German guard who stood by the board. "I am looking for the 'W' family. Missing: good friend. Looking for father: missing from depot. Looking for brother: he left last on Feb 12." None of the messages he read were of people he knew.

"Marc, Marc! Is that you?" he turned and ran straight into Marie.

"Oh my God!" she gushed. "What are you doing here? I thought you would be gone by now."

"Marie, I don't know what to say. You look great, by the way. It is good to see you again." Marc replied. He did not have an answer for why a wall went up inside him just then. He heard his response and voice, and it rang cold in his head, which conflicted with the fact that he had proposed to this woman in the spring of '40.

She hugged him and then said into his ear. "I am so glad to see you. I have missed you so much." Marc melted and his formality fell.

"It ... it ..." he stammered. "Marie, I really have missed you as well."

"Where are you staying? I have so many questions but, first, what are you doing for dinner?" she asked him next.

Marc then remembered why he was at the market in the first place and that, again, he had found nothing suitable to eat. She seemed different to him, but he pushed it aside in his mind, just as he tried to forget the war.

"Well, not sure yet. I am looking for anything but cat," he said with coldness suddenly in his voice.

"Come to my place tonight for dinner. I have some rations. Not much, but enough. And I have so much to tell you." She studied his contours and features. "You're so much thinner. I have some work to do to get you up to weight again. But you are still so handsome."

"Are you at the same place?" Marc asked.

"No, well, close. I am close." She got out some paper and wrote down the address. Marc looked at it and realized he knew the building.

Marc saw her shoes. They were new, with leather soles. "No wonder I did not hear you walk up. You have leather shoes. Where did you get them?" he asked.

"Well, where do you think? The black market, of course," she raised her eyebrows at him.

"Did they have men's shoes? Do they take trade? How many francs?" Marc's mind focused upon salvation from his hated wooden-soled shoes.

"I can see."

"It is just so hard to get any leather these days because, you know, they take it all away."

Over dinner, Marc explained how he did not get home. He talked about the ship, and the people aboard, the hospital and Officer Sean in St. Nazaire. Marc talked with Marie without any guard for the first time in almost two years.

"Are you in?" she asked him.

"In what?" he asked, perplexed by the question.

"The movement, silly. Are you doing any work with the heroes?" she said, her eyes bright.

Marc stopped cold and was not sure how to respond next. He studied her. Her question suddenly seemed to wake him up. Marc seemed to forget the world for a moment, how he'd been talking about all these things that had happened to him. He never actually thought of how it all related to Marie.

"No, Marie, I cannot get involved with that. I've already been interned once. When America entered the war, they arrested us all. The only reason

I'm back here is due to the hospital work." He then remembered and said, "Oh, and the strange fact the Germans have no idea what to do with someone who is both French and American. Otherwise, I would be working with the others." He thought to himself, *I cannot tell her the truth because I cannot protect her from it.*

"I am," she said in a proud tone.

"What? What do you mean by 'in'? In exactly what?" Marc pressed with a mixture of concern and suspicion in his voice.

"It is why I have come back to Paris. I am here to work, to help with the papers," she said, as if he should have known this fact. She looked down as though hiding something else from him. "And a few other things. You know, whatever is needed."

Marc crossed his arms, and his face set with fear. In his mind flashed the faces of others he had know who had disappeared. In addition to the random arrests that have taken place, there was the round-up of Jews at the ice rink in the summertime, the occasional round-up of innocents at the Metro who would be executed in reprisal for attacks on the Germans. His skin started to burn with nervousness that Marie could be next. His dream of sharing a life with her was shattered by the fear inside him that she, too, might be arrested, rounded up, or shot, that she could simply disappear in the night.

"You should stop. It is not something you should be doing or even talking about. It is not safe at all," Marc said in a low, hushed tone.

"Nothing is safe, Marc. I cannot just sit by and watch my country slip away. Nothing is safe," Marie said.

Marc realized she was right, and that she had changed. He feared her, but for a different reason than the guards or checkpoints. He feared her courage. To him it meant she would soon be dead or missing like the others.

A sudden wall of disconnection descended in his mind. Marc hated to face the ultimate fear of such work. Without any words to describe it, he retreated emotionally, yet still listened to her as she continued on. He had only remembered her as the scared girl at the movie back in May 1940, hating that she would become those people in the newsreel. Now, she seemed to jump at the chance to join the newsreel. Marc's stomach was sick, as if he had swallowed a bowling ball.

"I know the risk, but I couldn't live with myself if I did nothing at all," she said. She blazed with courage, and Marc burned under it in fear. He searched for some escape from the conversation.

"Do you have a bike? You will need a bike," Marc said next, trying to stir it away.

"I can take the Metro, and walk," Marie answered back, perplexed.

"Take the bike. The Metro is not that safe. If something should happen, they pick up the hostages from the Metro trains. Or, they set up spot inspections in the Metro. You will need a bike, Marie. I have an extra one."

"Marc, what do I do with my Metro tickets, then? Can you use them?" she asked.

"I never ride the Metro, and you need to live further out, but maybe they will not take your bike, being a woman."

"Take my bike?"

"If you can walk to work, or take the Metro, and if the Germans stop you on a bike, they could take it from you because, technically you should not need a bike."

"Things have changed."

"Yes, Marie, they have," Marc said, expressionless. All the desire he'd had to make love to her left him that night as a tide of fear over the future rushed onto the shore of his soul.

CHAPTER 28

June, 1943

Paris, France

"It is too early," she said to the agent.

"Does he trust you?" the agent asked, raising his eyebrows.

"Yes, of course. That is not the problem. The problem is that things have shifted. Time has gone by."

"He likely is involved. It is just a matter of how and with whom," the agent suggested to Marie.

"I agree, and this is why it is going to require time. If you just want to arrest someone, anyone, then sure, I likely can move this along, but," she paused and considered her next words, "if you want to get an entire ring, and how they do business on the front and back end, then this will be an investment of time." She looked at him. "But worth it because it will be above and beyond all the other small little fishes you have caught."

"And you, Elio, how are you doing?" he turned to one of Marie's counter partners in the Milice.

"I'm in. It took a lot of time, but I'm finally in, and soon I will have enough names to provide," he said glowing, "for a full arrest."

"Excellent. That will make some progress."

"They cannot win. They are just godless Communists and Jews. The right is on our side in this thing and, with patience, right always wins out over wrong," Marie said.

"The main one is blind. They have placed a weak, helpless fool at the center of their web. It is sick, really," Elio continued, "but getting past him was not as big a challenge as I thought it would be. He does not approve of me, but I have convinced the others before I got to him that I am trustworthy of their pathetic cause. Now, it is just time gathering enough information to ensure all of them are arrested. Marie is right. It takes time, and she has just started. I have been working on this for eight months."

"Elio, do you know if they ever ride the Metro?" Marie asked casually.

"Never. Only if they must escape, otherwise they walk or ride bikes," Elio said.

"Very interesting. I will keep that in mind. Thankfully, I have a bike now," she said.

"You should get some fashionable riding pants," the agent said, smiling.

"Yes, excellent idea, and if any naughty Germans stop me to take my bike, will you get it back for me?" she said, batting her eyelashes.

"Before I forget, I was reading one of the special papers about concerts. You could take him out to this special concert. It is invitation-only, and they are playing Jewish music. If you go, he might run into others he knows. I can get you an invitation, amongst our resistance contacts," the agent said, nodding then in Elio's direction.

"That's very thoughtful of you. I would love to take in a concert. Please do," she said.

The night of July 19, 1943, was busy for Jacques, for he had several stop-by guests that evening. The work with the papers had grown along with the circulation. The group had a goal for growth of 250 percent for the month of July.

The Bastille Day circulation became the largest effort ever. The size and scope surpassed anything yet done to provide people with information and hope. Several locations printed the papers. The distribution took place in the open, under guards provided by the Defense of France. The papers were passed out in the open streets, instead of through apartment buildings under the doors, or on the Metro seats, or in the market to be used for packaging. This day, they were passed in the open streets of Paris, directly in front of the watching Germans.

The Defense of France had grown now to over five thousand strong. The logistics of the organization had outgrown Jacques' ability to keep pace.

Elio was a recommendation to him via Georges and of Philip. A 25-year-old medical student at the university, there was something odd in his voice. Jacques could not quite place it, but it was as if his voice was off-pitch, like a bell that had cracked and then been repaired.

None of this mattered now, for there were other considerations to be made. The man had contacts and was eager and self-sufficient. Most of all, he had convinced the others of his trustworthiness even before he'd met Jacques.

Jacques did not sleep well that night. He was up until one in the morning. and then awoke at four, but then fell back to sleep again. He woke to hear his father's voice downstairs at five o'clock.

"Jacques, Jacques ... the Germans are here to see you."

Dr. Jackson sat across from Marc and Torquette at the table in late August 1943. Finally, there was a knock at the door, and Torquette checked to see who it was. It was R. She opened the door and welcomed him in.

"Bonjour, R," Dr. Jackson said in a dry Maine accent. R sat down at the table and took up the cards. He glanced at the cribbage board in the center of the table.

Torquette brought in a cup of weak tea. It was more hot water with some color than real tea, but this was all that now could be offered. The table was barren of any cheese, crackers or blueberries.

"Any more contact with DF?" Marc asked R.

"No, and yes. Well, I found a place for Georges to stay." R sipped his tea. "He tells me Jean is fine and remaining north, out of town." Marc nodded as R finished his report.

"So, any other ideas for contacts?" Dr. Jackson asked.

"Well, yes, there is another group that is much more official than DF. But, I am uncertain of them yet. They want other things from us and I'm not sure yet how to process that."

"What do you mean?" Torquette asked.

"I mean that they can take the pilots, but they also want us to provide information and be more active on the ground." He looked over to Dr. Jackson and then glanced back at Marc before he continued. "They have requested to see if there is a way for us to get passage into Saint Nazaire. They want us to provide a report on the base there for submarines." He then looked out of the corner of his eye at Torquette and then Dr. Jackson. The room went silent.

"The other request amounts to nothing but street reports of conditions here in Paris and the rest of France. That is well enough. But the trip to Saint Nazaire is a bit of a pinch, in my opinion," R continued.

"I know the city, but I don't think I can go there. They're not going to let an American pass back through for anything," Marc finally broke the silence at the table.

"We have some family near there. Maybe we can send Philip for a vacation?" Torquette said next. R's eyes perked up and then immediately glanced at Dr. Jackson for his reaction.

Dr. Jackson looked at her and then looked at the board. He took a peg and moved it forward. "Marc, are you ever going to teach us this game?"

"Do they want just a report, because maybe I can meet one of my friends from there?" Marc asked R.

"They want photographs," R said as if he had just dropped a five hundred pound bomb on the table.

"Photographs? Really?" Marc snapped back. "How about a sketch or oil painting? It would be easier. Philip can just take some paints and set up an easel and do a *plein air* oil painting of the base. Would that work?" He rolled his eyes and stared at the table as he continued. "Because I have no idea where we are going to get a camera or some film." Marc reached down and took the peg that Dr. Jackson had moved. He moved it backwards by two positions from where it originated and then looked away.

"I know where I can get a camera, but not the film. It takes 120," Torquette said.

R said, "If they want pictures, then maybe they can supply the film? Now, how do we get there?"

"Oh, that is not a problem. Philip has a crush on this girl who is a friend of ours and he will enjoy the trip. And Marc, you can give him some sightseeing pointers about Saint Nazaire. Marc lived there for about six months back in 1940." Marc's face stretched in shock that both of them were still even talking about this expedition.

"It is a small box camera. A brownie, so he can hide it in a lunch bag and no one will know," Torquette continued to explain.

"Well then, let me know when we need the film. As for birdies, they can take five on Tuesday, but one at a time, of course." R finished ignoring Marc's foul mood.

"Good, because our nests are full," Dr. Jackson said.

"Any eggs?" Torquette asked.

"Of course not," Dr. Jackson said.

"Since none can be found in the market, I thought I would at least ask," she said.

Marc took up the board and put it back in his bag.

September, 1940

Saint-Nazaire, France

"Long trenches. Long trenches will work and we will need a few more people," Marc said to the officer.

"I cannot spare any men, but whatever else you need, let me know," Officer Sean said.

"Well, we need shovels for one. I know there were a lot of supplies they left along the road, so, any shovels, and tarps, something to wrap them in. It is too much to deal with coffins. Besides, we cannot wait. The storm kicked them all up and now it is a complete mess," Marc said next. It only took a few days once the storm blew through the harbor for the bodies to come washing ashore.

"Understood. They can't fish now, so maybe the fishermen can help," the officer suggested.

"They are superstitious. I will talk with the one I know, but I have to be careful. It has to be put just the right way, but I think that will work."

"Do you have a plan yet?" the officer asked.

"Yes, we will dig the trenches and fill them as they come in. Not all at once, but slowly as we need to. We have so many now, I can fill at least a few rows. But, this will not be the only one. We cannot bring them to just this single yard. We will need other yards closer to where they come in."

"I mean for getting back home?"

"No. Well, maybe. I have thought of going south and then getting a fishing boat instead of a freighter. They are less of a target, of course, and I think I might get one that gets me to where I need to be," Marc answered in a sincere tone, which he actually may have believed.

"If you need my friend to call again to your family, just let me know," Officer Sean said. He studied Marc's expression for some indication of his intent.

"Thanks, I appreciate that," Marc said.

"But for now, it sounds like you will be around a bit more. I will see you tonight for cribbage."

"Yes, I will be there."

October, 1943

Paris, France

"I have a surprise. We can eat later," Marie said to him as he arrived.

"What kind of concert is this?" Marc asked, looking down at the handwritten invitation.

"It is a private recital and very beautiful. It is like a salon except for musicians," she said, taking his hand.

"Sounds intriguing, and if you think it's a good idea," Marc said.

When they arrived, Marc became still. He shoved his hands into his jacket pockets without speaking to anyone. The first few numbers, he was rigid and stiff sitting next to her. Marie watched with a glow of wonderment and complete relaxation. Marc rushed to leave when the private concert finished.

"Why did we have to leave so quickly?" Marie asked him, wondering what it was that had spooked him.

"I'm just hungry," he said, without any apology.

"I was hoping to visit a bit with such an interesting crowd of people."

"What do you say we eat out?" Marc said as they passed one of the main hotels. "It is pricey, for sure, but it has been such a long while, and I have enough money. Plus, the food, I am sure, is black market," he whispered, as if no one knew that fact.

Marc checked the prices first and then to make sure he had enough francs, and then they stepped into the restaurant. Marie instantly recognized the men sitting in one corner and made eye contact with the agent. Marc noticed her body tense up but then she relaxed a bit. Then Marc noticed the Germans in the corner.

"They will do nothing," he said to her.

"I just cannot stand them," she said in a near whisper.

"We can go, but any place good will have some, you know."

"No, no, this is fine." She patted his arm.

"What are they having?" Marc asked the waiter while looking over at the Germans.

"Rabbit, Monsieur," he said firmly.

"Excellent. Two, if you still have them," Marc told the waiter. "It is supposed to be a no-meat day for the restaurants, and here we are, rabbit. I told you all the good places are where they eat," Marc said to her, excited about the meal.

Marie began to wonder if Marc might not lead to anything in the way of resistance. She couldn't help but notice how relaxed he was in the restaurant with the Germans just a few tables over, and yet deeply uncomfortable around a private concert full of people from the underground.

The following day, the agent asked her, "Did you enjoy your rabbit?"

"Of course. It was all the more delicious considering it was surely black market."

"And the concert? Did your friend meet or see anyone of special interest?"

"Not one. If he did, he sure avoided them. Maybe that is why he was so uncomfortable. It was like he wanted to crawl away into an air raid shelter."

"You mean, as if there was someone there he did not want you to know he knew?" he went on.

"Exactly," she said emphatically.

"Sometimes, it is what is not said, the lack of hello that speaks louder than the warm greeting," he said.

"I never thought of it that way, but you are right. He was more uncomfortable around people he knew yet committed to never acknowledge than in a restaurant with Germans who could ask for his papers right on the spot," she mused.

"And the music?" he asked next.

"Wonderful. They did perform very well," she said, smiling.

"It is a pity, you know, because not all Jewish music is subversive. Perhaps one day someone will reconsider that decision," he said, then put out his cigarette to leave the café.

CHAPTER 29

"*Le Corbeau*, it is supposed to be very good," Marc said to Marie.

"I've not heard of it."

"Well, at least the theater will be warm," Marc said as he glanced over the crowd of people in coats, hats, and muffs.

"Do you think they will throw a fuss here?" she said as they waited for the German newsreels to play.

"With the lights on? I doubt it. This crowd just looks to be hungry for escape," Marc said, smiling back at her just before the lights dimmed.

"I cannot believe you took me to this movie. It was terrible," she said as they left the theater.

"What was so bad about it? I thought it was fascinating."

"It is just the whole suggestion of denouncing people. The writing of letters, and terrorizing innocent people, all of it was repulsive to me," she said.

"I never thought of it that way, but you're right. The subtext is there that people can turn against each other, and maybe even should for some causes," Marc said calmly. "Next time you get to pick, and I promise to be good about it."

"So, when do I get to come over?" she pressed his arm.

"I have no heat, and no food," Marc said quickly.

"That's fine, I understand."

"Marie, my apartment was bombed, so my place is not grand and, besides, I have a roommate," Marc said.

"You never told me. Who?"

Marc stopped and wondered what he would tell her. Would he say it was a friend, or a coworker? Should he say it was someone from art school, or just someone from the neighborhood?

"Oh, it is a sad story. I met him at the soup lines. You know, the public kitchens they set up. I used to know him from before the war, great fellow and excellent student," Marc went on creating the story as he spoke.

"Well, he had no place to go or stay. Nothing too bad happened. It's not like he's wanted or anything. He's not Jewish, or anything foolish. He works at the factory, you know, the Renault factory," Marc said, wondering if he had gone a little too far. "So, he's staying with me until he can get a better place."

"That's very sweet of you. I didn't know you would do that," Marie said.

"A lot of people, Marie, they're just hungry and cold. That's all."

"In the south, there was so much more food. I have to say, I am surprised that Paris is so barren of good food, yet so busy with plays and concerts," Marie said.

"Well, they take everything, you know. The only way I got these shoes is through you." Marc looked down at his feet. "So, in other cities, there is more to eat?"

"Oh, yes. I mean it is not a banquet, but nothing like this."

"I had no idea. I haven't left since I got back from the sea," Marc said distantly.

"You never talk about that."

"What?"

"The sea, I mean, what happened. Why did you not leave?"

A wave of nausea filled Marc and his skin burned as he recalled the mixture of salt water and oil. He focused his mind upon a small point inside of him for peace, trying to overcome his urge to scratch his arms.

They reached her apartment on the Left Bank. "I couldn't bear the thought of never seeing you again," he said. "Look, I need to get home before the curfew. I love you and we will go see whatever play you wish." He kissed her good night and walked quickly in the direction of the Latin quarter before she could say anything else.

Marc arrived at his apartment. He stopped by another safe house to pick up a small bag of supplies, which was not much. He bought a small basket of strawberries that were only half ripe, along with a few greens and a loaf of highly questionable bread. He went into the kitchen and then to the back room. He knocked and said, "It is me."

"Clear," came back to him.

He opened the door and Georges was sitting up on the bed. "I have some food, not much, but something for you. I need to get over to the hospital in the morning. I didn't see any Germans out today, so it looks like it has cooled down quite a bit. Maybe a few more days," Marc said.

"Thank you, Marc. Have you seen anyone else?" Georges asked.

"No, just Marie. What do you think about Lyons or going south?" Marc said from the other room.

"What do you mean?"

"What do you think about doing an escort south to Lyons? Marie says it is easier there, more food, fewer Germans, fewer problems. It sounds like things are a lot better outside of Paris. And you can be the guide for some birds," Marc continued as Georges listened. "You get out of Paris, take some birds with you, and get south where there is at least some room to breathe and live a bit."

"What about the checkpoints? How do I get past the checkpoints?"

"I am working on the papers. In a few more days, they should be ready."

A few days later, before leaving for work, Marc said, "I'm going to be home late. I'm seeing Marie for another play. Remember, don't answer the door."

"I won't. Trust me, I won't," Georges said.

Marc glanced at the cribbage board on the mantel just for a moment before he left Georges alone in the apartment.

November, 1940

Saint-Nazaire, France

"If I can make it north, I have a place and plan, but making it north is not easy, Joan, and I'm not sure it is even the right thing to do anymore. I think going south is even less of a good idea. The closer I get to Spain, the more important my papers will become, and then, eventually, I will have a problem of crossing the border." Marc continued to rationalize his plan out loud to her. "But even once in Spain, I don't know the language. I will stand out. I really will be a stranger in a strange land, and I think it is riskier than the Channel."

She nodded, in bed. "I'm sorry if I seem off. It has been another really bad day of it."

"You need to take it slow," Marc said.

"I have been."

"You were up running all around the other day."

"And?"

"And now you're down again."

"I cannot just lie about every day, Marc."

"If you feel good one day, maybe if you rest even more, you will feel better?"

"Crazy American ideas. If you can get to England, go. Take it. Take the chance and don't look back. Then, maybe get word back about me. You can get word out ..." she droned on over the pain.

Marc looked at her as he searched for the words. "Don't think about using the transmitter."

"What transmitter?"

"I know you have a radio, or at least almost a radio. I made one before, you know, back in school. I'm the one who got the supplies and I knew when you asked for them they were not for the hospital. Copper wire is not for bandages. The spool is not for wrapping gauze. You might be missing a few parts still, but I doubt it. But, if you are thinking of a transmitter, don't even do it," he said in a cold, steady voice.

She looked up at him with a blank stare and shrugged her shoulders. "Do you blame me for trying?"

"Not at all, but they are listening, too. They know the same frequencies. They are bringing the equipment into town now and setting it up, and if you send one spark out, just one single spark, they will know it came from here and damn near likely will have you triangulated so damn fast, you'll not even see it coming," he said.

She turned away to look at the sea. "You're right."

"You can listen, Joan, but never speak, at least not here, never here, for they will hear you. Things have changed while you've been in bed. There are new dangers now, new enemies, but do not think it was like it was in the past, because it is not. I see it now. Listen, if it works, listen with careful caution, but never speak, not here, not now. It's not time yet."

"Yes, Lazarus sur Mer, I hear you."

"Then be a good angel, and pray."

December, 1943

Paris, France

"That was terrible," Marc said as they reached her apartment.

"I thought it was amazing," Marie challenged.

"It should be called *Slaughterhouse Opera*, not *Antigone*. I've never seen so many people die on stage without the aid of a machine gun," Marc said.

After a modest dinner for Marie, she decided to try a new approach about the Resistance. "I'm very excited about this new paper project. I want to read for you what they are going to print," Marie said.

"Stop." He looked up at her. "I don't want to hear it, and I don't want to even know about it and I cannot believe you brought that here."

"What's wrong?"

"Marie, I don't need to know, nor do I want to know," Marc said, trying to regain his composure.

"Marc, what do you believe in? I mean, in that play, yes, all of those people die, but it was for something they believed in. What would you die for?"

Marc thought for a second and said, "I would risk my life so that someone might have a chance to live."

"That's it? That is not dying, but just risking your life. What would you die for? Would you die for freedom? Would you die for France, or America?"

"I told you, I would risk my life so that someone might live," Marc repeated firmly.

Marie looked at him silently. Her hands rested underneath her legs, and then she crossed her fingers.

"But not die. Why are you such a coward?" she snapped at him. "Why are you even here? Could you not make it down to Spain for the *Yankee Clipper*? Did your family not send the *Normandie* back for you?"

Marc looked directly at her and saw no way of avoiding the argument that had been building for weeks. She would drop hints and then talk about this or that, or make comments about "the movement" or "the group" or "the club" or "the brave ones."

"Are you willing to die for this?" he asked, picking up the paper.

"Yes, of course. I would rather die for truth than allow untruth to rule," Marie said passionately.

"Have you seen someone die before?"

Marie thought for a moment and collected her words carefully. "No. I am a woman, not a front-line soldier. I mean, I've known people who have died, but never seen it," she said in a voice that gave not one inch to backing down.

"Then you have no fucking idea what you are doing. How in the hell can you sit across from me and tell me you are willing to die for truth, and honor, and bravery, and all these high-minded ideas you are throwing out to me? Liberty, oh liberty, for the fucking liberty of France, and you have never seen someone die? You have never seen the look on their face, or the glare of their eyes, or heard their last words. What the fuck is this?"

Marie's mouth fell open. Then she scrunched up her mouth.

"You're acting like a schoolgirl. This is a big game to you, playing cat-and-mouse with the Germans and papers, with lots of noble ideas. It is just pranks. Are you one of the kids who mark up the seats on the Metro? Are you running down the street, Marie, and using chalk on the doors proclaiming 'Victory' or 'Long Live France'?" Marc pushed himself away from the table and stood.

"It would hurt my feelings that you called me a coward if, for one single moment, I actually believed you knew what the fuck you were doing, but you don't," Marc said, realizing he had started to yell.

"Oh, is that so. You don't think I know what I'm doing?"

"This is not some play. Actors find it easy to die for their cause when they know the curtain will bring them back to life another night. The only ones who seem to get it are the animals. Remember the look on that elephant? Remember the shock of those bears that broke free and ran into the ditch to get away from the bullets?"

"What elephants? What bears? What are you talking about?"

"They get it. There are no Germans, or French, or British. Just death to them. There is life and death."

Marie turned silent as her expressions fell.

"I said, I would risk my life so that someone else might live, because when that moment comes, when they realize they are not going to live, no one gives a flying damn about this war- the French, English, Germans, or

Americans. It is then only about someone they love, who they will never see again, and very likely will never ever know where they died or are buried," Marc's voice rushed upon Marie like a storm.

"That stupid play is a lie. Everyone dies with courage and honor, as if that is how that goes. Bullshit. There is no remorse, no regret, no sorrow on that stage, and you know why?" he screamed at her. "It is not real!"

"Is that so? You don't think people can die with courage for a cause?"

Marc got down very close to her face and in a low, growling voice said, "People who talk of courageous death never have faced real death. They have never felt death all around them, in every direction, and heard the cries."

"Is that what happened?" Marie said quietly.

Marc froze. He woke up and realized he needed to get back to some place sane again.

"Is that what happened to Allen?" Marie said, her face soft with understanding.

Marc closed his eyes and looked for a point of balance.

"I mean, I'm just guessing. I have no idea what you're talking about, with bears and elephants. I wasn't there, but you were. I can see it," Marie continued, her eyes slanted with concern.

"Yes, and many others," Marc said, swallowing hard.

"So, Allen died?" Marie asked cautiously.

Marc looked up and then looked inside of himself. "No, Allen got away."

"Did he get back to England then?"

Marc's face turned blank, as his mind became a quiet ocean of death. After a long pause, he said, "Yes, he got home. Look, I need to go. I'm upset and I'm sorry that I lost it."

"Marc, don't go. You need to talk more. I want you to tell me what is going on," Marie pleaded.

"No, I'm sorry. I need to go. Thank you for dinner. The pigeon, it was excellent, the best ever," he said, looking down at his plate.

"Pigeon? Marc, it was chicken," Marie said, looking at him again with concern.

"Chicken?" Marc gasped and touched the edge of the plate. "I had chicken?" He nearly started to cry. "Where did you get chicken? How do you get this food?" he pleaded, his voice squeaking. He looked around for his coat.

"Marc, please stay, you need to talk," Marie got up from the table.

"I'm sorry. I am so sorry. I need to go," he said, looking back at the plate. *I can't believe I tasted chicken,* he thought to himself as he walked out the door.

Marie sat down at the table and stared blankly at the remnants of their meal. Over and over again, she reminded herself why she was there, and what her job was with Marc. She continued to hold down any sympathy she had inside for him like a drunk attempting not to vomit on the street. She continued the mantra in her mind that she had told to the Gestapo agent so many times: *What do I care for these fleas upon a newborn puppy? France needs to cast them off forever.*

"A new Europe needs brave men, Marc. You don't make the cut."

CHAPTER 30

"I am sorry," Marie said to Marc in the market.

"Why? You didn't go mad," Marc said, trying to avoid looking into her eyes. "I'm sorry I got so upset, but don't think for a moment that I did not believe what I was saying."

"I know, I know, and I've been thinking, and you are right. I've been acting like it is just a game and not considering the risk, the cost, and I think it is because I just thought, because I am a woman, whatever trouble I would get into, I could just get out of the usual way, the way I have in the past," she said.

"That hasn't worked so well for the others. Your little plan is not a good one."

"I know."

"Enough. Not here," Marc said as he looked from left to right and back again for anyone who could overhear them speaking.

"What?" Marie asked, surprised.

"We're in public and you never know who is around or listening. Don't you get it, Marie?"

"I can recognize a German uniform when I see one, Marc."

"Marie, I know that. It's the ones without a uniform who are the problem."

"I want to make this up to you. Will you come over for dinner again?"

"Where do you get these rations? Did you hijack a convoy or something?"

"No, I just save a lot, plus I have a few connections."

"Can you get any extra meat?"

"Yes, I think so," she said next.

"We need some for the hospital. The meat rations are not enough for some to heal."

"Well, I thought it would be for you, or us. What about you?" Marie said, confused.

"I don't need it, but I know a few others who do." His face then changed. "God, that chicken was good. If you can work it, let me know. Otherwise, it's best not to eat much of it. Just makes you want more." Marie laughed.

"You said there was there more food in Lyons?" Marc said.

"Yes, a little more."

"So, you could get things there, in the market? Cheese? What about butter? Bread? Did they have bread that didn't have sawdust in it?"

"That is horrible. Sawdust? No, the bread was very good. There was less, of course, but you could get things, nothing like here."

"Paris is not so gay anymore. Milk—did they have milk? Oh God, I miss milk. Eggs, too?" he went on, as if dreaming of heaven.

"Marc, I want to get back to us tonight. I love being with you because it helps me forget. I just miss you and I'm sorry about the paper."

Marc glanced at her, reminding her just by his eyes to not mention papers. Marie gave a playful tug of his belt.

"No more talk. I know. So, will you come over tonight? I might have a tighter belt for you. You're so thin now."

"Look, I need to go, but yes." Then he left.

"I need to head south for a bit," he said to himself as he rode his bicycle to the south train station. He stood smiling, leaning against a post. Philip emerged from the crowd and walked up to Marc.

"Do I know you?" Marc said with a smirk.

"No, but I could use a ride back over to my parents' home on Foch Street," Philip said with a boyish grin.

"Is that right? You have had quite an adventure. All the papers are abuzz about you."

"Georges—how is he?" Philip asked as he climbed onto the handlebars.

"Gone south, vacation." Marc said.

"Jean—have you seen his friend Jean?"

"Nope, but I'm sure he's fine. Don't worry. They are smart, just like you," Marc said as he pedaled up the street.

Inside, Dr. Jackson had just come home from the hospital, and Torquette had finished brewing some tea.

"So, tell us all or we will tickle it out of you," Dr. Jackson said, threatening to grab Philip by the ribs.

"It went well. We climbed to the top of the church tower and I had the camera in my lunch bag," Philip said casually.

"Wow, you can see a lot from there," Marc said, remembering the town.

"Well, not a lot. There are the docks, but the town," Philip paused, "there has been some raids, so not all the buildings you told me about are still there."

"I never thought of that, but it makes sense now," Marc said with a tint of sadness. He wondered if Officer Sean was still there, and Joan, as he remembered them back in '40.

"And, there is something else I think you are leaving out," Torquette smiled.

"What?" Philip looked up.

"Smoochy, smoochy," she said, making a kissy face.

"Mother, it was serious. I had pictures to take for the war," Philip blushed.

"He is shy, leave him be," Dr. Jackson said.

Marc was a bit sad inside that, although the pictures Philip had captured of Saint-Nazaire would help their effort, the place in Marc's memory was now gone. The body of the town had been bombed out; the soul of the place had left.

He rushed into his apartment to get dressed for the night. He had a large selection of clothes to choose from. He'd been gathering them for other safe houses that might need pants or a spare jacket for a stray airman. Before leaving to walk to Marie's, he removed the cribbage board from his bag and placed it on the mantel.

December, 1940

Saint-Nazaire, France

The two brothers were in the habit of walking the shores. After the last storm, Marc needed to get out for a bit, so he decided to take them up on their long-standing invitation to accompany them. They walked along the road outside town and up over to the north shores of the bay, and then worked their way up a trail and over to the beach.

All along the sands, it appeared clumps of seaweed had washed ashore with the high tide. The brothers were shocked and one said out loud, "They've never been there before."

Marc's eye focused upon the bones that stuck out from the sand, as he realized the clumps of green seaweed were actually uniforms.

"The storm must've taken away the sand," the other brother said. There they were, about fifteen or twenty yards from the tide that had gone out, in various positions, embedded in the beach, all along the shore.

"There are too many to take," one brother said to the other.

"Yes, but we can get their papers, and give them to the authorities one day when they come back," the other brother said.

Marc had seen this before, and knew exactly what he was looking at, but just a bit surprised to see so many at one location like this. *The sand must have covered them up because I have never seen so many at one place before*, he thought to himself.

Marc and the two brothers walked down the trail to the shore, and then the threesome moved from skeleton to skeleton, checking for what papers they could find on the clothing that surrounded the half-buried bones.

There was no rush or hurry, and in between looking inside coats and pockets, Marc looked for shells along the beach or, most of all, the sea glass that he had collected over the months.

Then they walked back to town, each with their own collection of papers, though not all of the fallen had papers to be gathered.

"How many?" Marc asked.

"Fifteen, I think," one brother said.

"No, there were at least sixteen, and there might have been more," the other brother corrected him.

Once they were back at the house, they emptied out what they had collected. "Let's put it together more organized, at least so we know exactly what was found on each one," Marc said.

He was going through each of the wallets and papers, stacking them together and making sure they were in order. "Do you have an envelope, or something to bind them together?" he asked one of the brothers, and then he saw it. Marc stared directly at the wallet containing the papers of "Allen Lee Michaels," his friend whom he followed from Paris.

"Do you know which one this came from?" Marc asked quickly.

"No, not sure, I wasn't paying attention." The wallet looked so much like the others, truly ordinary, and decidedly British in its non-uniqueness.

Both of the brothers looked at it, and then at each other and then back at Marc. "No, why? Do you know him?"

December, 1943

Paris, France

Marie lit the candle on the table before Marc arrived. She put a small bow around the new, tighter belt she'd found for him and sat down at the table, closing her eyes. Within her imagination, she told herself the story that

Marc never cared for her and was only using her. She imagined if Marc had been with her when she needed him the most, he would fail with weakness. Marie imagined that Marc was not really Catholic after all, but Jewish, and had lied about it when he was at Notre Dame, and he had disgraced the holy sacrament. She repeated the mantra in her thoughts: *France is for the French, and only the true French.*

Marc knocked at the door. Marie prepared to answer it. She had completed putting on her makeup of loathing that gave her the emotional wall of protection she needed to commit to her betrayal.

After dinner, Marc noticed the corner of one of the papers sticking out of Marie's purse and just asked her in a very casual tone, "So, what is with the paper?"

Marie pretended not to know what Marc was talking about, but, at the same time, she was internally glad that he noticed it.

"What paper? I told you, no more."

"There is one in your purse. And it's not even well hidden. If they should come in right now, they would see it," Marc said as he pointed over to her bag.

Marie followed his eyes and huffed with frustration. "I forgot to take it out."

"What did you mean by no more paper?" Marc pressed, but in a low, rational tone. "Did you mean you are quitting, or just not going to tell me anymore, because you know it makes me upset?" He paused and looked straight into her eyes. "I mean, what is it, Marie? Can you even tell me?"

"I meant that … that …I meant that you were right. We are not going to talk about it," she said with a dramatic flush of frustration. "It puts you at risk and me at risk. It is not safe." She looked away and said, "This last round-up was tough. We lost some people."

"So you are still involved?" Marc asked.

"Marc, I have changed. You have changed. There is a lot that I cannot tell you. You may see me as a childish, immature girl who is playing a game of cat-and-mouse with the Germans, but that is just because when I'm with you, I feel innocent again," she glanced back into his gaze. "I feel young and I let down my guard. But you are the only one who gets to see that. I have to keep up my guard all the time. The other night, I let you rant and rave because, honestly, you sounded just like me," her heart was blank as her mouth spoke the words. "I am sorry. It's not as easy as me just quitting and walking away from what I'm doing. And, I cannot tell you everything, even though I wish I could," she finished.

"How will I know?" Marc asked.

"Know what?"

"Know when they have you?"

"You won't, Marc," she said after a long pause, "and I will not know when they get you."

"I'm not involved with the Resistance, Marie," Marc said.

"That does not matter. You think they just watch crazy French men and women passing papers around? You work at the hospital. I'm sure that men pass through there. Every time a plane goes down, they go out and search for the pilots. Where did they go? Who are they staying with? How did they get out of town? You don't think they are watching you?"

Marc took up the plates from the table and then started to wash them. Marie sat at the table, matching Marc's silence.

"You're right. I never thought about that. I guess because I haven't done anything like that," Marc said, "it never occurred to me."

"Your identity card says 'Winoc,' Marc. I'm not naive. I have my own, you know," she then paused, looking to see if he would acknowledge the truth.

"Do you like it?"

"Like what?"

"The name. Do you like the name?"

"I have a new belt for you," Marie said, and then paused for a moment as she stared at Marc's back. "I only know you are here, when you are here, and you will only know I am here, when I am here," she said as she got up from the table, and touched his back tenderly. "I wish I could change things. Oh God, do I wish I could, but I cannot. But, when we are together, then, let's be together."

Marc turned and took her by the waist into his arms. "You sexy criminal," he said, and kissed her.

The following morning, across town and away from Marc's normal routine, she met her superior at a street café.

"And how are things going?" he asked her sweetly. The agent was dressed just like every other man in Paris, except that his clothes actually fit.

"Very well. I don't believe it will be much longer. He now knows everything I want him to know, and I have demonstrated to him that I can see what he is doing, even though he might pretend otherwise," she said. She took out a cigarette and lit up.

"But it has not been easy, which, I have to say, is a bit of a surprise," she went on.

"What do you mean?" the agent asked.

"Well, he is guarded. And I get the feeling it's not just about what he might be up to, but more than that. I just do not understand men at times. I thought once you give it up, they trust you completely, but Marc has been different," she said.

"Do you think he suspects anything?"

"No, absolutely not. He was dense in '39, and is dense still."

"Why do you think he is so guarded?" he asked.

"Why do you think? I have a few ideas. Actually, I have quite a few ideas. He knows I am involved and at risk and knows that I keep secrets. I think he loves me, because he hates what I am doing," she went on while looking at people passing on bikes.

"What do you mean?" the agent asked.

"He hates the Resistance. He thinks it is foolish and stupid. He cannot stand the thought that I am involved with it, that I could be in danger."

"Interesting. Do you think that is because he is taking equal risk and knows the dangers and does not like to think of you doing the same?"

"Maybe, not sure. He's hard to read. He's not clear like the others. Constantly thinking, but about what, I'm not sure. Like some flywheel in his mind that will not rest," she said, her voice uncertain.

"Appointments? Errands?"

"Well, if he does, not with me. He is completely blank on any of what he does. I have tried to get him to talk about Saint-Nazaire, but he avoids it."

"What do you mean? Was he at Saint-Nazaire?"

"Yes, back in '40, when every rat in town was fleeing to their own ship. He got on some ship that sank."

"Ship, meaning that he was trying to get out by ship?"

"Yes."

"What happened?"

"I have no idea. I know it was bad. He was traveling with a British friend of his, a guy named Allen. For all I know, he might be hiding Allen as a spy. When I try and ask him about it, he just throws up a wall."

"What is most important to him? What is his most important object?" the agent asked.

"The board. He has a board with pegs in it. It is the only thing he has from Saint-Nazaire and he does not talk about it, but I saw it once. It is strange looking," she said.

"What does it look like?" the agent asked, intrigued by the object.

"It looks just like a piece of scrap wood, but it has holes in it, in a design, formation sort, and a few pegs," she answered.

"And he protects it?"

"You're brilliant. I never thought of it, but of course. It is the board," she said next in a flash.

"I think you're right. The board must mean something. It likely is a counting device, and that means it is connected to the others. It is a way of keeping track," the officer said.

"I'll try and find out more, but I need to do it in such a way that it appears I'm just trying to get to know him better. I would expect a little more from someone who once proposed to me," Marie said.

"What? You never mentioned that before. Are you engaged?" the agent asked, appearing shocked.

"No, well, maybe. It was tentative, until after the war, but I don't think Marc will be available then," she said, smirking.

"You really are something else. He loves you and, yet, you impress me with your devotion. If you were German, I could get you into the SS," the agent said with a smile.

"He doesn't love me, but he is hiding something and, as you know, I am very good at finding out such secrets. I will let you know when I'm ready."

"This is not too difficult for you?" he shifted in his chair while looking out on the street.

"No. Not at all! What do I care about some foreigner? I may have slept with him in the past, but make no mistake, he is part of the reason we became a weak nation. Jews, Communists, and foreigners—they are all the same. Godless ticks living off the blood of our country," her voice low, but intense with contempt. "I am actually enjoying this one even more than the others. He is not even brave enough for the Resistance."

He studied her intensity as she spoke. Her conviction was as strong or even more than some of the SS.

"I got my start at this café," the agent said.

"What do you mean?"

"I cracked a smuggling ring from here. It was two old women and three dogs in a flat not far from here. A priest would bring them strays, some airmen, but most of them were stranded from Dunkirk. They ran quite a show for a while."

"And, what happened?"

"Well, the American woman we traded for one of ours. Her British friend we just shot, but it took a while to get her. I think the priest got sent away. I am sure he has met his god by now. My hunch is that Marc is at least as big a case as those silly women, if not bigger. I think when this fish comes in, there will be a promotion."

"Marc may have come here to just paint and draw, but I'm sure he has other talents, and I think you are right. It will be a nice catch when we are done."

"Marie, before I forget, we've searched for your family in Tours, but with no luck. Have you heard anything?"

"No, I was hoping you had found them. Are you sure?"

"Yes, we've looked in more than a few of your suggestions, and no one has seen them. Do you have any idea where they might have gone?" He felt sorry for her because it was not the first case where people had become separated from their loved ones.

"There is one other place, but I don't know if you can help. Do you have any resources in the free-zone?" she asked, almost doubting the response.

"Some, but why?" he asked, perplexed.

"My mother's sister lives near Antibes by Nice, in the mountains just outside. I think maybe Biot, but it could have been Valbonne. I'm not sure, because she would talk of her but we never visited. She always came to Paris," Marie lowered her voice. "Look, I trust you. My aunt is a very devout and adores Petain but, she has lived there forever and her husband is buried there, so she would never leave. I think if they really are not in Tours, then they might be down near Antibes. I know it is a lot to ask, but do you think there is any way you can get in contact with scouts down there?"

"I will see what I can do. I can make no promises, but I know what it is like. This war has really stirred people up and getting lost is common," the agent said. He stood to go, leaving her to return alone to the Metro.

CHAPTER 31

"Philip, can you see who it is?" Torquette asked from the kitchen.

Philip walked to the door and opened it. The two men then quickly came inside the house without him even saying so much as "Hello." The dog went wild as Torquette came out to see who had come in.

"Where is your husband?" they asked her.

"He is at the hospital, of course. Is there something wrong?" Torquette asked.

"No, nothing, but we have some questions." Then the second man left and the first one sat down in the front room.

Torquette returned to the kitchen and held up her finger to the maid. She handed her the mail for others and the maid quietly left the house through the back door.

"Would you like some tea?" Torquette then asked.

"Yes, that would be nice," he said.

"Philip, you're going to be late," she said.

"He cannot leave. He must stay here until your husband comes home," the man said in a cool tone.

"Well, Philip, it appears you have a day off," she said as she put the cup down. Torquette moved to the drapes and flung them open. "There, that is better. Let some light in so you can see what you are drinking."

The second man then returned with Dr. Jackson. He smiled at Philip before he went to the porch. Outside, in front of the entire world passing by,

Dr. Jackson sat out on the porch smoking a cigar with the one officer while the second officer made a phone call.

"I hope this does not make you uncomfortable," the man said to Dr. Jackson.

"No, not at all. Why should it?"

"Well, perhaps you were expecting someone else today?"

Marc came riding down the street. As he neared the house, he saw that the drapes were perfectly open and a black Citroen was parked outside the house, a natural gas tank strapped to the roof for fuel. He decided to ride past and just look at the car, but he glanced up and saw the man standing in the front room. He then looked straight ahead and continued riding up the street.

Maybe it is family, he told himself as he rode to his apartment, but his stomach churned with another truth.

"We'll be going in the morning, so be sure to pack," the first officer said after he hung up the phone.

"Well, do you think it will be a long trip?" Dr. Jackson asked next.

"No, I am sure just a day or so to clear up some questions," he said with a smile.

"Will you be staying for dinner?" Torquette asked next.

"Yes, we will be staying the night," the officer said.

"Well, then, I will try do my best," she said as she returned to the kitchen. "Sumner, we must not forget to mail off the bills before we leave," she said, as she took all the clean dishes the maid had stacked and threw them back into the sink. As she filled the sink with water, she mumbled, "For all the lies we must tell to be true."

"Marc, it is tight. I have a question to ask you, and please do not be upset with me," she said after dinner.

"What is it? I don't have anything left, but if you need something, maybe I can work it out." Marc's heart seemed to stop as he waited for the question to fall.

"If I need to hide … If I need to not be seen for a bit, because it gets too hot, can I stay with you? Or, do you know some place I can stay?" she said quietly, almost pleading to him, while smiling and attempting to keep eye contact with him.

The question startled him. He'd heard the question over and over again in the past few years, but not from anyone so close to him.

Where was he going to stay? He had never asked this question of anyone. He always just assumed that if things got hot, he wouldn't have to worry about it because he would've been arrested and the problem of where to stay would be solved by the Germans.

"No, Marie, I don't, and you cannot stay with me," he said, feeling a deep sense of guilt. It sounded more like he had failed her or in some way had betrayed her already.

"But why? It wouldn't be long, maybe a night or two?" she continued to plead, watching his reaction. Her voice almost cracked. "I wouldn't ask, but everyone else is gone. I have no place else to turn, Marc," she said as she looked down and then up again into his eyes.

"I never thought it would come to this, or get this bad. Someone betrayed us from within and, now, I have no idea whom to trust anymore. I trust you, Marc, but I cannot trust the others," she said in a depressed voice. "I don't even know where they are anymore. Everyone has scattered," she said. Her words became softer with every sentence.

"Marie, it's not because I don't love you, or want to save you. It's because I cannot save you or protect you. I am not the one you want to stay with," Marc broke down, trying to explain to her why he couldn't protect and hide her. He tried to shake off a nagging feeling in the back of his mind that there was something Marie was holding back, but dismissed it.

"You need a place where you know you are safe, and with me, that is just simply not going to be the case. I don't want to lead you into danger."

"I see. I understand," she said, not looking at him.

Marc returned to his apartment, and after turning on the light, he looked at the cribbage board with a deep sense of doubt weighing upon him. The conversation with Marie seemed off to him, but he couldn't pinpoint the exact reason why.

December, 1940

Saint-Nazaire, France

Marc returned to the beach alone. He searched from skeleton to skeleton for the identification disk. He wondered if he'd ever find him, as it was likely the disk washed away or had been otherwise lost. Then he came to one of the bodies lying face up in the sand. Only the bones remained along with the uniform and the boots.

Marc took the disk and turned it over and there was Allen Lee's name on it.

Marc sat next to the body in the sand.

"So, what do you say? You want to come ashore with me to the real graveyard?" he asked, and then in his head he heard a voice say, "Not fair."

"Not fair, not fair," Marc heard between the waves.

The voice triggered in his mind. "You're right. Not fair to the others here on this beach, is it. Not fair I'm alive and you are dead. Not fair they put all those people on that ship. Not fair innocent civilians died. None of it is fair, Allen." Marc spoke out loud the thoughts streaming through his mind. "Not one fucking bit of it, the whole shitty mess is not fair." Then he stopped.

"Whom am I talking to?" he said in his head. "What was that?" He sat a bit longer. The tide was starting to come in. It was time to go. It was late and he needed to walk back to town.

He rose and said, "Look, friend. I'm going back into town to play some cards with the officer. You are welcome to come. I need a drink. I really need to get drunk. But, if you stay here, I understand. It is really beautiful on this beach."

The ocean waves started to reach further up the shore. Finally, one just touched the lower part of Allen's boot sticking up from the sand. "It looks as if your ocean blanket is coming back to tuck you in for the night." Marc watched the water with a peaceful fascination. It comforted him in a way, like visiting hours at the hospital and the nurse coming in to tell the guests they must go.

"I think Officer Sean cheats. It's not fair the way he plays cribbage, but I have come to enjoy it. He is a funny German. He just wants the war to be over so he can go back to America." Then Marc walked away, never to return to that beach again. He knew that his friend would not appreciate being buried alone without his friends along the beach. Then Marc remembered the last time he saw Allen. It jolted him like the bomb back on the ship. He'd seemed so real. He could see him as clearly as anyone else that day in the hospital. But he'd been so sick. Doubt returned and he settled into believing that it was just that he had wanted to see him. Marc wanted to know that Allen had made it.

"Another round? You are certainly enjoying yourself tonight," the officer said, holding a curious stare.

"I'm better at the game when I feel a bit relaxed," Marc lied through a slur.

"I think you have something there."

May, 1944

Paris, France

Marc folded his shirt neatly and then placed it on the ship's plates. He removed his trousers and folded them like he was putting them back on a store rack. Then he removed his boxer shorts. The officer said this was his best chance.

Marc turned and a peacock rose out of the porthole, followed by a second, then a third. He had no idea who, why, or even when the peacocks had got on the ship. Why they were so important that they could escape through a porthole and not the men perplexed him. Just then, he heard a bell sound. *"Bling! Bring-bling!"*

Marc looked up and Allen, his friend, was riding the bicycle on the side of the ship, his dress uniform perfect. "Marc, Marc!" he called over as he rode the bike down the plate of the ship, swerving around portholes like some kid riding around cones in the street, swerving past the peacocks as they strutted down the plates. "Marc, over here!"

"Allen, is that ..." Marc felt drunk struggling to speak.

"Marc, this is important. Do you have a smoke?" Allen asked, looking deep into Marc's eyes. Everything around Allen seemed to recede as Marc focused upon his friend.

"No," Marc whispered as loudly as he could.

"Don't move, Marc. Don't move one single inch," he said, looking over Marc's head. Allen's voice penetrated Marc's entire body. It pierced his bones. The peacocks circled Marc and the bike in a dance. The sun sparkled off the chrome bike. Allen waved his hand over Marc's head and, just then, a monarch butterfly flew in front of Marc's face. *Where did a butterfly come from way out here in the middle of the bay?* Marc thought.

Allen said to Marc in the clearest tone, "Be careful of the butterflies."

Marc awoke and immediately jumped from his bed. His skin itched. Wide-awake, he ran to the sink to wash. There was nothing on him to wash, but he scrubbed his arms. He breathed deep and fast, and his heart raced in his chest.

He stopped washing his arms and looked at his face in the mirror. He then closed his eyes, again seeing Allen in his mind's eye. He held onto his face. It had been now just under four years. He wanted to shake the dream, but could not resist the temptation to share a few more minutes of sweet friendship with a familiar face unburdened by the trials of life and war.

CHAPTER 32

"There is someone out in the garden for you," the orderly said to Marc.

"Who is it?" Marc said.

"Don't know, but says he knows you."

Marc walked out into the hospital's garden. He looked around and almost left, believing whoever it was had already gone.

"Are you Marc?" the man said, emerging from a bush.

"Yes. How do you know my name?" Marc asked the airman. None of the airmen whom Marc had assisted over the years ever openly asked his name like this, and when he did give it, it was short, such as "M," or even Winoc. Many times Marc concealed that he was even from America as his own personal joke on the airmen.

"Dr. Jackson told me that if he was not here, to ask for you," he said. A trigger inside Marc closed all the doors of trust. *Could this be true?* he considered. The man seemed American, and was in a flight uniform but, still, how in the world did this man know ahead of time to ask for Dr. Jackson, and how is it that Dr. Jackson had told him that Marc would be a back-up?

Nothing like this had been discussed in the past, but perhaps Dr. Jackson knew something was coming. Perhaps his arrest was not so much a surprise to him, as it was to Marc.

"Is that so? When did you talk with Dr. Jackson about this?" Marc asked the man, still trying to decide who he was under the uniform.

"I didn't. He is not here. But according to what we were told at the base, if we could make it here, we were to ask for him, and if not him, then you," he explained next.

"You were told this where? What base?" Marc pressed quietly.

"The airbase, in Britain, before we took off on the mission for the factory," he said.

"What factory?"

"The Renault factory, you know, the one that burned to the ground a few weeks ago."

"You've been down that long?"

"Yes. I was staying with someone who then brought me here."

"Is that so," Marc said. He pondered to himself. Could it really be true? Could it have traveled all the way through the previous airmen, through the hospital, down to Lyons and through to Spain, and back to England? He had been doing this now for a few years, so, anything was possible. But the idea that Marc was actually now a person who was known to British and American air forces, as well as Dr. Jackson, Marc found a bit odd, but plausible.

"Here, it's in here," the airman said. He pulled from his pocket a small officers' guide, which Marc had seen before. "See?" He pointed to a page with a small detail about the American Hospital in Paris, and Dr. J, and Mr. M. Marc grew alarmed and horrified that they would be so stupid as to print that in a book that could fall into enemy hands.

"Look, are you able to help with a place? I haven't had any food and have been on the run for a bit. The people I was staying with couldn't keep me and they brought me close enough to the hospital. Can you help me get to the next leg out of Paris?" the man asked.

Obviously, the airman knew not only about his mission but what to do if he should be downed. And it was 1944. Back in '42, even '43, this was simply not the case. Marc's guard eventually dropped to the familiar American accent.

"Yes. Stay out here until I come for you. I need to get some stuff," Marc said.

The airman returned with Marc to his apartment that night. Marc had a change of clothes at the hospital for just such occasions, so he was able to pass through the streets of Paris without too much problem. Marc had become remarkably adept at bypassing the checkpoints. The airman was appreciative and a bit chatty at times that night.

"Do you play cribbage?" the airman asked Marc while looking at the board on the mantel.

Marc glanced at the board. "Sometimes. It was a gift."

December, 1940

Saint-Nazaire, France

Joan rolled over to her side. She looked at the clock and told herself, *Five more minutes*. The clocked chimed at the top of the hour. She started to lift herself out of bed, looking out the window.

"What a stormy day. Maybe I will not take a walk," she said out loud to herself. A knock came to the door.

"Yes."

"Breakfast."

"All right," she said as she fell back into the bed.

Marc opened the door and brought in the tray. He set it up on her lap and then took the seat next to the bed.

"Is something bothering you?" Joan said.

"I have something to tell you. I am going back, Joan. I have made the decision," Marc said.

"Oh, back to England?"

"No, I am going back to Paris."

"But I thought you were going up to England and then back home to America? There is nothing back in Paris for you, Marc, nothing but trouble, that is," she said, and then let out a small moan of discomfort.

"I have decided to go back to Paris. I know other Americans there, and I think I might be able to help out with the American Hospital." He sounded rehearsed to Joan.

"Sounds like you have this all thought out. I didn't know you wanted to go into medicine full time. I could use the help around here, Marc. Why not stay in Saint-Nazaire?"

"Joan, there is nothing here for me to do. The other nurses can help. There is no more work to be done with the yards. I need to go back. There, I might be able to make a difference." The words fell away from his mouth over her covers and out the windows to the sea.

"What has changed? What is the hurry all of a sudden? I mean, you were going to go up to England and stay with your friend, Allen." She held her stomach as it cramped. "Why do you all of a sudden now want to go to Paris? What are you running from, Marc?" she whispered a little too loudly, unaware that Marc had heard her.

"I'm not running away, Joan. I just need to be someplace where I am needed. I cannot go back to America and just resume my plush life in New York and forget about everyone I know in France. There are Americans in Paris, not many, but still, and I just think that's the best place for me right now," Marc's voice stood firm.

She listened and then said, "You found him, didn't you. You found your friend and now …"

"Yes."

"I understand now. I have appreciated you here these months. Without you, I would have had to deal with that German officer directly, and you made that a lot easier," she went on.

"He's not as bad as you make him out to be. He's just trying to survive like you are."

"When do you leave?"

"Maybe tomorrow. I'll find out in the morning."

"Do you know why you are going?"

"Yes. I think back in Paris, I can help at the hospital, and help others who are trying to make it through."

"Not even close, Marc, not even close," she said, looking out at the sea.

"Joan, I can't go north. Even if Allen were alive and I had a place to stay in London, I can't get across the Channel." He sounded like a child complaining to his mother. "I can't really go south. I have no proof of my American citizenship. I lost everything on that ship out there." He then looked out and checked if the tide was low, where the superstructure haunted the coastline. "If I even got over the border, I don't know anyone in Spain and would not know where to go. And, besides, after everything now, I cannot go home. At least in Paris, I can do something."

"Marc, listen to me carefully. Do you know why I dragged you from the ocean that day? Do you know what drove me when I was nearly eight months pregnant to convince a French fisherman to go out there and get you swimmers? I got news for you, friend. It wasn't because God called me and said, 'Hey, you got to save these chaps.'

"I saved you, not because I was trying to save you, but because I was trying to save the one whom I had lost in the past. I was trying to save the one soldier who died who I thought I could save if only I had done this, or that.

"And that dead soldier, whom I could not save—drives me in ways I can't quite get at. I lost my baby, Marc, because I was so driven by that need to save him. That is why I was out there that day, and dragged you from the sea back to my hospital. Angels do have demons, you know.

"And you are exactly the same. You're not going back to Paris to help others. You are going back to try and save Allen, but he's dead. So, now to make up for the fact you are alive, you are taking his place and going back to

Paris to help others through," she said as she picked at her food. Marc shifted his weight and crossed his arms.

"Maybe you have something. Is that wrong?" he asked.

"No. Not at all," she paused and stared at the ocean. "I used to think it was wrong, but I don't anymore. It is just part of who I am and why I do things. What is wrong, Marc, is lying to yourself. What is wrong is telling yourself it is some other reason and justifying your motives with some false ideas. That is wrong."

"I see," he said. "I think I understand what you're trying to tell me."

"Marc, go back to Paris and find what you need to do. Help as many people as you can. I would if I could get out of this bed," she said. "Just don't fool yourself as to why you're going back to Paris."

"Thank you for understanding. I will be back in a bit for the tray." Marc then left the room. Joan picked at her food a bit more. She looked again up at the window and caught a break in the clouds.

"Oh, maybe there will be a break? Ha, some angel of Saint-Nazaire I am! I can't even part the clouds."

I don't think he heard a word I said, but all the same, it would make no difference. He is going to do whatever he wants, because I would, she thought as she gazed at the waves.

"Oh my Lazarus sur Mer, I raised you from the dead of the sea, and now you are searching to go do the same."

May, 1944

Paris, France

"So, do you play the game?" the airman asked him pointing to the board.

"Yes, at times, but not lately," Marc said.

"I would love to play cribbage. It would help me relax," the airman said.

"I would, friend, but I don't have any cards," Marc said in a distant voice. Marc weighed the options of telling the airman of the possible danger he was in by staying here, or keeping his silence.

"Pity. What happened to the cards?" the airman asked. Marc then remembered that the Jacksons were arrested. *How could I have forgotten so soon?* he thought. The cards were always at their apartment and Marc would bring the board.

"Some friends borrowed them and have not returned them yet," Marc said, deciding to smile and push away his sadness.

The next morning Marc told the airman, "Stay away from the windows and do not let anyone in, or answer the door ever. Understand? You are not safe here, but safer than out in the garden. I need to head to work but will be back soon." Marc started to leave.

"Sorry that I don't have anything to eat. Things are very tight right now, but I will see what I can get from a friend coming into town," he said, careful not to mention her name. He left a cryptic message for his American friend Drew that he needed to repair some socks. She lived south of Paris on a farm. He never called for supplies for himself, but only when he needed them for an airman.

"When do I head south?" the airman asked.

"I don't know. You are an unexpected surprise, so I'm winging it right now. I will be right back," and Marc left then to meet Drew downstairs.

"I need your help," Drew said to Marc.

"What is it?" Marc asked. He took the basket and quickly peeked inside. "This is great, Drew, my God, thank you."

"I have one who is being a problem and I need to knock some sense into him. He is acting really arrogant and cocky, like some do, and seems to think he is king of the house," Drew went on in a low voice.

"Give me a minute and I'll go with you," Marc said to Drew as he ran upstairs to put away the supplies. "Listen, I need to go help my friend out a bit, and this is all you have. I cannot cook for you right now, but I will be back. Look at me and listen," Marc said firmly to the airman. "This is all, it has to last, and you have no idea what it took for me to get this. I will be back. Stay away from the windows and do not answer the door," Marc finished.

The airman looked at the basket full of eggs, some vegetables, and bread.

Drew walked with a determination about her, and Marc did not say a word as he followed. She wore her hair up, in a bun, but looked younger than her true age. She had worked in radio, and Marc had met her through other safe house contacts. Normally they would muse about America and the war, but not today. Drew was on a mission.

They walked quickly up the stairs to the flat and rang the bell twice, with one knock. A much older French woman opened the door and they started to greet each other in French.

"You, we are taking a walk. Let's go," she said to a tall, handsome captain Marc had never seen before. He looked a little shocked, and was maybe twenty-one years old. He glanced at Marc and could tell he was the same age, but gave him a slightly dirty look. Marc suspected he believed he was French.

"Where are we going?" he said in a New England accent as they walked down the stairs.

"Shut up," she said curtly.

"Silence," Marc said firmly.

After walking a few blocks, she turned into a small alley and they walked down until she was sure no one could see or hear them. She turned quickly and faced the handsome young captain.

"You have been one hell of a fucking prick. They tell me you expect to be waited on hand and foot and you are not appreciative of our food," she growled.

"They are not giving us what you bring," he said, shocked.

"It has to last. It is all we have and it has to last for your trip out of here. They cannot give you everything," she continued on, staring angrily at him.

"This is just a gimmick for you people. You are being paid. If I am a pain, then why don't you just give me to another house?"

Drew's eyes narrowed and she glanced at Marc. She took a deep breath and tried to calm herself.

"They get 100 francs per day, per man, and it costs 800 francs per day, per man, to live in this rat hole of a city. You are right. It is a gimmick and we are the ones being played."

The airman fell silent. He backed up against the wall and looked away from Drew, first toward Marc, and then to the ground.

"So, if you want to go someplace else, this man is with the Milice, the French Gestapo, and I can trade you right now for a handsome reward that will go a long way to helping support more sensible characters than you."

When they returned to the apartment, the captain barely looked up at the woman he was staying with. Drew assured the woman there would be no other problems, but if there were, to call her quickly.

"Thank you, Marc. You are such a good actor," she said to him before they parted.

"You are a tough bird, Drew," he said, smiling.

"You need some more ass-kicking with your new bird?" she joked.

"No. I'm not sure of him yet. I need to teach him a bit of French at least. Look, Drew, the Jacksons are now gone. If I don't call you, don't chance anything with me," he said.

"You got it, but I hope to hear from you more," Drew said before she left.

CHAPTER 33

"It's me, all clear," Marc called out as he entered the apartment. The airman came out of the back room.

"Don't worry, I made something for myself but I was sparing. Thank you for everything. I want you to know that. I know this is a big risk for you," he said.

"Thanks. Risk is everywhere these days. Look, can you speak any French?" Marc asked.

"Some, but not well."

"What do you know?"

"Well, voulez vous couche avec moi chez soir."

"Do you know what that means?"

"Sort of."

"Don't ever say that sentence again. What else do you know?" Marc asked.

"Let me see. There are all kinds of sentences in the back of my pocket guide," he said as he took out a small four-by-six brown pamphlet with the seal of the American Eagle on it, as well as *A Pocket Guide to France*.

"Uh, look, that will not be much help. So, you've never spoken French?" Marc said.

"Wait—I have something else," and the airman took from another pocket a very small American Red Cross map of Paris. He opened it to the section where it had a list of simple questions. Marc covered his mouth in shock. He took both the pocket guide and map away from the airman.

"Listen carefully. If you take these things out, they'll know you're an American. See, American Red Cross? And see here, it says down here 'War and Navy Departments of Washington, DC.' I'm sorry, but you cannot have these with you ever." Marc took them and put them under the cribbage board.

"Now listen. Say you get stopped walking along the street, or on the Metro someplace, by a German, and before he says one word, what do you say?" Marc asked the airman. He looked back at Marc with a blank stare.

"*Vous sie haben fumer*?" Marc said next. The airman squinted slightly.

"'*Sie haben*' is German, not French," the airman protested.

"Yes, and *vous* and *fumer* are French for 'you' and 'smoke.'"

"You are telling me to ask in German and French, mushed together like that, for a smoke?" The airman looked perplexed.

"Fuck yes, I am. The German thinks you are either American or British. But if you ask for a smoke using both German and French, he will know, without ever asking for your papers, you are from Paris," Marc said.

"*Foomay*," Marc said lifting his head a bit. "Think fuck you, but instead say '*foomay*.' It's not just what you say, but how you say it, as well."

"Wouldn't I want to say it the correct way, to show I am really French?"

"No. You want to talk like a fool. Otherwise the German will start speaking in French to you as well as the Parisians, and then what? Do you want to die and sound good, or be an idiot and live?" Marc said. He hated dealing with Americans now, with all of the attitudes they had about the Europeans.

"Why a smoke?" the airman asked.

Marc studied him closer and began to doubt some of his sincerity, but decided that he just was another young stupid flyboy who survived his crash. "Because everyone wants one here, and the Germans have the best rations," he said.

"I have to go into work. I'll be back at the end of the day. Stay away from the windows. and, if it makes you feel any better, here are your little books back," Marc said as he took the pamphlets from under the cribbage board.

December, 1940

Saint-Nazaire, France

Officer Sean finished filling out the rail pass, and then turned to another folder on his desk. He scanned the list of names alongside the various graveyards that he requested Marc to prepare. A small package rested on the corner.

"The American is here," his secretary said.

"Send him in."

Marc entered and sat down. He took a deep breath and waited in silence. Officer Sean finished looking through the file and put it to one side. He inhaled deeply and smiled at Marc.

"I am not happy about this, Marc. Not one bit. I am more than a little disappointed that you want to return to Paris. I thought you were getting along here quite well and I had found myself a cribbage partner for good." He studied Marc's expression to see if he had changed his mind. "You really want to return to Paris?"

"Yes. I think it's best," Marc said.

"Why?"

"I can't get home. I can't get to England. I don't have any papers for the border to prove I'm American. At least in Paris …"

"Why? I can get you papers for Spain if you need them. Why Paris?"

"There are Americans in Paris and maybe I can help with the hospital there."

"I knew you were an American even before you did. The day I came into Joan's hospital and you told me that Eleanor Roosevelt was the chancellor of Germany, I knew right then you were American. The nurse told me later that you thought I wanted to know if you were the father of her baby. Who else would have ever thought of such a crazy thing?" the officer went on, looking down at his desk, talking more to himself than to Marc.

"Why?" he snapped at Marc as he looked up.

"I can't stay here any longer," Marc paused and looked into his eyes. "I need to get away from the sea. I need to get away from the yards," he said, trying to hold back his emotions. "I found someone the other day, and now I just need to go." His upper lip quivered.

"Was that why you got drunk? I had never seen you drink before, so I knew something was wrong," the officer said in a softer tone.

"Yes. I needed those drinks."

Officer Sean began to speak, but then stopped. He shifted his weight in his chair and then leaned his elbow upon the desk, leaning in toward Marc.

"I do not understand you. I will tell you something that most people do not know. I wake up everyday with a plan on how to get back to America. I cannot do a thing about it, because if I leave, what will happen to my parents? But you, Marc, you can leave, but you won't. I understand that you need to leave Saint-Nazaire. I am shocked you have been here this long. I am sorry if you found a friend in your work."

Marc's eyes turned away from Officer Sean. He looked up at the new portrait of Hitler that had replaced the previous head of state.

"Marc, look at me. What siren of Paris is calling you back there?"

Marc sat considering the question. "I know Americans in Paris who I can stay with, and, maybe, she will come back. I knew this woman and she went south with her family, and maybe. I know it won't be easy. I know it's going to be hard in Paris. But, I need to be where I feel like I'm needed. I just cannot stay here anymore."

"I have your pass. I had already decided to give it to you. I just wanted to know why. I understand what you are saying and maybe you are right. But I have another question for you." He paused. "Do you see who I am?"

"What do you mean?" Marc asked.

"Marc, I want to win the war, but it is a different war than the British, French, or Germans want to win. I think you just see my uniform and think I am a Nazi. It is not true. It is not easy being a slacker German. I just want to stay put. I don't want a promotion, and I do not want to leave my post. I am just trying to stay put and stay alive. If I live through this, then I win the war, my war against death." He gazed deeply into Marc's eyes.

"And I am not the same kind of German you are going to meet back in Paris. They want an Iron Cross, Marc. They want promotions and commendations," the officer said as Marc sat, unblinking, listening to every word.

"They want glory, heroism and, most of all, they want destiny, to shake his very hand. Just remember, if you find yourself someplace you never expected, you made the choices to put yourself there. I made the choice to return to Germany after school, and now here I am. Now, I just want to know, do you see me, or do you just see this uniform?"

"I see you. I know you are not the same as the others. I wish everything could be different. I wish it could be 1939 again. But ..." Marc stammered.

"Oh, yes, who would not love to go back to 1939? Here is your pass and here is something else I have for you. It is a token of my appreciation for your help. You made things a lot easier for me here working with the French and that crazy British woman, and I have appreciated playing cards with you, as well." Officer Sean then gave him the pass and a small package.

"Go ahead, open it. It will not explode," the officer joked.

Marc opened the package and it was a small wooden cribbage board made from a piece of oak.

"I know, not what you expected. It is not chocolate or cigarettes or extra rations, but I thought you might like it now that you seem to know a little bit about the game," the officer went on.

Marc studied the board. "Thank you. Where did you get it?" Marc's voice cracked.

"I made it," he said, as if it were obvious.

"Where did you get the wood?"

"One of the soldiers got it for me. I think from the beach. Why, is there a problem?" the officer asked, perplexed.

Marc looked up from the cribbage board made from an oak handrail and said, "No, it is perfect. Thank you. This means a lot to me. You have no idea."

"And, Marc, thank you for the work on the file. The list of graveyards is impressive. But one question—why are there two lists?"

"One is alphabetical, and the second is by size and distance from the ship's sinking."

"The list, starting then with Angoulins-sur-Mer and ending with Pornic, is by number buried and distance from the ship?"

"Yes. The ones at the top have only one or maybe two graves, and are towns up or down the coast, and the ones at the bottom are where most of them are buried and closer to Saint-Nazaire."

"Eight hundred fifty-nine, and the rest got away?"

"No, most died. These are just the ones who came ashore."

"How many do you think were aboard?"

"I have no idea. At least seven thousand, but it could have been more."

"You're very lucky."

"Yes, I know."

"I hope your luck continues in Paris."

Marc placed the board in his bag and shook Officer Sean's hand. He then walked to the train station with his travel pass, on his way back to Paris.

Officer Sean sat back down at his desk. He picked up the folder and began to look through the file. He then removed his glasses and stopped.

I did the same damn thing. I needed to feel needed and so I returned to help at home, and now here I am. I see a damn fool because I am a damn fool, he thought as he began to laugh. "I am so needed now, there is no possible way to escape."

May, 1944

Paris, France

There came an unassuming knock at the door. The airman stood and walked over where he knocked back twice. A single knock then came back and he then opened the door to Marie standing in the hallway.

"Voulez vous sie habben fumer avec moi ce nach?" he said in a perfect American accent.

"Who taught you to talk like an idiot?" she asked.

"Your boyfriend, of course," the airman said.

"If you said that to me, I would run away thinking you are crazy," she said as she entered the apartment.

"That is the idea and, frankly, he is very smart," the airman said, smirking.

"We will soon see just how smart he is. Have you found anything?" she asked.

"Well, not much. He has some food now, and a lot of extra clothes for an unexpected guest such as myself, but I haven't found any maps, names, contacts, or anything. The cards are gone, as you know."

"What about the board?"

"It is just a board with nothing on it. No compartment, no marks, nothing."

"Is there anything strange about the holes, or number of holes?"

"Maybe. I mean, there are seven up both sides, and I think normally there are six. It is a custom-made board, of oak. It is not a board that he would have bought," he said as he gave it to her.

"So, either he had to have made it, or they made it, but it definitely is not just any board for cribbage," she said.

"I believe it is just a block of wood."

"He will be here soon," she looked down at the street through the window. "Are you ready with what we rehearsed?"

"Yes, absolutely. It'll be fun. He actually believes I am from America. My accent is as good as any other boy from corn country," he said with pride.

CHAPTER 34

Marc walked through the door as Marie stood behind a door in the hallway. The airman sat on the bed in the back room, away from the windows, just as Marc had told him. She came out, and Marc stood shocked and said, "Marie, what are you doing here? How did you get in?"

"Marc, Marc, I had to. I had no place to go. I needed someplace, I am sorry," she pleaded.

"How did you get in here?" he asked again, completely stunned and unable to process this new surprise.

The airman came out and said, "She pleaded at the door, and was banging and banging, until it was so loud, I thought it would draw others. I know you told me not to let anyone in, but she said she knew you and told me that she …" He then stopped, as if he was pretending to have done something bad, like a dog that had crapped on the carpet.

Marc stood in silence. His guard was up but, at the same time, there was now nothing he could do. *Who had followed her? How long would it take to find her, and then all of them?* he thought. His mind raced through a number of problems.

"Marc, Marc, listen to me. I have a plan. I need to get out of town, and so does he. We can pose as husband and wife, and no one will know. I know this looks bad now, but it can work out. And you can come, too. We can meet up once we get out of town."

"I need to think," Marc said, sitting down and closing his eyes.

"She has a good point, Marc," the airman said. Just then, Jacques flashed across his mind and his stomach felt uneasy. The airman's voice had a confidence in it that betrayed him. It lacked any fear.

"Marc, I know we can do it, but we need to know how to get past the checkpoints," Marie said. Marc's mind went blank, and then he thought of the dream. He opened his eyes and looked at Marie and the airman. They appeared to expect him to actually have a plan for this. As if all Marc had to do was say, "Oh, yes, no problem, you will be escorted at eight tonight. Want some tea until then?"

He went to the bathroom and started to wash his face in the basin, and then looked up through the mirror into the room and saw Marie looking at the airman. He continued to then wash his face, with the nausea worsening by the moment. Marc fought off the nervous need to wash his arms.

"Marie, what happened?" Marc whispered when he went back into the front room.

"They came for them. They took everyone. I missed the meeting and they were all gone, Marc. Everyone. And I don't know if they will talk, but I am sure some will. I should have seen it. You were right and you told me, but I did not listen."

The airman appeared to just listen and act as if he was embarrassed by everything. Marc noticed his silence.

"So, they're coming, Marie. You know that, right? You know they will find you if you stay here."

"Yes, I know. I am sorry to put you in danger, and him. I had no place else to go, Marc. I am so sorry." Marc could no longer pretend not to hear the lie in her voice. She was lying to him, and he realized that the airman was in on it all. His stomach grew still as he could see that they were not coming at all—they were already here in his apartment.

"I have a plan," Marc said as he walked back into his bedroom. He searched through drawers, opening and then slamming them shut. His mind spun furiously to develop some kind of new plot for his guests. Then he remembered the night before and the questions the airman had about cards and the board.

"Where are they?" he complained.

"Where is what, Marc? What are you looking for?" Marie said, standing in the hallway.

"The cards, the cards! I forgot the damn cards. They must have them," he said. He then turned and looked at her. "Do you have something to write on?" he said, desperation in his voice.

"Yes, I have something. I have some scraps." She pulled paper from her purse. It was a small, nearly brand new tablet of precious paper. Marc smiled as he looked in her eyes.

"Excellent," he took it to the table and then started to draw. "Now, listen to me. This is very important." He held up the paper that now held a small drawing of an animal. "Show this card, and when they ask at the border, tell them, 'I am the weasel.' They will let you pass. I would give you the real card but it is lost, so this will have to do." Marc couldn't believe his own act. He had somehow plunged himself into her lying and just mirrored it back to her. "They will know who you are and let you pass. But, Marie, don't tell anyone else, and if you are captured, it is important that you eat the paper, or destroy it. You can never tell them you know me. Understand? It would put so many others at risk. You have no idea."

She stared at him with wide eyes. The airman looked as if he believed every word from Marc. "I love you, Marie, and I want to be with you and the only way I know is by giving you this card. It is the only hope. But remember, if they catch you, tell them nothing," Marc finished.

She took the card and said, "What do I do?"

"Hold the card down in such a way that no one can see. When the border guard asks for your papers and identification, give them this card and look straight at him and say, 'I am the weasel.' It is that simple. Once you say that, everything will go as agreed. It is the secret code, Marie. Tell no one." Everything in him went cold. He knew now that he was playing her game, but there was no way for him to win.

She never loved him. She was false. Everything was false and a lie. Marc now just wondered when the Gestapo would come through the door, because he was sure they were waiting.

"When do we go, Marc?" she asked.

"Now. You cannot stay here or waste a moment. If you hurry tonight, you can make it out. I so want you to stay, Marie. I love you and I wish I could go, but it would only make it more dangerous."

As they got up to go to the door, Marc took Marie and kissed her, and said, "Be careful. They are everywhere. If you see me again in prison, remember we do not know each other. It is for your own safety, Marie."

"Marc, I love you. I will, I promise, I will."

Marc turned to the airman. "Be careful. Take care of her, and say nothing with that accent," Marc said. The airman nodded in agreement. He seemed almost as if he was lured into a trance of believing everything Marc had said.

"Marc, do we need the board?" Marie asked. Marc said, "No, the board always stays with me. Without the board, all is lost."

And Marc was then alone in his apartment but for how long, he was not sure. His mind raced with fear of the possibilities. And then doubt began to creep in.

Maybe Marie was being honest. Maybe he had just sent her and that airman to their deaths with his stunt. But everything inside him, his full intuition told him that the voices lied. There was such a lack of sincerity in them he thought, as he closed his eyes. It was remarkable how well the trick worked. No wonder Jacques was in charge of recruiting.

Again, doubt crept back into his mind, and with the worry, came fear. Eventually, it all seemed hopeless. But still, never before had an airman known his name, and Marie seemed to show up just in time.

Marc left the apartment and walked to Notre Dame. He sat in the empty cathedral. There was no service, and no priest present. Marc struggled to find inside himself some faith that his prayers would be heard, but there was nothing inside him that said yes. He noticed that the window had finally been removed. Maybe the workmen believed by taking down the little window of hell, heaven would someday reappear?

At first he was going to return to his apartment, but instead decided to take a walk. He checked to make sure he had his papers with him, just in case he should be stopped.

The play *Elois* had some tickets, which was rare in those days when it seemed like everyone sought the theater to escape the hunger and fear of the war. The characters came and went on the stage. Their miniature lives seemed to pass in front of him. One loved another who did not see the love. Another wanted someone else who wanted someone else. As he sat alone in the packed theater, he thought that hell is not a place underground, or a window in a cathedral, but other people.

Marc walked aimlessly through the streets back to his apartment, lost in thought. Did he make a mistake? Or did he just not want to accept the truth, that it was he who was led to his own death by such a simple love?

"Halt," he heard from behind. He stopped in his tracks, thinking, *This is it, the moment where they finally find me.*

"Papers. It is past curfew. What are you doing out here?" the guard asked him sternly.

"Walking to my apartment after seeing a play," Marc responded, wondering when others would spring out.

"These papers are excellent. I am sure they are a forgery," the guard said in dry, dispassionate French.

"But that name, it is authentic, so perhaps the people who make the fake papers are so good, we now use them ourselves. Which play?" the guard asked as he looked at Marc's fake identity card.

"*Elois*, over at the Temberea," Marc answered obediently.

"Ugh, horrible play. Depressing," the guard grumbled. "Why are you so late?"

Marc looked at him, perplexed. *Is he going to arrest me or talk about the nightlife?* he wondered. "My girlfriend left with another man," he said with a monotone voice.

"And you saw that play? Why?" the guard looked at him, shocked.

"I didn't know what it was about," Marc said, and then realized that the guard was going to let him go as he handed back his identity card.

"Get inside. I don't want to see you again out tonight. Go find something to drink like a decent Frenchman," and the guard then walked away, leaving Marc in the street just a few doors down from his apartment building.

CHAPTER 35

Marc stood in the hallway on the landing, just outside his door. He stared at the threshold for any hint of movement inside of the apartment, but it was darkly silent. Decision after decision rushed through his mind as he stared at the doorknob. He thought how odd it all seemed, like a surprise birthday party, except it would be instead for his arrest and execution. After the wave of past decisions leading to this door washed by, another wave of should-haves rose up inside him, but there was no time left.

Marc stepped forward and took his key, turning to the left four times, until the door unlocked. He closed his eyes and then opened it. Marc then walked across the threshold, but still only silence. He shut the door behind him loudly to challenge the darkness.

After standing in the dark for a few moments, hearing nothing but the echo of the empty room, he hit the light button on the wall next to the door, and there was nothing.

There were no Gestapo agents waiting for him, or German soldiers to take him away. There was no one in the back room, or bathroom or kitchen. He walked into the front room and saw the cribbage board, which stirred a storm of doubt up inside his soul.

December, 1941

Paris, France

"I have no idea who he is," Dr. Jackson said to Marc as he sat across from him at the hospital. "I'm sure he is one of the thousands of soldiers left behind, who hid in the woods after Dunkirk, but who knows. He probably stripped his papers and identity disk so, if he was ever caught, they would not know he was British."

"How do you know he's British? He could just be some kid, and some family is looking for him now." While the sadness of death still troubled him, he was growing ambivalent, as it had become so common.

"He is British. The lady who brought him said he spoke only English and no French, and she only found him in her barn a week ago," Dr. Jackson said, looking back at Marc.

"How did he die?" Marc asked quietly.

"Blood poisoning. Something bit him, probably a few weeks back, and he never healed. Either that, or he got a bad cut someplace. Being weak, the body just did not fight off the infection. If he had got here maybe a few days ago, he would've had a chance," Dr. Jackson said, looking over Marc's back to make sure no one could hear them in the basement morgue.

Marc looked up at Dr. Jackson, without any emotion. "Why are you telling me about this?"

"Because I think you should give him your name for burial," Dr. Jackson said in a low whisper.

Marc's eyes suddenly widened, and he looked down at the dead man on the slab.

"I would if I could, but I am a doctor here," Dr. Jackson said, "and I cannot so easily just die. But you can die, and be 'reborn' so to speak. That way, if someone should come for us Americans, at least you have a chance," Dr. Jackson said softly yet intently.

"I don't know. When do you need to know?" Marc asked next. His mind started to work out the details of what could happen, how he would get word back home that he was alive yet dead at the same time.

"Tomorrow, my place, depending on the drapes, of course," Dr. Jackson said, and then walked out of the morgue, leaving Marc to think.

May, 1944

Paris, France

Marc laid in his bed listening to the silence of the room close in around him. He played in his mind every possibility of escape, but each one ended with someone likely paying a price for his flight. He thought what would happen to innocents and the people at the hospital, yet they had no idea of his activities. He checked and rechecked in his mind if there was any way he could be traced back to other safe houses.

What if I was wrong, and Marie and the airman were real? How arrogant of me, he thought, to condemn and judge someone based purely upon the tone of a voice. He considered the possibility that the reason no one was in his apartment to arrest him was because they were being tortured themselves while protecting his name.

Between the dreams of doubt and the fears of escape, Marc fell asleep early that morning.

Marc woke with a jolt. He was surprised to still be free. It was morning. He stayed in bed for an hour and then finally got up. It was too late to go to the north or south. Running seemed pointless to him. He bathed in the cold water, dressed, and went to the hospital on his bike. He looked around the apartment before he left with the same strange feeling he had back in June 1940, before he and Allen left the embassy for the train station. He noticed that the airman had left the supplies. Marc took some of the bread and cheese for breakfast.

"Hungry men would never leave food behind," Marc said out loud to himself. "No, Marie, you do not need the board," he said, looking at it on the mantel.

December, 1941

Paris, France

"My God, Marc, I love you," Sylvia said to him as he came in through the door to the shop.

"I came as soon as I got the message. What can I do?" Marc said, looking around at the bookstore.

"Start taking the books upstairs as I unload them," she said as she pulled books from the shelves.

"How much time do we have?"

"I have no idea. I just know not much. They could be back anytime," she said in a rush of tears.

Within the hour, a few more of her friends arrived and the books began to make their way up the four flights of stairs to the attic. By morning, all of the books were gone, and Marc was helping a carpenter pull down the shelves. By noon, he had started to paint the empty walls.

"Sylvia, why couldn't you have just sold him the book? I mean, all of this just because you crossed one German over a book?" Marc asked her.

"Marc, it is not that simple. My entire business is built by word of mouth. If I do that, then there will be more Germans and more books and, sooner or later, someone will complain about me selling Germans degenerate literature, and I will be the next book bonfire out in the street," she said, dipping her paintbrush in the can.

"You don't know that for sure. No one has complained yet, and they have been here for over a year and you have had other German customers. And you do not just sell degenerate books," Marc said, wondering if the lack of food or warmth had finally caused her to crack.

She looked at him like a fool and then let out a snort. "Marc, it is that degenerate work that sells. It is time to wake up and see what is going to come. America is now in this war, and we have no idea how long we are going to be free to live in Paris."

Marc dipped his brush into the can and started a new line on the wall. After a few minutes more, he said, "I have a chance to die officially, and then get a new name."

Just then, the painter came back into the room with more paint. Sylvia put down her brush and moved over to Marc and took his arm. "Come with me," and then said to the painter, "Maurice, we will be right back. I need to show him something upstairs." Marc and Sylvia walked up to the fourth-floor attic where the books were stacked for storage.

"Are you?" she asked looking at him.

"I don't know yet. I have to decide soon, though. We have an unknown and the doctor thinks it would be best that we take my name and use it for the death certificate," Marc said to her quietly, shocked that he was even considering the idea.

"You should. Don't be stupid. I would die in a heartbeat if I could, but look at all this. I am stuck, but you can do this and no one will know differently," she said intently yet low.

"But what if word gets back to my parents? What then?" Marc eyes squinted.

"I have a sister, in California, and I can get a message through her to your parents and all will be fine. It is even better then, because they can officially report the death to the Americans and it will look all the more real." Sylvia sat upon a pile of books.

"What about papers? I don't know anyone," Marc complained.

Sylvia's eyes became wide and bright with excitement. She stood up and then drew close to him and clasped her hand over his ear in a whisper. Marc then drew back and looked at her face in near disbelief. He took a deep breath and his eyes again focused.

"I know him," Marc said with a nod.

"Then do it! Don't worry about the rest. I can take care of your parents and get what else you need," she said, looking at him, confirming the agreement.

"Now, let's get back so if they return, there is no more bookstore to sell any books." They walked downstairs to finish painting the room.

That same afternoon, Marc rode his bicycle out to the Jackson home. The drapes were arranged in just the way to indicate it was safe to come inside.

May, 1944

Paris, France

In the hospital basement, near the laundry chute, one of the agents said to the other, "How can we be so sure he will not change his routine?"

"What if he does? Then we will get him someplace else. There are only so many ways south. But, why should he leave today? Last night, instead of running out of town, he ran to a play," the second agent said.

"I hope you are right."

"Stop worrying. This will not take long."

"Did you bring a gun?"

"What for?"

The younger agent looked up at the experienced agent and then down at the briefcase. "You don't have a gun in there?"

"Oh God, no, of course not. Those are just the case files for the arrest."

"What if he runs?"

"You will run after him."

"What if I lose him?"

"We will just call ahead, and then pick him up later someplace else. Besides, they love it when they have a good chase."

"I thought you had a gun. I thought they always give the senior ones a gun."

"What for? They don't have any more bullets, and they need to ration what ammunition they do have for more important matters. I used to have a gun, but that was sometime ago. If you know what you are doing, you do not need a gun. It is altogether unnecessary. I have made numerous arrests now just making sure I choose the right location."

"What if he has a gun?"

"He won't, and if he does, he will pull it on you first."

"That is not funny."

"I am not trying to be funny, just honest."

Marc arrived through the back door of the hospital. Before he got started in the kitchen, an orderly came into the room.

"There is a basket below ready for your attention," he said to Marc.

"Very well. I will get it later."

"If you can now, that would be great because we are very low now on clean sheets."

Marc nodded and then removed his apron. A strange peace came over him as he approached the door to the basement. *I wonder what new surprise I might find*, he thought to himself as he opened the door.

He walked through the door into the large room where three baskets were lined up along the wall.

Then he knew for certain. All the doubt and self-pity flew away. The door slammed behind him, and from the baskets arose a single agent dressed in a suit.

"Were you expecting someone else?" the agent asked.

"I was expecting no one at all. Who are you?" Marc asked but he already knew the answer. All the doubt evaporated in a single instant as the agent rose from the sheets.

"Mr. Rémy, or Tolbert, we thought you might be expecting an airman?" an older voice came from behind him near the door.

"No, I was expecting to find a lot of dirty sheets that need to go out to the cleaners. What is this all about?"

"That is why we are here. I need you to come with me to the station. We have a few questions to ask you about some visitors you have entertained. Perhaps you were not aware of their activities? It does happen."

"Now?"

"Yes, now, unless you don't feel like going?" the older agent said as he lifted up his briefcase and tapped his hand against it.

"Will this be long? They need me to prepare the lunch," Marc said. He knew the answer would be a lie.

"No, not very long, but my assistant will let them know, so if it takes a bit longer, they will not be waiting for you," the older agent said to Marc, maintaining constant eye contact.

"Will I need anything from my flat?"

"Don't worry. We will send someone for you if it comes to that."

"Well, you have everything covered. How thoughtful."

"Thank you, and now, please, we have a car waiting," the older agent said, as he gave a quick smile to the younger agent.

CHAPTER 36

Marc stared at the monstrously ugly painting that hung upon the wall just to the left of the agent: a peasant women knitting under a greenish-yellow light within the canvas. Marc could not tell by just looking at the painting if it truly was a drab, pea-soup green, or just required a cleaning.

"Who is R?" the agent demanded firmly. Marc remained silent. "Would you please be so kind to tell me who 'R' is?" the agent then repeated in a firm, yet polite, tone of voice.

"Are you French?" the agent then asked.

Marc simply nodded in agreement while still holding a captivated gaze upon the painting.

"I see. And are you an American?" the agent asked.

Marc shifted his body weight and his posture improved before he could stop himself. He then froze in a state of uncertainty if his movements had betrayed him. *If I answer yes, then it will lead to eventually confirming that my French identity is false,* Marc pondered. *If I deny my nationality, it appears no harm could come from this,* so he shook his head from side to side, in disagreement.

"Very interesting. I think you are an American. Are you sure you are not an American?" the agent pressed again while looking at Marc's identity card and papers.

Marc held his face still, not letting any emotion reflect in his eyes or his mouth. He steadied the rudder of his heart until nothing deviated inside him.

"You are not Marc Tolbert then, born in Paris, raised in America, and returned to Paris for studies in 1939?" the agent calmly stated.

"I find it rather remarkable that Marc Tolbert died, just a few days after his country entered the war, and the death certificate was signed by none other than Dr. Sumner Jackson of the American Hospital here, while you have been working there. It is amazing, don't you think?" the agent continued calmly, looking at a file. He looked up at Marc, checking to see if anything about his posture told him that he had a change of heart.

"Well, perhaps it is just an amazing miracle?" the agent said.

Marc held his silence as the agent continued to look through the file in front of him.

"Winoc Rémy is a very authentic name, after all. Britney? I think so. Winoc is some kind of saint, I believe," the agent mused on, talking more to himself than to Marc.

"Marc, are you positive that your name is Winoc Rémy, and not Marc Tolbert after all?" the agent pressed again, almost in a fatherly tone.

After a few minutes of silence, the agent then turned back to his file and said softly, "Well, it appears he is French."

Marc's eyes fell away from the painting of the woman in the sickening green light, to the cribbage board and cards placed neatly upon the desk in front of the agent.

December, 1941

Paris, France

Marc walked up to the door and knocked twice. The door opened and there stood Torquette, a warm smile on her face. He sat down at the table across from Dr. Jackson.

"I think it is best, it is insurance. You hope never to use it, but if you need it, well, it is a good thing," Dr. Jackson said to Marc.

"But they have not done anything yet, so how can we be so certain they will round us up?" Marc said. He still had not made the decision, even though Sylvia had certainly made him think hard about it.

"We can know nothing for certain, Marc, except we cannot trust everything will be in our favor," Torquette said.

"Once you sign the certificate, you know it will be reported to the embassy, and the State Department, and then to my home. What if the message gets home before I can get word back?" Marc said.

"I can delay that process. We can forget to report something, or take some time on that part. Torquette has a sister in the States, and we can send a note requesting some supplies for our friend, passing along word to your parents," Sumner offered as a solution, "and this is only during the war. Afterward, we will correct the records and they will understand due to the circumstances."

"Sylvia offered the same," Marc said distantly.

"Have you thought of a new name?" Torquette asked.

"Sort of, but I am open to suggestions," Marc smiled.

"So, you have decided then," Dr. Jackson asked, looking at Marc directly.

"Yes. I'll do it, but on one condition. He is given a good burial and I pay for a marker. It is the least I can do since the fellow is giving me the opportunity to die and be reborn," Marc said, looking at Sumner.

"I have a feeling that the dead are going to become very popular for the purpose of resurrection," Sumner said as he looked at his wife. "Do you have a contact yet that can get you a new identity card?" Sumner asked next.

"Yes. I have a contact for papers. I actually know him from before the war."

"Excellent, now a name. What shall we call you?" Torquette said with a smile.

"Winoc," Marc said without hesitation. Torquette looked puzzled, and Sumner's face held a blank stare.

"I rather liked Marc. I was thinking more of a last name," Torquette said, looking at Marc with a motherly gesture.

"Oh no, Marc is so common. There are so many. I finally want a unique name. Winoc is it. I am certain," Marc said proudly.

"Well, Winoc it is. How did you come by the name?" Sumner asked.

"I was reading about the early saints of France, and discovered the story of Saint Winoc of the northern region who took in refugees from the war. He is a forgotten saint, but one all the same, and I rather like what he is known for," Marc said.

"I now like it as well. Winoc is beautiful. And I don't know anyone else called Winoc," Torquette said, looking at Sumner.

"Since you are choosing saints, can I recommend then a good French last name?" Torquette asked next.

"Please, I would be honored." Marc said.

"Rémy, after Saint Rémy, who baptized and converted the king of the Franks to Christ," she said.

"It appears you have a new name, Winoc Rémy. It certainly is unique," Sumner said, amused.

May, 1944

Paris, France

"I am sure we can pull it off," Marie said to the agent.

"I am listening. So far your catch has not said one single word."

"The key is perception. If he perceives that I am getting the same treatment that he is, then half the battle is won. Once he knows, his own emotions will work against him until he has to confess to save me from his own crimes," she said in a low, cold tone. "It works. We have done this before and you know it works. It is just we have never carried it this far before."

"You're right, but I think it is a good idea. We can put him along with another unrelated arrest that we can sacrifice," the agent said. "Actually, I like it. We could get some interesting results."

"Once he sees me, with the airman, and also with someone he does not know, there will be confusion. He will not be able to disassociate the other's death with my possible death," Marie said.

"Well, sounds like you have quite a date planned out."

"The key is planning and setting it up ahead of time. He is terrified of water. I really don't think it will take even half of what I have planned," she said with a smile.

The door flew open to Marc's cell, and he woke to the guards screaming at him. He struggled to stand at attention. The same drama played out over and over again nearly every hour for three days, until finally, the door flew open, and Marc did not stand. The guards dragged him from the cell and kicked him in the hallway. Marc then woke up.

He fell asleep in the car, but awoke as the car drove down what appeared to be Victor Hugo Boulevard. Inside the house, they threw cold water on him until he was drenched, and then threw him on the floor outside a door that led to the basement.

Beyond the door he could hear the screams of a man and slaps of a whip. The door flew open and the man was thrown to the floor next him, bent over upon himself in agony. Then, Marc was taken down into the basement. He did not get a chance to see who was standing beyond the light. His shirt pulled off, he stood with his hands against the wall.

The first slap of the whip ripped down his back with a terrible force, followed by the next. His hands pressed into the wall until he was not able to keep from screaming.

All along the basement wall, the imprint of hands could be seen, pressed into the sides of the asbestos lining.

Marc felt the blood trickling down his back, down through his pants. His own hands now were impressed deep into the wall in the company of those who preceded him.

They dragged him up the stairs and threw him onto the floor of the hallway. He struggled to look up, and sitting in front of him was Marie. He closed his eyes and tried to again fall asleep to her screams but his consciousness would not wane. The first man moaned and rocked back and forth on the floor.

Marc's body flew up against the right side door of the back seat. The second man then flew in, striking him. Marie then collapsed upon him and the door slammed shut. The agent in the front seat kept constant watch upon them as the driver sped through the streets in the early morning hours.

Marc kept half an eye out on where they were driving. He realized they were going down Avenue Foch and then turned down Rue de la Pompe.

"This is a side of Paris you don't see often," Marc mumbled.

The agent barked, "Shut up!"

The car stopped and the driver and agent pulled them out one by one, taking them up to the house. Marc could see the number "180" near the door.

Inside, a woman dressed in a long, red satin evening dress, greeted the new guests.

"Oh my lovelies, how sweet you all look. Oh, they have mistreated you so much," she said in a sugary tone.

"House rules are still the house rules, so everyone must strip, now," and her tone turned harsh upon the last word.

Three men then started to forcefully strip the three prisoners, and just as they finished, another knock came at the door. The woman answered it.

"Just in time for the party, sweetie," she said, as another agent then brought in the airman from the garden.

The four of them were then tied down to plush chairs, arranged in an outward facing square in the center of the room. A man then began to play classical piano.

Marie sat in the chair directly behind Marc, and she started to cry. Then the airman started to yell, and the other man whimpered, his voice sounded muffled. The woman came to Marc, and then started to cut his hands. She used a board with razors attached.

"Patty cake, patty cake, baker's hands," she said sadistically, as she cut open his palms. The music filled the room with an upbeat polonaise by Chopin. Then a second man forced Marc's hands down deep into a plate of salt. His hands felt as if they had caught fire, and the music reached a crescendo. In the midst of the pain, the notion came to Marc that the key was A-sharp.

A wet towel, stained with blood, then was placed over his face. His knees could not help but strain against the ropes. He had lost all control of his body, and it seemed to now have its own consciousness, independent of his thoughts. His legs and torso shook violently.

The man next to him gurgled and gasped as water splattered over Marc's shoulder.

Then Marc felt the cold water pouring down upon his own face. He struggled not to breathe, but his body reacted to the water and it poured through his nose and mouth, choking off all air. He began then to choke, and his esophagus burned of acid. The bright polonaise then slipped away.

He stood naked on the side of the Lancastria. All around him he could see young men getting ready to jump, and then he noticed the one man. He was completely nude, and he stared at Marc, a small smile on his face. Marc noticed that his skin had a golden hue to it, and he appeared to be the man who was sitting next to him just a few moments before. Just then, he heard from behind him, "Bling, bring-bling", and he turned. John was riding the bike down the side of the ship, and then right up to Marc.

He took the bike and held it up to his eyes, and it transformed into glasses.

"I can see you," he said to Marc, "and now you can see them," and placed the glasses upon Marc's face.

He then touched Marc's shoulder, guiding him to look down on the plates of the ship, and just beyond the steel surface, he could see himself in the room, in the chair with a towel over his face.

His body was now on the floor and Marie was over him. The airman was also kneeling next to him.

Marc looked back at John. John then took his right hand and placed it on Marc's heart, and he could see the words before they came to his ears, "Go back."

In a rush, Marc fell through the ship, and back into the front room of 180 Rue de la Pompe. The music had stopped and he was throwing up water onto the floor. Before he could see anything, the two other guards had taken Marie and the airman to one side, as if they were still being tortured.

The woman in the satin evening dress pulled him up into the chair with another man, and started to slap him around. "You have had so much fun." Marc continued to cough up water and gasp for air at the same time, while his body shook intensely.

After a few more moments, he regained some semblance of consciousness. His mental focus reasserted itself and he began to wonder if he should look.

They piled them all into the car waiting outside, throwing their clothes into their laps, but the other man did not follow. Marc recognized his face as the same face he had seen on the side of the ship. It sickened him that they had killed the man, and the thought crossed his mind that the two naked people next to him were not people at all, but just ghostly shells of humans, less real than the dream he had of the ship.

CHAPTER 37

The guards took the three of them from the natural-gas-powered, black Renault into the Gestapo prison, and put them into separate cells. Marc continued to cough up water, and his throat twitched with minor spasms. A complete sense of dread began to descend upon him, as each muscle in his body shook with tremors.

Sitting up, he fell asleep just for a second, or longer, but then woke up in a panic, fearing death. The door flew open, and a guard shouted at him to get up.

Walking down the hallway, his sense of time and space completely warped. It seemed as if it took a year to get out of the cell and down to the interrogation room, yet he had no memory of the year that had just past.

"Mr. Rémy, Winoc Rémy, how are you feeling?" the agent said in a very soft tone. Marc sat up, but his mind drifted into a timeless ditch of instantaneous sleep.

He awoke to a gentle slapping on his face. Marc was startled and wondered how much time had passed. *When did she get in here?* Marc thought as he saw Marie sitting next to him. Marc could not shake the nagging feeling she had been there for a while.

"You are Marc Tolbert. I know you are Marc Tolbert, and so do you, so let's just stop entertaining that myth." The agent moved to his desk.

"And Mr. Tolbert, it says here that you arrived in France on June 19, 1939, and that you were even on a diplomatic trip to see … what is this? I am impressed. You have had quite a tour of Europe."

"And your cell name, or code name, is 'the Weasel,'" the agent then said with a tone of confidence.

"Oh, Marie, you shouldn't have," Marc slurred out the words, like mud mixed with stones.

"I am sorry ... I am sorry ... Please, just tell them," Marie pleaded. "They don't want you, but 'R.' They don't want me or you, Marc ... please."

"Marie, Marie ... I told you ... I told you ..." he said with a mixture of tears and smiles, "and you swore you would never tell." He shocked himself with the words. Marc felt amused that he had found the courage to hold her accountable at last, but then he crashed into a despair when he looked at the board and thought of all the times he had met at the Jackson home. His courage came too late for all his friends that she had betrayed before him.

December, 1941

Paris, France

"So, who is this man who can get you papers? I did know someone but he is now gone," Dr. Jackson asked.

"Sylvia told me about him. I helped her shut down the store, and confided in her my opportunity to die. Don't worry. She is trustworthy. I told her I had no idea where to get papers, and she told me of him," Marc said.

"And you knew him?" Torquette said.

"Yes. I met him in 1939 at Fontainebleau," Marc said.

"Is he a student?" Dr. Jackson asked.

"No, he is an instructor. I took life drawing from him, and then again in Paris. In fact, he is the one who introduced Marie and me back in 1939."

"I do not believe we know this man," Torquette said, looking at Sumner to confirm.

"Does he have a name?" Sumner asked next.

"Yes, but when I spoke with him before making my decision, he asked to keep his name in confidence. He is only known by 'R.'"

"Do you think he could join us sometime?" Dr. Jackson asked.

"I'll ask him, but I believe he would. He is very good with papers, and has contacts with people who can get across into the free zone."

June, 1944

Paris, France, Fresnes Prison

"Who is 'R'?" the Gestapo agent asked. Marc almost fell asleep. *Is this the same agent? Yes, it is the same agent,* Marc realized.

"Marie, how long did it take you to line this one up?" He heard his own voice, but did not recognize it.

"I didn't do it, Marc, I swear. Just tell him, please … they don't want us," she pleaded in a pathetic tone of voice.

"Oh, come on, Marie, I know … you can trust me. How much did they pay you this time?" His voice echoed in his own mind, and for a moment, he questioned if his words were just thoughts, or if he'd spoken them aloud.

"Please, please, oh my God, please, I cannot believe this is happening," she started to cry. Marc started to laugh. The agent's eyes never once left the drama.

"Oh, Marie, I love it when you cry. But more, please … you should cry a little more for this …"

"Marc, Marc, I had to. I had to do it. Please, I love you. I want a future with you. They don't want us. They just want 'R,' they will let us go if you just tell them who 'R' is. I had to think of us. I just wanted to be with you, please, Marc, please. I just want things to go back to the way they were before. Do this, please, for me," she screamed out between her sobs.

"You know, it was quite prophetic that night he posed us the way he did, you with the rope, and me as Gaul."

"Fuck you, Marc," Marie's voice rained down on him like a bomb. The agent's head snapped up and looked at Marie, his eyes bright and wide.

"Fuck you! How dare you judge me! Who the hell do you think you are? You're just a little boy. You don't belong here. You are not a solution. You are just another part of the problem, and the only one with a rope around your fucking neck is your own self-righteous self."

"Marie, Marie," the agent stammered as he rose from his chair.

"I am at least helping to build a new and stronger France. A France that does not go to war with horse-drawn cannons, or leaves its cities to be bombed. We became weak because of people like you. No more. Not any more."

The agent walked toward her as he drew his hand to his mouth. He stopped and then turned to the door.

"How fucking dare you judge me, you lying sack of shit! What are you? Who are you? At least I am fighting for something, something strong and right, a new, united and stronger Europe, free of worthless garbage—a France where horses don't run wild in the street over the bodies of children …" Marc's eyes rolled to the back of his head as he passed out.

June 13, 1940

Orléans, France

"Marie, don't be long! Meet us in the town square afterward," her mother said to her.

"I won't. I just want to check in with my friend and make sure everything is fine," she said. Marie walked down the narrow streets of Orleans, leaving her family to go visit her friend from the art school. Finding the apartment building, she rang the bell.

"Annette," she called from outside.

Annette opened the door. "Marie, I am so glad to see you. Come in! What are you doing here?"

"We are going south, maybe to Bordeaux, I think. We had to leave Paris. It is all very sad," Marie said.

"It is shameful what has overtaken France. Just shameful," Annette said.

"I know, I am sick over it, but we need to have faith."

"Marie, open your eyes. We have been betrayed from within. Our own government of old fools has done more for the German army than Hitler. Can't you see this?"

"I know, but it is not just that, Annette. We trusted the British again. They drew us into this war, and now they are running back to their island."

"It is absurd, and I, for one, look forward to the end."

"Don't say that, please."

"Marie, France is going to lose. How can we not? Just look at what is happening, right here in Orléans. The government tells everyone in the district to bring in the horses. What do they do? Round them all up in the town square. Does the army ever come to get the horses? No. Who will feed these horses? Who will give them water? Look at what our country has come to? We turned our back on God, Marie. The government kicked out the church from the schools and look—rot. We are as rotten as a fallen log in the woods."

Marie's mother, father, little sister, and brother came into the town square. Gathered all around were horses. "Mommy, I want to pet the horses," the little girl said.

"Papa, are they giving rides?" the son asked.

"No, we are going to the market. We need to get something to eat for the long trip," he said, as they made their way around the square to the other side, to where tents had been set up along a side street.

"There is no petrol. Are you walking? You should stay here in Orleans with us. It is safer than the roads. At least when they bomb here, there are shelters below," Annette continued.

People in the market looked up, as they could hear the buzz of the planes from somewhere above. No one was quite sure of the direction. People in the market started to get excited, and Marie's mother had let go of her brother and sister for just a second, not knowing they had walked back toward the horses.

The father looked up at the sky, and then back at his wife, who was trying to buy some fruit. Just then, the planes came down on the town square and the sound of their guns spit down upon them.

"What is that?" Marie asked.

"Oh my God, it is another raid!" Annette said. "Get away from the window!"

Marie left the window crisscrossed with tape, and ran for the door.

"Why are there no sirens?" Marie asked.

"See, I told you! It is a farce. We cannot even sound the alarms for the raids."

The father spotted his two kids, just maybe forty feet away, not even to the town square yet. He ran for them as the planes then came in over the square, shooting into the horses. They went wild and broke free of their ropes.

A bullet got her father in the chest and belly. Another bullet got her mother in the back of the head. But the horses got Marie's little brother and sister.

Marie ran from the flat, and had just reached the end of the small street that led back to the town square. The horses ran wild down the street past her as she hugged the side of a building. Once they had passed, she ran down to the market, where she found her family, just where they said they would be waiting for her.

May, 1944

Paris, France, Fresnes Prison

"You are worse than even the Jews. Soon France will be free of you Jews, foreigners, and Communists!" *When will she stop?* Marc wondered as he awoke. "What are you, Marc? You are just a coward running away from home, running away from death, always running away. You talk of price—

what have you lost in this war? What price have you paid? You're just a fucking rich Yankee kid, lost in France, pretending to be someone."

The agent opened the door and called down the hallway for the guard.

"I bet you even pretended to believe in God just to get me. You are even less than the Jews, you piece of shit." Marc slumped in the chair in a state near delirium.

A guard appeared in the doorway. "Take her out of here," the agent told the guard.

"I will go, don't worry. You will get your answers," Marie said to the agent.

"You should have left Paris when you could, Marc," she said hatefully, "and never come back." The door slammed shut.

"Too much *Au Jour d'Hui* for her, or *Action Français. Français, Français seulement*," Marc said with a laugh, in a mocking voice. He took a deep breath as he looked up at the agent and then passed out cold.

The agent fell back into his chair. He ran his fingers through his hair and closed his eyes in frustration. He looked up at Marc in front of him, out cold.

"Let's take a break. Yes, I think a break would be good. Do you mind?" he asked Marc, slumped over unconscious in the chair.

The agent then studied the cards and the board behind him. He walked back and forth in front of the desk, his eyes scanning everything he had laid out. The answer is here, he thought. Then the idea struck him. He looked back at Marc slumped over in the chair.

"I will be right back. Please, make yourself comfortable. I promise not to take too much longer," the agent said, smiling at Marc.

In just a few moments, he returned to the room with another woman, a guard, and a typewriter. He began to talk very fast in German and the woman translated it into English. He then motioned the guard to wake Marc with a glass of water. Marc woke with a violent thrashing.

"Please try to stay awake. This has been the fourth time we have tried to move through these charges. I need you to focus," the agent said as he pounded his fist upon the desk.

CHAPTER 38

"*French, Français seulement,*" Marc spoke up, smiling and laughing. He felt a euphoric rush of energy once Marie had left the room. He was not even sure when she had left, but eternally grateful to the guards for his rescue.

"You are an American, and therefore our conversation must be in English," the German agent said.

"I was born in Paris. I am a citizen of France as well as America. I have been here for five years and I want to understand what you are charging me with. Can you please read the charges in French?" he said in French. He sat up, as if prepared for a birthday cake to be brought to him, for his candles to be blown out.

The agent nodded and then began reading over the charges. The translator's French was even better than her English.

"You are charged with conspiracy against Germany, aiding and abetting the enemy, distributing false papers," and the list went on and on and on. The details were mind-numbing to Marc as he listened to them, from his job at the hospital to his relationship with Marie. *How odd to include her*, he thought, and realized then they had prepared this ahead of time. *I think I might have just had a nap*, he thought as he lost track of the woman's voice.

"Dr. Sumner Jackson, who is the snake, Torquette Jackson, who is the turtle, Marc Tolbert, who is the weasel." Marc then puckered like a weasel, twitching his nose. He started to laugh out loud. Officer Sean was right. Everything he said about the Nazis had been right, and he was watching it right in front of his very eyes. The entire thing played out like some bizarre comedy.

The German agent then stopped. "Do you have anything to add to these charges, Weasel?"

Marc was shocked by the question because he had no idea that he would have an opportunity to add anything. The possibilities intrigued him. "You know almost everything. I am shocked at how detailed it is. I am stunned that you figured it out," his voice came from another source, as if his body had been possessed from far away.

The agent smiled. "Yes. We are very thorough. You are not in the hands of the Milice here, Weasel," he said proudly, his tone calm and even.

Marc looked at the huge chart behind the agent, with the cards laid out on the table in front of him and the cribbage board.

"I am not the weasel," he barked, deciding to pick a fight.

The agent looked exasperated at Marc. "You are the weasel, Sumner is the snake, Torquette is the turtle. We know you are the weasel!"

"Because she told you," Marc said slowly.

The agent smiled, "Not only that but, Winoc, your first name starts with 'W,' and that means you are the weasel. You are smart, very smart. You are the weasel." *The man is insanely stupid*, Marc thought, even in his delusional sleepwalk.

"I am not the weasel," Marc repeated in a sluggish tone.

"You are the weasel. The snake is the doctor who cares, who heals the birds. Torquette is the turtle who keeps them in her shell for protection, and you are the weasel who covers up the tracks and takes them away. Weasel, who is in the henhouse now? If I ask you, I am sure you would tell me it is the cow. Now, who is 'Rabbit'?" the agent demanded of him. He almost pleaded, as if for his own life. "You have told me before you know."

"You want an Iron Cross, you got to do better than that. I am not the weasel," Marc said. He felt unsure of himself as he struggled to remain focused. His mind burned with a singular desire to fall asleep.

"You are the weasel, don't lie. I am not a fool. Tell me who is 'Rabbit'?" he asked again in a fatherly tone, full of concern and sympathy.

"I am not the weasel, and there is no rabbit," Marc said, looking up at the board and all the various cards and names that meant nothing to him at all. It was completely and utterly a uniquely crazy fantasy of the German officer, created from the random things they had gathered at the two houses. Marc never expected any of these cards to mean anything at all, but here he was, fighting over them, screaming over them.

"You are the weasel, Marc! I know that! You know that! Marie knows that—everyone knows that. Who is ...," the agent continued on.

"I am 'R!'" Marc's voice burst open.

The agent froze at the desk. He turned around and looked at the board. Marc knew he now had the agent, because he never considered this possibility before and never expected Marc to confess to being 'R.' He could see how the agent was looking at the relationships, and trying to work them out. He could hear the German officer in his head. "Yes, give him what he wants. He wants that Iron Cross, Marc. This will go straight to the top, big report, important finding, critical to victory, promotion and medal ..."

"Marie is the weasel," Marc spurted out in laughter.

The agent turned and said, "You are lying. Marie is not the weasel. You are the weasel." He was disgusted. "I do not believe you. Look at you. You are doing it now, covering up, and playing tricks trying to get out of this. You are a trickster, Marc. Just admit it."

"*Marc, Marc,*" Officer Sean said as he came out from behind Marc. *When did he get in here?* Marc thought to himself. He smiled with warmth for him, feeling safe that he was in the room. "*Pay attention to me and work with me. He wants the Iron Cross and you want the bread. Now, Marie is the weasel and you are 'R.' What is 'R?' Look, come on, Marc, I got some bread here for you,*" Officer Sean said. Marc could see the Gestapo agent right through him.

Marc looked down at the table. The cards sat spread out in front of the cribbage board next to the plate of bread the agent had placed for him. His mind ran blank. He then looked up at the agent and said, "The rabbit is dead, but I am 'R.' I am the raven," he said with just the right tone of defeat in his voice. The words rolled out from him with a complete sincerity. *Of course he is the raven*, Marc thought as he heard his own confession, but it surprised him that he had even said it, for he had no idea what it meant.

The agent turned back and looked straight into Marc's eyes and then down at the cards. He scanned them quickly, finding the raven card. A smile broke across his face.

He snatched it up and tagged it to the board. The rabbit card he tossed back down upon the desk. The agent then stepped back and studied the cards.

Marc watched in total amazement at what a thoroughly insane pile of utter bullshit they had come up with from just a bunch of cards and names. He was slightly amused by the fact that he had to solve it for them. He felt a deep sense of well being that he was solving their problem while borderline insane, plus satisfied that he was able to include Marie's name. The agent had his Iron Cross, and Marc had the last word about Marie.

The agent stood stunned and captivated by the beauty of his cards. It was as if he totally forgot that Marc was sitting in the room, waiting to be led to his cell. He took one last look at the cribbage board.

"You are lying. You cannot be the raven. You gave Marie your card. You told her, you are the weasel," he snapped back at Marc.

"I am the raven. I steal the food, clothes, and supplies for the nest. I fetch for the turtle and the snake." Marc was careful not to look up into the agent's eyes until he said, "But the weasel is whoever must take the birds away. I did not tell Marie I am the weasel," Marc was breathing deeply and his heart raced in his chest from the exhaustion. "I told her to say *she* is the weasel, because she had a bird to take away."

The agent then picked up Marc's identity card and saw for the first time the initials, "W" and "R," for Winoc Rémy. He slammed the card against his head, and then down upon the table.

"You are both. You are a raven, but also the weasel, but only the weasel when you need to be. It is brilliant!" the agent said.

Then Officer Sean from Saint-Nazaire looked at Marc with pride. "Good job, Marc. He is going to get his Iron Cross. You have given him the promotion, the one he wants and needs. Now the bread is yours for the taking," and then Marc saw him walk through the wall and out of the room.

The agent stood stunned at Marc's confession. He had everything now: the snake, the turtle, and the raven. He had them all, and the weasel he had as well, and just did not know it. And he was proud because, now, not even Berlin had cracked this code. He had all the answers. The days and nights finally had paid off, and he was able to crack Marc himself without Marie's help.

Then Marc asked what he had never asked before. He said words that had never come from him in all the days and nights of questioning.

"May I … May I now … have that bread," Marc asked while looking at the plate next to the cribbage board.

The officer turned away from the board, and then down at the bread. He quickly picked it up and brought it to Marc and said, "Yes, you may, my raven." Then he went to the door and called a guard, and then told the secretary to change the charges. He even brought in a sausage for Marc, and he ate it while they read the charges in French, *"Marc, who is the raven, is charged with ..."*

The agent believed it. The woman believed it. Even Marc believed it as he ate their food. Yes, I am the raven, the stealer of the food, and you have your Iron Cross, but you will never get this sausage back from me, he thought. It is mine now, all mine. Marc wondered if Officer Sean would return to play a game of cards as he devoured the precious sausage.

Marc stared at the board, which he had carried with him from 1940. He knew this would be the last time he would see it, and thought of the first time he had seen the wood.

"I suppose you must hate her," the agent said next. Marc looked up from the board. "It is a curious thing that she saved your life not once, but twice."

Marc's body jerked a bit at the thought, and his mind did not have any memory of these supposed salvations from Marie.

"And how do you see that?"

"If it was not for her, I would have treated you as a Frenchman, and had you shot. But she is the one who helped us prove you are really an American so, for a while at least, you will live," the agent said with a smile.

"That is only once," Marc said, half asleep.

"Oh, yes, and she helped you breathe earlier. Apparently, you had a little too much to drink while listening to some music," the agent said.

Marc felt the bottom fall out from inside of him, but then resisted the pull of despair. He gazed at the board and decided that this new path would eventually lead him out of this hell, just like he had turned that day and made it to the side of the ship. He thought of his mother, father, and sister back in America, and how much it would hurt them if he was gone. He made a pact with himself that he would survive.

"There is one other thing," Marc said.

"What is that?" the agent asked.

"The board, it is from the banister of the ship that sank."

The agent eyes squinted, and he looked down as he scratched the back of his head. "I will be sure to add that to the report."

"Thank you," Marc said.

"For what exactly?" the agent said.

"For taking the board away from me."

"Oh, Marc, I assure you, we will take far more away from you than just this silly board," the agent said. The guards then took Marc out of the room, and that was the last he would see of the railing from the ship.

Two days later, Marc was removed from the prison in Paris and moved south to Moulins. He was surprised to see Dr. Jackson and his son at roll call. It was good to see they were alive, but painful for him because he felt responsible for their arrest. He had not betrayed R, but his blindness to Marie had betrayed the Jacksons.

He now was a raven. He had become a bird between worlds that sees outside of time. He knew that it was due to Marie that they were betrayed and denounced. If only he had not trusted her, this would not have happened. If he had only let go of 1939 and seen who she was now, not in the past, not whom he'd met before. But letting go of the dream of loving her was harder than letting her go, as she walked out of the prison interrogation room. He would not be in this hell of watching Dr. Jackson and his son stand for prison roll call, had it not been for his greed.

Marc had tried to steal time. He'd tried to steal back the past that he lost. Now Dr. Jackson and Philip were like doves, innocent and pure, with white feathers. He had once been a dove, long ago, but then he fell into the sea, and his feathers were stained black as the night by the oil. Now, he was the raven. Marc felt neither life nor death, but only his own self-loathing. All the others in line were men, but he was a bird of death. Marc now stood at Moulins in a raven's hell, watching doves pay for the raven's sins.

CHAPTER 39

July, 1944

Moulins Prison, France

The cell door flew open as Marc scrambled with the other prisoners to stand at attention. The guard came screaming in a rage, pushing through each of the men, first grabbing one and then Marc. He slammed Marc against the wall outside the cell and slammed the door. Then he kicked him twice in the butt and once in the back of his knee, all along pushing him down the hallway with his rifle.

Marc began to tremble with fear. He had heard the screams, and seen men leave his cell, gone from roll call, never to return. He crossed the threshold of a room to his left, and received a blow to his head. His ears rang from the blow.

The guard then ripped his shirt off his back, and forced him to kneel on a bench. Marc suddenly felt the overwhelming need to urinate. He held back, and tried to focus and concentrate. His eyes looked up the wall and he could see the splatters. Just then, the first strike of the whip fell upon his back. Every muscle inside him seemed to contract in a spasm and then a second, third, fourth, and fifth blow befell him, slicing open his flesh. Before the thought of screaming had reached his mind, it had left his mouth.

The guard stopped as a second guard came in the room.

"You fool, he is the wrong one," he yelled at the man with the whip.

"This is the one you asked for. Renee, the Parisian," the guard protested.

"Renee is a girls name you idiot. This is the American, you fool. Get him out of here and get me the other one," the German guard yelled at the Frenchman.

Marc slammed down on the floor of the cell as they threw him back in. The guard then searched quickly through the other prisoners as the other German watched. None of the other prisoners was Renee from Paris. The other five were not the man they wanted. The door slammed. The darkness of the cell surrounded Marc. None of the other prisoners came near him.

Soon, across from his cell, Marc could hear the commotion of another search. Hollers came under the door as he heard the same shuffle with blows down the way. Then screams followed in the distant cell. But they did not stop. Marc thought, *they must have found poor woman Renee*. The guards did not inspect the cell again that night. At the morning roll call, Marc struggled to stand upright. He could also smell the pungent urine smell on his pants. He had no memory of urinating on himself.

Marc saw Dr. Jackson at roll call each day. He had been there longer than Marc. Once he also saw Philip, his son.

"I heard from another they are in Paris," one prisoner would say.

"They have to be. Soon they will be here, in Vichy," another prisoner would say.

"They landed, largest landing ever. There is nothing that can stop them," yet another.

The rumors never stopped. Marc listened, but never spoke about them. He wondered if they were bait. He questioned the reality of any prisoner who was not whipped or handcuffed or beaten.

Dr. Jackson had a look of concern for Marc as he showed him his hands. They agreed never to speak if they should ever be arrested. Marc knew it was dangerous to talk of any Resistance work in the prisons. The only ears you could trust would be your own, and even they were a betrayal of screaming tortures night and day.

"That is a bad infection. How did you cut your hands?" Dr. Jackson asked him, as if Marc were no different from any other prisoner.

"Don't recall. Sort of blocked it all out," Marc said next.

Dr. Jackson cleaned Marc's hands and drained the small abscess of pus. Then he treated the wounds with an iodine solution, and dressed Marc's hands with bandages.

Marc looked for the words to say to him. He rehearsed a few variations in his mind. Then he would pull back and realize that by telling him that Marie betrayed them, it would only open up more questions, and cause him more pain. But Marc felt he needed to tell him, and that he had a right to know. The courage would then pass away and he'd slip back into silence.

"Keep the faith, my friend. It won't be long," Dr. Jackson said to him as he finished.

Marc thought as he left that he would tell him another time, but the opportunity never came about.

"What are you here for? You're the American?" a new cellmate asked.

"*Je ne sais pas*, I don't know," Marc said shrugging his shoulders.

"Yes, you do. You must. What did they charge you with?"

Marc sat in silence in the dark, staring at the shadowy figure. He shook his head from side to side, slowly repeating, "I don't know."

"I'm here because of smuggling. They caught me, but before they did, I was able to get quite a few away," he said proudly, looking at Marc.

"Soon, we will be out of here. Just watch. They don't have much more time. They feel it. You can see it. Come on, what did they get you for?" he asked Marc again.

The more he talked, the more Marc turned inside. Marc thought to himself, *He is practically giving me a full confession. Why would he speak to a total stranger like this?* Marc listened to the man's voice, his quiet confidence. He lacked the fear of every other prisoner in the cell. The others remained silent. He had not asked any of the others why they'd been arrested. Only Marc.

"Enough, I will tell you," Marc finally said, as he moved over near the man. Then he said to his face, just loud enough for everyone else in the cell to hear. "I was hoarding the real nickels, you know, the coins. They caught me. I had a whole can of them in my room under the bed." Marc smirked at the lie, but knew that hoarding of coins was a serious charge. Sometimes they gave people three months hard labor. The other prisoners chuckled a bit. Marc could see that the man knew it was a lie, but he laughed all the same.

A few days later, the man was transferred to another cell, and no one spoke or asked Marc anything else about his charges.

Marc considered jumping into the river as they marched toward the train station, but it was not deep enough. He watched along the way for any possibility of escape. The entire prison was in a long march. Dr. Jackson had left two days before with around two thousand others. The German guards yelled constantly. Marc could not understand where they got the energy. Shouting so much had to be exhausting.

The train cars looked like they were carriages for animals. The tops were rounded, and the slats were covered with wire. So many men were crowded into the car, there was no room to sit. The door slammed shut, leaving the men in the sweltering heat. Each one had a loaf of bread and a piece of sausage, but there was no water, and just a single bucket in the middle of the car for waste.

Marc leaned against the forward wall of the rail car, trying to get as far away as possible from the bucket of waste in the center. The train stopped, and then would start up again, to pass another train stopped on the tracks. Eventually, in spite of the smell and heat, he fell asleep leaning against the wall.

Marc awoke to a commotion on the other side of the car. Some prisoners had found a way to escape. One by one, a man would throw himself from the moving train as it rolled along. Marc's heart pounded with excitement. The men just in front of him held their breath, waiting until it was their turn to jump. Marc had no idea how long the men had been tossing themselves through the open slats, but there were at least twenty now that had dropped out of the car because no one now was pushing or leaning up against him.

The train then came to a stop. The men started to panic, pushing and shoving for a chance to get out. Then a shot rang out and the back of one of the men exploded into the rail car, spraying the air with his flesh and blood. The men moved away and down from the hole in the side of the car. The Germans screamed and shouted just outside. Marc could hear running and shots in the distance.

The doors of the car flew open and the German guards shouted for everyone to get out. Marc fell to the ground and then stood at attention as he was counted. His throat was ablaze with thirst, and his stomach churned. His eyes scanned to the right and left, studying the movement of the other Germans. His mind raced with fear if they were going to shoot the rest of the car.

One soldier then started to move through the men making a selection, one to the left and one to the right. The man tapped his shoulder with the butt of the rifle and directed him to the right. The train car door was opened, and Marc climbed in with twenty-five other men. There must have been a hundred in the car.

The ones directed to the left went to the car just behind the one they'd been in.

The doors slammed shut, and then the guards shouted at the cars in German. Marc could tell they were going to shoot by the anger in their frantic shouting. Then one soldier on each side of the train ran past the two cars and released a clip of ammunition into the walls. At least three men slumped to the floor in Marc's car. Two or three others were shot but not killed. The Germans then left, and the train started down the tracks again. This was the last of the three nights before they reached the new camp.

CHAPTER 40

The train started to stop more and more frequently. About noon of the third day, the train finally came to a full stop. The doors opened and the men piled out onto the ground. The bucket had long since overflowed with waste, which now covered the floor of the car. Six men lay dead behind Marc, as he walked toward what appeared to be an enormous camp. He could see that the train had picked up more cars along the way.

SS officers walked down through the line, and with a whip, lifted the chin of each of the men. The older ones and truly young went to the left to form another line.

"If you are sick, or need care, then go to the left. We have a hospital for anyone injured," the man said in German, with a sweet and enticing voice. Most of the men did not understand German, and their faces wore perplexed looks. A few who appeared healthy went to the sick line, but the SS picked them back out and placed them in the line to the right.

"Only those who need care, please. There is not much room in the hospital, so only the sick and weak," Marc heard as clearly as the day the man asked him, "Do you believe the French and German people can know peace?" The line to the left then parted from the line to the right.

"Place your clothes carefully, because there will not be much time after you get out of the shower," Marc heard over and over again. The men walked then into the shower room, and the door shut behind them. After a few minutes time, scalding water fell down upon them. Men yelled out in pain from the burning water.

The door on the opposite side to the showers opened, and they all left to line up outside. It was now seven at night. Three hours passed as Marc stood in roll call waiting, standing, the entire time naked.

He listened to the noises of the camp, which were unlike anything he had ever imagined. It was not actually a camp to him as much as a strange city.

A group of prisoners then came to the block of naked men and led them through the camp to a long house. Inside, each prisoner sat down in a chair while another prisoner ran shears over his head. Soon the floor was covered in the discarded hair. Men began to cry and sob. The razors burned Marc's scalp. His emotions died inside of him, and his mind bleached dry with exhaustion. A sense of dread filled his chest as he pondered whether he had died and was now in hell.

In the next room of the long house, Marc dunked himself in the vat of soapy water. Men vomited. Others refused to get into the baths. The guards would then beat them.

In another long house, Marc was nearly running through it, as prisoners tossed him trousers and a shirt, and he was given some wooden clogs. Nothing fit exactly and the clothing had rips and tears in it.

"You are to wear these bands at all times. If you do not, you will be shot," the prisoner yelled at them.

Marc took the armband, with a red triangle on it, and pulled it up and over his left arm. All of the prisoners he noticed had the same shirts on. Each had a red triangle with "P" next to it.

The summer sun blinded Marc, now seven in the morning. There had been no sleep and there was a new roll call. The SS stood behind a desk in front of the block of prisoners, going through the names of the manifest and calling each prisoner forward, one by one. A doctor came to the guards and the interviews stopped.

"We are in great need of medical help here. If you are a doctor, or a nurse, then please step forward. If you have any medical training whatsoever, please tell these men and you will be given a very good work assignment," the SS officer said. Marc heard the disingenuous call in the man's voice.

"What is your profession?" the guard asked Marc.

"Craftsman."

"What do you make?"

"Metal, I work with metal."

"Machinist then?" he snapped.

"Yes," Marc responded without any emotion.

The guard then looked toward another SS officer, and then pointed and said, "Over there."

Marc had overheard other prisoners talking. Rumors were flying about what jobs they were going to do. He felt physically exhausted, though his mind was still alert. He knew he absolutely did not want to say anything about hospital work. There was no hospital here.

Marc marched with about two hundred men out of the camp and down the road for several kilometers. Soon, the group marched into a new camp. It was late afternoon, and Marc stood again for another roll call. Then the men were divided amongst the guards. The camp returned to the compound and Marc became part of a larger roll call. His mind had sunk into hell. He was now convinced he would never sleep, or eat, or even be allowed to die.

After the long roll call, the camp prisoners broke, and Marc walked through a new line where he was given a slice of dark bread and a cube of margarine. He devoured it.

In the barracks, he found his slot in the bunks.

"Marc," he heard from across the way. "Marc, is that you?" he heard a second time.

Marc then looked across and squinted, "Georges?"

"Yes, it is me, Georges," the man said back. "In the morning, not now, Marc, in the morning, we can talk." And Marc finally slept.

"Jean is in another block," Georges said as they got ready for roll call in the morning. "If you can make it, Marc, three days, you can make it three weeks, and, if that, then three months," Georges said to Marc as they left the block.

"I have been here now three months, and they say that means I have a chance at surviving the war. Did you hear anything? Is it true, about the Americans?" Georges asked.

Marc just turned and nodded.

"You can talk here, Marc. We are all the same," Georges said.

Marc realized it was pointless now to keep silent. He had remained silent yet had been shot at, beaten, and tortured. "Yes, it is true. In June sometime. I am not sure when. That is all I know."

Marc's words carried, and there was a strange, silent affirmation from the other prisoners as they lined up for roll call.

"Eyes right, caps off!" the commander yelled across the blocks of prisoners.

Three days became three weeks, and then three months. At night, Marc collapsed into his slot, then he scrunched to the side as his bunkmate piled into the slot with him. He closed his eyes and fell asleep so fast, there seemed to be no transition between life and death.

Morning came, and everyone rolled out to line up. Marc stood near the rear of the line for the soup. He had tried to stand near the front and ask the prisoner to dunk the ladle down deep into the pot in hopes of getting a little bit of potato, but he would not. So, Marc tried to hang near the rear in hopes of getting something from the bottom once all the top soup was gone. He stared intensely at the soup as he approached. Marc willed the ladle to go down to the bottom and bring him the precious solids. His plan worked, at least for this morning. His inner will had manifested for him a bowl of soup with precious potato.

At the factory, once the guard left the room, everyone slowed their pace. Marc matched the others in the room, glancing over at Georges and Jean, who had been assigned now to the same machine room.

Marc took the bread in his hand that night and then broke off a small piece and tucked it away into his pocket. The rest he ate quickly. A man had died in the block, but the *kapo* had told the guards he was sick. The *kapo* would then take the rations for himself.

Marc's mind became blank with pain. He had no thoughts now except bread, soup, and water. He thought again—maybe he was right and he had died. This was hell after all, but there was nothing but sleeping, eating, roll call, and work.

Marc climbed into his bunk. He placed his soup bowl under his head. Jean and Georges climbed into their spots. If the *kapos* believed someone knew someone from before, they would separate them. Marc felt rich having two friends near. Men would talk endlessly about past celebrations or dinners. Others would shout at them to be quiet, as the thought of food brought too much pain. Marc focused just on the present, using bricks in his mind to wall off the past. Most of the men who'd been in Marc's railcar had disappeared over time.

Bombs dropped near the camp to the north that night. The noise brought shock waves to the building. Marc wondered if he could hear the machinery in the factory being torn apart. In the morning, work would be canceled.

"I am sorry. The factory is gone, but you all may have as many pancakes today as you want," the German commander's proud voice echoed in Marc's mind.

"Marshmallows—can we have marshmallows, too?" Georges or Jean would ask.

"Yes, of course," the guard would say, as if it was silly to ask such a question.

"Marshmallows for all this day!" the commander said over the loudspeakers. The camp went wild.

Marc must have fallen asleep, just between the bombs falling and the camp getting all the food they wanted from the German guards. He was back on the *Lancastria*. He folded his clothes on the side of the ship. The water rose up the plates, coming toward him.

Then out of the portholes they started to come. First the ones down by the creeping waves, but soon all along the side of the ship. They rose from within until they spilled out into the ocean all around. The waves turned white with the angora rabbits. The black plates of the ship disappeared under the rabbits, covering up the snapping rivets as it sank further into the sea.

"Bling, bring-bling," he heard and turned. Sister Clayton rode on the chrome bike down the side of the ship and the rabbits parted for her, like Moses and the Red Sea. Beside her, on both sides walked a dog, followed then by the boy and the girl from Belgium.

They all stopped right in front of Marc, and up from a porthole rose the burly Scotsman holding out a silver platter with the white angora rabbit upon it. Marc knew it was wrong to think the rabbit was food. Rabbit, at first, seemed so wrong to eat in Paris, but not by 1944. Rabbit was like steak to all who could afford it. Is this for me? My own rabbit? No, no, I should not think of it that way. Marc remembered that the rabbit was to be the Scotman's daughter's pet once he made it back home.

Sister Clayton then got off the bike. It fell into the rabbits all around her. She walked toward the Scotsman, Horus, keeping eye contact the entire time with Marc. He could see his words, but could not hear them. He only heard them in his head, but could see Horus's lips move. Sister Clayton took the rabbit and then handed it to the little girl. She petted it and then handed it to the little boy. The boy looked up then into Marc's eyes, as he walked toward him, lifting up the rabbit, the words reaching Marc's mind before he said them with his mouth, "Bon Chance."

CHAPTER 41

February 15, 1945

Monowitz, Subcamp III of Auschwitz

The *kapo* ran through the block yelling, "Roll call! Roll call now!"

Marc awoke from the dream with a jolt. As he climbed down from his slot and grabbed his soup bowl, he could not shake the sight of the little Belgian boy from his mind. The freezing morning air blasted his face as he passed through the door of the block, running with the prisoners to the main assembly area to line up again for roll call.

"Number present?" the guard asked the *kapo*. Marc heard his voice, distant and preoccupied.

"Block eleven, forty-five present, two infirmary, two dead and one missing," the *kapo* said to the guard. The guard just nodded. Marc glanced at the guard. *Normally one missing meant a search for the prisoner*, Marc thought, but the guard did not request a search at all.

"One missing?" the guard asked the *kapo*.

"Yes, one is missing."

"Very well."

Marc knew something was wrong when he did not send them all to search for a missing person. Normally it was a suicide, but nevertheless, the rules were, alive or dead, they must be counted. Marc became anxious as each block reported their counts. The mood among the guards changed. Their arrogance had faded and their faces betrayed they had a problem to solve.

"We are evacuating the camp. Those too sick to leave will be left behind, and once the Communists arrive, they will surely kill anyone left, so if you wish to survive, you must go," the commandant said.

"One hour, the final roll call will be in one hour. Now break," and his words set off a bomb of activity in the camp. Prisoners took extra shirts and pants, anything they could wear. Some looked like clowns from some circus graveyard, their feet wrapped in think bundles of extra clothing to protect themselves from the snow.

Marc stuffed into his pocket two pieces of bread and two pieces of sausage, which were the only rations. He felt rich beyond all measure to be trusted with so much food. Marc stood in line with his bowl for soup, as the prisoner hurried to fill each bowl. Men would gulp down the thin, watery stew in just seconds, and the truth in their eyes said this time, it was a matter of life or death.

"You must march or you will be shot," the commander then said at the second roll call. Marc knew it was not for him. It was for the others, but not him. Marc's mind wore the feathers of the raven, a dead bird that yet lives. *Those words are for the doves because ravens never die,* his mind told him.

Oh, if the doves are shot, maybe I can steal their food, the raven thought to himself. But then, Marc stopped the thought and tried to let that part go. The more he resisted the thought, the stronger it grew. A peculiar madness fell upon him like clouds of snow. *Yes, shoot the doves who cannot keep up, and we will take their food, and then we ravens will have their pancakes with marshmallows.*

Marc clung to the food in his pocket. *If you are real good, maybe a dove will give you some bread before it falls,* another voice said inside him. Marc pretended the voices were not his own, but the thoughts of other prisoners he now could hear.

Georges arrived with Jean back at the main square just as the blocks began to form again for the final roll call. Jean wore several layers of shirts, and Georges's feet were bundled up to his ankles.

"Marc, Jean, come. Let's march up front. Let's not be looking at what is going on behind us." Marc joined them.

"Block 5, march! Block 9, march!" It started to snow again. "Block 11, March!" Marc, Jean, and Georges began then to march through the camp gates.

"Halt," the guards called out after a few kilometers. After several minutes, the command came: "Turn around, and go back."

"Are we coming or going?" Jean asked the open winter air.

"Halt, halt," the guards then called out through the line, striking a note between fear and anger.

"Right, attention, turn around and go forward," another officer commanded next.

Soon two men made a break for the woods but did not even get twenty yards before they were shot dead.

"They don't know where we are going," Jean whispered to Marc.

"Quiet, you're right," Marc said.

But soon, this business stopped and the march went on and on through the woods and along the road, which had mainly snow with some exposed patches of dirt. And from time to time, Marc could hear a shot behind him. Sometimes close, but usually in the far rear of the line.

A shot then rang out from the woods and all the guards looked up at once. Then came a second and third shot. The guards knew it was not one of their rifles. All at once, the same thought came to their collective minds: "A patrol!"

"Run, you lazy dogs, run!" and everyone started to run. Marc's body ached, and his head caught fire with pain.

Why am I here? Marc asked himself. What have I done for this? And then, it came to him. I am not here. I will not be here. I will become invisible and go away, his mind said as he walked mentally through another door.

A football then landed in the snow in front of Marc as he was running. *"Get the ball, Marc, get the ball!"* and just then his classmate Stephen ran past him and snatched the ball from the snow. He was dressed in his game uniform, complete with pads and his leather helmet. *"Marc! Marc, I am going long! Throw me a pass,"* and he gave Marc the ball and ran ahead of him in the snow, way past the guards, and disappeared.

"Give me the baton, Marc, hurry! They will be here soon," his friend Ralph said to him. He was dressed in his track clothes. *"Marc, you are doing great! We're winning the race, man,"* he said, running ahead with the baton. Marc could see cheerleaders on the side of the road. Even the guards were waving to them.

Just about then, from someplace in the line behind Marc, it came up and out from the snow. The prisoners let it pass and the guards gave a nod of approval as the car approached. It was a bright red 1928 Stutz, a seven-passenger limousine. Marc's father ordered it brand new from the factory with a custom interior. In those days, you went into a showroom and you ordered the features on the car. Each one was made for that special customer. Marc's father wanted club seating in the rear. "You know, like a train, or a stagecoach," he'd told the salesmen.

They had never made one that way before. The president of the company liked it so much, he delivered the car personally to Marc's parents' house.

"Breakfast, breakfast, Marc. Breakfast is ready," he heard. It was his mother's voice.

"Son, time to eat," he heard his father call from the driver's seat. The car pulled beside them, and his little sister, Elda, open the door and said, "Get in here, Marc, before it gets cold."

Marc climbed into the car and sat in the back seat, and there, on the center table, were pancakes, glorious pancakes and syrup, marshmallows, toast, and orange juice.

"Marc, will you read me a story?" as she handed him the book. Elda loved to hear a story in the car and Marc never could say no. Marc remembered that she loved the car so much that they would often go into the garage and sit in it, just to read a story. "Skip to the good part, Marc. Skip to the good part, please," she pleaded.

"Don't do it, Marc," his mother said, looking through the center divider window.

His father said, "Listen to her, she knows."

"Please, please, Marc, the good part, please," the car backfired then and shook.

"What was that?" Marc then started to look out the window.

Marc's mother turned and said, "That is enough now, Elda. Get out and play with one of the nice guards," and as the car backfired a few more times, Elda climbed out to run with the prisoners and guards in the snow.

"Marc, don't let your breakfast get cold, and pay no attention to those backfires," his father said, looking at Marc through the rearview mirror.

Three of Marc's friends from school came into the car next and sat across from him. He had forgotten about them. *Oh*, he thought, *how good it is to see them again.*

"Marc, let's sing a song," and they all sang a tune from way back in grade school, and it was so happy and cheerful. They were clapping and singing, with a clap, clap, bang, bang, and the car would backfire again. It was so much fun to clap and try to match the backfire of the car. It was like the car was clapping with them. And then one said, "Roll out …"

Marc's father turned and said, "Stop it! Stop it now. Enough of that. I do not want to hear that song again," then Marc's friends were not so happy and they got out of the car, as well.

The car drove on right down the center of the column of soldiers and prisoners running in the snow on the road, and Marc sat in the back of the car, with all those pancakes.

And then his mother said, "Oh, look, it's Veronica! Over here, Veronica, get in the car and talk with Marc, will you please?" And the car rolled up alongside Veronica as she ran in the snow, holding a gun to one of the guards. "Take this rifle, you naughty guard, and I will be right back," she said, and then climbed into the car.

"Marc, I am so sorry about leaving you the way I did." Marc felt a little better, because when she ended things, she never said those words. "And if I'd known for a second that you were going to go to Europe and study art, I would never have left you," she said, and Marc felt even better.

"But, Marc, honestly, I have a confession. You were so good, and you believed me when I said I didn't want to have sex before marriage, and so, I thought maybe you might be a little funny, you know," then Marc felt odd inside and not quite sure how to take the comment, but stared at the food in front of him.

"But, Marc, now that I saw you went to France and got a girlfriend even worse than me, I know you are swell, and I missed out on a good deal." Marc stuffed another pancake into his mouth. "I am so sorry, Marc, if what I said to my friends ever got back to you," and Marc felt vindicated. Finally, she saw him. Finally, she wanted him again. Finally, he could drink some orange juice.

"And, Marc, now that you have been arrested, charged, and are in prison, you are really hot. I mean, Marc, you are a real catch," she said. He had finally proven himself to her. She saw him now. He spread jam on a piece of toast. The car backfired again, and Marc looked up from his food.

"Pay no attention to that, Marc," his mother said.

"Look, I need to go and shoot one of the naughty guards, but when you get home, call me. Please. Call me. I mean it," she said as she left.

"Thanks, Veronica. Have fun, and don't get pregnant, honey," his father said in between backfires of the car.

"Oh look, honey, more friends from France. Stop and let them in," his mother pleaded with his father.

It was Allen, David, and Dora from the *Normandie*. *How odd*, Marc thought, *I don't remember introducing them before.*

"Marc, I got home by plane, the *Pan Am Clipper* all across the ocean. Only got sick a little bit," Dora said to Marc in her seductive tone.

David said, "Marc, it is so good to see you. Thanks so much for the francs. I got home by the *Manhattan*," as he then turned to Allen.

Allen sat in the middle, a calm smile on his face. A large white angora rabbit sat on his lap. *Allen was not on the* Normandie *but the* Lancastria, Marc remembered. "See, I am dead," he said. "They cannot hurt me anymore. It is all just a show." He then grabbed another pancake and put into his pocket for later.

Allen said, "Marc, I'm sorry if I frightened you that day in the hospital. I just wanted to encourage you to make it, my friend." Marc's mother looked back with concern at Allen, her eyes showing she was cross.

"Thank you for sitting with me on the beach that night," Allen said. Suddenly a jolt ran through Marc and the car backfired violently.

"That is enough. If you cannot talk nice, you cannot talk at all," and the car let out several backfires, and his friends turned into white doves cooing on the seats. The car shook and backfired even more, and all three turned into large ravens. Marc started to look out the window at the other prisoners.

"Marc, don't look out there," his father said.

"What was that?" Marc asked, searching the snow.

"Marc, pay attention now, eyes forward," his mother said.

The ravens were ranting and raving, back and forth, back and forth, their heads bobbing up and down. "Craw, and rall, crawa, and rall EEE," back and forth, and all fear had washed away from Marc. He ate another sausage and drank down a large glass of orange juice. Both of his pockets now overflowed with pancakes.

I have enough for Jean and Georges now, he thought to himself. "I am not afraid of you, ravens. You do not scare me anymore," he said out loud to them.

"Crash rally, crash rally, crash rally," like dogs sounding an alarm they called out. "Guard, guard!" his mother called over to the car. The doors opened and the guards shot two of the ravens and they disappeared instantly in a puff of smoke.

"Thank you," his father said politely.

"Why is the car backfiring so much, Mom?" Marc asked as he looked out the side window.

"You missed one," Lynette, his mother, then said. But the guards left the car. She turned to the large raven and stared into its eyes. It was silent, with its beak sticking through the center divider window, wearing a large top hat and red-buttoned vest.

"Don't you dare shit on those seats," she said.

Then the raven turned to Marc, and he laughed. Shit on the seats, shit on the seats, how funny. Here we are, in the middle of Germany, with a raven in the back of the Stutz, and my mom makes a joke of it. I so miss her. She could make anything funny. Oh, how good it is to laugh, Marc thought as he laughed hysterically at the scene before him. The car chugged a bit and backfired twice. Marc tried to stuff another piece of toast into his shirt pocket, and grabbed another sausage from the plate. He then started to look out the window again, and the raven lifted up its wing and blocked Marc's view.

Marc got up close to the raven and stared at its eyes. He thought, *Beak to beak, raven to raven in the back of my parents' Stutz.*

"I am the raven," Marc chuckled, and, just then, the raven turned into the Gestapo agent. Marc fell back with surprise against the seats of the car.

"You are lying. You are not the raven. You are very smart, Marc. I believed you. I so believed you, because when you said you were not the weasel, it was true, and I heard it in your voice. But I was confused then, and when you said you were R, the raven, I believed that, too. You tricked me, Marc. You lied. You are not the raven after all. I have had to study this case very hard. You are a tough one, Marc, a real tough trickster," the agent said.

"You got that right," his mother said.

"Glad someone else sees it," his father said.

"Marc, I have new charges," the agent said, and then the secretary came into the car with her the papers.

"New charges, oh good, honey, new charges. This should be good. Real good," his mother said.

"In French or English?" his father asked politely. The car backfired loudly and Marc looked again out the window, concerned.

"Marc, pay attention to me," the Gestapo agent said to him.

"What was that? It sounded like a gunshot," Marc asked.

"Absurd. Look at me, and listen," the agent said.

"English, please," his mother asked the agent.

"French sounds so much better to me," his father complained.

"How about Dutch?" the agent offered.

"No, English, and can you make it with a southern accent because Marc is into guilt, Southern Baptist English, please," she asked real nice-like with a smile.

The agent then started to talk really fast and the woman said in a long, drawn-out southern drawl, "Marc Tolberrtt, y'all here are charged with carousing around with the wrong kind of women, and looking at 'em naked in drawing class, an' skinny-dippin' without a license in French waters with citizens of the British crown before they have had a proper tea and, most of all, sex before marriage in a foreign country, and a whole bunch of other things that good Catholics frown upon and, most of all, what any good Southern Baptist would give their right arm in a heartbeat for a chance at doinn' without getting caught and, worst of all, repeating the same mistake twice with a woman, thinkin' you know what the hell you are doin'. How do you plead upon this copy of the book of French phrases for Mormons?"

Marc's fears dropped, and he could not believe how absurd it all sounded and, most of all, how true it was.

"Book 'im. Guilty as charged and thank God, too," his mother said through the center divider window.

Then the secretary said, "So recorded now in the great records of Germany, under the command of the Great Virgin Mother, Eleanor Roosevelt."

Marc smiled as he stuffed his face with another piece of toast wrapped about a piece of golden brown sausage dipped in maple syrup.

"Oh look, speaking of the wrong kind of women, Marie, Marie, will you come over here and have a little visit with Marc?" The car chugged and backfired.

"Don't talk with her, Marc, it will only make things worse for you," the Gestapo agent said as he left the car.

"I be seein' you in church real soon now," the secretary said as she waved her hanky to him while leaving to follow the agent into the snowy woods. Marc assumed they were going to watch the circus. Marie climbed into the car, fully clothed, no less.

"You really do your best work naked," his father said.

"You are something else, Marie," Marc's mother mused to herself.

Marie turned to Marc, but he closed down. He knew what she wanted, and he was determined not to give it to her. All of these pancakes and sausages were his. He grabbed the extra toast from the plate, and the jar of jam. *I don't care if it was chicken that night, all these pigeons are mine,* he thought as he guarded the food in his pockets.

"Marc, I am so very sorry. This is entirely my fault and I never wanted this to happen and ..." Marc focused on every single word that came from her, holding back everything inside of himself. He knew she wanted the food; he could see it in her hungry eyes. He knew she came for the marshmallows.

"But ..." *Yeah, but what?* he thought. "But can I have some jam? Can I have a sausage?"

"But, Marc, you have to understand something. You had a role in this, too, and I could not have done what I did if you had not let me do it. So, you see, Marc, you are here because you allowed me to do it."

Then the words came from within Marc. "Marie, *fuck off.*" The car shook with a backfire, and the sky outside grew dark.

"That is enough," his mother said.

"Time to go, Marie. Nice having you," his father said.

"And, Marie, if you are ever in New York, be sure to go to the Empire State Building," his mother said.

"Oh, yes, good idea, and you can see all of New York, Marie," his father said.

"And it is so much taller than the Eiffel Tower," his mother added with a smile, "and you can JUMP. People do it all the time, all the way to the ground," she said, bristling with a wide grin.

"Thanks, Mr. and Mrs. Tolbert, that is a great idea. I might need to get out of France after the war, and it could be good for me to get away," Marie said.

"Oh, you're not just pretty, naked, but a smart girl, too," Marc's father said.

Marc checked his pockets to make sure she had not stolen any of his food.

"Game time," Marc's mother said as the car rolled passed a group of German guards. They ran slower now, and an officer broke away and stepped into the car. Officer Sean now sat across from Marc.

"Marc Tolbert, you are the worst cribbage player the New England Catholic Church has ever produced. I was so hoping that when Joan pulled you from the sea that day, you would be someone I could finally play cribbage with, while wasting my time in Saint-Nazaire," he said, and then dealt the cards, just like he had done all those months back at the port, after a day of Marc digging in the church yard.

"I used to think I was lucky, but I was wrong," Officer Sean said with a smile. "The bad cards just seem to go to you each time I deal them." Marc picked up his hand, which was crummy as usual.

"So, I have an idea," the officer said, grinning. "We will trade hands. I will give you my cards and you will give me yours," and then he took Marc's cards and started to laugh. The car then shook and backfired again. Marc looked out the window, worried.

"That sounds like, like, someone was shot," Marc said, covering his pockets of food.

"Marc, eyes forward. Pay attention and no more looking out the windows," his father said, looking at his eyes through the mirror.

"Marc, this is great. I have never had such a bad hand before. You really do just have a shitty hand of cards," the officer joked, "but, Marc, I've got good news. These cards are not that bad." The car chugged and sputtered. His mother looked back at the hand, and his father looked through the rearview mirror at him.

"Marc, my plan did not work out so well for me. You are alive but I am dead," Officer Sean said as he glowed with a golden light.

In a flash, Marc was then staring at himself. He was a little boy sitting across from himself in the car, wearing his schoolboy knickers. Outside, it was the golden hour, that timeless period of the day. The light had a warm, blue tint to it. His mother and father sat in the front seat and they drove through the hills of Maine, going off to the cabin. Marc, the boy, held a children's book on his lap, and he did not look at Marc, the prisoner. The car did not backfire at all. Marc, the prisoner, could smell that it was brand new, shiny and fresh inside the car and outside; he could smell and taste the woods as the wind passed through the open windows.

Then Marc, the boy, looked up at Marc, the prisoner, and said very softly, "We are here."

"Halt. You have run twenty-one kilometers," the guard said, exhausted.

The prisoners started to collapse in the snow all around Marc. Jean and Georges swayed back and forth, struggling to remain standing.

"Don't lie down, don't fall asleep," Georges said to Jean.

"Fall in, by fifty, five per row," the call went out. Men stumbled over the bodies of those who collapsed into the snow. The train waited on the tracks with the doors open.

They packed them one hundred per car. Men wailed and cried through the next three days as the train moved slowly westward, deep into Germany.

Jean started to cry, and then became very quiet. "We can stop for lunch here, Jacques," he said, gazing into a far-off distance as he spoke to his old blind friend from Paris.

Georges shook him over and over again. "Jean, Jean, wake up," but nothing worked.

"Yes, I have the food," Jean said in a whisper.

Marc remembered then the food. He searched his pockets but found nothing. Where did the pancakes go? And the toast? It was all gone. He was numb with pain, and he dared not sleep because he could see death come upon those who fell in the car.

"That fucking bitch got the pancakes," he murmured under the groans of the others in the boxcar. He knew she must have taken the food from him. Marc found a small crust of bread in his shirt pocket but he feared bringing it out for Jean.

They will jump me and kill me if they see it, he thought as he looked through the boxcar at the ravenous men. Men jumped upon the bodies, searching the pockets for any extra rations of bread.

Marc loathed himself for losing the food to Marie. He hated that he was not brave enough to bring the bread out of his pocket. Drifts of shame built up around his feet like the snow that fell through the roof and slats. Marc kept checking his pockets, as if the food would return.

"Jean, get up, get up now, please," Georges pleaded with him as he slumped down. "Get up, Jean, get up."

"Here, we can stop here for lunch now. The view is beautiful," Jean whispered just above the sound of the railcar clicking along the tracks.

CHAPTER 42

February, 1945

Buchenwald, Germany

Marc watched the doors on the car next to his slide open. Boys, or just maybe teenagers, started to pile out. The guards gathered them in front of a pile of dirt at the rail yard. Marc looked away as they started to shoot the kids. He could not resist looking up through the slats. He saw a group of boys run just beyond the guards and disappear into the forest.

A day later, Marc's car doors slid open. The guards yelled into the car, "Everyone out!"

Georges moved toward the door and Marc followed. Jean lay on the floor of the car, among the dead. Marc gave no thought any longer to Jean, for he was convinced that he would soon be joining him in a winter sleep.

Marc could not escape the echo of Georges calling out to Jean. "Get up, get up. You cannot sleep here."

There were no machine guns for Marc and Georges, but instead a ragged horde of ghostlike creatures playing various instruments. These ghostly figures were the welcoming band to the camp.

Marc felt haunted by Jean lying in the railcar they'd just left. *Maybe he was sleeping a very deep sleep?* he thought. Marc's own body ached for sleep and food. *It would've been just a bit more and he would've been in the camp,* he thought as the memory of Jean quickly passed away. *Maybe he is right behind me? Maybe he was not yet dead.* The thought clung to Marc, like a child dragging along, holding his leg. Just then, one of the twenty-eight men left alive, marching toward the gate of Buchenwald, fell face down dead. The doubt disappeared, and Marc accepted that Jean actually had died.

"Jacques, Jacques," the man called through the block.

"Yes, what is it? I am here," Jacques answered back.

"Some new arrivals have come, and there are some French among them from Paris. They are held up in the small camp, but maybe you know a few? Thought you would want to know."

"Let Yves know. Tell him I need for him to take me down there, and check. Do you know any of the names?"

"I will find out. There are only twenty-seven. If you do know any, well, you will need to move fast because they are in very poor shape."

"Go get Yves and try and find out the names," Jacques said to the prisoner clerk. He wondered if any of them could be someone he'd known from Paris. It was another lifetime for Jacques. He was the head of a resistance group, and writer for an underground paper, but that was another lifetime ago. Now, he just sits at the door of his blockhouse in charge of sweeping the floor after the men leave for the quarry.

That evening, before the last roll call, Jacques and Yves walked down into the small camp to search out the new arrivals. Yves stood taller than any of the other prisoners, and he was nearly bald. His face wore wrinkles, but not due to his age.

"Are you Georges from Paris?"

"No."

"Are you Georges from Paris? We are looking for a friend," Yves asked another prisoner. He pointed over to two men lying down next to a wall within the camp theater.

"Are you Georges from Paris?"

"I am Marc, New York, but yes, Paris. This is Georges, from Paris. Wake up, Georges, wake up," Marc said, shaking him.

"Jacques, is that you?" Georges said.

"Yes! I thought it might be you. Can you get up? Can you walk?" Jacques asked. He could hear the moans of the men, dying from exhaustion. Then he could see in his mind's eye Marc helping Georges to stand.

"Look, we have come to get you. Stay right here," Jacques said. He pulled out some camp money from his pocket and stuffed it into Yves's hand. Yves patted Jacques on the shoulder and then guided him over to Marc, placing Jacques's hand on Marc's shoulder.

"I will take care of it," Yves said.

"Marc, we need to get you out of here. Yves is going to go talk to them now."

"They said we are here for a few days, to make sure we are not sick," Marc slurred.

"How long have you been here? When did you arrive?"

"Uh, they said we will have jobs soon," Marc's voice drifted off into the distance of thought. Jacques gripped his shoulder, trying to give him some hope.

"Let's go, now," Yves said after he returned from the guard.

"Can you help Georges?" Jacques asked.

"Georges, Georges, come along. Let's go. You are coming with me," Yves said, grabbing him by the elbow and lifting him to his feet. Yves took from his pocket two armbands, giving one to Jacques.

"Marc, put this on, over your arm," Jacques said to Marc, stuffing the armband into his hand. Yves took another armband and pulled it up over Georges' arm.

"Now, let's go, before anyone else comes in," Yves said firmly.

Yves supported Georges as he walked toward the door and out of the theater. Marc walked with Jacques, holding his shoulder as they followed Yves. Outside, Yves looked for any sign of other guards. At the gate between the small camp and the large camp, the keeper said, "Who are they?"

"Friends," Yves said, stuffing camp script into his hand.

"French?"

"*Oui.*"

"Wait here," the gatekeeper said as he walked toward a man standing against the wall of a blockhouse. After a few moments, he returned to the gate.

"Jacques' block first, then after roll call, take them to block twenty-seven. Make sure to get the armbands back to us once they are in for the night."

While at Jacques' block waiting for evening roll call to finish, Jacques asked Georges about Jean.

"Yes, I did see him. He got away," Georges said to him. "He escaped, Jacques, he escaped!"

Jacques could hear the lie. It was such a sweet way for Georges to tell him. So sweet of him to lie that Jacques could not bear to let him know that he knew it was a lie.

"He escaped," Georges said a second time. Jacques not only knew it was a lie, but that Georges actually believed it to be true.

"Marc, is that so?" Jacques said, reaching out his hand for Marc's. Marc took his hand to his face and shook his head from side to side.

"He got out of the train, I saw him. He walked away into the woods, but the guards did not follow. He escaped," Georges said in a euphoric voice.

"I am so glad he got away," Jacques lied back. "It will not be long. We need to have courage. In a just a few moments, we are going over to a new block. Good French—they will watch after you. You need to eat some more, Georges, please. Another piece of bread."

"He escaped, Jacques. He got away," Georges repeated again.

"I know, Georges, I know," Jacques said softly. "I will see if I can get you any more rations. You need strength."

Each day there was roll call before the men would march out to work. Georges fell sick again and could not make roll call. Then, even work in the quarries came to a stop. The guards only showed up for roll call.

Georges burned inside and begged for water from Marc. "Eat. You need to eat some soup," Marc begged him. He got extra bread from Jacques. But he just grew weaker with each passing day.

A prisoner doctor came into the barracks to see Georges, and Marc pleaded with him to do something. "There is nothing. Stop giving him your food. You need it for yourself."

Marc stirred awake in the middle of the night. Georges said over and over again to the top slats of the bunk, "Three months and you can survive the war, three months they said, three months." His voice became softer until Marc fell back asleep.

The rule was if someone should die during the night, the others still needed to carry the body to roll call to be counted in the morning.

"Georges, Georges, wake up," Marc pleaded. "Please, Georges, wake up," but he was gone. Everyone in the blockhouse had already left for the roll call. Marc tugged at Georges' body and pulled it to the edge of the bunk. He then gave a great heave of strength, and then collapsed onto the floor with Georges' body on top of him.

The door flew open and Yves stood in the doorway. "Marc, you need to get out to roll call, now."

"I need help. He is too heavy for me to carry," Marc cried as he struggled to get out from under Georges.

"Is he dead?" Yves asked.

"Yes. I have to get him out of here. I cannot let Jacques find him," Marc pleaded. Yves then helped carry Georges out of the blockhouse to the main assembly area.

Afterward, he helped Marc put Georges on one of the flatbed trailers, hidden and away from clear view of the rest of the camp.

"They took him to Dora, you understand me?" Marc said to Yves. "No matter what, when Jacques asks, they took him to Dora," Marc cried as he walked away from the flatbed filled with bodies.

"Marc, he will know. They are not even making selections for Dora. Why?" Yves said.

"Please, tell Jacques he got better and they took him to the other work camp," Marc shouted at Yves.

"Marc, I will, but he will also ask you," Yves said with a hushed tone.

"I know. I know."

"Don't you think it would be best to …"

"They took him to the Mittelwerk-Dora camp. He got well and they put him to work. I will it to be so," Marc shouted at Yves, shaking.

"I understand," Yves said, walking back with Marc to the block.

Inside, Jacques sat waiting after roll call.

"Where is Georges?" Jacques asked Marc, holding the extra soup and bread. "Did they take him to the infirmary?"

"He got better. He got better, Jacques, but they selected him for work at Dora," Marc started to cry and sob. "At roll call, they took the strong ones off to Dora."

Jacques sat and listened to Marc's cracking voice. He could tell by his tone that Marc was lying to him, but at the same time willing himself to believe the lie first. The voice frightened Jacques, for it did not seem like it was human any longer, but the voice of a tree struck by lightning.

"Marc, it will not be long. We can hear them now. We will get Georges out of Dora. Don't worry, he will make it, and so will you, just a few more days, Marc. We know. It is true this time," Jacques said carefully to Marc. *It is true, but does he believe it? The voices of this place are unlike any I have heard before*, Jacques heard from within himself.

"I have some bread for you, Marc, a little extra. Please, you need it," Jacques said. Marc broke off a small piece and put it into his pocket, and then ate the rest quickly.

CHAPTER 43

April, 1945

Buchenwald, Germany

"I just cannot forgive myself. How could I have been so blind?" Marc said to Jacques as they sat outside the blockhouse after morning roll call.

"Marc, I am blind. I was trusted by all of the men of the Sons of Liberty and the Defense of France with the job of making sure that no one joined who could not be trusted. And I was given that job by the others due to the fact that I am blind." He raised his voice like a prophet from a mountaintop. "I see not with my eyes, but with my ears and mind. I see things with my ears that eyes cannot see, and this was my job.

"I should have been more forceful. I should have been more emphatic," Jacques said. "I should have insisted that he not be allowed in," and then Jacques' voice lowered a bit, "but I was told that I was too cautious and that he had good references. So, I relented, and Elio became a part of the Sons of Liberty and, ultimately, our betrayer.

"Instead of listening to my gift, I listened to my friends who were gifts to me in life, and now, I am here with you in this place. I have lost now those friends because they trusted me," Jacques pressed the words into Marc's ears, still uncertain if Marc continued to believe his own lies or had accepted that Georges and Jean were now dead.

"Marc, I am able to discern trustworthiness by voice alone, and yet I made a terrible mistake, so how is it that you are holding yourself to an even higher standard of omniscience?" Jacques said, wondering if any of it had gotten through to Marc. He listened for any indication that Marc was indeed receiving his words, as they basked in the warmth of the early morning sunlight.

"We all knew and accepted the risks, and it was foolish to think we were going to cheat our way out of paying the price. You and your friends did the same," Jacques went on, trying to bring Marc around.

"I trusted her, Jacques. I trusted Marie, and then I was blind to what she was doing until it was too late. Because I was blind, an entire family was arrested. I saw them in prison." He turned into Jacques' face.

"I so much wanted to tell Dr. Jackson about what had happened, but I couldn't. First, I couldn't bear to tell him that it was my girlfriend, a French Catholic woman, who had betrayed and denounced us." Marc stared into the yard as ghostly men passed by, moving in every direction through the camp. "And I couldn't tell him because we had agreed beforehand, if we ever were caught, we would not talk about it if we should see each other. I trusted her, and because of that, they paid," Marc's voice trailed off.

"Marc, I trusted far more than you did, and far more have now paid. We cannot know everything nor see the future. Remember, I am better at seeing blind a person's heart than you are able to see with sight. Yet, my luck ran out," Jacques said, feeling a sense of healing inside of himself with those words. *Perhaps I needed to hear myself speak those words, even more than Marc,* he thought.

"Even though we knew the risk, I did not think we would end up like the others. I somehow believed we were special, that we would somehow prevail," Marc said.

"We all did, Marc. We all believed we would walk on water. We sank, but it is not because we lacked faith. We sank because we had the faith to get up out of the boat and take the step. You did not fail your friends. You did not get them arrested. You just had faith, Marc. That is all. I had faith. Jean, Georges, and all the others had faith. Everyone you see here had some faith.

You had faith in Marie, and you gave her your trust. She betrayed that trust and now you are here. Faith is not a sin, Marc. Giving your trust is not losing your soul," Jacques said, his face tilted toward Marc. "Losing the ability to trust and have faith is losing your soul." Jacques realized that he could open the cell door, and even point the way, but only Marc could take the step and walk out of it. He put his hand on Marc's shoulder and, then took a deep breath. Jacques almost started to add to his words, but then stopped. *Maybe I have said enough, and it will just take time for him to hear the words*, he thought. He decided to just enjoy the warmth of the sun.

April 11, 1945

Buchenwald, Germany

Marc and Yves guided Jacques as he went from blockhouse to blockhouse.

"Do not go, stay. Do not go with them, no matter what they say," Jacques said.

Rumors ran rampant through the camp, but the guards were gathering up inmates to march out. They told the men that if they stayed, it meant death.

The following morning, there was no roll call and the guard towers stood empty. A group of inmates had managed to get a radio communication out to the nearby advancing Third American Army.

Marc felt self-conscious as he saw the first of the American soldiers come through the camp. The men were healthy and appeared strong. *They walk without any fear*, Marc thought. But it was not long before Marc noticed a different kind of fear in their faces, as they saw the bodies waiting to be cremated, men covered with head lice, and the walking dead appear in the doorways of the blockhouses.

Men cried when they saw the soldiers. Many of the soldiers gave over all their rations to the prisoners. They would eat with a certain uncontrolled hunger until they'd stop, unable to eat any more. The prisoners became sick, and a few died from gorging on the food.

A group of mäusle men, or walking dead, came out from a blockhouse to see the soldiers, and then they walked back down the row of buildings to wherever it was they'd come from.

Marc said to Jacques, "God is not three persons in one. That is a lie. God is five persons and walks in the same direction."

"What do you mean by this, Marc?"

"They have come out to see, the mäusle ones, the ones without anything but bones and skin, and they are walking away from us down toward their blockhouse. I have no idea what holds them up, or drives them forward except that they are gods. They must be gods, Jacques. But not three in one, up in the sky, like the priest says, in church. No. God is five—no, wait, six. I did not see the one behind the others. At least six, and separate, walking in the same direction, here on Earth, not in the sky like the priests lie about in church," Marc said, his voice quivering.

"Yves, what do you think of Marc's new sight of God?" Jacques asked.

"I see the same, but a different number. There must be more than six gods walking. Maybe seven, eight, or more," Yves said.

"What makes you say that?" Jacques asked.

"Marc, and yourself. You may not be as thin, but that is only due to lack of time. If those are gods, we can see that because everything else has burned away," Yves said.

Marc realized that he was not much different from those men. Maybe just a few weeks more and he would be exactly like them. It shocked him as he realized why the sight of the soldiers made him feel uneasy. *They are fully alive, not just half,* he thought.

"Marc, Yves has spoken, and it is official, you know, for he is a priest. You must be a god as well, because only a god's eyes can recognize and see another god here in the flesh," Jacques said.

"Jacques, maybe now all the eyes I see will be the eyes of God?"

"What a gift, Marc, to see God. It takes a special sort of sight. Why can you see God just now?" Yves asked.

"Because I am not dead, but I am not alive. I think it is because I am between the two," Marc said.

"I understand. I feel the same way. Do you think after we leave, we will return to just the sight of the living?" Yves asked.

"No. I don't think we will, nor do I believe that we can," Marc said.

The soldiers began to stack crates of supplies near the camp's front gate. No one rushed the food. A new spiritual order came over the men, with a certain kind of air to it that could not be smelled, but could be felt.

CHAPTER 44

April 19, 1945

Buchenwald, Germany

"Forward, march!" the leader called out. Marc stood with Jacques and Yves as the group moved forward. Jacques held Marc's shoulder for guidance. The French flag flew over the men.

Another group of men had the flag of Poland, and yet another the flag of Russia. The entire camp changed over the short course of just eight days.

Blockhouses had signs outside of them detailing what can happen to Hitler. Men's attitudes changed about survival. A tall, wooden obelisk stood on the quad, as Marc's group paid their respects. Fifty-one thousand stood out, written in black paint against the whitewashed wooden structure.

Later that evening, Marc, Jacques, and Yves walked around the camp, upon Jacques' insistence.

"I want to remember this sound, the sound that came after we became free again."

"Does freedom have a sound, Jacques? How is it different from before? Men are still dying, you know, the ones who are beyond the point of recovery," Yves said.

"Yes, I know that. But the sounds have changed. There is no resistance in their voices."

"The ones who are still dying?" Marc asked.

"No, all of us. The resistance in our voices is now gone. I forgot how, when the occupation began in Paris, this strange anguish emerged in the voice of my friends. I had never known or heard such a collective anxiety before Paris fell."

"And now you no longer hear it?" Marc asked, as he searched his own memory for some voice of innocence before the war.

"Yes, it has left. I hear pain and sorrow. I am not telling you all is now healed, but now I can hear freedom," Jacques said.

"Things have changed. Men now have hope," Yves said.

"It is remarkable how quickly the men have changed from prisoners to comrades," Marc said as they passed one of the blockhouses with a group of Russians dancing inside.

"Freedom was all I had known before, but I could not hear it, because I had nothing to compare the sound of freedom to. Now I know how to recognize this sound, because I now know the sound of resistance, not just from the voices of others but from within my own voice. Where is the music?" Jacques asked a man passing by.

"The small camp, in the theater," he answered him as he walked past the blockhouse.

"I want to hear the concert. What do you say, Marc?" Jacques asked.

"Yes, it will be nice. It has been a while," Marc said after pondering the opportunity for a moment.

They walked together, Marc leading the way for Jacques and Yves down toward the small camp, where they used to keep the Jews before the Liberation. Then they came to the doors of the small theater across from the camp brothel.

A large ensemble took the stage, and the tune *Dipsy Doodle* played. The theater stood packed full of Americans from Patton's Third Army. Marc, Jacques, and Yves found a seat near the back, as the band played *Solitude*, and then *In the Mood*.

Then the band played *Bugle Call Rag*, and the men went wild with shouts, hollers and whistles.

"Why don't they like it?" Jacques tugged at Marc's striped uniform sleeve.

"They do like it, Jacques. In America whistling means you like the performance, not like France at all."

A smaller ensemble then took the stage. They played *Honeysuckle Rose*, and then *Confession*. The mood shifted and became more relaxed. The music shifted Marc's mood, and he thought, *When was the last time I just enjoyed music without any fear?*

The band continued with a minor swing. Jacques listened to the music, smiling, his face tilted upward. Yves sat with his legs crossed. Marc thought about his friend Dr. Jackson and his family. He hoped that they were still alive.

Then they started to play *Les Yeux Noirs*. It was sweet to Marc's ears. He thought of Paris, and when he first arrived there back in 1939.

A young Frenchman took the stage and began to sing in a wonderful voice. The first number was *Ménilomontant*, and it brought so much happiness to Jacques as he tapped his foot. Then he sang *La Polka du Roi*. The men of the Third Army listened and gave thundering applause after each number. *Joseph, Joseph* followed after that number, and then *Zafouket Na Klarinet*.

The young Frenchman sang the song *A Tisket, A Tasket*, and the men found it hysterical. Smiles and laughter filled the small theater, which had been a place of such horrible sorrow. Marc then remembered this was the place where Jacques and Yves found him and Georges. *Georges and Jean should be here*, Marc thought. Then he changed his mind and decided he was wrong.

"Georges and Jean are here, you know," Marc said.

"Yes, I know. I was just thinking the same thing," Jacques said.

The concert closed with a wild rendition of *Tiger Rag*. The men stood for the number, and the entire room shook with the excitement of the band and the singer. For Marc, the concert was a sweet memory, like an eternal moment of time of freedom. He had found the freedom to enjoy himself again, even if only for a while, and most of all, the freedom to confess to Jacques in a gentle way his lies regarding Jean and Georges. The timing seemed predestined to him, like he had fallen into just the right moment, where he had the freedom to speak of them as passed, but also a way to speak of their presence as eternal.

CHAPTER 45

April 23, 1945

Ravensbrück Concentration Camp for Women, Sweden

Torquette shook inside, out of fear of what was to come next. The guards called the entire camp together for a spontaneous roll call, and she knew by their voices this was a selection.

"*Français seulement, Français seulement ici, maintenant,*" the guards called out. Slowly, all of the French women of the camp lined up separately. Torquette's stomach boiled with fear. She thought of her husband and her son, and the last time she'd seen them at Moulins. A scab on her face, from a rat bite the previous week, bled.

As she reached near the front of the line, she saw the guard mark the back of women with chalk.

"The final selection," she thought to herself.

On the back of her coat, the guard drew down from the left and then the right, in heavy white chalk, a cross. Then all the women with a white cross on their backs gathered to one side. Rumors went wild through the group, as some cried and mumbled they were going to shoot them all.

"The Swedish Red Cross has agreed to care for your needs. You have been selected to be turned over to their care," the guard said. Torquette began to cry, because she had prepared herself to die and now she knew she would live.

May 3, 1945

Bay of Lubeck, Germany, S.S. *Thielbek*

Philip looked up from the deck of the ship. He could hear planes overhead, but could not determine their direction just yet. The holds and lower decks of the ship contained a world worse than any he had seen in the other camps or prisons. Guards began to shout out commands, and men started to run back inside the ship as the planes opened fire.

Pandemonium broke out, and soon the ship began to roll over. Philip jumped into the sea without his father. On the shore, machine gun fire rained down on the swimmers. Philip made it out of the water just past the gunners. He recognized another prisoner, and asked him, "Have you seen my father?"

"Yes, he was swimming toward the shore over there," he pointed back toward the ship. It burned, sinking into the sea. Only fifty prisoners survived, and Philip soon accepted that his father, Dr. Jackson, was not among the survivors.

May 7, 1945

Buchenwald, Germany

"Tolbert, Tolbert?" Marc heard as he stood in the crowd surrounding the American soldier passing out the mail.

"Here," Marc said, moving toward the soldier to get the letter, the first since December 1941. He quickly tore open the American Red Cross telegram seal.

"Start: Dear Marc, I am well, living with auntie in California. Mum gone in '42, and Papa last year. I am so thankful for you to be alive. I believed I was alone. More to follow. Love, Your Sister, Elda: Stop. Richmond, California. USA."

"What does it say?" Jacques asked Marc.

"Everything is great. My sister misses me," Marc said, and his voice trailed off a bit. Marc quickly stuffed the letter into his pocket while looking around, as if he had a secret to hide. His jaw became stiff and his eyes hollow.

"Do you think you are going back to America?" Jacques asked next in a neutral tone.

"No. I believe I am going to stay in France for a bit longer. We need to get ready. The trucks are going to be here soon, and today is our day to leave," Marc said, quickly taking Jacques with him back to the blockhouse.

"Did you get good news from America?" Jacques asked.

"Yes, everything is fine," Marc said, trying to measure his voice.

"Is that so?"

"Do you have everything you need for the trip?" Marc asked.

"I am leaving what I have here."

"But, don't you want to take ..."

"It stays here. I am not going to hold on to anything," Jacques said.

That afternoon, Marc, Jacques, and Yves boarded the trucks that took them to a city near Buchenwald, called Eisenhart. In the lobby of the hotel, piles of pants, shirts, and jackets, along with shoes and socks of every imaginable size and color, laid waiting for the men. They stood mulling around the piles, uncertain of what to do, as if the clothing intended for them seemed too good to be true. Marc started to sift slowly through the garments, looking for something that might fit. He felt self-conscious, aware of his camp uniform, as he picked up some dark slacks and a white button-down shirt.

Marc then took Jacques with his new garments up to his room. Yves took the room opposite to Jacques, Marc next door. Yves had not spoken much since the concert. Marc could tell by his mood that this silence was not directed in anger at Jacques or Marc, but inward toward himself. In his room, Marc opened the closet door, but resisted closing it after he had put away his new clothes. Anxiety arose inside of him with each hour in the room. The bed did not welcome him, and he felt unworthy of the clean water.

Eventually, he took a long bath, overwhelmed by the idea that all of this warm, clean water was for him alone, without anyone else waiting or watching him in the room. The bed's warmth and comfort pained him until he found the space to let go into sleep.

Early in the morning, he awoke from a deep dream, hyperventilating. Marc was back at Monowitz, before the march. He was near the fence, and one of the guards took his cap off and threw it toward the barbed wire. The guard taunted and mocked him to get the cap, or he was going to have him hung for sabotaging his uniform. But Marc could not get the cap, because he knew the guard was going to shoot him if he went near the fence.

He sat up in bed, drenched in sweat. Marc sat confused for a moment as he struggled to decide which was more real, the dream or his room. The dream took him back to the day in Monowitz, when the same guard took off his cap and threw it against the fence. An air raid siren had gone off and the guard disappeared into a bomb shelter. Then Marc ran for cover. He stole another cap later from the oven room. It was still difficult for him to shake the dream that had no siren of salvation.

Marc put on the pants, and cinched his new belt all the way to the last hole. He then put on the shirt, buttoning the collar, followed by his socks and shoes. When he walked, the shoes slipped, even though they were, at one time, his size.

Marc gazed at the striped wool shirt and pants that he had worn from the camp. He then remembered the telegram and took it from the pocket, along with the small square piece of brown paper used as a pass from the camp. As he turned, he caught himself in the mirror. The shirt did not fit but just hung on him. The collar circled his neck like a loose tire. He looked like some kid wearing pants meant for a giant. A swell of emotion started to overtake him, and he could feel a breakdown coming as he looked at himself. He was in better health than many, but still he weighed one hundred and fifteen pounds when released. He had gained twelve pounds since April 11, but it had not been easy.

"No, NO, NO, goddamn it, NO!" he shouted as he pounded his fist into his hand with the telegram and small pass. *Why did I survive these camps, but my own parents did not even survive back at home?* raced through his mind. He gained his composure and said to the mirror, "I think you have gained some weight," and then turned away. The camp uniform sat piled in the chair. Marc thought to fold it, but then stopped himself. He turned to leave it as trash, but stopped at the door.

"Jacques is right. I should just let it go," he said softly to the walls of the empty room. Marc closed his eyes and then looked back at the uniform again. He then tore off the small red triangle and number and put it into his pocket with his camp pass and telegram.

Jacques basked in the sunlight and wind in the back of the truck with Marc and Yves as it drove down the roads of Germany.

"Where are we now, Marc?" Jacques asked.

"We have left Coblentz, going west to Luxembourg."

"We have passed the Rhine, then. I guess I missed it," Jacques mused. He must have been so happy that he could take a nap and let go of knowing exactly every detail of a trip to someplace unknown.

They arrived then at a camp for displaced persons at Longuyon, in northeastern France. The next morning, the sudden jerk-and-stop motion that Marc made as he walked, shocked Jacques.

"What is wrong?" he asked Marc.

"Uh, just waiting," his voice cracked. Jacques' ears scanned the station. He could hear the footsteps stopping, but none climbing onto the platform.

"Come along now, please, one at a time," a French voice called to the men. Jacques could feel Marc's shoulder tense up and his movements became forced.

"Where are you going? This is the right train to take back to Paris," he heard a voice to his right call out.

The word *train* split the air in Jacques' consciousness. *Of course*, he thought as Marc lurched forward in the line, *it is the train they fear*. Another man then brushed up against him, walking away.

"You sang the other night, didn't you?" Marc asked a young Frenchman sitting across from them.

"Yes, for the soldiers. Yes, that was me up there," the young man said. Marc looked at him and guessed him to be just about eighteen or nineteen years old, his stature far shorter than Marc's. His eyes smiled with warmth.

"Were you in show business before the war?" Jacques asked him.

"Yes, I sang and danced. I had a small band of friends. I don't know what has become of them." His voice grew quieter. "I must be an orphan now. I am sure of it."

"I can understand that feeling," Marc said, his voice clear.

"Did they get your parents, too? They rounded us up and put us in train cars, like animals. They were screaming and yelling at us like a bunch of lunatics back in Paris. Are you Jewish, too?" he asked next.

"No, but my parents passed away during the war. It really is not the same thing, but still. Actually, I am rather lucky because I have one sister left. You must hate the Germans?" Marc then asked.

"No, I don't hate the Germans. In fact, I don't want to hate at all. I am finished with all this hate. That is the problem, you see, people hating other people. We all need to stop hating. I do not want to become like the people who hated me just because I am Jewish," he said with a passionate voice. "Do you believe in God?"

"No, not in the one I cannot see. You know, the one in the sky," Marc said dismissively. Jacques sat and listened to them speak, deep in thought. *It was so odd that Marc could casually tell a stranger that his parents died, yet would hide the fact from me.* Jacques even wondered if Marc was aware of the fact that he had told Jacques nothing of the death of his parents.

"How can I believe in someone like that after everything I've seen?" Marc went on, trying to shake off the question. Yves looked up at Marc and smiled, nodding his head in silence.

They arrived in Paris at the East Gate station. Crowds of people waved French flags and threw flowers at them as they left the train. The buses drove through the streets of the city and then arrived at the hotel.

"Where are we, Marc?" Jacques asked, trying to get his bearings.

"Hôtel Lutetia. We are on the Left Bank," Marc's voice squeaked out with the tension of a piano wire.

"Why are you so tense? Is something wrong? You don't seem very happy to be back," Jacques asked.

Marc pulled him to the side, and then cupped his hand over Jacques' ear so he could hear over the noise in the room. "This was the Gestapo headquarters. They brought me here the first night of my arrest."

"Marc, I will be outside," Yves said.

"Are you all right?"

"Yes, but I can't go in. Can you tell them that I am outside and need someplace else to stay?"

In the hotel lobby a woman screamed "Robert!" Then the teenager on the train turned and screamed back. Marc understood them speaking in French. She was Robert's sister.

No one called out Marc's name. He checked the list to see if the Jackson family had arrived, but he could not find them among the names.

"Name?"

"Marc Tolbert."

"This will be your room, and here are the instructions."

"I can't stay here. Neither can my friend Yves. He is outside. Is there another place?"

"Oh. Yes, I understand. We have had other requests. Let me go and check what can be done."

Marc walked back outside and found Yves and Jacques, with Jacques' family. After a small conversation, he went back inside the hotel.

"We have other places, but they are full. In a few days we can move you. I am sorry, but you will need to stay here for the next few nights. If there is a room that you wish to avoid, perhaps we can do something," the clerk said.

"No need. We have a place now for a few nights. But we'll take the other location when it becomes open."

"Excellent. Here are your papers and Yves'."

To celebrate, Marc and Jacques went out for a drink and smoke at a local café. Yves came in a bit later and joined them. Marc continued to eat whatever was given to him, and ordered more. He rolled in satisfaction, so happy for the glorious food.

"Marc, you should be careful. Remember what they told us," Yves said.

"It is no use. I've tried. He is like a goat now?" Jacques said.

A group of British soldiers sat close to Marc and his friends. The soldiers broke out into a chorus of singing.

"Roll out the barrel…" Marc felt as if he'd been shot in the chest. The lyrics pierced his mind and he started to feel nauseated.

"Roll out the barrel and we'll have a barrel of fun," the voices terrorized Marc. It was more horrible than any of the bombs or guns during the war. His legs began to shake, and his stomach knotted into a ball.

"Roll out the…" Marc ran from the table, hand clamped over his mouth. Shooting cramps ripped through his stomach as he doubled over. He reached the bathroom just in time to vomit into the toilet. Marc heaved violently, coughing up blood into the bowl, as his entire body shivered.

Yves came running for him. "Marc, what's wrong? What's happening?"

"Make them stop, please for the love of fucking God, make them stop singing, please…," he pleaded.

"Marc, you're bleeding." Yves then ran back to Jacques. "He's bleeding and vomiting up blood. He has gone mad."

"We need to get him to the hospital," Jacques said, getting up from the table. He followed the voices singing in the bar, finding one of the soldiers.

"Can you stop singing for a moment? My friend is very sick and needs some help. Can you help us take him to the hospital?"

September, 1967

Saint-Nazaire, France

"Please be seated," Jacques said to the gathering by the graveside.

"We are gathered here today to celebrate the life of Marc Tolbert. Born 1919 in Paris, France, to Eldon Tolbert and Lynette Bonnet of Paris, at the end of World War One."

"He grew up with his family in New York, and in 1939, returned to Paris for studies. Marc never returned to America, but stayed in France after the war and switched his studies to medicine, becoming a doctor for the American Hospital in Paris. As you know, he passed away May 3, 1967, of cancer. He is survived by his sister, Elda, who is here with us today from California," Jacques said, smiling and looking out toward the gathering.

"Marc asked me if I would be so kind to deliver some words for him today, and I, of course, agreed. I met Marc in 1942 in Paris, during difficult times. He was in need of some help, and I was in need of helping some people. His name at that time was "Winoc," but among friends it was always "Marc." I asked him if there was anything he would like me to say today, and I will do my best to pass on his wishes." Then Jacques' voice changed slightly.

"First, we become our decisions over time. We choose to love, or we can choose to hate. We can choose to forgive, or we can choose to take revenge; to have hope, or we can choose to fall into despair. But, regardless, we become our choices we make over time," Jacques said. The words were true, he thought, but how difficult for people to accept.

"Second, the tests in life reveal to us who we are becoming in this world. Each of us faces tests in this world and when they come to us, they are like a light from which there is no escape," Jacques paused, pondering the words and then added, "In that light, you will discover what kind of person you are becoming by the choices you make. Be grateful if you do not like what you see, for you have been given a chance now to change your choices." He noticed that his voice came back to him with an unexpected tone, as if he were speaking toward trees or hills.

"Third, there are no shortcuts. You cannot cheat these tests, swap, or trade them with others. You are the only one who can pass them," Jacques said, completing what Marc had spoken to him before he passed. But the words seemed incomplete to him, alluding to something more as he stood in front of the gathering.

"There are those who believe that faith, hope, and love are things we do, in order to lead blessed lives. They are like tricks that earn us a prize from God, such as an easy life. If we play the tricks just right, we will be blessed with love, find riches, and be successful." Jacques remembered the precise morning the bill came due for his tricks on the Nazis when they came to arrest him.

"It is not true. Faith, hope, and love are states of being, and when you are these states of being combined in one moment, you can pass any test that life may bring to you, even the test of when it is your time to stand for your own death." Jacques felt as if he had found the note he was searching for.

"Marc knew this, I am sure, because he practiced it in so many ways, before, during, and after the war. I will miss him, as I am sure all of you will. He was a living example of the type of light you would need in dark places such as Buchenwald." Jacques could not shake the feeling that his voice had bounced off something larger, just beyond the small gathering.

CHAPTER 46

June, 1945

Paris, France

"Son, would you like to pray?" the priest asked as he stood over Marc in the hospital. Marc awoke startled from a deep dream. "Would you like to pray?"

"No, I'm resting now," Marc whispered.

"It would be good for you to pray, son. When was the last time you confessed your sins?" the priest pressed, his stare cold. Marc's body tensed in the bed. He wanted the priest to leave.

"Confession—when was your last confession?" the priest asked impatiently in French.

"I have no sins to confess to your god," Marc said. The priest looked perplexed by the answer.

"Son, we all have sinned and fallen short of God. Now, please, I am busy and have come to pray over you."

"Which camp were you in?" Marc asked like a child.

"I was not in any of the camps. Why does that matter?"

"I no longer need your prayer."

"Are you turning your back on God?"

"No, but I don't need you to tell me how to feel, or when to pray."

"So, you are a Jew," the priest said with a smirk.

"I did not say that."

"It is a pity that you did not learn the fear of God from your experience," the priest said, smacking his prayer book back into his hand. The words struck Marc as wholly out of touch with any idea of God.

Marc watched the cleric leave the room. He sat up in bed. At first, he was irate at the rudeness of the encounter, but soon he started to laugh.

"I thought he was going to stuff the prayer book down my throat. The nuns back at my school would have smacked me silly."

Jacques walked into the room, his arm looped through Yves'. "I hear you are feeling well today. Soon you will be out of here," he said as he greeted Marc.

"I was close, real close, Jacques. It was scary there for a moment," Marc said, his voice relaxed.

"I was worried. You were close, and it scared me quite a bit," Yves said.

"Yves, is this the end of your grand silence?" Marc asked.

"Yes. I'm still not sure of what I will do now, but my silence is over."

"Are you returning to your old parish?" Jacques asked.

"No. I can't do that now. I no longer have a parish. I'm not like the one who just left, at least not anymore. Marc, did you pass through to the other side?"

"It was so odd. Two of me stood on either side of the bed and they would watch me at night. If I started to breathe funny, they would then move in as if they were going to take me away. I watched them all night, but then I had a dream, and they were gone when I awoke." Marc's face showed fear mixed with wonderment. It was as if he could not quite believe himself.

"What kind of dream?" Jacques asked, his curiosity piqued.

"It was real. I mean, it felt as real as this right now. But it was nothing like this place at all. I think I really did die," Marc said looking up towards them from his bed.

"What was it like?" Jacques asked.

"Beautiful, It was beautiful," he then paused and said, "but, I'm worried for Dr. Jackson. I'm not sure if he made it."

"Why is that?" Yves asked.

"He was in the dream, and I think he drowned," Marc said.

"That is amazing. Philip has returned. I checked back on your friends and he told me the same thing. I was not going to tell you but it appears your friend already did tell you himself. We really are all connected in some way," Yves said to Marc.

Upon his release from the hospital, Marc walked with Jacques down to a new café. He had enough strength, and had regained his ability to hold down food, so he felt confident the typical small portions from the French café would not challenge his stomach.

Marc, Jacques, and Yves sat outside, in the July sun of 1945. They talked about their post-war plans. Jacques wanted to go back to school and become a professor. Yves decided he would return to school, but still did not know exactly what would replace the priesthood.

"I think I'm going back to medical school, but first I need to pass my baccalaureate here," Marc then said.

"So, not back in the States?" Jacques pressed him.

"No, you heard me. I'm staying here," Marc said intently.

The waitress came over to take their order, and it was Marie. She looked down at the pad of paper on her tray, and after a moment, looked up at the three men. She smiled at Yves and Jacques, but her face changed as she looked at Marc.

"Is your name Marie?" Marc asked, knowing for certain that the answer was yes. A storm then rose up inside of him. He was hit with so many thoughts at once, he struggled to find a single one to follow.

"No, my name is Brigitte."

"How odd. You look so much like a woman I met in '39. Her name was Marie. Perhaps you know her?" Marc pressed, knowing it was her, maintaining eye contact as her eyes avoided his.

"I am sorry. I do not know any "Marie." Are you ready to order?"

Jacques and the Yves ordered, and then Marc said, "I will have some pigeon, if you have it."

"Fine, I will check for you," she said, her voice punctuated, her face strained with tension. Her eyes glanced quickly down to the left as she turned away.

"Is that her? Your voice tells me so," Jacques said.

"Yes, of course it is her. I would know her anyplace. And that lying voice, well, of course it is her."

"Who? Who is she?" Yves asked Marc.

Marc fell deep into thought. It was as if nothing existed around him. He could see nothing but blackness and then the flame of a match touching a candle. The light of the flame revealed her face, and he was sitting at a table across from her. A lovely plate of roasted bones sat on the table in front of him. He wanted to eat those bones. He was hungrier for those bones than even the bread or extra soup, or chicken, or any other food.

"She was once pretty. Not so much now," Marc said, distracted by the scene in his mind. Jacques kept silent, the words passing over him.

The light revealed to Marc that they were in a room of bones. Bones stacked up all around him, just like they were in sheds at Buchenwald. Marc's mouth watered for them. Marie stared at him with a wanting smile.

The bones talked and had names. Marc knew the bones and hated her for it.

"Was she a girlfriend? Did you leave her?" Jacques asked again, but Marc wasn't listening to him.

Marc's soul shuddered to eat. He wanted that plate, the roasted bones of revenge. He wanted to eat for what happened to Allen, Georges, Jean, and the Jacksons.

"Just be honest with yourself. You are doing it for them, whom you could not save," Joan's words came from behind the bones.

Marc froze. *How old am I?* He saw three lives, like precious eggs in a basket. He saw the egg he had before the war, then the egg of the war. He gazed last at the final egg, for his life now before him. *How old am I now?*

The screaming man on the radio kept his promise, Marc thought. It was a thousand-year reign. It was even more than a thousand years. Every day in the second egg was a year. Marc was only twenty-six, yet felt the weight of a thousand years in his soul. The second egg was denser than lead.

"If you are someplace you never expected to be, always remember it is due to your choices." It was the officer from 1940, before Marc returned to Paris. He heard the officer's voice snake from deep within the wall of bones.

Marie stared at him, smiling. He could feel her wanting him to eat. She had brought him to this lovely dinner to dine, to feast upon revenge. She wanted him to have these tender roasted bones. Marc knew if he tasted this dish, she would have his third life.

Marc bent down toward the flame, taking it up in his breath, and then blew it out completely.

"Marc, Marc, are you listening?" Jacques touched his arm. "Are you there, Marc?"

"Yes, I'm here," Marc said calmly.

"She had a lot of fear in her voice. Do you think you are going to say anything?" Jacques asked.

"There is nothing to be done. Nothing would be changed by it, Jacques. No one would be brought back," he said as he thought of Jean in the boxcar. *Pointing the finger at Marie would never raise Georges from the ashes,* he thought. *Allen would not be brought up from the sands of the beach, and the Jacksons would not be saved by it now.*

"Did you love her? Sometimes it is hard to let go of love when there is no closure. It is easier to let go of the person than the dream," Yves asked innocently. Marc knew he was quite unaware of who Marie was to Marc.

Marc's leg bounced. He knew inside that he did love her, but also knew that this was not the woman he'd met in '39. She was a ghost, and he could not love a ghost. Yves was right. It is harder to let go of the dream of someone than the flesh.

"Yes, I did at one time, but she changed, as have I. We are not the same people we were when we first met," Marc said.

"That does happen," Yves said.

"Marc, why don't you share your vision with us?" Jacques then asked.

"It is just a dream, Jacques, not a vision," Marc smiled.

"It is a vision, Marc," Jacques insisted.

Just then, a second waiter returned with their order. "Where did the woman go?" Marc asked.

"Oh, she needed to use the restroom," the waiter said dryly.

CHAPTER 47

June, 1945

Paris, France

Marie walked quickly back inside the café and then up to the bar. "Can you take this out, please? I need to use the restroom," she asked the bartender. He looked a bit shocked by her request, but let it go as she walked away toward the restroom.

She shut the door and turned the lock to make sure it was secure. Her heart pounded in her chest. She was sweating and had become nauseated with fear. Marie turned and looked at herself in the mirror. Her face pale, she realized Marc would say something, and that meant arrest followed by a trial. Her mind raced through the faces of those who would be drawn down upon her. She had seen the same thing play out over and over again in the past year. Others—war criminals—noted in the papers, imprisoned at Drancy.

Marie lifted the toilet lid and vomited into the bowl. She continued to heave over and over again until there was nothing left in her stomach.

They were no longer content to just shave heads. That was all just games when Liberation came in the summer of '44. Now, the people wanted lives. People knew where their loved ones had gone once they were shipped off to Germany. She started to cry, even as her stomach continued to heave up empty air. A total and complete curtain of dread fell upon her from the ceiling.

She scanned her memories. The entire war started to flash in her mind. The images and emotions raced through her consciousness.

Then she found the curve. Her mind's eye fell into the rut as wide and deep as the British Channel. Marie held it in her mind, tenderly, with love.

A new wave of sorrow overtook her as she cried. She cried harder than any other time in her life. She cried out all of her pain into the rut of her memory.

"We are going to leave soon on the train, but we need food, Marie. The market is open, since there have been no raids," her mother said to her. Her mother's face was beautiful, and she could touch it. "Can you meet us in the market, and then we will walk to the station?" she then asked. Marie could see her father, sister, and brother in the background. They all looked healthy and safe.

She cried and cried looking at them. They were always with her, less than a second away. She always could come back to this moment and see them, the last moment she saw them alive.

"Tell Annette hello, and we will meet you at the market," her mother said.

Marie stopped. "No, I am going with you."

"But I thought you were going to visit your friend first?" her mother said, perplexed.

"No, I want to go with you. I will visit her later," Marie said in her mind. She jumped through into the past and went right back to the one decision she regretted the most. With everything inside, she wished to pass into the dream of her family, to go back to June 13, 1940, to be back in Orleans.

"All right, then, let's go to the market," her mother said. Marie's heart filled with peace. She knew that she would then share in the holy communion of the horses, and never have to taste any of these bitter days of life during the war.

Outside at the café, Jacques grabbed Marc's forearm and squeezed it. "Will she be back?"

"I don't know. She did not look well. If you need anything, please call on me," the waiter said before he left their table.

"She cannot even look at me," Marc said. He started to feel the same sadness. He knew there was nothing he could do to go back. He just wanted to go back to the summer of '39, but there was no passage to it.

Marc scanned his mind for the last honest words that she'd said to him. Was it in front of the agent, as she left? "You should have left Paris, Marc, and never come back." She'd spoken with such venom. He questioned if she honestly did ever love him before it all came undone.

He then caught his breath as the words struck him. He couldn't avoid them or deny their truth. She was right that day, outside the movie theater. He realized that they had become the people in the newsreel: simply broken. He closed his eyes and tried to steady himself.

"It will not be long, you know. I don't need to do a thing?" Marc mumbled.

"What do you mean?" Yves asked.

"She is out in the open, working in a café. It will only be a matter of time before she meets someone else," Marc said, thinking of the eventual outcome of this terrible newsreel of his life.

"There are other women, and, besides, maybe you will get together with her again," Yves said, unaware of the impossibility of such a disastrous reunion.

"Yves, I will tell you later. It is more complicated than that," Marc said.

"Marc, tell us the vision again," Jacques asked.

"You mean Marc's dream?" Yves said.

"It is just a dream, Jacques. Not a vision," Marc said, looking down at his plate.

"Marc, it is more than that, much more. Please, I love hearing you tell me about it," Jacques pleaded.

Marc sat silent for a moment and gathered his thoughts. *The dream felt more real than even life*, he thought while he pondered Jacques' pestering.

"When I was in the hospital, I think I got very close to dying. And these twins, who looked just like me, stood on either side of my bed, looking at my chest, ready to take me away. I couldn't sleep but just stared at them as I breathed. I hadn't felt like that since the sinking. I thought maybe I was dead, and then I thought about what would've happened had I died. Then, they were gone and I was back on the *Normandie*, going home ..."

Marc woke in a leather chair of the smoking lounge. He was naked and covered in oil. His life jacket had come untied.

He started to focus his eyes, and all around him were horses. A horse's snout then prodded him in the chair. His mother and father were riding the horse. His mother said, "Time to get up, Marc, you have a ship to catch."

He stood up and found the entire room filled with horses, in between the leather chairs, surrounded by the gold lacquer murals along the walls.

Marc felt compelled to walk toward the doors of the lounge. In the corner sat a woman, with what looked like her family. They were laughing and enjoying lunch. The woman looked back at him and smiled. He hesitated and recognized her face, then walked through the doors into the main lounge.

Rain fell down from the wide-open sky when he passed through the doors. All of the oil from the broken Lancastria fell away from his skin under the showers. In the lounge, he saw elephants in a circle, lifted high upon their hind legs. People gathered around and watched the show, between the towering glass fountains of light.

The murals came alive, the gods sharing the circus with all the people. Marc caught the eye of Jean, and then he saw Georges. He walked through the room with no shame or concern that he was naked. He removed the life jacket, but carried it in his hand.

The gods stood in each corner of the lounge, beholding the magnificent circus act. The sky above held a golden sun. Angels flew down close to the fountains of light, dipping in jars, and carrying the treasure high into the sky. The bears danced with the children, and the lions gave rides on their backs. Even wearing the rags of the camps, the people were glorious and bright. The little Belgian boy with his sister sat laughing at the show beside their two dogs.

Marc walked down the stairs and toward the dining room. The doors were wide open. As he approached, a single white angora rabbit came hopping up the stairs past the passengers. The rabbit stopped in front of Marc and then went around him. Marc laughed out loud and felt the overwhelming joy from the room.

"I know your name. This way, please," the agent from Paris said to Marc. "You are welcome here," he said with a smile. Marc followed him through the vast dining room. All of the tables were filled with men, women, and children in all kinds of dress—uniforms from all sorts of nations. The solid blue floor shimmered like water, and Marc thought he was walking on the ocean. On each side rose the fountains of lights. The beams of the dining room gave way to a cloudless sky.

Then he came to his table. Dr. Jackson stood and hugged him. "I was not able to swim, but Philip made it." He looked healthy and strong.

Officer Sean stood up and greeted Marc next. He'd been playing a game of cards with the Scotsman, and the other John, the other British man Marc had met on the Lancastria.

Allen came over to the table with a tray of drinks. "Marc, I have those drinks from the bar," and Marc took one along with all the others. "Let us toast together," Allen said.

Marc took his glass and raised it with the others to the large, looming statue in the center of this dining room. It seemed even larger now to Marc than when he had first seen it going to France. The golden lady, however, was not a statue but alive, holding out an olive branch above the diners.

"To peace everlasting, my friends!" Allen called out. "To peace everlasting," they echoed back.

CHAPTER 48

September, 1967

Saint-Nazaire, France

"And they toasted to the golden goddess of Peace, raising their glasses together and said, 'to peace everlasting,'" Jacques said as he finished telling the vision. He could not put his finger exactly on the emotion that rushed through him. *Perhaps it was the hope of the vision that he loved, and that the dream Marc had, captured his own heart back in '45,* he thought.

Then, the full weight of the twenty-two years bore down upon him like boxcars on a train pressuring the engine as it screeched to a stop. He stood in silence before the gathered mourners, deep inside of himself. Jacques tried to remember the last time he heard Jean's voice.

"Those were very sweet lies he told, very sweet," he whispered to himself just above the dead silence, as he remembered how Marc refused to say they had died. The silence lasted only a moment, but for Jacques, it opened a deep well of time. He remembered all those rowdy brave voices gathering in his apartment in 1940, his young band called the Sons of Liberty. He smirked at the cocky arrogance of their innocent offerings of bravery. He lingered over all those young voices long past, lost in the war. They were all still alive, though only in his consciousness. Georges and Jean were not gone. He just hadn't listened to their voices for twenty-two years.

No one at the graveside seemed to be in any hurry for Jacques to finish. They waited patiently for him to find himself again. Dora held a card from

David back in the States. Nigel sat next to her, holding their two canes. Marc's sister, Elda, sat in the front row, next to Jacques and his family.

Jacques then caught himself. He stood tall before the people and said, "I have always loved that vision, that dream of Marc's from those days, of a ship going home, with both friend and foe reconciled under the presence of something we were all fighting, praying and hoping for, that beautiful goddess called Peace."

The echo of his own voice sounded strange to him, as if there was something more just beyond the people gathered, as if there was a second congregation standing all around. They were standing around them, and above, in every direction: men in uniforms left to drown in the sea, women and children dumped into the sea by the flipped lifeboats, the nameless refugees who disappeared from the earth as they boarded that ship. Jacques doubted his ears but they did not lie.

His speech complete, Jacques moved back to his seat.

"As you know, Marc was not particularly religious, and that is why he asked me to speak instead of a priest. Please join us inside for a reception with Marc's sister, Elda." Jacques took the hand of his wife to guide him back into the reception room.

Marc's soul felt the sudden release as the rate of time increased.

"Why did I have to go back? If I had just let her go, I would've always had the Marie of '39, but I went back and lost her, and all those people paid," he cried out in anguish over the guilt and shame he'd held inside all those years after the war.

Then the light of days flashed in the sky. Marc stood with the assembly of those known unto God from the *Lancastria*. The priest held the staff with the clock atop it. The dial sped up and the years passed. Marc looked up at the priest, recognizing him as Yves from Buchenwald. He had lost contact with him after the war, but never forgot how he'd helped him carry Georges' lifeless body to roll call.

Marc stood looking back at the grave. It bore the title of his request. He'd been emphatic that he had given his true name to someone unknown in '41 and would not take it back. The grave marker stated simply, "Known Unto God." Marc's service as a medical doctor flashed before him far faster than the years of the war.

"Joan was right. I was trying to save those whom I'd lost," Marc said. Then the rate of time increased again, until Marc could no longer read the clock. His life played out over and over again, much to his horror, in what appeared to be an endless loop.

"Why are you condemning me to this?" he yelled at Yves.

"I condemn no one," Yves said.

"Is this it? I am condemned to watch my life over and over again? I am in hell. Are you my judge?" Marc said with rage.

"You know that is not true," Yves said.

With each spin of the clock's dial, Marc's life replayed before his eyes. "What siren of Paris, what siren of, what siren, what siren, what, what, what ..." Marc heard Officer Sean each time, as he stood dumbstruck by the flashback of the years.

"The siren was from within my own heart. I betrayed myself long before Marie," Marc said in reflection.

Yves stepped closer to Marc, and Marc looked up at him. Yves cocked his head a bit with a curious smile, which struck Marc as odd. Then a spark came alive within Marc's eternal deathwatch of his own life. *My own betrayal begets my own forgiveness,* he thought. Yves nodded his head in agreement, staring into Marc's eyes.

"Will you?" Yves asked.

"Yes," Marc said.

"Yes, what?"

"Yes, I will forgive myself."

"When?" Yves said as he stepped back and nodded at the spinning clock. Marc looked at the clock as his life played out before him again haunted by this question. In a flash, he saw the burden over his head, held by his own hand, placed there somewhere in time that he could not see or remember. Now he knew why it had never left him, and how to be free of it if he could bring himself to the words.

"I forgive myself," Marc said.

The clock stopped, as did the flashbacks. Marc stood with the dead of the *Lancastria*, surrounding Yves who held firm to his staff.

"What day is this?" Marc asked.

"June 18, 2040," Yves said.

"Why are we here?"

"This is the day of healing, the last day you must see before you can let go of this life and be free," Yves said. Marc's attention felt drawn to across the Channel, to London.

A older clerk walked slowly down the long corridor of the new building created to house the records in London. He opened a door and walked into an office.

"Yes, what is it?" the younger clerk sitting at the desk said, looking up at him.

"There is a request for these records," he said, holding a file.

"And that is a problem?"

"They were sealed."

"So show them the records. You don't need me for that."

"But the rules are that they need to be reviewed first, even if the seal has expired," the older clerk said with a smirk.

"You are such a pain. You are interrupting my work for this?"

"I have never seen you work. Please, look at the seal," the older clerk said.

"What is this?" He snapped the file from the new clerk's hand.

"Bloody right, I say. You need to get off your bum and review this file."

The younger clerk looked at the front of the file, at the one-hundred-year-old seal of Winston Churchill's office. He opened it and began to read the documents inside.

"Come on, now, what does it say?"

"Oh, I had no idea. This explains everything," the younger clerk said, scanning the papers. He folded the file and handed it back.

"That's it?"

"Yes, of course. It's time. Show them the file."

"Why was it sealed for a hundred years? I've never seen any records from the war still under seal."

"You can read it now, too. I'm not sure why it has been kept sealed for a hundred years, but I believe I understand why they thought back in 1940 they needed to keep it sealed that long," the younger clerk said.

The older clerk then returned to the front desk to deliver the file over for the small crowd gather in the waiting room.

Marc's attention returned to Saint-Nazaire. The priest was right for it was a day of healing for the wounds of official silence from the British for the sinking of that ship, and all the years he had spent trying to change what could never be changed. His soul radiated a beautiful golden light, with all of the others gathered for this day.

"Your watch is now complete. The time has come for us now to go. Will you all please join me for the final prayers?" Yves bellowed out. Marc felt a sweet change inside himself called freedom.

"May the Peace of the Lord within you heal you of all your wounds by day or from night, by love or from war."

All the people gathered known unto God said with a unified voice, "Thanks be to God."

www.ingramcontent.com/pod-product-compliance
Lightning Source LLC
Chambersburg PA
CBHW020328180626
46812CB00001B/103